"A political thriller to match what happe. .... Utilizing
his experiences from government and campaigns, Avrashow brings a real-life
quality to the characters. Having served for sixteen years in the California
Assembly, I can unequivocally state—Avrashow nailed it."

— HON. RICHARD KATZ,
Democratic Leader, California State Assembly (ret.)

"*Center Stage* is both fascinating and entertaining; it is a MUST-read."

— AURA E. MARTINEZ,
author of Creating a Lifetime of Wellness

"It's hard to put this book down."

— DOUG KRIEGEL,
Emmy Award-winning journalist

"An intriguing spin on the phenomenon of celebrities-as-candidates."

— BOB RONKA,
Los Angeles City Councilmember (ret.)

"I have run campaigns and been a candidate. *Center Stage* takes you right
to the center of the chaos, drama, personalities, and comedy of a campaign.
If you like *American President, The West Wing, Madame Secretary*, and *VEEP*,
you'll love this book."

— FRED GAINES, ESQ.,
Mayor/Councilmember, City of Calabasas

"An impressively entertaining and carefully crafted novel from cover to cover.
Center Stage is extraordinarily and unreservedly recommended."

— *MIDWEST BOOK REVIEW*

"*Center Stage* is a must-read. Avrashow draws on his extensive experience in California politics to craft a thriller to satisfy political junkies and general readers. The pages turn themselves in this fast-paced insider's view of a most unusual candidate and his campaign for the Senate."

— S. FREDERIC LISS,
award-winning author of
The Fire This Time, A Novel

"Juggling the dramas of a Senate campaign, *Center Stage* is a suspenseful novel about a rock star candidate with a party-filled past."

— *FOREWORD* CLARION REVIEWS

Praise for
CENTER STAGE

"In the tradition of Allen Drury and Richard Condon comes the next great author of political thrillers: Wayne Avrashow."

— MICHAEL LEVIN,
New York Times *bestselling author*

"An entertaining political thriller—smart and engrossing."

— *KIRKUS REVIEWS*

"Avrashow's book is an entertaining reveal of an unconventional candidate and campaign. It's filled with drama, hope, and conflict."

— ANTONIO VILLARAIGOSA,
Mayor of Los Angeles (ret.)

"Wayne Avrashow has written a political thriller that draws on his considerable experience...a great read."

— ZEV YAROSLAVSKY,
Los Angeles City Councilmember (ret.)
and Los Angeles County Supervisor (ret.)

"Political drama, complex relationships, and a page-turning narrative all compete for your undivided attention in Avrashow's entertaining debut."

— ELIZABETH L. SILVER,
author of The Execution of Noa P. Singleton

"A riveting page-turner... *Center Stage* has all the elements to be developed into a memorable film dramatization."

— PETER SAPHIER,
former executive at Universal Studios and
Paramount Studios; co-producer, Scarface;
acquired the novel Jaws *for Universal*

"I served with Sonny Bono in Congress, and Tyler Sloan would be a fascinating candidate for the United States Senate."

— HON. HOWARD BERMAN, ESQ.,
United States Congressman, former Chairman
House Committee on Foreign Affairs (ret.)

"As an elected official, *Center Stage* is a compelling read...I was rooting for Tyler Sloan. A thrilling ride of an unconventional campaign, and I'm hoping it becomes a movie or limited series."

— JOHN LEE,
Los Angeles City Councilmember

"Pin-sharp and compelling, with wry humor and real authenticity. One of my top five books of the year (so far!)."

— ROBERT PARKER,
bestselling author of Far From the Tree

"*Center Stage* is a pulsating political thriller that's filled with wry humor and hits all the right notes. Candidate Tyler Sloan rocks!"

— MICHAEL H. RUBIN,
author of the award-winning thrillers
The Cottoncrest Curse *and* Cashed Out

CENTER STAGE

A Political Thriller

RealClear
PUBLISHING

A division of RealClear Politics

Center Stage: A Political Thriller

Previously published in substantial form as *Roll the Dice*

For more information, please contact:
Amplify Publishing
620 Herndon Parkway #320
Herndon, VA 20170
info@amplifypublishing.com

CPSIA Code: PRV0121A
Library of Congress Control Number: 2020918087
ISBN-13: 978-1-64543-794-9

Printed in the United States of America

To Bret and Grant, the greatest sons imaginable;
to Ann, for her support, love, and editing;
to my brother, Craig, a connoisseur of fiction;
to Zev, where the journey began.

CENTER STAGE

A Political Thriller

WAYNE AVRASHOW

ONE

May 4, Washington, DC

It was the perfect funeral.

The perfect weather appeared as Washington, DC's, rain had ceased, and the sun struggled out from behind gray clouds.

The perfect blend of grief and respect cascaded down the rolling greens of Arlington National Cemetery as the attendees awaited the eulogies that would cite Nevada senator Ted Garvey's patriotism.

Tyler Sloan arrived after most of the mourners had already been seated, and a standing-room-only crowd had formed. With his arrival unnoticed, he quietly observed his father, Mike, being escorted to his seat. He moved closer to locate a position where he could hold a clear view of the service. With his plainclothes security aide following close behind, Sloan walked past the numerous Nevada and Washington public officials sitting stiffly on folding chairs. As he proceeded, a synchronized nudging of elbows and whispers mounted in his direction.

"It's Tyler Sloan."

"That's Tyler Sloan."

"Tyler Sloan? Here? Why?"

The last statement had been louder than the others. Suddenly the mass of cameras and photographers positioned atop a not-so-distant knoll shifted to fix on him. Photographs of former governor Mike Sloan, the vice president, and various senators were "journalistic cool," but those of Tyler Sloan were "tabloid heat."

Sloan stood erect, squinting into the modest sunshine. His brown hair was full, tousled, and flecked with the faintest touch of distinguished gray. He had basked in celebrity for decades, from his early days of singing at high school dances to sold-out arenas around the world. No longer merely a star with wall-mounted platinum albums, he was also a global financial mogul. He was pleased when last month's *People* magazine had included him on the list of the "World's Most Beautiful People" but winced when the article described him as a "charming, *middle-aged* rogue."

Despite his comfort with the attention, Sloan sought refuge from the piercing gaze of a woman who repeatedly turned in her seat to glance at him. The polite glances eventually morphed into a lingering stare. When she winked at him, he cast his glance away. His eyes fell again on his father.

Sloan appreciated his father's aura as a political statesman. As a child, he had studiously read every newspaper clipping of his father. That reading had rendered him the only kid in his third-grade class who knew the meaning of the word *gravitas*. Now he noticed the slight stoop of his father's shoulders. He had always marveled at his father's energy, but Garvey's death was a stark reminder of his father's mortality; the two men were but a few years apart.

The late senator Garvey and Mike Sloan had served together in the US Congress. Sloan's childhood memories included sitting at his father's desk in the congressional chambers while Garvey played card tricks with him, never grasping how Garvey was able to pull the ace of hearts from behind his left ear.

The senator's death had shaken the nation's political equation. Nevada was now the Senate's tipping point. The political buzz was persistent yet uncertain. With the Democrat Garvey in office, the equally divided Senate had allowed the Democratic vice president to cast a deciding vote to break a Senate tie. However, with Garvey's passing and the upcoming election to fill the now-vacant seat, a Republican victory would equal fifty-one votes and Senate control.

All but one camera returned its focus to the podium when the service began; a single camera remained focused on Sloan. The final eulogy was given by Garvey's brother, who battled through tears as he shared childhood memories that were usually far removed from the public domain. When the priest concluded the funeral rites, he stood beside the family to witness the twenty-one-gun salute. Garvey's middle-aged daughter sobbed almost as loud as the shots that rang out.

Sloan dabbed his moist eyes with his handkerchief as the casket holding the deceased senator's body was lowered into the ground. The instant the casket disappeared, Republican Chris Collins and Democrat William Rogers, whom everyone called Billy, began to "work" the mourners. The two leading contenders for the Senate seat appeared united in false grief, and Sloan bit his lip at their lack of shame.

Collins, a former television news anchor, walked toward Sloan with a quickened pace, discreetly waving as she approached. Her blond hair shone, her skin glowed, and her blue eyes sparkled. Television was her manifest destiny. Critics acknowledged her translucent beauty, but Sloan could peer through her transparent looks into her empty soul.

Collins effusively greeted Sloan, who returned a perfunctory embrace. "Cherry blossom season is fantastic," she said with inappropriate glee, gesturing to a nearby tree with her dark sunglasses. "Can I count on your help? We've known each other for a long time."

"We know each other well—*very* well," Sloan replied with a hint of mischief.

"I never…" Collins's words squeezed out through her tight lips. "I never want to hear that again."

Billy Rogers dutifully trudged up the small incline toward Sloan. Upon seeing his approach, Collins grazed Sloan's hand with her own and walked toward the cameras. Her appropriate somber countenance had returned, her dark glasses once again fastened securely over her griefless eyes. Her real political skill was in projecting an illusion of concern.

Despite the increasing wind, Rogers's slick black hair withstood any movement. His hairline ended in a sharp widow's peak, the most angular feature on a short, stocky physique that resembled a fire hydrant. "It's coming this week," he said with determination. "There is a rumor the governor might go off the reservation with his appointment. But I'll get to the Senate, appointment or election."

Without malice, Sloan privately dismissed Rogers as a mere pedestrian pol. He equated the lieutenant governor's political skills to those of a casino pit boss—the politician's former occupation. In the media-driven political orbit, the mere fact that Rogers "did not look like a senator" was a deep career wound.

"Join Team Billy," Rogers said quickly. "Sing a song at our Mandalay Bay fundraiser."

Sloan was well versed in candidate-speak. He translated phrases of "needing your help" and "wanting you on our team" as pleas to open a checkbook or, in his case, to make a strategic public appearance.

"Not now," Sloan replied tightly, turning away.

* * *

Many in the funeral crowd gradually dispersed. Others remained standing in small circles, sharing remembrances. Sloan walked down the incline to Garvey's family, aware of the remaining mourners' collective gaze following his every step.

He extended both of his hands to Garvey's grown son, whose eyes expressed a lost battle against tears. Sloan gently placed his hand on the man's wrist. "Our dads shared a noble profession."

Garvey's grieving widow was moving closer, her steps slow and halting. One lift of the black veil off her face revealed her moist and drawn eyes. A slow reach to grasp both of Sloan's hands. Her words were almost inaudible before a slight smile emerged. "Ted was so pleased when you sang for him," the widow said, referring to how Sloan had honored the family friendship by performing at the senator's last fundraising event.

Sloan hoped his nod and modest smile brought her comfort.

Garvey's widow returned the veil to her face, walking away with her children's assistance.

Sloan saw his father approaching and went to meet him. Formally he was "Michael," but everyone referred to him as "Mike." Mike Sloan. Mike had once told his son he was politically fortunate—one or both of his names fit snugly on a political button or bumper sticker.

Sloan raised his arms hesitantly to exchange a hug but drew them down when Mike offered his hand for a shake. As the cameras focused on the two, Mike lifted his chin and straightened his posture.

"You lost a dear friend," Sloan said, adding a gentle touch to his father's shoulder.

"Loyal. Ted was loyal. Served with him for…" Mike's voice cracked in sorrow. "Twenty years in the House. He was with me in my governor's race—campaigned with me in New Hampshire. He's the reason I won the Nevada caucuses. If I'd had a dozen Teds, I'd be president today."

Sloan silently recalled meeting with his father at the Democratic National Convention the day after Mike had lost the nomination for president. Describing his father's mood that day as "despondent" would have been charitable.

"Hey, come to Las Vegas," Sloan said quickly as if the idea had just occurred to him. "My residency at the MGM ends on May 14."

There was a pause.

"I've seen you sing," Mike said.

A longer pause followed.

Sloan forced a lighter tone. "Not in this decade."

Mike sighed with a discernable weariness. "I'm attending too many damn funerals."

"Come to Vegas," Sloan said again, attempting to lighten the mood. "Riley will join us. You can't say no to your granddaughter."

"Some folks today have no shame," Mike said, seemingly oblivious of Sloan's gentle urging. "A few people here told me to move to Nevada to run for the Senate. It's a special election, only serve eighteen months, not the worst idea."

"You retired from that. Stop and smell the roses; time to enjoy."

Mike's vision turned to the rows of grave markers, of heroes laid to rest. "Smelling roses can put you six feet under." His eyes narrowed as he looked at Sloan. "I heard a rumor you may run. Imagine that."

The men exchanged silent stares. A funeral and his father's unknown reaction dictated this was neither the time nor place to voice his plans. Sloan's only certainty was that he would not run for political office to hear the applause; his pockets were already stuffed with the currency of adulation.

"Imagine that," Mike repeated, searching for a response. "Of course, when a man hits fifty, he knows what's best. No need to consult with his father, even a father who's won a few times down the track."

Mike had always praised his son's skills in mastering the entertainment world but never failed to contrast those with the political skills required to master the political game, or as he referred to it, *the game.*

"You know your game; I know mine," Mike stated confidently, then added with a tinge of regret, "I've won every election—but my last." The subtle regret floated harmlessly away, no response necessary. "Son, our worlds are different; our *games* are different." His tone conveyed comforting paternal counsel laced with smugness.

"Not too much difference," Sloan replied.

"You think you can do this?" Mike queried. "*Really* do it?"

Sloan heard far too much doubt in his questions. For an instant, he thought of citing how he had testified before US Senate Committees, authored an opinion piece for the *New York Times,* and helped resolve a musicians' union strike against a chain of hotels on the Strip. Instead, a light squeeze of his father's shoulder. "We'll talk."

TWO

May 14, Las Vegas

The MGM Grand Garden Arena was filled to capacity. Sloan took a bow after his third and final encore. He raised his arms, careful not to mimic a preacher or an egomaniacal rock star wringing one last cheer. In a long-ago interview, he'd described the perfect concert as "orgasmic." Tonight was *that* kind of night.

Sloan allowed his breath to slow. His lean body was fit but slightly fuller than it had been in years past. The sleeves of his black shirt rolled up on his tight and tanned forearms. His carefully coiffed hair was modestly damp from the string of up-tempo songs where the drums cranked louder, and the thumping bass masked the imperfections in his voice. He was confident he still had the "pipes" but also aware that backup singers were his saving grace. Once his voice was described as "edgy" but now too frequently termed "raspy."

"Tonight is the night, my friends." The next words would deflate the crowd's energy as if the helium was seeping out of the balloon. He let the air out. "This is my final concert."

The crowd was hushed. A rolling wave of audible moans filled the theater. Shouts of disbelief rang aloud. Sloan gazed through the floaters in his eyes that slightly blurred his vision; they would pass.

"Others have done a Goodbye Tour, came back to do a Farewell Tour, then an Encore Tour, and then the Last Encore Tour." Sloan held a dazzling smile. "Some get the band together for the Final Hurrah, and then the ultimate Last Hurrah tour. But that's not me. Las Vegas is my home; I'm not going anywhere. Let's just say *au revoir*. I'll see you all again."

Sloan took his time, methodically walking closer to the edge of the stage, reaching down to graze the hands of those in the front row. "You made my dreams come true," he continued. "Your dreams…you all need to…" The audience craned forward in delicious anticipation as if this were a secret they all shared. "Capture Your Dream!" he shouted.

The shout-out expected—the title of one of his penned rock classics. They thundered as one with a return volley: "Capture your dream!"

Sloan pumped his fist, and then again as his grin exploded.

* * *

Sloan sat alone in the back of the hotel's stretch limousine, which drove him to his Lake Las Vegas home. His security man and the driver sat in the distant front seat. Filling the limo's refrigerator were chilled water bottles from three continents. He nibbled from a platter of red and gold raspberries, slices of papaya, crackers, and imported cheeses. The hotel staff was ever ready to satisfy his culinary desires.

He flexed his right wrist, a slight but nagging injury that was too slow to heal. His palms were often tight. His body no longer responded to his every wish. When he was young, he had done three shows a night. Now he scheduled intermittent nights off to recharge.

Years ago, the songwriting had flowed effortlessly with memorable "hooks"—now, that writing was labored. The few songs he wrote held deeper meanings. No throwaways. Many of his songs were of romance tinged with regret, of the moment when one stares across the room at their spouse with a reflective certainty that the embers of their once-unified dreams could no longer be lit.

His audiences demanded to hear his old hits. He calculated the number of times he had sung "Baby's Fire"—far too many. A disjointed smile spread across his face at the song's various interpretations. To maintain his interest in "Baby's Fire," he had performed it with horns, done an acoustical version, and often added a country flavor with a steel guitar. His songs were his babies. He loved them all. Yet how many times could he sing them all?

He had accepted his limitations. He winced at the memory of last year's Super Bowl halftime show, when a rock music contemporary had slid across the stage and needed his guitarist to help him rise from the floor. Wearing a bemused smile, he rubbed his knee, still aching from his last run.

Sloan fixated upon his political trump cards. Fame rested comfortably upon him. Fame could be an unforgiving, harsh mistress, but he was confident he had mastered its tempo. He had a lifetime of observing his father's political prowess. He had met three presidents before his twenty-first birthday, able to garner media coverage with a mere utterance or appearance. His campaign could ace that sweet spot between policy and celebrity, a political magnet for the disenfranchised on the right and the left. His opponents would play within neatly defined political boxes, yet he could dance unrestrained. He was the nothing-to-lose candidate.

* * *

A week later, outside the security door of a Victorian residence in San Francisco's fashionable Pacific Heights, Sloan buzzed the intercom. "Is Mike Sloan's campaign manager available?"

"You're early," Tony Martino's gruff voice responded as the iron gates opened.

Martino waited for Sloan at the front door. A considerable weight bulged from his midsection, and a baggy shirt hung below his waist.

Two years earlier, President Bret Reed's approval ratings were tanking, and the political punditry had universally dismissed his reelection chances. The president then summoned Martino to serve as his campaign manager. With Martino at the helm, Reed had ridden Big Mo to a narrow reelection victory. Martino was hailed as the political genius du jour and remained the "go-to guy" to negotiate with the Reed administration.

Martino enthusiastically patted Sloan's back as the two entered the unkempt living room.

"Hey, loved that movie you were in. Gonna do another?" Martino asked.

The movie *Last Song* had earned Sloan an Oscar nomination for supporting actor. He'd played an aging rock star now resigned to performing in Holiday Inns.

Sloan grinned. "I'm thinking of a new role."

Dotting the room's walls were political photographs. Three black-and-white pictures rested on the fireplace mantel. One framed image showed Martino as a young boy with his parents in front of Brooklyn's Ebbets Field, the long-ago-demolished baseball shrine. To the left was a brushed silver frame with a photograph of Governor Mike Sloan peering over Martino's shoulder as he reviewed election returns. On the right was a framed photo of President Reed and Martino in an eerily similar pose.

Sloan noticed a week's worth of shoes neatly aligned in one corner, confirming this was a single man's home.

Martino explained how he preferred corporate consulting as opposed to the frenzy of a campaign. "It's more money and less brain damage."

"You're simplifying your life, like Thoreau," Sloan replied cheerfully.

"A rocker quoting Thoreau." Martino was impressed. "I like my pace. Today my toughest decision was at Starbucks." Martino patted his stomach. "That Caramel Mocha Frappuccino is my downfall."

Sloan looked for a place to sit barren of magazines, newspapers, and books. His eyes settled on one computer screen that displayed the latest poll results from RealClearPolitics; another screen showed ESPN's baseball scores.

"Handicap the Nevada Senate race for me." Sloan was removing a sweatshirt draped across the back of a love seat. He sat and propped his feet on the edge of the ottoman.

"Rogers is capable, but zero charisma," Martino replied. "You don't want to be stuck next to him at a party. Collins is the feminists' nightmare, an articulate conservative woman. Chris could go national, but..." He paused. "She's not authentic, not much warmth there."

"Which side would you rather have?" Sloan asked in a tone that demanded an answer.

Martino nodded at the "force-you-into-a-corner" question. Political consultants were loath to acknowledge the obvious—that their party's candidate was a near-certain loser.

Martino spoke with confidence. "We'd energize your dad's network if you jump in against Rogers. Or pass, you make a lot of dough, and women still throw themselves at you."

"Still?" Sloan asked as Martino sputtered an explanation. "Still?"

Martino walked around the room, adjusting a frame that hung at a slight angle. Sloan thought it odd that one frame would disturb Martino when so much of the room appeared amiss.

"Your dad would have been a hell of a president," Martino said.

Sloan had often heard similar comments, never certain which ones were heartfelt. He appreciated Martino for serving as the keeper of the flame for Mike Sloan.

"Mike would burst with pride if you ran. What's his take on it?"

Sloan grabbed Martino's jacket, which lay on the couch. He tossed the coat to Martino. "Can't be late to meet Grant for dinner."

* * *

Before they entered the Villa Florence on Powell Street, Martino told Sloan that if he were to run, he should announce soon, or Rogers and Collins would "dominate public attention."

"Public attention?" Sloan scoffed, then added in his best Robert De Niro voice, "*You* talking to *me*?" With that, he swung open the restaurant's door and entered.

Taking note of his presence, the bartender shouted out like a UFC ring announcer, "Ladies and gentlemen…Ty…leeerrr Sloooan!"

A small group of Japanese tourists began singing Sloan's "Got to Believe" in fractured English, and a young father was nudging his son closer to the newly retired rock star. Sloan signed the boy's black-and-orange San Francisco Giants satin jacket with the gold Sharpie pen provided.

As they were escorted to the restaurant's private dining room, Sloan saluted patrons with smiles and obliged a few selfies. He exchanged high-fives with a group of well-suited young men and autographed a woman's copy of the latest *Rolling Stone* magazine, which featured him on the cover adjacent to a banner that read, Exiting the Stage.

Sloan turned back to Martino. "Want to rethink your *public attention* analysis? This campaign could be fun."

"*Fun?*" Martino dismissed the thought as the two sat down. "I've heard every description of campaigns, but for a candidate, they are not fun." Martino studied Sloan. "You have a gift in dealing with people. They worship you."

"*Worship?* Let's not go there."

"You'd be a *rock star* candidate." Martino appeared to enjoy his choice of words, leaning forward across the table with a smile and ending with emphasis, "A *real* rock star."

"Keep staring, and someone is going to think you're proposing," Sloan said. "What's your fee to run it?"

"Man," Martino momentarily objected, "it would take *beaucoup* dollars and some real political mojo to win it."

Sloan elaborated that he had named his company *blue* without a capital letter, and the Silicon Valley venture capitalists loved it. He had a string of successful investments in budding technology firms that generated lottery-like multipliers. Sloan boasted about *blue's* success. The company employed nearly a thousand people with a song publishing division, auto dealerships, a beer distributor, restaurants, and real estate holdings, and the *blue* nonprofit foundation owned motels that housed nearly a hundred people who were formerly homeless.

Wayne Avrashow

Sloan slid his phone across the table, displaying a website with the net worth of celebrities. He gained perverse pleasure as Martino's eyes enlarged while he read Sloan's entry.

"*Mama*, you're loaded," Martino blurted. "*Nine hundred million?*"

"Well…the market's down." He smiled. "My dad ensured that I still own my song rights, and those babies still get covered. Even with Spotify, Apple, and all the downloading, I'm still receiving wire transfers. I'll start the campaign with a million-dollar check."

Martino modestly shook his head. "Not close."

"*Cuanto?*" Sloan asked and then raised two digits. At Martino's abrupt dismissal, he opened his palm to signal five.

"Try north of fifty million," Martino said without missing a beat.

Sloan involuntarily shuddered. "You serious?" He reflected on the amount, hopeful his ability to get free media would lessen the need for paid media.

The private room's door flew open as Grant Zimmer entered. Zimmer was the sun around which political and celebrity planets revolved. A Google search would fail to locate the words *timid* and *Zimmer* in the same paragraph.

The waiter closed the door to ensure their privacy.

Zimmer opened his small tablet and read aloud. "Listen up: Ted Richman's column in tomorrow's Las Vegas paper the *Review-Journal*. The headline is Tyler Sloan's Encore?"

"Richman's no longer the big kahuna—but the man won a Pulitzer," Martino said, then added with notable condescension, "Do Vegas slot players bother to read?"

Zimmer read the column aloud: "Beyond each party's base, Nevada voters have scant excitement for either of the leading candidates, Chris Collins and Billy Rogers. Today undecided wins. Whispers persist that Tyler Sloan is pondering a race against Rogers, or he may launch an independent bid. Candidates outside of the two parties usually collapse, but politics are in Sloan's bloodline. Politicos are wondering—what's the next song on the Sloan playlist?"

As his personal attorney, Zimmer had fought the battles that allowed Sloan to glide gracefully above the fray. He was the ferocious lawyer anyone would want on their side—the pushy, arrogant lawyer who would be feared and hated if he represented the opposition.

Sartorially decked in elegant Italian suits, Zimmer extended his arms to flash diamond cuff links. In contrast, Martino's loose-fitting clothes and well-worn tennis shoes stretched the intent of business casual dress. Martino's role as campaign manager would instantly legitimize Sloan's campaign, but their relationship had little depth.

"I met with the president," Zimmer said with his usual directness, seemingly disappointed that the mention of President Bret Reed did not generate more enthusiasm. "The *president*," Zimmer repeated slightly louder. "Ever heard of him?"

Sloan motioned for more.

"The libs are pounding on Reed to support Rogers now and clear the Democratic field." Zimmer spoke rapidly. "But the president sees Rogers as too far left to win the general election. He knows you're our party's best hope."

Sloan snapped to attention. "The *president* said that?"

"*Emmis*," Zimmer replied. His use of the Yiddish word for "truth" amused Sloan.

Martino offered an impromptu political tutorial: "Billy Rogers gets appointed to fill Hodges's seat, an incumbent's edge in the election—"

"Boys"—Zimmer was theatrical in his interruption—"a little wrinkle emerged…Rogers is not getting appointed. The Republican state attorney general made the governor an offer he could not refuse—no charges would be filed against him for malfeasance if he appointed a caretaker to the Senate seat and set a date for a special election."

Zimmer explained that the two parties would hold caucuses to select their nominee, the Democrats on June 18, the Republicans two days later. The general election would be August 22.

"Do Rogers or Collins know this?" Sloan asked.

Zimmer's tone was dismissive. "Need-to-know basis. Let's organize now for the Dem caucus."

"I'm not a Democrat," Sloan replied. "I've been registered *Decline to State* for years."

"One form, one signature, one minute, and—boom—you're a Democrat!" Zimmer's response was intense.

"With my baggage, it would be tough to get fifty-one percent, but I could snare forty in a three-way race as an independent. It's the perfect political storm—people don't trust either party." Sloan paused to study the men's reactions. "I'm running as an independent."

Sloan brushed aside their pleas to reconsider. In two weeks, Collins, Rogers, and the president were all speaking at the Teamsters' convention in Las Vegas. "*I'm* introducing the president that day." Sloan added a wink at the two.

The political wizards exchanged puzzled glances.

"I called in a chit for my campaign appearances for Reed," Sloan explained; noting their reaction, he was proud that he had one-upped his presumed experts.

Zimmer gently questioned Sloan's readiness for a campaign.

Sloan detailed his trips abroad and meetings with foreign dignitaries, estimating he had dozens of photographs and correspondence with international leaders.

"How do we include those in TV ads, Facebook, social media, mailers?"

Zimmer and Martino exchanged glances as if Sloan's naivete was overwhelming.

"Remember what I told you," Zimmer said quickly. "It's not what you know, but what they *think* you know. In thirty seconds…why are you qualified?"

Sloan cited a book he had read on the differences between structural and evolving politics. He offered details before halting, chagrined at the look of disbelief his advisors were shooting him.

"Tyler…" Zimmer was deliberate. "Not since the days of the Roman Empire have we had philosophers in the Senate. What will *do* in the Senate for some *schmuck* in Reno?"

"No, the big question is, *why* are you running? Answer that," Martino commanded.

Sloan drew back slightly from the table. "No offense, guys, but you two know how to manipulate the system. You can access any door in Washington." His vision scanned both men. "How does the middle class, the working mom, or the down-and-out get heard? Who rattles the cages for them?"

At Zimmer's slight smile, Sloan asked rhetorically, "You know the differences between the two parties?" Sloan spaced his thumb and right index finger a millimeter apart. "Different special interests and different lobbyists. Pick your poison."

"A little rough, but we'll poll it and work on it." Martino nodded.

"No polls or focus groups; I know my audience—just get me out there."

"It's more than retail politics. The media wants details, at least some details," Martino noted. His voice grew taut. "The microscopes will come out when you get closer in the polls. If a poll shows you might win, the media *proctoscope* will do a thorough exam. Reporters will interview a bunch of gals who hung around backstage." His index finger menacingly jutted forward across the table. "Strap yourself in tight, buddy boy; it'll become ugly. But *if* I'm in—I repeat, *if* I'm in—I'm the first to wake you, the last to tuck you in."

Sloan crossed his arms over his chest. A penetrating stare at Martino.

"You get a two mil bonus if I win. Are you in?"

Martino fell uncharacteristically silent.

Sloan chafed, interpreting the silence to confirm that neither man believed he could win.

"Listen," Sloan began. "You both know there were *a lot* of women, I smoked pot, and it was public when I checked myself into Betty Ford. I never did psychedelic drugs or anything with a needle. All I do now is taste a little wine."

"Manageable, all manageable," Zimmer accented it all with a dismissive gesture. "You're the first to complete a college degree between rock tours and rehab sessions."

Sloan hesitated, alternating glances between the two. "Years ago… Collins and I had a fling."

A momentary silence stilled the private room.

"That's a new one," Martino replied cautiously. "When? For how long?"

"About twenty-five years ago, only a couple of romps."

The two advisors held their silence; their disbelieving faces were mirror images.

"And…" Sloan added slowly, pausing to gauge the reaction of his two advisors.

"And?" Martino interrupted. "There's more?" His hands grasped his forehead dramatically.

"There's a tape of Chris, another woman, and me," Sloan said hastily.

"A threesome sex tape with Collins?" Martino's voice was spiked. "What the hell?"

Sloan extended his palms out in a comforting gesture. "An old rock buddy of mine filmed it; he has the video. He's coming to town. I'll get the tape from him."

"Talk to me," Zimmer urged. "How long is this tape? Who was the second gal? Is it graphic? Does Collins know about it?"

"She knows. We were together in my hotel room after a concert. Chris was drunk, and no one had a stitch of clothes on. I haven't seen the tape in years, but I remember I was in the shadows, hard to see me—but my voice was clear. Chris and the other woman sang Buffett's 'Margaritaville' for the camera. Perfect song for the occasion." He paused. "I know it's strange."

"Strange?" Zimmer said with disbelief. He rose from the table and paced. "Strange? I've had clients with underage women, hookers, gay lovers, drugs—I've seen it all." His voice slowed. "But none were on a ballot."

"Forty years in this business…" Martino's voice trailed softly.

"Get that tape," Zimmer commanded. "Pay any price."

"I'm on it. As I said, I'm meeting him next week," Sloan replied.

"Any price," Zimmer said sharply. "Pay any price."

THREE

June 4, Las Vegas

Sloan walked briskly past the flower-filled lobby of the Wynn Hotel. He paused to appreciate the carousel composed of one hundred thousand fresh flowers and to gather his thoughts; this was the first public appearance since reporter Ted Richman had floated his possible candidacy. Martino puffed behind as the two walked toward the charity dinner at the hotel's Lafite Ballroom.

Upon entering the foyer, Martino took one step back and adroitly grabbed two pizza-inspired hors d'oeuvres from a passing waiter's tray. With his Jell-O-like jowls and disheveled appearance, no mistaking him for the candidate, but his curly gray hair and fleshy face were respected fixtures on the political scene. Notwithstanding the evening's formality, Martino wore his signature sneakers.

"Richman is here," Martino told Sloan, popping one of the pizza bites between his lips. With the semichewed tidbit still in his mouth, he added, "He'll follow you around, but no interviews—not yet."

Sloan playfully jabbed Martino's shoulder. "Controlling the candidate wasn't our deal."

Walking across the lobby, Sloan noticed heads turning in his direction. He flashed a generous grin as he joined a group of guests.

One man introduced himself as the executive director of the Nevada teacher's union. He cited with pride how the union formed a coalition to defeat a bill in the Nevada legislature that would have implemented school vouchers.

"Why not try vouchers in one district for a couple of years?" Sloan said matter-of-factly, but friendly.

The man stared daggers at Sloan and then turned away abruptly, muttering under his breath.

Ted Richman approached. "You irritated that guy. He's the union's leader."

"Is it a rookie mistake to say what you believe?"

"Your dad did not raise a rookie. You getting in?" Richman queried. "Tell me if you need to go on background; Mike can vouch that this reporter plays it straight."

Sloan viewed Richman's ever-present fedora and sport coat as the hippest imaginable for a man of his age. He held his gaze on Richman. "Rumor has it you're a loyal guy."

Richman's expression displayed the reporter's first hint of a smile.

"You and my dad had…the arrangement."

Richman began recounting his fond memories of covering Mike Sloan's campaigns. "Back in the day, there weren't as many African American reporters, but Mike was always good to me. I was a young black punk reporter that thought he knew it all."

"I understand there was reciprocity to that kindness."

At Richman's uncertain gaze, Sloan noticed the veteran reporter's hearing aid. He inched closer to repeat his comment.

The reporter wore the smile of a Cheshire cat. He offered that Mike would share political gossip and information that he would attribute to an informed source, a high-placed official, or a campaign insider.

"And you returned the favor?" Sloan was easy in his inquiry.

"Mike didn't do it because of some affirmative action bullshit; I earned it. And, yes…we appreciated each other's insights."

"Ready for the sequel?" Sloan wore a mischief-laced smile.

"Only do it for a man named Sloan. Anything you want to share?"

"I'll see you at the Teamsters' conference. The day Reed is speaking." Sloan held his hand over his mouth. "Nothing specific, but in that day's paper, you can drop one hint, inference, or rumor." Sloan paused for effect. "I'm announcing that day."

"I won't quote you, background only, but why? Why are you running?"

"Washington is poisoned with hyperpartisan BS. Nothing gets done. *Nothing*."

The two men exchanged concurrent nods before parting ways. Sloan deftly walked through the room until the lobby lights flickered to signal dinner. Politicos scurried in an elaborate dance, speaking with one person while simultaneously scanning those standing behind—the full political minuet. Sitting at the dinner table froze mobility like a thoroughbred restrained on the bit, so some candidates remained in the lobby until the last possible moment. Then they not-so-casually moved through the entire room to "find" their seats, collecting business cards and contact information.

Disdaining the candidates' dance, Sloan met with Grant Zimmer in the lobby. Zimmer held a stationary presence to receive those who wished to pay him homage on their way into the ballroom. "Look around." Zimmer grandly gestured around the hotel's lobby. "The Italian tile, the chandeliers…breathe in; they pump in fragrance to mask the smoke; God is in the details."

From his coat pocket, Sloan removed several business cards pressed into his hands tonight. His cell phone was receiving texts with contact information. Following Zimmer's praiseworthy idea, he sent texts to himself or jotted brief notes or graphics to trigger his memory. His campaign staff would send emails or short notes to each, relying on his keywords or drawings.

"What have you got?" Sloan asked Zimmer.

"Thousands of names for an email the moment you announce. My people can bundle ten million for you in a month. We'll be ready."

Sloan paused. "Ah, that's not the campaign I want to run."

"At least meet them," Zimmer protested. "There's no one you'd have to apologize for."

"I'll meet them, but that's my only promise."

* * *

"Warhol was wrong; my fifteen minutes has lasted thirty years," Denny Morgan stated to Sloan, a couple of days following the event at the Wynn.

The lead singer of the long-disbanded rock group The Screams, Morgan had come to Las Vegas for the Hit Masters Convention. As it neared midnight, Sloan and Morgan sat isolated in the convention's meeting room at the Orleans Hotel. Morgan's white shirt, dotted with numerous green stars, and red pants aligned with his crimson boots.

Called the "Ultimate Survivor" by critics, the Hit Masters Convention gathered together all the "one-hit wonders." In the convention room, music videos of the hits played continuously from wall-mounted television screens, and nameplates identified each hit master's name, group, and musical instrument. Attendees wandered from booth to booth to chat with their favorites and purchase autographed photos taken decades ago when the artists still surged with youthful promise.

"Tyler, my man, my three-minute masterpiece 'Get Up' was number two on *Billboard* for two straight weeks, but there was one bastard I couldn't knock off number one," Morgan said with wry admiration. "Yeah, the nameplate is demeaning, but it's still better than having to introduce yourself and getting that blank who-the-hell-are-you stare."

Sloan allowed Morgan to vent. The singer's fate was similar to Sloan's character in *Last Song*, the down-on-his-luck singer clinging to his long-ago bragging rights.

"The good news?" Morgan chuckled. "I still get laid here. I sign photos downstairs and tits upstairs. The asses get softer every year."

Morgan's hair remained the same length and color of years past, but his weathered face and rare smile were the tell; the big-hair band singer's best days were in the rearview mirror.

"Not like the old days." Sloan smiled as the waitress rested bottles of mineral water on the table.

Sloan noticed Morgan's ravaged teeth. He recalled his friend had scant discipline when the white lines were laid out before him. Morgan could be a poster child for the 1980s antidrug "Just Say No" advertising campaign.

"After the last song, I walked off as the final chords hit, no encores." Morgan's voice turned melancholy. "I thought it was cool to leave while the crowd was chanting for more. Now, I'd give my right nut to hear it all one more time."

"Keep in touch with your old band?" Sloan asked innocently.

Morgan emitted a series of clicking sounds. "That…would be difficult. One guitarist died, the other is in prison, and our drummer is a born-again freak living somewhere in Montana. My piano player sued me for using the name The Screams on tour. I won, but it cost me one hundred K in legal fees…no reunion tour is on my horizon."

Although sympathetic, Sloan grew tired of Morgan's refrains of what *could* have or *should* have happened. He asked about the videotape.

"It's a DVD now," Morgan answered. "I had all my old VHS tapes converted years ago. Both Rogers and Collins had their people contact me. Collins's assistant got pissed when I didn't confirm I had it; she started hinting about you, me, and…Kenny."

The name was an unexpected and unwelcome historical jolt. Kenny was a notorious cocaine dealer to many in the music industry. Sloan dismissed Kenny's role as a mere hanger-on when he started at the small clubs on the Sunset Strip—the Roxy, the Whiskey, and Gazzari's.

"Her assistant wasn't asking about clubs," Morgan continued. "She asked about those wild parties at the house in the hills off Sunset Plaza Drive. Remember your hot, red-haired backup singer who blew her nose and spewed blood everywhere? No one ever saw her again, and no one dared to call."

An awkward pause followed.

Morgan lowered his voice to relay that Collins's team had offered him $50,000. His quivering voice and darting eyes concerned Sloan. "I'm broke, only scratching out a living here and there."

Sloan reached out to pat Morgan's wrist.

"Rogers's guy offered a hundred K. Can you match it and help me out on something?"

Although Sloan had expected the need to pay Morgan, the meeting began to resemble a shakedown. He curled his finger for more.

"I've got bits of songs we wrote together back in the day, in that studio in the Valley."

Sloan heard Morgan's boot tapping against the metal legs of the table. Sloan could not recall any history with the songs.

Morgan turned to the screens mounted on the wall and mumbled about a play on *SportsCenter*. He pressed again for Sloan's help to "polish our songs."

Sloan nearly blanched at Morgan's phrase "our songs." He kept to his task. "No copies? The DVD?"

"Damn it, Tyler, you think I'd double-cross you and make copies? Back to the songs: don't diss them; they're good, but snippets. They need your finishing touch. I'll stream an album, *Denny Morgan Sings Tyler Sloan.*"

Morgan's foot tapping was now more pronounced. Sloan glanced down at the table as Morgan's boot pounded disturbingly loud against the table's aluminum legs.

"Tyler, my band blamed you for our downfall, that tour where we opened for you."

Sloan braced himself for an ugly turn.

"We were never the same after being bounced from that tour," Morgan said. "After that, The Screams were on the bad-boys list, but without the hits."

Sloan understood his opportunity was fleeting. He masked his exasperation and reached across the table to pat Morgan's wrist again. "Denny, you were in a bathtub filled with champagne and two groupies instead of onstage rehearsing. You were doing lines when you should have been at the sound check. My manager booted you guys without telling me."

"Dude"—Morgan's tone spiked with resentment—"you weren't exactly Pope Tyler."

Sloan saw fear, anger, and subtle loathing imprinted on Morgan's aged face. The best move was to appease him. "My man will call you. I'll match Rogers's one hundred K, and I'll work on *our songs* right after the election; that'll generate another payday for you."

FOUR

June 8, Las Vegas

The Teamsters Union played the ultimate political weapon—leverage. Twenty thousand Teamsters were jammed into the Events Center at Mandalay Bay to link President Bret Reed with their legislative agenda.

In an anteroom outside of public view, Teamster president Bob Carney stood with his hands on his hips to meet with the two senior aides of Chris Collins and Billy Rogers.

Carney's suit hugged his large frame as he impatiently tapped his foot. "I agreed to *five* minutes." He tugged at his necktie, appearing unaccustomed to wearing one as the knot remained slightly off-center. A glance at his watch. "You're down to four, and I haven't heard squat."

Collins's aide, a well-groomed young man, gestured to the Rogers aide, a stylishly coiffed young woman. "Our candidates are not entering the room unless you assure us that Sloan's not speaking. I've got Chris on hold, and she's got Rogers standing by."

Carney looked askance at them.

"We have no idea, and you have no idea what Sloan will say," the young man added hurriedly. "You read Richman's piece. What if he announces right now? Right now!"

Carney smiled benevolently. "You got both of your candidates on ice? Keep 'em chilled." He wagged his finger close to each of the staffers' faces, alternating between them. "You two ever go to a boxing match? Today the president and Sloan are the heavyweights in the main event. Your candidates are the lightweights on the undercard. I don't know what the singer's going to do, but it would be a hell of a note if he announces in front of my people." With that, he drew a hasty retreat, slightly bumping the male aide.

* * *

A large, hulking man abruptly obstructed Sloan's walk to the elevated stage at the Teamsters' convention. Sloan held his ground as the man moved closer.

The man looked down at Sloan and said in a deep bass voice, "You did drugs and antidrug commercials."

Sloan agreed. The man was candid and accurate.

"Let's keep kids from messing with drugs," the man continued as he stroked his bushy black beard. "Send a National Guard team onto ships along the coast wearing pirate gear. They'll land on a beach and teach kids about boats and drugs at the same time. Kids love pirates."

Sloan recalled his father's comment about politics attracting "characters one slice short of a loaf." Sloan firmly shook the man's hand. "Ship ahoy, mate."

Sloan walked past the media section, accustomed to public stares and cries of wonder at his presence, but uncertain how to respond to the media's interrogative shouts. He played it safe with smiles and waves. Now tossing in random "hey" and "good to see you."

Richman's column in today's *Review-Journal* had resonated: "Watch Sloan; all political eyes are on Sloan."

Sloan wore his political uniform of a Canali navy pinstripe suit and white shirt. Dismissing ties as barbaric, he opted for an open collar. His hair swept back, posture erect as admiring stares tracked his every move. His stride was purposeful as he walked onstage, past a swarm of Secret

Service agents who had engulfed the arena, and found his name posted on a folding chair toward the center of the stage.

Chris Collins was delivering her remarks with pitch-perfect tone and cadence. Republicans were breathing rarified air as Collins led in the early polling. Sloan studied her; she bolstered her words with gestures, well-timed pauses, and full smiles—a performance that held all the spontaneity of an Olympic synchronized swimmer.

Rogers's remarks were an octave too high as he nailed every touchstone of the progressive agenda. When he began citing a tedious laundry list of his voting record, Sloan's confidence spiked; his opponent was as thrilling as a mashed potato sandwich.

Sloan rose from his seat as Rogers and Collins cast steely glances toward him in a prefight staring down of an opponent. Sloan returned a playful nod to Rogers and a quick smile toward Collins.

The union delegates greeted Sloan with a thunderous ovation. Many delegates hoisted preprinted signs in the air that read, "I Believe!" Approaching the podium, Sloan stooped to autograph numerous Teamster baseball caps thrust toward him.

Sloan understood that public speeches were not analogous to the child's game of skipping rocks on a lake's surface and watching the resulting ripples. Once released in the public domain, the speaker "owned" those ideas, and proposals dismissed as "silly" could guillotine a public career.

"Good to be back," Sloan opened with a broad smile. "I haven't been on a Vegas stage for…what? Five weeks?"

Sloan noticed the near-hypnotic nods of a middle-aged woman who gazed upward from the front row. He understood. When her pedestrian life brushed with his celebrity, she would hold an ephemeral wisp of status to share on social media and to regale her coworkers at tomorrow's coffee break.

"My father was elected governor of California with the endorsement and support of the Teamsters. My dear friend Louisa del Mar is a proud Teamster."

Sloan gestured to another female delegate sitting below. On cue, the Hispanic woman stood and waved toward Sloan, then turned, beaming toward the crowd.

"Louisa embodies the American dream," Sloan continued. "She supplied food backstage for my band. We're partners in Louisa's, the best Mexican restaurant in town. Don't tell me about the Teamsters; our restaurant proudly employs Teamsters."

The political media gorillas were punching their laptops. Cameras were focused.

Today, Sloan would make his bones distancing himself from the political status quo. He understood the mood in the hall; the International Brotherhood of Teamsters had over one million members, and none dined on caviar and truffles at a Georgetown political salon where the pampered bemoaned "income inequality" but failed to relate to the struggling middle class. Sloan seized the moment to throw red meat to the hungering crowd.

"Democrats and Republicans claim to represent you"—Sloan raised one finger in the air—"but those candidates stuff their pockets full of campaign contributions from Wall Street bandits whose actions foreclosed homes and shuttered hotels that ripped through Nevada like a tornado. That's not me…no, that's not me." He waited for the cheers to diminish slightly. "You're not happy with do-nothing politicians. Neither am I! Let's take them on!"

Sloan paused, aware that his delivery was a pace too fast, a too-rapid drumbeat. He modestly slowed the tempo. "You'll have to educate Mr. Rogers and Ms. Collins about what you do. Not me. I know how important my Teamster brothers and sisters are. Right now, I'll introduce you to some of your members."

Sloan pointed outward, calling on those Teamsters to stand who had worked with him on his movie, on tour, at the restaurant, or the MGM. Dozens of Teamsters rose and pointed back toward Sloan. Fists were clenched, the room filled with cheers.

He located President Reed's staff, the advance woman who stood to the side of the stage. She frantically waved her hand in a circular motion, signaling Sloan to wrap it up. His allotted warm-up time to introduce Reed had long passed.

"Now." He held the word as if he were in a recording studio, stretching the word for emphasis. "Now," he repeated, "those political jokers spent twenty-five hundred bucks to install each digital security camera in our public buildings." Sloan reached into the pocket of his suit jacket to retrieve one small digital camera. "Yesterday I bought the same security camera…but I only spent sixty dollars." He paused before tossing his verbal grenade. "I got mine at Best Buy."

"Give 'em hell, Tyler!" A shout rang out from the crowd.

Sloan raised his hands high and wide, bouncing on his toes, cheers fueling his energy, the crowd loud enough to demand an encore. Not content with a marginal victory, he flipped the backgammon cube to raise the stakes, set to deliver the concluding paragraph he'd finalized the night before.

"Ten days from now, the Democrats will nominate Billy Rogers; two days later, Chris Collins will be tapped by the Republicans." His voice rose. "I'll quote an English statesman from the eighteenth century. Edmund Burke said, 'The only thing necessary for the triumph of evil is for good men to do nothing.' I will not be idle; I will act."

Sloan glanced to his left to see Rogers tilt awkwardly in his seat. He turned to his right to watch the smugness stamped on Collins's face dissolve. Worry marred their expressions. Sloan relished the brief lull.

"Today, I announce my candidacy to be Nevada's next senator. I will run as an independent, not tied to petty partisanship or beholden to any party."

The room hushed, their reaction delayed, as if the news was too startling to digest. Then cheers erupted as delegates thrust their Teamsters' signs in the air while others exchanged high-fives. Many rushed to the stage.

Sloan felt the same dopamine rush as he had onstage when he was performing. He was nodding, the adulation surging, a crush of chaos, the room ripping apart at its seams. The audience was playing its role, and the cameras cherished the visual.

"Now..." Sloan continued, seeing the crowd's fury unleashed. "Now...we honor a great president."

Sloan motioned for the brass band to play "Hail to the Chief."

President Reed strode deliberately onstage to a massive ovation.

Sloan's voice strained above the rising din as he fully extended his hand. "President Bret Reeeed!"

The loud ovation propelled Reed to the podium.

Sloan stole a glance at his opponents. Rogers's eyes darted in every direction, his face near crimson. An aide grasped his arm to force him to remain seated. Collins sat mute, her face devoid of expression.

Remaining at the podium, Sloan thrust his hand forward to greet the president. Their vigorous handshake cemented the coveted photo op. Holding Reed's hand, Sloan whispered an intentionally unintelligible message. Reed leaned forward, smiling as he asked Sloan to repeat his comment. Photographs kept to their task during the prolonged handshake, ensuring a lengthy time frame to capture images of the Reed-Sloan coupling.

Reed leaned close and whispered to Sloan, "Son, you've got some onions."

"We good?" Sloan added, covering his mouth as he leaned close to the president.

Reed returned a slight but perceptible nod.

Sloan moved to the edge of the stage as Rogers approached with an open hand, muttering under his breath, "Gutsy to run with your history; get out—you'll be destroyed."

Sloan held his smile and gripped Rogers's hand tighter. "Buckle up, Billy. I'm in."

* * *

Later that evening, Sloan sat on the piano bench in his custom-built home in a gate-guarded community amid the manufactured lakes of Lake Las Vegas. This house held his grand piano, while a smaller version was at his condominium on the Strip. He tapped the ebony and rosewood keys. Yoga and other relaxation techniques had their place, but the initial touch of his fingers on the keyboard was his salvation. Right here, right now, he was unfettered and alive.

Today mirrored those times when he'd left a recording studio confident he had another hit song. His modest goal for the day had been to be politically credible, not dismissed as a rock-star dilettante. Today had cemented his political legitimacy. He wore a smile of contentment. He had awakened this morning with lingering doubts, acknowledging his irritation at hearing the doubt from his father following the funeral. No more. Not after today. Still holding skepticism, but hopeful he had pleased Mike.

He presumed that he'd be dismissed by the talking heads and their conventional wisdom, as well as by the wise men and women of the two entrenched political parties. But after today, they—the mysterious and omnipresent *they*—had to realize that Tyler Sloan was ready to frolic in their political galaxy. He could play the game.

FIVE

June 10, Las Vegas

It was a sun-splashed chamber of commerce morning, as Sloan and Zimmer rode in a private helicopter hovering above Las Vegas Boulevard.

Sloan gestured toward the city sprawled out below. He liked to think of an individual's interpretation of the Las Vegas skyline as a Rorschach test. The symbols of the world dotting the Strip's hotels—the Eiffel Tower, Manhattan's skyline, Caesar's towers—could be hailed as symbols of how humans conquered a barren desert. To others, they represented materialism on crack.

Zimmer marveled at the far-reaching suburban sprawl that approached the distant mountains, sharing his observations with Sloan over the communication headset.

"I brought you up here to drive it home; this city and state are far more than just the Strip," Sloan replied. "The economic recession hit us hard; it was a bursting bubble that inflicted a lot of pain. We had too much. Too much retail. Too many houses. Too many hotels. Look out there, as far as you can. Every third house was financially underwater." He paused. "Remember this for our campaign: voters were scared; some still are—we're more fragile than most cities."

Sloan pointed toward construction sites, and Zimmer's eyes followed. The city was once again sprouting hotels.

"We're a different city," Sloan continued. "Our founding fathers were Moe, Bugsy, and Benny. We love our independence, and that's why I'm going to win. We're tolerant…a ton of strip clubs; you can wager on dice, cards, sports, anything that moves; shoot away at indoor ranges; go out, kick up some dust in the desert…we're tolerant."

As the helicopter began its descent toward its station, Zimmer was quick to note, "Your dad called last night. He's pissed off."

"I sent him a text message before I announced," Sloan replied innocently, but Zimmer returned a piercing stare.

"You can't just leave your dad a text message," Zimmer admonished. "I thought you two buried the hatchet."

"No hatchet, just a lot of miles between us." Sloan paused. "I didn't know what he would say, and I didn't want to hear him mock my chances. He always had higher hopes for J.R."

Zimmer was slow to comment. "I know you believe that your dad wanted Mike Jr. to follow in his footsteps, but he knew—in his heart he knew—that your brother just wasn't cut out for a politician's life."

Sloan shrugged. "Dad and I never talk about J.R. It's too painful."

"You did everything; you tried to help him."

Sloan steadied his gaze on Zimmer. "When we speak, it stays between the two of us even when it's not about business?"

"Of course. I'm your attorney," Zimmer said, then added with a gentle chuckle, "and your rabbi. So, you're privileged on both fronts."

"Cindy's not stable," Sloan blurted. "I can't have an unstable ex-wife during a campaign. She knows nothing about politics, could name more fashion designers than senators. She has no discretion, never had much, but it's at an all-time low." Zimmer's sympathetic nod encouraged Sloan to continue. "We have a great daughter. Riley's the best. When I was on tour, Cindy was such an attentive mother. Now it's a different story…" His voice trailed off. "She respects you."

"She needs more help than I can give," Zimmer counseled, his eyebrows rising.

"Talk to her. You'll need to keep her happy during the campaign—at least as happy as possible. We need her to keep a low profile."

* * *

The next day Sloan chartered a plane to take him to his hastily called press conference in Reno. During the flight, he read various reports of his candidacy on the internet. *The Washington Post* headline blared, Tyler Sloan Announces for Senate: Entertainer Stuns the Capitol. One Teamster delegate sarcastically referred to Sloan as "Senator Songboy." The article concluded, "Sloan's announcement was a theatrical, ultra-high-definition appearance while his opponents were grainy black-and-white images from a bygone era."

A political columnist from the *Los Angeles Times* raved, "Tyler Sloan was the rock star boys wanted to hang with, girls wanted to romance, and parents accepted. Our governor's son was no Boy Scout, but he confronted his problem and beat it. That alone earns my respect. To paraphrase an old Sam Cooke song, 'We don't know much about history, don't know much biology,' but we'll soon find out how much Sloan knows about governing."

Sloan looked up from the laptop, a smile playing on his lips. "Martino, you couldn't have written this any better."

Martino was clearly not buying into Sloan's glow. "Trust me, Elvis, today is the best press coverage you'll ever get. We get a week's honeymoon—*maybe*." He paused for the moment, appearing to weigh the sensitivity of his next topic, then spoke. "You need to talk with your father. Zimmer told me he's pissed. Smooth it over; we can't have him tell the world he was clueless you were going to announce your candidacy."

Sloan nodded in agreement.

Martino's tone kicked up a notch as he began filling Sloan in on the staff he'd hired from the president's campaign who were not with the White House or Rogers.

"When do I interview them?" Sloan asked.

"Interview? They're already hired. A half dozen of them are on this plane."

"Run it by me next time," he said without hesitation. "I sign off on all major decisions."

Martino returned a curt nod. The plane began its descent to Reno-Tahoe International Airport; Sloan sensed the pressure change, both in the cabin and in Martino.

"Hey, put your hand out," Martino commanded. "I'll teach you something before we land."

Sloan closed his laptop, but he did not comply. "I know how to shake hands."

"I've seen you with your posse," Martino snorted, dismissing the term. "You bump fists, slap palms, or do some chest-pounding bullshit. One day, you're going to shake one thousand hands. You don't want to get red or swollen knuckles. You've got to protect this area." Martino grasped Sloan's right hand and squeezed between his thumb and forefinger. "After a few hundred shakes, this fleshy part can be rubbed raw. Never squeeze a woman's hand and don't get too close and invade her space. Your biggest worry is the crusher."

"A WWF wrestling guy?" Sloan asked. "Come on."

"No, some big bruiser who wants to prove his manhood by crushing your hand like a grape. Shake a big guy's hand first and get out quick. Move on before he realizes it."

Sloan was pained to understand the importance of the lecture. Martino waved him off as he began to object. "Listen," he warned. "If you see a whole row of hands at a rally, just touch fingers to avoid some idiot squeezing or scratching your knuckles." He winced at the thought. "Be careful not to get the knuckle-crunch."

"The knuckle-crunch?" Sloan laughed, mocking the phrase. "You're playing with me."

"The first hand in the shake controls the grip," Martino responded knowingly. At Sloan's wave of dismissal, Martino snapped, "Take this seriously. You don't want to be like Teddy Roosevelt." Martino paused with a seeping smile that cried for a response.

Sloan sighed with resignation. "OK. I'll bite. What happened to Teddy Roosevelt?"

"T. R. shook eight thousand hands one day at a White House reception."

"Bull."

"You don't want to know what happens after eight thousand dirty, clammy, sweaty, sticky handshakes." Martino's expression soured. "We'll have antiseptic hand wipes for you. Use them *after* you get in the car." He wagged his finger. "*Never*—and I mean never—use them in public, or you'll look germophobic." Martino reached out to playfully punch Sloan's shoulder. "Didn't Johnny Cash teach you that when you were on his TV show?"

"I missed that lesson. I was busy backstage with a country singer that night."

"Let's hope that story doesn't pop up on-line."

"No worries. It went viral years ago," Sloan said with a wink.

* * *

The next day more than ten thousand students pressed together, a crush of humanity at the Quad at the University of Nevada in Reno. The throng assembled at the foot of the stairs in the grassy area surrounding Brown Hall. Dozens of Sloan for Senate signs and banners dotted the campus.

Standing backstage, Sloan overheard one man jest to another, "Here comes the reality show." No doubt, Sloan was the man's intended target.

"Excuse me?" Sloan moved toward him. "The reality show?"

The professor shrugged. "I'm a political science professor, and, no offense, Mr. Sloan, but the United States Senate is the highest legislative body in our nation. I take politics seriously."

"So do I," Sloan replied curtly.

* * *

Martino moved within inches of Heather Sanders, a former Reed advance staffer. "Is the laser show ready the instant Tyler walks onstage?"

Her eyes enlarged; she held a look of terror, anticipating the worst.

Martino's gaze passed over the half circle of young, polished aides who remained at rapt attention. "Well?" Martino snarled.

"Sloan vetoed the lasers," the staffer responded meekly.

"What?" Martino thundered. "I hold the only veto. Do you see my veto pen?" He paused briefly and then barked. "Don't be intimidated by him. He's just a frickin' candidate." His last few words were drowned out as the college band started playing Sloan's "Believe."

The rock star candidate walked to the lectern atop the concrete steps. Cheers, hoots, and hollers reminiscent of a cage-fight event set the tone. Sloan opened his speech by discussing health care coverage.

As Sloan spoke, inflatable microphones stamped with Sloan for Senate tumbled from Brown Hall's top steps and into the masses below.

"Where did *those* come from?" Martino and the aides watched from the sidelines. Turning to the aide, Martino gripped the young man's shoulder. "Why isn't he doing a little light chat instead of some policy crap? Did you go over his speech?"

The young man hung his head sheepishly before his courage returned. "I'm supposed to tell Tyler Sloan how to work a crowd? Mr. Martino, when my aunt was in college, she got so excited at one of his concerts that she threw her bra onstage! My own aunt! I'm supposed to tell that guy how to excite an audience? I'm thrilled when a girl responds to me on Tinder." He gestured at Sloan. "That guy wrote the book on babes."

Martino's worry multiplied as Sloan's speech remained focused on various issues. The crowd grew increasingly restless. No one had attended to hear a public affairs lecture.

"Let's talk about restructuring the debt of suffering countries," Sloan continued.

Several students tossed the Sloan "microphones" in the air in mock defeat. With each remark, their enthusiasm was deflating. When Sloan finished and walked away from the lectern, Martino turned on the staff.

"What the hell just happened? Who briefed Tyler this morning?"

Several aides confessed their participation.

"How long?" Martino pressed.

One aide volunteered that the briefings lasted many hours. The aide added, in a tone too smug for Martino, "He claimed you wanted him to have more details. Don't blame us."

Martino bit his lip, took a step toward the aide, his face red, his voice sharp. "Remember 'Let Reagan be Reagan'?"

The blank expressions told Martino that the aides had failed to grasp the historical reference.

"Think Obama was briefed for hours before he went on campus?"

"Maybe," one brave aide replied, seeing Martino's glare. "I don't know."

"Look at that guy with the Sloan microphone you bozos shot out to the students," Martino barked. "He's dry humping that girl with our microphone. Make it guitars or something else next time. I don't want to see some woman or man going down on a Sloan mic on YouTube."

"But he's a singer, not a guitarist," the aide mildly protested.

"Change it," Martino commanded, "or I'll stick one of those mics down your throat, or worse."

* * *

Sloan chose to be alone on the return flight to Las Vegas. He scrolled through various text messages on his phone and then surfed the internet for the reactions to his speech. He knew he had failed but hoped commentators would report *something* positive. All were mediocre reviews; the only plus was most reports praised the overflow size of the rally.

His fist banged the plane's armrest in frustration. When did it turn? He had not "bombed" in decades, let alone with a college audience. His thoughts ran, but answers were elusive. He reached for his phone to call his father.

"Hey, Dad," Sloan said when Mike answered.

Silence.

"I'm sorry I didn't have a chance to speak to you before I announced."

No response.

He apologized again.

"Son." Mike Sloan finally spoke. His voice resonated deeply, a voice sufficiently full to star on Broadway. "My son announces for the United States Senate without telling me?" The volume cranked louder. "I heard it from goddamn CNN. C-fucking, N-fucking, fucking-N. Don't you think I deserved a phone call from you and not from a reporter?"

"I sent you a text."

"A *text*?" Mike bellowed. "I prefer a phone call. Please don't like me on the Facebook?"

Sloan cracked a smile at how his father often inserted *the* before websites.

"One phone call is asking too much?"

Sloan appreciated the moment of silence before his father went on. Mike's voice remained edgy, but the volume flattened. "You don't want my help? I get calls from candidates every week asking for advice or wanting me to make an appearance for them. Last week a guy called a doofus running for mayor of Twin Falls, Idaho. Twin fucking Falls."

"Of course, I need your help," Sloan admitted. "I'm playing in your sandbox, not mine."

Neither man mentioned that morning's *New York Times* columnist, who opined that Sloan's hiring of Martino was a psychological plea for acceptance to his father. The column detailed numerous "issues" between them that went beyond the usual father-son generational differences.

"Remember who worked his ass off so you could play in our garage with your band? Your mother and I put up with that pain-in-the-ass drummer Dion."

"Derek."

"He was a goofball, just like that long-haired kid Bill who played guitar."

"Will."

"And their names are important?" Mike grunted. "You didn't exactly pay your dues on this. Starting off with the Senate is not easy."

"Dad, I've won three Grammys, had dozens of albums on the charts; I was nominated for an Oscar and enshrined in the Rock Hall of Fame."

"And that affects the price of potatoes in politics?" Mike questioned.

"In today's world, that means I paid my dues. Right or wrong, that's how it is." Sloan continued.

"You think it's easy to get elected to the Senate?"

"Dad," Sloan's voice remained patient. "You think Rogers is smarter? Think Collins can think past a sound bite? I've got this."

"You've got this?" Mike repeated with more sarcasm than Sloan wanted to hear.

Sloan ignored the retort and changed the subject to the safe topic of his daughter, Riley. He filled him in on Riley's honor student status and mentioned she had a boyfriend. He confided he wasn't quite sure where he stood on that development.

"I love that little muffin." Mike gave the conversation its first glimmer of warmth. "Listen, son, if you need my help, call me…if not, well, then talk to whoever you want."

Sloan knew he had to improve navigating his relationship with his father. "If you have any ideas on how to help the campaign, I'd be glad to hear them." That was insufficient. "More than glad; please let me know."

SIX

June 12, Las Vegas

Alone in his home, Sloan studied his reflection in the full-length mirror. He could not recall the last time he had failed in public. *There was no other Reno.*

He shuffled through the many index cards listing a series of points that he had used in Reno. Too much policy, he was too intent on proving his worth. "Damn," he spat; no one could hear—this was for him. A quick decision, he would campaign without the prep, polish, and packaging; each speech would have one card with bullet points. He decided to paint each address with broad rhetorical brushes, tossing in verbal grenades at the two parties. He would simply speak, not memorize.

He stood in front of the mirror and did various run-throughs out loud. The stopwatch on his phone reinforced that he was too lengthy. He wanted ten minutes: a six-minute speech, two minutes for ad-libs, two minutes for crowd reaction, and he was out. He sipped from his mug, his witch doctor's potion of hot water, honey, ginger, ginseng, and slippery elm to protect his vocal chords. He gobbled down his numerous vitamin and mineral supplements, a daily regimen that included cayenne pepper and oil of oregano pills to boost his immune system.

He comforted himself—he was back onstage. The opener had to grab the audience; the closer had to leave them exhilarated.

* * *

The usual suspects moved single file through the Caesar's Palace villa Zimmer rented. The meetings had balanced flavors of a Vatican visit and a sit-down in the back room of a New Jersey strip club. Flanked by Martino and Zimmer, Sloan endured almost a full day of fifteen-minute meetings with potential bundlers—supporters who could raise campaign contributions that totaled at least $100,000. Sloan was bored during many sessions, returning his focus when feeling Martino's foot press against his under the table.

Johnny Romano sat across from Sloan. At Romano's side was his father, Dominic, sitting in a wheelchair—Dom to his friends and family. The younger Romano was ruggedly handsome, his features exaggerated, his nose, face, and hands oversize. His loose-fitting multicolored Versace shirt and numerous gold bracelets screamed Vegas wealth.

"Papa deserves all the credit." Romano gestured to his father before he traced the family tree. He began by citing how his grandfather had acquired vacant land on the Strip in the 1950s, and his father had been the driving force to parlay it all into a string of off-the-Strip hotels, two more in Reno, and numerous adult entertainment clubs. Romano omitted mentioning any of the legendary family's "ties" to the city's historic unsavory characters.

In his prime, Dom had been affectionately called "the Duke" based on his physical resemblance to the midcentury quintessential movie star John Wayne. That moniker was now ancient history as his weakened body remained bound to his wheelchair.

"My dad always took the family to the Sunday breakfast buffet at the Dunes Hotel. Remember the Dunes?" Romano asked Sloan in a voice louder than necessary, seemingly to ensure that his father heard every word.

Sloan gestured toward the elder Romano as if they were old friends. "The Dunes had that tall, bearded man on top of the hotel entrance, wearing white robes and a turban. When I was a kid, I asked my parents if that man ever shaved."

The elder Romano alternated between laughs and coughs.

Sloan watched as Dom's hand returned to rest on his knee. Although the room's temperature was comfortable, a worn plaid cotton blanket lay across his lap. His frail appearance unnerved Sloan; Dom was only three years older than his father.

"You knew Michael Jackson?" Romano asked with apparent interest.

Sloan seized the moment by citing the time Jackson had joined him backstage. Under Romano's gaze of admiration, Sloan shamelessly traded on his celebrity. "Michael told me…" Sloan hesitated for effect. Romano was leaning so close to him that he was teetering on the edge of his chair. "Michael told me that he wanted to be immortal, a dancer-singer-actor. Only on film can you be immortal."

Sloan eyed the beaming Romano. He had created a link between himself, Jackson, and Romano. He was ready to close the deal.

"I hope I can—" Sloan began.

"We're aboard," Romano replied quickly. "My group will support you."

Sloan rose to signal the end of the meeting. "We'll party together in Washington after my election. I'll show you the note Michael sent me."

* * *

As the time neared nine at night, Sloan rose from his chair. He listened patiently to Bob Carney, president of the Teamsters. The Teamsters' endorsement was still open. Carney urged Sloan to lend his public support to a Teamsters' organizing initiative with technology companies.

"An hour ago, I met with a high-tech firm executive who blasted your boys," Sloan said lightly. "He claimed some Teamsters were a little rough in picketing their firm."

"A Teamster getting physical?" Carney wore a pained expression. "Look, most of my labor brethren are supporting Rogers, but he's too liberal for my guys. Collins turns off my minority members. Might have to say no to both."

Carney handed Sloan his business card. "How about one of yours?"

"One of my what?"

"Cards. Your business card."

Sloan stared uncertainly. "Never needed a card. I don't have one."

Carney tilted his head in disbelief, and Sloan flashed him a smile. "Not to worry," he said, grabbing a pen and jotting his cell number down on the back of Carney's card. He added a *Call me, Tyler Sloan*. "When I get to the Senate, I'll autograph and send you my first card."

Carney smiled, accepting the card, tucking it into his pocket, and exchanged a firm handshake with Sloan.

Once Carney was gone, Sloan gathered his tablet and headed for the door. He turned to Zimmer. "I'm done."

"Wait!" Zimmer protested. "Jefferson Jackson is on deck. His friends call him J. J."

"I guess everyone calls him Jefferson?" Sloan joked. "The man doesn't blink without a motive. He's a smooth character, good at marketing, advertising He's Don Draper, and I'm not buying."

Jefferson Jackson was the chief executive officer of Gala Corp., a New York Stock Exchange–listed firm with casinos and hotels in Las Vegas, Atlantic City, the Bahamas, Midwest floating riverboats, and the Chinese territory of Macao.

"I know he's a prick. He tries to intimidate people with his size," Zimmer snarled. "He doesn't mess with me, of course. At least listen to him; Gala is a great client for my firm."

Sloan sat back down. He'd hear what J. J. had to say.

Jackson's words unfurled like rare silk. His drawl conveyed the friendliness that sucked in the naive and propelled cynics to hold their wallets. His shiny forehead and receding hairline nearly glowed.

Regardless of time or place, the well-groomed Jackson smelled barbershop fresh. Men of an earlier generation would term him "dapper."

Jackson's hand reached out to rest on Sloan's shoulder. Sloan retreated at the gentle squeeze. Jackson was tall and husky and habitually leaned forward when he spoke. He was "Texas big."

"I was hoping you'd run; this Senate race is the whole enchilada." Jackson's bushy eyebrows darted upward. "Neither of your opponents is Phi Beta Kappa. Rogers can't win unless you and Collins each take two legs and toss a live kitty in the Bellagio fountains. When—I mean, *if*—you return to the stage—"

Sloan's retort was sharp. "I'm winning this race, and I'll be in DC."

Jackson kept charging. He dwelled on pending federal legislation that would allow Gala to joint venture with Native American tribes in a national chain of casinos while concurrently reducing the standards to permit more tribes to qualify for gaming. "Poor Native Americans have suffered too long,"

Sloan was impressed. Jackson said his last statement with a straight face. He and every political candidate in Nevada from Senate to sheriff were aligned in opposition to efforts to reduce the state's hold on gaming, already battling online casinos and the national spread of sports wagering. Nevada had to draw the line.

Sloan's response failed to deflate Jackson, who inched closer as if physical proximity could sell his case. "I've got an independent committee ready to air ads your team might want a little distance from."

"Don't do it." his voice spiked. "No ads, no committees. Got it?"

"But your father—" Jackson began.

"Is Mike Sloan on the ballot?" Sloan asked brusquely.

* * *

"Do you want to win? Do you *really* want to win?" Zimmer sputtered as Jackson's exited. His exasperation was shared by Martino, who grunted in agreement.

Sloan waved off the pressure. "I appreciate what you guys did today, but it was torture."

"Torture?" Zimmer snapped. "Raising five mil in a day is torture for you? The president never said that. Today will result in *millions* more to an independent committee."

Zimmer detailed how the Democratic speaker of the house, Bernard Pinkerton, was mobilizing his fundraising team behind Rogers, and every future Republican presidential candidate was scheduled to land in Nevada to raise money for Collins.

"Cut open the head of every elected official, and you'll find politics and policy," Martino said, his tone intentionally sinister to reassert his standing. He referred to Pinkerton with the unflattering nickname often used by Republicans: "But Pinky is all politics."

"I need a shower after today," Sloan bemoaned. "Each one linked their support to a bill. I hate raising money. I'll write the damn check, outwork Collins and Rogers, and get more media time than both."

Sloan could not discern if Zimmer's stare was of admiration or pity. "Love your optimism," he replied. "In a campaign, we look under every rock for support. J. J. was practically crying when he left."

"Don't cry for me, J. J.," Sloan mocked in a falsetto reminiscent of *Evita*.

"There's humor in this?" Zimmer replied with a straight face.

Sloan glanced down at Zimmer, though both men were standing. Their difference in height was noticeable, but Zimmer's ferocity and tendency to gesture upward with his index finger appeared to reduce the gap.

"J. J.'s a big boy; he's heard *no* before," Sloan said firmly.

"You can't make a half-assed commitment," Zimmer replied with his upward motion.

"Half-assed?" Sloan fumed, turning away to diminish the tension. "I walked away from millions of dollars and cheering crowds every night..." He paused. "I didn't do all that to spend the next ten weeks begging for money—no more fundraising. I'll write every damn check. I'll raise money on-line, a hundred-dollar-max contribution. Watch. This thing will explode."

Sloan walked outside to get some air. The warm desert evening air soothed his nerves. He watched through the glass doors as Zimmer's hands flailed in frustration, and Martino returned a series of nods. The two appeared to gather in a conspiratorial huddle before walking out together to meet him. Sloan braced himself; he would not be intimidated.

"Look." Sloan interrupted the moment Zimmer began. He alluded to the often-rumored but never proven reports that Zimmer and Martino had planted moles inside the opposition campaign. "In Reed's campaign, you guys knew what the Reeps were going to say before they said it."

Martino's words were measured. "We got lucky."

"I need that same luck," Sloan said. "Nevada is where people get lucky."

Martino sighed in exasperation. "I heard you, but I ran one poll. There's good news, but…"

"Don't sugarcoat it; give it to me," Sloan said firmly.

Martino confirmed Collins's significant lead over Sloan and Rogers, but the undecided vote was much higher than usual, and Sloan's name ID was "off the charts." Martino clicked off numbers, numbers, and more numbers. Political operatives genuflected to the numbers with a reverence reserved for a deity.

"It sounds like all of your polling told us what we already know," Sloan said, his tone indicating that he would not be interrupted. "The bottom line: I'm famous, and no one knows who to vote for."

Martino shrugged and followed it up with a smile. "Not a bad synopsis. I've done my homework on you. When you checked out of Betty Ford, your career was skidding. Yet one report had your mood as *ebullient* that day. One reporter said, 'Sloan didn't find a pony in the room; he found Secretariat.'"

"Is there a question amid that pop psychology?" Sloan asked.

"I need to know you better. I need to ask you some questions." Sloan waved him on, and he continued. "Any arrest when you were young or lately?"

"No and no." Sloan's answer denoted the seriousness of the question, and he headed back inside the villa.

Martino and Zimmer followed.

"You tried cocaine?" Martino asked, trailing behind.

When Sloan ignored him, Martino asked again with more bite. "Don't blame me; the media will ask these questions. They'll be two op research teams talking to everyone who was backstage or in your band. A blogger in his pajamas will down three beers and allege that the two of you did blow with seventeen-year-olds in a hot tub."

"Obviously, that would be a lie, but go on," Sloan replied with annoyance.

"Do you have a girlfriend now? A current squeeze?" Martino pressed.

"A *squeeze?*" Sloan smiled. "A little dated, my friend. I see a couple of women, but nothing serious."

"Are they stable? Are they married?" Martino asked.

"Yes and no. Both are age appropriate." Sloan paused. "Close enough."

"How many times have you smoked pot?" Martino quizzed.

Sloan turned to Zimmer. "Didn't Obama smoke pot? Clinton? Bush?" He sighed. "Understand my life. My first house was in Laurel Canyon; the little Canyon Country Store was my second home. Rock bands and groupies." His hands were moving. "Guess what happened."

"Damn it, Tony," Zimmer snapped. "The only question I have is, where's that damn sex tape?"

Martino vigorously nodded. "I'll get to that." This was his domain, and he would not be rebuffed.

"Get to it today," Zimmer snapped. "I don't want to wait until tomorrow, especially if you wear that same damn shirt you wore the last two days."

Martino waved off the insult. "How many girls have you been with?"

"Been with?" Sloan asked with a wry smile.

"Slept with, had sex with, fucked," Martino said tightly. "Don't make me work so hard."

"I was immature. I was like the deli man at the busiest meat counter in town, yelling *next,* and three women raised their hands."

"Was it the thrill of the chase?" Martino asked with a dollop of understanding.

"The chase? That chase was rigged like hunters on a cordoned-off ranch. But that's in the past. I've grown up."

Martino accepted the explanation and then pressed, "How many?"

Sloan rested his hand on his chin as he mentally multiplied the number of tours by the number of years. "Early on there were tours with other bands. We played clubs every night, the Teenage Fair at the Hollywood Palladium, then halls, arenas, and stadiums. No shortage of women."

"Ballpark it." Martino was firm.

Sloan glanced at Zimmer. "More than a hundred."

"A little more than one hundred?" Martino kept on it.

"Hundreds." Sloan bit down on his lip. "Not thousands, hundreds."

"*Madonna mia!*" Martino paused nervously. "Are we talking two hundred or…more?"

"Hundreds." Sloan paused. "Let's leave it at that."

Martino eyed Sloan; it was a hard glance. "You must know if it's closer to one hundred or one thousand?"

"I couldn't tell you exactly, but closer to one hundred."

Martino's jaw dropped, his mouth agape. "Hundreds of *different* women?"

"No, some repeat customers there, on tour and around the studios."

"Holy shit," Martino replied, and his mouth snapped shut. He opened it to say more but closed it again. "Anything that could be a problem?"

"Like?" Sloan asked.

Zimmer chimed in, "Men, underage girls, diseases, or jealous husbands?"

"No men." Sloan chuckled. "Once, when I was young, I got crabs, you know."

"No, I don't," Martino replied bluntly. "Any husbands of these gals?"

"Get a clue, Tony!" Sloan exclaimed. "Girls come backstage, you think we conduct interviews? Think Grant ran security clearances on them? Ask them what their favorite perfume is? I'm sure some were married, but…"

Martino nodded; he wanted more.

"Some guys hooked me up with their wives, their girlfriends." Sloan was matter of fact.

"Jesus H," Martino muttered.

"I was there, Tyler's counsel," Zimmer chimed in. "No legal filings, not even a shakedown for harassment or nonconsent." He glanced at Sloan. "Thank God."

"That's what's important." Sloan regained control. "Look, I'm a bundle of stuff. Vote for me, and you buy the whole bundle." He clapped his hands. "Let's move on. You've got enough."

"Let's all focus," Zimmer said, pressing downward with his palms to soften the tension.

"So, the tape…" Sloan said. "Morgan hasn't delivered."

"We can't trust him," Zimmer interceded. "I called him and left two messages, no response. I'll put some men on it."

SEVEN

June 14, Las Vegas

First poll: Collins 30%, Rogers 20%, Sloan 15%, Undecided 35%

Sloan sat alone in a conference room in an industrial park near Las Vegas's McCarran Airport. "Damn," he blurted as he scanned Martino's analysis of the campaign's first poll results. He quickly jotted his thoughts regarding each poll question, which included comments such as "wrong question," "likely voter," and "need push question." When he finally glanced up from the report, he was surprised to see Martino standing in the doorway, holding a box of doughnuts.

"Didn't want to disturb you," Martino said, moving into the room and placing the doughnuts in the center of the brushed-aluminum table. "Miles Judson is ready to unveil his new media plan."

Sloan slid the notated report to Martino. Sloan noticed when Martino held a powdered sugar doughnut, and the white powder fell upon his campaign manager's shirt collar.

"Judson can wait," Sloan said with an edge. "This firm whiffed. My dad taught me how to read polls before most kids knew their math tables. It's not great—I'm only at fifteen percent—but the horse race is not my focus. Not now."

Martino defended the polling firm's experience and cautioned him that the poll was only meant to be a "quick-and-dirty snapshot."

"Do one more poll with push questions about negatives on all three of us," Sloan said. "Also, ask the voters how much they care about a candidate's religious beliefs."

Martino gave him a puzzled look.

"Humor me," Sloan replied. "I live in Vegas; I understand odds. I know I'm the underdog. But I've got two mediocre opponents and a short campaign. Collins has a base, but she's like my saccharine aunt, giving me her phony smile while nagging me for not writing a proper thank-you note."

"There's positive news," Martino replied. "The campaign is fluid, baby. More than a third are undecided." He paused. "Carney has the Teamsters on hold to see if we show some traction."

Sloan waved his hand at Martino for more details. His tone was laced with reluctance, but Martino continued, "Carney said he wants to make sure he's not booking passage on the *Hindenburg*."

Politics equaled perceptions. Sloan understood that he was being viewed with political curiosity, but not yet as a potential senator.

Outside the room, Judson barked commands to his staff. His sarcastic voice carried to Sloan's ears. "That guy is a condescending, pompous jerk. His first media plan was junk. He doesn't get me or the campaign."

"It's too soon to tell. Give the man a chance," Martino implored.

"It's my first campaign, but not my first rodeo. I need to see something real *today*."

Martino nodded glumly and then changed the subject. "Your dad has been calling me daily since your announcement."

Sloan didn't bother to hide his surprise. Of course, his father would call Martino rather than him, even though he'd given him an opening during their last call.

"Today Mike asked if I polled his numbers with Nevada voters," Martino went on. "You need to ask him to come out and campaign for you. He wants that ask."

Sloan had no chance to respond as Miles Judson strode into the room. He had the air of a man whose life would be incomplete without a beach house. Trim and in his mid-forties, he wore a cream-colored Armani suit with a rose-pink T-shirt. Judson's assistants distributed copies of the advertising plan and proposed commercial summaries to Sloan and Martino.

"Simplicity sells," Martino said bluntly. "Let's target the masses who don't recognize the beauty of the fat lady singing at the opera. We need to reach men watching poker tournaments and women watching fem shows on Lifetime."

"Really?" one of his assistants shouted back as another aide knocked over a water bottle. Fortunately, it was still capped. Sloan shot Martino a pleading glance to tone it down and then asked to see the contrast ads. "It's basic political math—voters are more likely to vote *against* a candidate than *for* a candidate, so what do you have?"

Judson gave Sloan a condescending smile. He removed his thin, gold-framed glasses to emphasize his point. "One wrong utterance on your opponents," Judson said with certainty, "and you're ground meat."

"Nonsense," Sloan rebutted. "Wait too long, and I'm *dead* meat."

Martino leaned across the table for a buttermilk doughnut, took a bite, and spoke as he chewed. "We need simple spots, two-by-fours to hit 'em over the head."

"Remember your history, Judson," Sloan said bluntly. "When Bill Moyers wanted to portray Goldwater as being too reckless, they aired a child picking daisies with a mushroom cloud as a backdrop—without naming names. LBJ won in a landslide."

"That's *ancient* history," Judson responded sharply, his face reddening.

Sloan was quick to reply. "You did the media for Thacker last year in Michigan. You know Thacker never responded when Rondo hit him."

"Most people call Rondo a slimy SOB," Judson responded icily.

"Nooo"—Sloan drew out the word—"most people call him *Senator* Rondo. Where's Thacker?"

Martino let out a snicker, the crumbs of his third doughnut—a glazed one—spewing out across the conference table. He brushed them away and then retrieved, from an oversize envelope, a gray board displaying color photographs of each candidate. Collins's photograph resembled a Hollywood portfolio shot.

"Find a picture of her that's less flattering," Sloan insisted. "My God, half the men in the state will want to date her."

"And half the women will want to know what makeup she's using," Martino added.

"*Really*?" Judson's aide shook her head. "Are you aware of what century you're in?"

Martino was content to smile. "*Every* picture of her is flattering." He glanced at the aide. "You agree we can change that?"

"You want to contrast?" Judson said as an aide began the PowerPoint presentation. The first image showed Collins's new ad with dogs on her front lawn. "Collins does not even own a dog," Judson said with a knowing smirk.

"You're questioning her credibility because she borrows a dog for a TV ad?" Sloan's palms turned up in exasperation. "I'm campaigning for the highest legislative body in the land—not master of the K-9 corps."

Judson continued about Collins's ad, but his confident veneer had been damaged. Martino, meanwhile, was being fueled by his doughnuts. "Wire the pooch to see if he's got some inside dirt on Collins. Maybe the doggy, the poor mutt, needs more walks."

"Dump that ad," Sloan directed.

Judson was obviously not accustomed to the pushback, his murmur intelligible as he clicked his remote. Photographs of Judson's past ads aired. The first showed a scholarly woman standing in front of a school, surrounded by children, speaking about educational reform. The second ad showed a beefy first responder standing inside a fire station, pledging support for his candidate. The last ad showed a woman in a hard hat walking through a manufacturing facility.

"Pabulum," Sloan said glumly. "None of these ads are *me*. Give me something with optimism, and I'll hit it out of the park. Like me talking to voters."

Judson held silent as if silence was a sufficient answer.

"The old Doors song 'Break on Through,'" Sloan continued, "we have to break on through."

"Not sure what you mean, but…" Judson's voice trailed. "We know our business."

Sloan shot a hard glance at him, irritated by his placating tone. He could sense all eyes on him. The silence of Judson's assistants spoke volumes: this political neophyte, dilettante rock star had absolutely no clue.

Sloan suddenly pointed to the more outgoing of Judson's assistants. "Who am I?" he asked. "Am I some frickin' accountant you put in front of a school yammering about how great teachers are?"

"You're the talent onstage," Judson stammered. "We're the talent with the message."

Martino paced the room, propelled by the sugar-laden flour nuggets flowing through his system. He retrieved a fourth doughnut, this one covered with pink sprinkles. Sloan gazed upward—he had seen enough.

"I banned pink food backstage," he said with a wag of his finger, his mood lightening only for a moment. He held a hard and lingering stare at Judson. He rose from his seat, the signal to terminate the meeting. He motioned for Martino to follow him out of the room. "We'll get back to you, Miles."

* * *

The Las Vegas morning air had succumbed to the early summer heat. Sloan glanced at his handheld odometer, which indicated he had run 5.5 miles. He'd met his goal, reaching the self-imposed extra 10 percent for each of his exercises. The run had cleared his thinking of yesterday's dead-end meeting with Judson. With a series of deep breaths, he walked to the rear of his home.

Sloan smiled when he saw his thirteen-year-old daughter, Riley, reclining by the swimming pool—a smile that instantly flattened when he saw his ex-wife lounging nearby. Riley and Cindy had been staying in nearby Henderson with her sister.

Cindy stared away as he approached. Her coolness had become a game. He would cheerfully call out greetings, testing her for a glimmer of warmth, trying to squeeze civility from her. He realized that when they spoke, he was taking more than his quota of deep breaths.

He rationalized their marriage had served one purpose—Riley. Their paths crossed on life's journey, their daughter made it all worthwhile, but their paths never truly aligned. Despite his doubts, they'd married when she'd told him she was pregnant. He had tried to make the two disjointed parts into one, but those puzzle pieces had never fit.

He looked closer at Cindy; it had been quite some time since he had last studied her. She remained thin and attractive, her wardrobe always fashionable; she would never lack for male attention. He recalled how he had teased her about her changing hairstyles. That slight push would inevitably provoke her to proudly remember her modeling career, which had required different styles. Cindy would strike a pose and recall her pride and joy of walking down a runway.

"Senator? You want to be a senator?" she asked in a tone revealing her displeasure. She fixed her vision on their daughter. "I couldn't stand going to some yahoo 4-H club in Reno."

"You enjoyed the Yahoo holiday party in San Francisco."

Cindy returned a sarcastic smile before launching into a litany of reasons why she "detested politics" in a voice laced with scathing displeasure. "Politics is a mean-spirited meat grinder—don't need it, don't want it, and don't like it. You'd be happier if you don't run. And if *somehow* you win…"

She continued, clearly oblivious to how her comment stung. She motioned toward the house, where Martino was visible through the sliding glass doors, talking on his cell phone. "That is one *nasty* guy. When I was in the kitchen, I heard him laughing about ways to screw people. I'm sorry I voted for President Reed."

Sloan gave her a knowing smirk.

"Well, *if* I had voted, I would have voted for Reed," she corrected, peering through her sunglasses. She began posing questions without expecting answers. "Remember the guy in the tree at our wedding? That nut photographer who posed as a doctor to get pictures of Riley at the hospital? Our marriage was five years of hell."

"Hell?" Sloan knew it was fruitless, but could not resist. "You never objected to attending concerts with me, going backstage meeting your favorite bands…you seemed to enjoy the time Aerosmith let you sing backup onstage, the gowns you wore to movie premieres, the Oscars, and Grammys. Five years of hell? You were treated like royalty." He could add a dozen more examples…but why?

His words died on his lips when Riley dove into the pool; she'd obviously been annoyed by their exchange. With loud, boastful cries, she counted off each lap as she touched the pool's edge. Sloan recalled her delight as a little girl, watching him exercise, asking if she could join him so they could both "break their backs." Riley's own athletic skills were maturing; Sloan gazed with pride as she appeared physically and mentally sturdy. He chastised himself for exposing her to his rift with Cindy.

When Riley emerged from the pool and gathered a towel around her, she reminded him that she still had not shed her girlish mannerisms. "Daddy," she repeatedly cooed, holding up the sunscreen bottle.

Riley's fair skin had been rendered pink by the sun. A series of kisses on her back before applying more sunscreen to her shoulders. He'd once spent months trying to write songs for and about her before realizing it was far better to actually spend time with his daughter.

"Tell Mom about your latest weirdo fruits," Riley whispered in his ear.

Sloan shook his head; he had no interest in sparking another argument with Cindy.

"Mom." Riley was undeterred. "Did you try any of those mango nectarines Dad has in the kitchen? They're awesome. We took some when we hiked Red Rocks yesterday morning." When Cindy returned a blank stare, Riley continued, "How about a papple? A combination of pear and apple." When Cindy's foot tapped with annoyance, Riley turned to her father. "Daddy, those black apricots were delicious."

Cindy tossed her legs over the lounge chair and stood up to put on her cover-up.

Sloan lowered his voice but kept his smile. "You know my tastes drive her bat-crazy. Why do you want to irritate your mother?"

Riley pondered the question as if it was the most important one she had ever faced in her thirteen years. "I don't know," she said slowly, then laughed. "It's just fun."

Sloan kissed her forehead before rising to his feet.

Cindy shot them both a suspicious look.

"My best to Gene Claude," he said, as he passed Cindy on his way inside. He took a perverse pleasure in mispronouncing the names of her boyfriends.

"He's French—it's *Jean-Claude*," she snapped.

*　*　*

Sloan met briefly with Martino before a half-pleasing dinner with Cindy and Riley.

When he was alone, Sloan turned on his tablet to hear *In the Office,* a favored political podcast, which was also syndicated on nearly one hundred radio stations. The host, Larry Dinkowitz, used the pseudonym Dr. D, often referring to himself as the "good doctor." He was a political factor throughout the Southwest and Mountain states. He dominated Nevada's airwaves with his antiestablishment views.

Sloan mused that while the host was never a doctor, Bruno Mars was born Peter Gene Hernandez, and his career worked out.

"This Senate race is fascinating," the phone caller was saying.

The host interrupted in his gravelly voice. "The Democrats have a loyal one in Billy Rogers. He's a true believer. But check him to make sure the man has a pulse."

"I like Chris Collins; she's a patriot," the caller responded.

"I wish she would say something that doesn't sound like it was vetted by twelve handlers and the Republican National Committee. She's always *on*."

"How about the singer?" the caller pressed. "I heard he and his dad, Mike Sloan, have some father-son problems."

Sloan turned up the volume.

"I'm Dr. D, not Dr. Phil. I expect the ol' governor to be on the stump soon. The Republicans may not like Mike Sloan's politics, but he reminds me of a friendly uncle."

"And how about the singer?" Sloan asked aloud.

As if the host could hear him: "You ask about the singer? Let me tell ya, Tyler Sloan will make it a fascinating campaign. Pay attention to him. He's smart, crafty, and talented—he's the one to watch."

EIGHT

June 16, Las Vegas

The blinding sun forced Sloan to don his sunglasses the moment he stepped outside. He walked along the lushly landscaped pool area of the Bellagio Hotel and entered a private cabana to meet Las Vegas's mayor, Elizabeth Javier.

The mayor gestured to the television. Sloan looked at the screen to see Chris Collins. His opponent wore a pleasing and plastered-on smile, speaking to an interviewer in front of the reflecting pond and the ornate, Roman-inspired columns outside the Forum Shops at Caesar's Palace.

A full description of Collins depended upon one's shade of America. To Red State partisans, she was charismatic and capable, but to their Blue State brethren, she was a vapid, fading beauty queen.

"Man up, Billy Rogers," Collins chided, her eyes growing wider, appearing proud of her verbal lashing. "Nevada's economy is fragile. Rogers and his big-government, socialist lackeys should get out of the way of the job creators."

"Man up? Socialist lackeys?" Sloan repeated with a puzzled shrug. "And she's leading?"

Javier maintained her gaze at the screen. "I disagree with *everything* she says…but she knows how to say it to energize her base." She added with a touch of awe. "That woman's hair is always meticulous, perfectly styled—it's a miracle."

Javier's political prominence was turbocharged. The previous week, she'd been listed in a *Time* magazine article as "a leader of the twenty-first century." Sloan had heard the mayor referred to by others as "well put together." He recalled the *Las Vegas Review-Journal* editorial that delighted in Javier's detour to the bathroom for one final touch-up before a city hall press conference. The media grew weary and left the steps of city hall before she finally emerged. The next day's editorial jested, "Our city can relate to a youngster's disappointment over a rained-out baseball game. The mayor's press conference was canceled due to hair spray."

"Your campaign has to step it up," Javier said, turning her attention on Sloan. "You don't want the chattering class going, *Tsk, tsk, poor Tyler Sloan should have stayed onstage and left politics to the pros.*"

Sloan mocked a boxer's stance. He raised one fist and playfully jabbed the air with the other. "Don't worry; I'm looking for the first cut eye. I'll nail 'em both."

"Did you hear what that sore loser from the mayor's race said?" She did not wait for a reply. "He said our city's changed so much that pretty soon the city council will be filled with Z's—Rodriguez, Gomez, Hernandez. How can a black guy be such a racist? He said, 'Wake up and smell the *frijoles* that kicked me out of office.'"

Sloan shook his head sympathetically but held mum, wanting no part of that feud.

Javier shared that she was troubled by his speech in Reno. She advised, "You're a rock star. Flaunt it; celebs win. No more long speeches."

"I overreacted. I heard one professor backstage refer to me as a reality-show candidate. My overpaid, pompous aides pumped me with too many details. It was an off night; not every song McCartney wrote was 'Yesterday.'"

"A *New York Times* reporter was asking about our friendship. He asked if I was ever backstage with you? If I knew anyone you dated... I need that grief?"

Sloan waited with trepidation.

"I got your back," Javier reassured him. "I told him we're friends, but I have no clue about your love life. How would *I* have a clue about *that*?"

There was seduction in her tone. Their attraction to each other never dissipated. He gazed at her full lips and luxurious brunette hair— yet this was neither the time nor place to retrace those steps.

"I never noticed your baby blues," she murmured.

Sloan and Javier met years earlier in a tale that rivaled a tired soap opera plot. He'd been the headline act at San Francisco's Cow Palace and, for good measure, had the unique privilege as the son of the state's governor. She'd been a Berkeley College girl from a dusty New Mexico town too small to be described as a city. She had parlayed her academic achievements and sultriness to earn an internship with Sloan's record company.

The two shared equal annoyance with the opening act's lead guitarist, who painstakingly organized his guitar picks in neat rows within his guitar case before demanding "*Only* green M&M'S." Javier had earned Sloan's admiration by "accidentally" filling the bowl with all colors of the candy *but* green.

"Judson's media plan is weak," Sloan said, pulling himself back from the memory. "Ever hear of the media consultant Bree Baker?"

"She was in last month's *Esquire* profile, 'The Women We Love,'" Javier replied with enthusiasm. "She puts *cojones* on her clients."

"Implying something?" Sloan glanced below his waist.

Javier flashed the smile that disarmed political opponents. "Politics agrees with you; it's your..." She paused, turning away to gaze through an opaque curtain to view the pool.

"My *raison d'être*?" he said, bemused by her statement.

"I remember what you told me one night." She cupped her mouth with her hands and spoke in a reporter's voice: "Here's Tyler Sloan sloshing through the frozen tundra during his primary campaign in New Hampshire."

"Your endorsement would be sweet, or just stand next to me and coo your support."

"Labor and the party will crucify me if I went against Rogers. Sorry, Tyler, but an independent means you're a dish that's not on the menu."

Sloan had learned from his father when to ignore comments that did not advance his cause. "It's no secret you want to be governor. Grant Zimmer and I will help—a twofer."

"Where's Mike Sloan in that deal?" She was obviously intrigued. "A threefer? Your dad has a lot of friends here. His endorsement would be huge. Let's both think about it."

"Do not; do not commit to Rogers. I'll talk to my dad."

* * *

A few days later, Sloan met with Zimmer in Sloan's new Las Vegas campaign office. They'd rented a vacant floor of suites in a high-rise office building in the Hughes Center, framed by Sands Avenue and Flamingo Road.

Zimmer confessed his failure to get a response from Denny Morgan.

"I didn't play it right with that son of a bitch," Sloan replied. "I've tried to reach him, but he hasn't returned my calls or texts. It was all BS that we wrote songs together; he saw my doubt," he mumbled. "We have to get that video."

"I've got a call into LA's best private investigator. They'll track down that weasel," Zimmer added with unfiltered confidence. "They never fail."

"And then?"

Zimmer's sinister smile alarmed Sloan. "Damn it! Finesse it, Grant. This could backfire on us! Morgan could sell it to Rogers or Collins just to fuck me. Tell him I've got two new songs for him, and we've lined up a producer." Sloan paused, wanting Zimmer's buy-in on his next statement. "I'm firing Judson. We need a new approach to our media, and he's too old school. I'm calling Bree Baker."

Zimmer's face pinched to recall the name. Sloan showed him Baker's work on YouTube from the previous year's insurgent campaign. The handheld camera and rapid cuts produced edgy ads that bore a closer resemblance to a music video than a packaged political ad.

"She was the media advisor on the biggest upset in the country last year," he explained. "She got outspent ten to one, but her candidate took out the Democratic majority leader in the Oregon primary."

Zimmer urged patience; he was clearly not enthused by a single congressional race.

Sloan reached for his cell phone. "Stick around; I'll need your input."

"I'm sure your melodic tones will suffice." Zimmer smiled.

Sloan punched in the number and was pleased a female voice answered immediately. "Is this Bree Baker?"

"Who's this?" the woman responded.

"Is this Bree?" At her silence, Sloan added, "Bree Baker, the political consultant?"

The line went dead. Sloan shrugged. After a moment, his cell phone rang; the phone number showed "Restricted." He answered, ignoring his rule about restricted numbers.

At his greeting, the same voice asked, "Are you the guy who just called me?"

"Glad you called back—"

"Listen, dude, this is a new phone, new number. Two questions: Who are you, and how did you get my number?"

"I'm Tyler Sloan," he began and then stopped. Dumbfounded, he looked at Zimmer. "She hung up on me. What the hell?"

"Remember my line about not sticking your *dick* in crazy? Well, don't hire crazy." Zimmer laughed. "What's plan B?"

Sloan held up a finger. He tried the number again, speaking rapidly the moment he heard her voice. "Bree, Tyler Sloan, don't hang up."

"Right," she said sarcastically. "Dude, if you're Tyler Sloan, how did you get my number? I got this phone yesterday."

Sloan was pleased that at least they were talking. "My security team got your number. It's nothing sinister. It's about my campaign."

"This sounds like a prank call. Am I being punked?" Before Sloan could reply, she quickly said, "Hold a sec."

Sloan stared at his office wall and the framed grainy photograph of Fremont Street from the early 1950s, when downtown ruled the city. When Bree returned to the line, he told her, "This call is quite important."

"My mani-pedi appointment is important too."

A mani-pedi? Sloan mouthed to Zimmer.

"*Meshugenah.*" Zimmer gazed upward. "Crazy girl."

"Are you that Moveon.com guy from the Hilton in Portland? Or the dude from the *HuffPost*?"

"For the last time, I'm Tyler Sloan, I'm running for the United States Senate, and I need your help."

A moment of silence; Sloan thought he connected.

"I was with my parents in Vegas last year. We saw your show. Or at least we saw Sloan." Her voice was rapid. "Prove you're for real. Right now, sing the song you opened with."

"I open with different songs. I can't recall the exact song from one show."

"Sing, or I'm hanging up," she snapped.

"OK, OK." He was quick. He thought for a moment, then sang, "Don't care if I get knocked down, only care if you're around." A moment passed. "We good?"

Silence. After a moment, Sloan looked at his phone; the call had not been terminated. He glanced at Zimmer.

"Oh, my God. No fucking way." Her voice rose. "You're really Tyler Sloan." There was another pause. "Awesome. Tyler Sloan singing to me? I'm an idiot."

"Ms. Baker, let's talk about my campaign. I need your expertise."

"You need *me*?"

"I loved your work in Oregon. Viewed every download. With your help, I can win this." Without prompting, he added that Tony Martino was his campaign manager.

Bree rapidly fired her opinions, terming Rogers as a "dull uncle" and Collins as "a phony Effie Trinket." At Sloan's silence, she added, "A loony bitch from the *Hunger Games*."

He was amused at the generational gap to her reference; he thought of Collins as a smiling Nurse Ratched.

Bree pushed to understand her exact role in the campaign.

"If we click," Sloan said, "you're the media advisor. You're in charge."

"Total charge? Listen, I sort of, kind of…committed yesterday to a candidate running in a special election for a Florida congressional seat. I'd have total control there."

"A puny Florida congressional? My race is for control of the Senate. We'll get more media in a day than that race will get in a month. What were you going to make in Florida?"

She began to cite an ethical issue in revealing the amount, but Sloan interrupted. "If I retain you, I'll double that offer. This is the biggest race in America. The president's best friend, Grant Zimmer, is in my office sitting across from me. Help me win this, and your stock will rise like a hot IPO."

He winked and handed the phone to Zimmer.

"Young lady." Zimmer's voice rolled melodically. He smiled at Sloan. "The president raved about that campaign you did."

"The president?" Bree sputtered. "Awesome, what did he say?"

"Now, now." Zimmer's voice soothed, "Bret is a dear friend, and I always respect our confidences. I can tell you the president was impressed with your work—very impressed."

Sloan retrieved the phone and confirmed the date she would arrive. "Text me your flight info, and my driver will meet you at McCarran."

* * *

At her Malibu home late that night, Cindy kissed Riley's cheek good night and walked down the hall to the master bathroom. Opening the medicine cabinet, she searched past the clutter of cuticle scissors, nail files, aspirin, and over-the-counter medicines. She grasped the small, circular container of Lortab, which Dr. Goodman had prescribed for her migraine headaches. She momentarily held the plastic bottle before returning it to the shelf. This was not a "migraine moment."

Next to the Lortab was a larger container with tonight's drug of choice—Vicodin. She removed one pill.

She could recite the warning label by rote: "Do not take with alcohol or nonprescription drugs without consulting your doctor." She mocked aloud a refrain from one of Sloan's songs, "Sugar tonight, give me sugar tonight, my baby." She placed the pill in her mouth and washed it down with water from an Evian bottle.

Returning to her bed, she turned on the television, clicking the remote until she found a biography about Meghan Markle. Cindy had written letters to Markle with advice on how to live in the royal family, disappointed she never received a reply. She purchased numerous coffee table collections of photographs of the royal family.

Her anger grew as she thought of her ex-husband. Despite the years, her hostility had not abated. She was unable to fathom why Sloan would subject himself to the campaign turmoil, the criticism, the constant scrutiny. She recalled how her attorney was forced to argue for an increase in spousal support, but now Sloan was spending millions for an inevitable defeat, perhaps a humiliation. She speculated how Riley could use that money in her trust fund.

During the long stretches of extended tours, she visualized the constant stream of women lusting after Sloan. She thought of the old axiom that political power was the ultimate aphrodisiac. She fixed on the image of women flocking to her ex-husband, the rich, handsome superstar attempting to seize a political prize. Her thoughts grew hazy, her body warm, as she pulled the quilt to her chin.

NINE

June 17, Washington, DC

The national political media elite gathered for their monthly High Noon Club in Washington, DC's, Willard Hotel. Richman was the senior political reporter of the *Las Vegas Review-Journal*, but it was his Pulitzer Prize and three decades at the *Los Angeles Times* that earned him entry to the club. The balance of media was the biggest of the Big Feet: network broadcast reporters; print media from the *Washington Post*, the *New York Times,* and *Wall Street Journal*; and online media from *politico.com*, *Yahoo,* and the *Huffington Post.*

The group sat in a conference room near the circular round robin bar. The club's rules were clear: no staff; no prepared remarks, notepads, or recording devices; and the newsmakers' comments could only be used as "deep background."

Several men glanced, some discreetly, as television reporter Tammy Keller entered the room. One male reporter seemed fixated on Tammy as she brushed the lint off her cream-colored skirt, which was hemmed one inch above modest.

Sloan was confident he could handle each of these dozen reporters, but he remained wary of Ted Richman, despite the reporter's past relationship with his father. Martino had described Richman as "possessing the media's best bullshit detector."

Sloan was no virgin in press relations. He seized on the question and listed his business credentials at *blue*, his foundation's charitable work, and his global investments. "Substance will decide this election, not a party label." He sighed with relief, confident he'd handled the first thrust.

"*Substance?*" Richman belittled the word. His red fedora and caustic tone were visual and audio echoes in the small room. "Voters want *substance?*"

Before Sloan could respond, Tammy Keller shot out, "Did you answer a question last year regarding your net worth by stating, 'It depends on the day'? Today. Your net worth today?"

One of Sloan's female advisors had dismissed Tammy Keller as "a bimbo with a cute figure." The comment was indicative of the gender culture clash in which women used the word *cute* to describe a woman's body that caused male tongues to stiffen.

Keller was a former beauty contest winner who later practiced law in the US Attorney's Office. She was a ratings-generating machine as a political affairs reporter for FOX News. She possessed the skill to unearth stories with the proper dose of skepticism. Perfectly cast for the medium with voluminous near-black hair and sea-green eyes, and few missed her constant hint of cleavage. Yet she hadn't received her Columbia University journalism degree for her Vogue-ish high cheekbones; she drilled down on Sloan.

"No one knows their net worth."—Sloan trod carefully; wealth often bred resentment—"not to the penny."

"Maybe." Keller was leaning forward to secure her role and seemingly Sloan's attention. "But I'd sure be within a million or two."

A ripple of laughter spread through the gathering, and Sloan metaphorically kicked himself for adding the damning last phrase.

Sloan was confident he had ripped through the next series of less-personal questions, before the youngest reporter in the room, evidenced by his trendy tattoos, introduced himself as Josh David Mack. Mack went on to cite a string of various songs Sloan had written. "The lyrics in those songs hint at hostility toward women," the reporter concluded.

Sloan patiently explained how songs conveyed the emotions of tension, anger, and other conflicting emotions on both sides of a relationship breakup. "Josh, those are just songs. They're fiction."

Mack's follow-up was quick. "You have eight executives in the C-suite at *blue*. None are women. Why is that?"

The room of reporters turned to Sloan; this question had spiked their interest. He had adroitly handled this morning's issues on terrorism, the Middle East, the economy, and national security. Now he was faced with *this* question?

Mack was a dizzying, sartorial rainbow—his eyeglass frames were green, his jeans a bright turquoise, and he wore a maroon plaid shirt. Youth had its privileges.

"We had four women," Sloan replied.

"Not today." Mack's tone was rushed.

Sloan identified and praised two female executives at his firm who had voluntarily taken leaves of absence to have children; one retired last month, another was on medical leave. He saw no legitimate controversy but was uncertain at the question's edgy tone. "Two great women simply chose to raise their babies. I hope and expect they'll return. We're filling one position, and one is open. No issue there."

"Mr. Sloan," Mack continued with an edge, "we decide the issues in this room."

Richman hastily clapped his hands together, confirming his authority.

"One last one," Mack inserted without a glance at Richman. He sputtered, seemingly to avoid interruption. "How much did you raise at your meet with lobbyists at Caesar's Palace?"

"I returned all the checks." Sloan was pleased with the softball question. "I'm only accepting one-hundred-dollar contributions. Not a penny more. My campaign is free of special interests; the voters care about that." Sloan flushed with confidence, swiveling in his chair to await the next question.

"Care?" Mack replied in a mocking tone, and Sloan swiveled back. Mack drew his hands across his chest to emulate a banner headline. "Tyler Sloan Says, 'He Cares.'"

Sloan noticed Richman's hard stare at the young reporter. Richman held his thoughts, seemingly content to stir his Scotch on the rocks before raising his eyebrows at Sloan concerning Mack's gamesmanship. Sloan forced a smile to mask his unease, uncertain if Mack's derision was meant to reinforce his own professional standing or to mock Sloan's candidacy.

"Tell us a specific example of what you term *government waste*," an ABC reporter asked.

Martino's advice had been drilled into his mind: "They won't quote you verbatim, but don't trust the bastards." Sloan equated the warning to the famous *Miranda* case: "Anything you say can and will be used against you." Sloan peered down the table; the reporters looked like hunters in pursuit of a fox.

"You raised the issue; you can retract it." Keller winked to a colleague to note her "gotcha." She then glanced toward Richman, seeking approval that he would not grant.

Sloan mentally scrambled before recalling the news report of the night before. "The House bill to build new navy helicopters is pure pork," he said, "and the Senate should reject it."

With that, Richman grabbed the large bell used to close each High Noon Club meeting since the first gathering twenty-six years ago. At precisely 1:00 p.m., he rang the bell three times to signal adjournment.

Following nondescript good-byes to the reporters, Richman halted Sloan's walk to the door. The reporter said softly, gruffly, "You're a damn interesting candidate."

"Screw interesting," Sloan whispered to Richman. "I'm in to win."

With his security detail and aides trailing behind, Sloan left the meeting and walked to his waiting car on Pennsylvania Avenue. With a wary glance at the men in black, Tammy Keller approached and asked if she could "hitch a ride."

Sloan agreed. As they rode, the reporter sat a tad closer to him than was respectable, her long legs crossed provocatively. Noting that his aides were purposely looking out the windows or down at their phones, he eyed Tammy cautiously; even a blind man would take notice of her.

Tammy lightly grasped the ends of her thick hair as she praised Sloan's handling of the interview. Her sparkling green eyes conveyed currents of electricity as she methodically twirled her hair with her fingers. An edge of her red, lacy bra peeked out from beneath her blouse.

"I'm flying out in two days to join your opponents'—Collins's and Rogers's—campaigns. I'll be back covering you in a couple of weeks." Tammy's head tilted, her full lips curled with intrigue. "Do you need to fly back…now? Or do you have time for an informal chat?" Her words were sufficiently innocuous to allow them both a graceful exit.

Sloan's aides remained silent. They were paid to harbor no judgment. Paid to hold their comments.

"I've got the busiest schedule known to man, but I'd be happy to drop you off wherever you want." Sloan was cheerful and friendly.

Her lips curled in a model's pout. "*Ladies' America* tonight, but first, I have a meeting at the Capitol."

"Take this lady to Congress," Sloan barked to the driver.

* * *

A half hour later, Sloan strode along the tarmac to his plane at Reagan Airport in Washington. He felt his phone vibrate. The caller ID said "Mike Sloan." Sloan had once had the contact listed as "Dad," but thought it too childlike. It briefly occurred to him after Ted Garvey's death that any call could be *the* call, so he answered.

"Dad, I'm getting ready to board a plane back from DC."

"You think you can trust those jackals?" Mike's voice was unyielding. "Did Obama trust O'Reilly? Trump trust anyone except FOX? I had a great rapport with the press, but I knew when to keep my mouth shut."

"Meaning?" Sloan braced for the impending reply.

"Your comments at lunch about wasteful navy helicopters are all over the Capitol."

Sloan muttered profanities.

"A lot of those copters are going to be built outside of Atlanta," Mike added. "The senator from Georgia has a different view than yours."

"That was all off the record..." Sloan's voice trailed.

"Right," Mike added with a dismissive grunt. "Buddy Jennings, the Republican senator, called. A reporter tipped him off."

Senator Edward "Buddy" Jennings was the Republican minority leader clinging to his position amid rumored challenges to his leadership.

"Jennings is out as the leader if Rogers wins and the Dems take control," Mike continued. "Buddy's betting on Collins but wants more than one horse in the race for fifty-one votes. You're his saver bet."

"Who leaked it to him?" Sloan pressed.

"He protected his source, wouldn't give me a sniff. He said you betrayed him, claimed he protected you when you testified in his committee on *downshifting* of songs—excuse me, downloading. Son, know the rules of the game."

Mike's last comment was condescending. Sloan was tempted to shout but held the phone away from his mouth to collect himself. He wondered if Richman could have called his father, and Mike was protecting his old buddy Richman. "Dad, exactly when did Jennings call you?"

"The time? I'm not a secretary. Next time I'll take notes."

As Sloan boarded the plane, he bit his lip, angry at himself for appearing as a neophyte in front of his father. Although chastened by the duplicity, Sloan was reminded of the obvious: information was power and readily swapped. He dismissed Richman as the source; he possessed a shred of honor and would not have leaked the comment. He focused on Mack, the man with the snide questions.

As Sloan sat on the plane as it taxied down the runway, he was angry that support was lacking from his father's response. Mike still treated him like a child. He wondered if fate had taken a different course if Mike's reaction to J.R. would have been empathetic, if Mike would have provided the wise counsel he willingly offered other candidates in the past decades. As the plane began its takeoff, he stared out the window; racing by were decades of memories, struggles of their relationship.

TEN

June 18, Las Vegas

Sloan had seen Bree Baker's images on-line, but none did her justice. He extended his hand to greet her as she entered his Las Vegas campaign office. She wore an unstructured pink-and-black jacket, crisp black jeans, and a rose-colored T-shirt scrawled with Chinese script without apparent meaning. He noticed her multi-strapped high heels. Her wardrobe reminded him of his younger backup singers…at rehearsals.

She returned his scrutiny and his firm grip. Her emerald eyes rose gradually from his shoes to his hair. She walked around his desk, lingering to gaze at his empty in-box and full out-box. Though it was after working hours, the cleanup crew had not yet removed the trash or the crumpled papers—those missed baskets—lying to the side of the trash container.

After a brief exchange of perfunctory questions and answers, Bree summarized her last two years, culminating with the upstart campaign victory in Portland, Oregon.

"Miles Judson didn't pass your test?" she asked with a knowing smile.

"My test? Miles was the definition of a failing grade. His ads could have been used by any candidate from Boston to Boise." He added lightly, "I'm a different type of candidate."

"I schooled Miles in Portland," Bree replied. "His stuff was yesterday's news. His ads were like a dude I once dated; it was the lighthouse syndrome. The light was on in the lighthouse, but no one was in the lighthouse. His ads were pretty little clouds of media puff, nothing there."

"He bragged about awards he won for his work." Sloan waved his hand, dismissing the very idea. "Not bragging, I've received more than my share, shiny plaques don't win elections."

Bree studied the wall of mounted photographs behind Sloan's desk. She inched closer to gaze at a photo of Sloan and Riley, taken years before, standing hand in hand with Winnie the Pooh at Disneyland. She tilted her head in uncertainty at the framed photographs of Sloan with Democratic *and* Republican officials.

He sought reassurance that his reputation would not be marred. He recited criticisms from the defeated candidate in her congressional race in Oregon. "Did one of your TV spots imply the incumbent was mentally ill?"

Her pause troubled him. "Mentally ill?" Her voice began slowly—too slowly for Sloan. "Not really. But after that rip, he couldn't father a child."

"A little too negative?"

Her fingers signaled a smidgen of error. "I know my rep." Her hand waved theatrically. "My friends say, 'I'm choked with the ambition of the meaner sort.' Shakespeare, *King Henry the Sixth.*"

Sloan was intrigued. Bree Baker was a Red Bull–jolt of confidence.

He studied her as she continued to walk around the room. She was slender but not thin, petite, but not short. Her confidence oozed as she discussed her strategy, gesturing with her fingers and then a balled fist to emphasize her point. Her eyes widened; her voice firmed. "It's simple: you campaign like a rock star, and I shoot video of you like a rock star." She smiled. "Not like a rock star, in this case, a legitimate rock star."

Describing her as attractive was a coward's play. One profile described her as "a politico dominatrix wielding high-heeled stilettos." Sloan mentally slapped himself from his distracting thoughts. He pressed her to analyze his campaign. She cited a litany of failures:

despite his nearly one million followers on Twitter, the campaign staff had not posted in a week; there was little capitalizing on his celebrity; and Sloan's speeches were bogged down with policy.

"Who's dropping the ball?" she asked with a gentle scolding.

He chuckled. She was prepped; she was good—really good. He was tired of the sycophantic campaign aides who laughed too quickly at halfway-witty remarks and never dared to push back. Bree would not fall into that trap.

"Contrast ads?" Sloan asked.

"If we ran against King Solomon, we'd charge he was a vicious butcher." She wore a bemused expression while adjusting the black beret that rested atop her short auburn hair. "If he threatened to cut the baby, we'd charge he favored the rich mother, play a little class warfare. I'd dredge up the king's background." Her expression was infused with Satan's pleasure. "Rogers is no angel, and Collins is no saint. My ads will flatter you. 'In thy face, I see the map of honor, truth, and loyalty.' Again, *King Henry the Sixth*."

"The one with honor, truth, and loyalty makes the final call."

"You said *total* control," she replied abruptly but without pouting. A notable sigh of exasperation followed to emphasize the foolishness of his comment.

The two exchanged brief stares. Control of the media equated to control of the campaign. That decision was now—right here, right now. Bree spoke of when her mom was a little girl, accompanying her grandmother to Portland State University when Bobby Kennedy campaigned there for the presidency. Her mom and grandmother regaled her with the story of the grinning Kennedy and his tousled hair, and how her grandmother grazed Kennedy's cuff links.

"Dude, when you're firing"—she pointed at Sloan—"you provoke the same frenzy."

He smiled at her choice of words. At her pause, he urged her to be blunt.

"Your speech in Reno," she began slowly. "Your hands," she stated and stopped.

"I don't need you to critique my manicure. Go for it."

She elaborated that since their phone call, she'd been on YouTube studying videos of him performing and on talk shows. She noted that his hand gestures were spontaneous, punctuating drumbeats, other times rehearsed cues to his band; on talk shows, his grasp appeared to reach out to caress the audience. "There was none of that in Reno. You locked your hands on the lectern, released once in fifteen minutes. You never gesticulated, didn't appear to be yourself."

Her analysis did not require psychotherapy. Sloan understood a speaker gripping a lectern was a pitiful man without confidence. In Reno, he was not onstage, standing at the podium as a candidate, and Bree had verbally slapped his face with the reminder. Despite his repeated viewings of the speech, he'd failed to detect that flaw. Now a short, silent curse. His appearances were his livelihood, yet he'd missed the obvious.

"I was too rebellious to be the most popular girl in high school," Bree noted with apparent pride. "You're popular, you're *da man*; you'll win if people see and touch you."

He was listing stances on specific campaign issues, braking at her headshakes and frown.

"It's high school, dude. You're the prom king. Forget issues."

Sloan shrugged; he had come to a similar conclusion. "I need to protect my brand—I sign off on everything," Sloan pressed while scanning her advertising budget and fee. He winked at her. "This dude makes the final call."

Her expression showed pity for the headstrong but foolish candidate. She pressed for total control, promising not to embarrass or indict him.

Time was his enemy. Not deciding was its own decision. He patiently explained the importance of how he envisioned the campaign would unfold, his role, her role, and how his lifetime of work could not be besmirched by one wrong ad or any scandal.

"You're patient when you explain things," she replied, "just like my dad. It's quite a coincidence the two of you share the same birthday, but you're two years younger."

He held his flippant thoughts. At least he was younger.

"Everyone has a movie in their head, a movie that they wish their life would be," she said. "I'll help you star in that movie."

"No movie in my head; I've lived and loved every scene. I need your help in this scene." He closed hard. "Your choice is simple. Come to Nevada and play with the headliner, or run that Florida campaign and fall off the radar screen."

Her smile widened. "Dude, you have six million followers on social media; we should be posting every day, many times a day."

"When should we start?"

"Yesterday."

* * *

"Why are you running?" Lee Parker, the host of *Not Too Late*, leaned back in his chair. His conversational tone was his modus operandi for prying, revealing tidbits from the unwilling.

Although based in Los Angeles, *Not Too Late* was airing a week of shows from Las Vegas's Rio Hotel's Crown Theater. The site often hosted Frank Sinatra's Rat Pack impersonators; the location proved *death was no reason for Las Vegas stars to fade.*

Sloan hesitated at Parker's question. He sat on the set's couch with Parker safely behind his desk. Last week, Sloan was grilled by the harshest political media critics in Washington, yet no one posed this obvious question. Sloan's personality was not that of his bass player, the one who retired to a Caribbean island to operate bars and fishing boats. He mentally dismissed the notion he was running to avenge his father's presidential loss; a talk show was not the place to air a father-son relationship that he had never fully grasped.

"I want to give back." Sloan explained public service was a "noble profession." Yet that cliché was too contrived. He switched, disdaining the power of lobbyists and special interests. He leaned forward to mock how this conversation could somehow be held in private. "Just between us boys, I have views on the left and the right. At heart, I'm an independent guy. In Washington, all the two parties do is posture and bash each other, but I want solutions. I'll fight for solutions, not fight for ideology."

The applause sustained until the commercial break. Sloan owned the room. Just before they aired again, Parker leaned into Sloan, his mouth covered to obscure his words. "A lot of your fans are here tonight, and they want to hear you sing."

"No songs tonight," Sloan demurred. "I'm focusing on my campaign."

"We didn't book a political commercial. One song."

Sloan was returning polite rebuffs to Parker's relentless requests.

"I'm not some organ grinder's monkey, singing a song if you throw a banana," Sloan hastily replied as the show's band concluded its musical interlude to signal the end of the commercial. Aware his answer was too intense, Sloan added. "I'll tell some old war stories."

Parker ignored Sloan and asked the audience if they wanted Sloan to sing.

There was no "middle"; either he sang, or he spoke. The audience cheered, and the band began to play, neither waiting for Sloan's decision.

"Billy Rogers rode a motorcycle when he came onstage," Parker pressed as the band burst into the rock classic "Born to Be Wild." "We played blackjack with Chris Collins last night on the casino floor. How about *one* song?"

Sloan remained seated, smile fixed. He knew how much time he'd been allotted. An Oscar-winning actress was backstage and due to appear after the next commercial break. He would *not* sing; singing on command was a slippery slope that would diminish his seriousness as a candidate. He rose from his seat and walked to the front of the stage. He turned to the band with a smile, and his hands prompted them to stop playing.

"I loved performing—I hope I've brought you joy—but now I have a different agenda." He spoke jovially, though he was uncertain how he would be received. He told of encounters when he first came to Las Vegas, dishing the "war stories" he'd promised the host.

"Thank you for everything." He smiled and waved to the crowd. He blew a kiss toward Parker and walked off stage to thunderous applause.

* * *

The next day, Sloan's song "Taking It Back" cranked from the speakers outside the Summerlin Shopping Mall. He'd written the song to reflect the battle between quarreling lovers, but now it had been morphed into an inspirational cry for people to take back their government. Thousands had gathered for the outdoor campaign rally. The Las Vegas suburb was an urban planner's dream of twenty-two thousand acres—neatly planned, neatly carved, and neatly built.

"I'm gonna rip it up!" Sloan said enthusiastically to his staff as he climbed atop the makeshift stage in the shopping center's parking lot.

Many in the crowd wore T-shirts or caps embroidered with Sloan's name as they chanted in unison, "Tyler! Tyler! Tyler!" He walked along the edge of the stage, high-fiving his supporters.

Sloan pumped his fist in the air as he approached center stage. Greeting him was Sky, lead guitarist of Sloan's first band, Liberty. The guitarist was dressed in patriotic rock star chic: red leather pants, a flag-themed bandanna on his head, and a flowing turquoise cape draped over him. His wrap-around metallic sunglass held blue-tinted lenses, and tattoos covered his arms. Sky stood, legs apart, hands raised high above his head in a Messiah rock star pose.

"I was down and out." Sky's voice dropped, referring to his well-publicized bouts with Jack Daniels and any drug within reach. "Tyler personally drove me to the rehab center and walked me in. Action, mates, not just words. Tyler told me that I could have it all"—he smiled sheepishly—"just not all in the same night."

The audience was momentarily uncertain how to react but then roared, taking their collective cue as Sloan and Sky shared a sustained laugh. Sloan braced himself. Sky was ad-libbing, and Sloan knew his bandmate had no discretion. The two had parted professionally years before, as Sloan's music had blended rock and pop while Sky maintained his harder rock cred.

Sky turned to Sloan with a clenched fist of affection. "Tyler Sloan always tells me, 'It's always a good time to do right.' And that's how I live my life."

Sloan held his smile, never heard that statement before.

"Change the world," Sky proclaimed, quoting one of Sloan's songs. He dramatically thrust his finger toward Sloan and then the crowd. "Change the world! Elect Tyler Sloan!"

Sloan and Sky embraced again and then raised their hands together in a victory salute. This was not Sloan's father's political rally. Sloan saw Martino to the side of the stage discreetly making a fist, the sign to keep his remarks brief and tight.

"The Democrats and Billy Rogers want to raise your taxes and take your money. You want that?" Sloan asked loudly.

"Nooo!" The roar was loud and sustained.

"The Republican party and Chris Collins want to snoop into your personal life and preach valuuuuuuues," he said, mocking the word. He nearly shouted, "You want that?"

"Nooo!" The crowd kicked the body politic.

He pumped his fist upward. "Together, we can't be stopped!"

Slingshot machines hurled "Sloan for Senate" T-shirts into the crowd.

A daytime laser show dispersed rays of colors into the air as the Chuck Berry standard "Johnny B. Goode" cranked loudly, its lyrics altered to "Tyler B. Goode." Sloan walked the length of the stage, slapping hands with those in the front row as Sky did a Chuck Berry duck walk as he left the stage.

* * *

"Twenty thousand were here today." Martino smiled later as he walked Sloan to the waiting car. "Rogers and Collins couldn't draw that many if they went on Oprah and gave away cars."

"I had vigor today," Sloan said in a Kennedy-esque accent. He laughed. "Vigor."

Sloan's body tightened as a man approached with a steady gait and steely stare.

"Chris wants to meet," the man said in a muffled voice.

"Rails?" Martino moved to intercede. "What the hell are you doing here?"

Sloan momentarily relaxed at Martino's recognition.

Rails stood with his back rigidly straight and posture erect. He wore his hair in a sharp crew cut that resembled that of a Nixon-era Republican. His flat stomach and barrel chest belied his forty-plus years, his build resembling that of a National Football League defensive back. His features were sharp and angular, and his glossy black shoes and the crisp crease on his khaki pants blared military precision. Rails looked ready—*always* ready.

Martino spread his arms around both men to secure a hint of seclusion.

"We need a friendly chat about that old video you two gentlemen have." Rails discreetly slipped Martino a hand-folded note. "Here's the time and place."

Sloan stared at Rails and then diverted his glance, not wanting to appear worried. He remained mum, but he felt his throat tighten.

ELEVEN

June 22, Las Vegas

**Poll: Collins 31%, Rogers 20%,
Sloan 16%, Undecided 33%**

Sloan readied himself for the rising fastball. The mechanical lever sprang forward, and the hardball fired. His swing was level as the ball jumped off his aluminum bat. He smiled in perverse pleasure at the stinging sensation in his hands. He was keenly aware of his father's presence among the crowd, the elder Sloan joined for the day.

At eight a.m., the desert sun was soft and innocent. The Strip's casino gamblers were crashing from alcohol with dashed dreams and the mental grime of sleep deprivation. Slot machine addicts were numb after an all-night binge of mesmerizing sounds and lights that had slowly but surely drained last week's paycheck. Sloan dabbed perspiration as he walked out of the batting cage. Bree's crew and a horde of media filmed every gesture.

"My dad and I went to similar cages in LA." Sloan casually gestured toward Mike. "Glad to have my dad here." He relayed his childhood memories of being with his father in batting cages.

The media held little patience for his glossy memory trip. "Did you once say a great concert is better than sex?" a reporter shouted.

Sloan noticed one of Collins's aides nudge another in anticipation of his answer. Both of his opponents had their video trackers recording each of his appearances. Every word and motion was captured.

"Well, ah…I've enjoyed both," Sloan replied to hushed laughter.

Afterward, Sloan and Mike drove together to their next appearance. Mike was clearly not pleased, and Sloan hesitated to ask what was wrong, not desiring a lecture if his father thought he had somehow failed with the media. Finally, unable to withstand the silence, he said, "OK, what's on your mind?"

"This game is filled with cheap shots," Mike advised. "Remember the stories about how I flubbed my answer on cloud computing? Your last answer back there was *not* what you want. You should *never* joke about sex, race, or religion."

"I never joke about race or religion. Sex jokes? Maybe once with Judson's staff."

Mike motioned for more details. Sloan estimated that only a few people had heard his comment comparing a tightrope walker to a man getting oral sex from an elderly woman—"Neither should look down."

"Good one." Mike's smile disappeared; his tone sharpened. "Never use it again."

* * *

That evening, Sloan and Mike shared Riley's fourteenth birthday dinner in Sloan's high-rise Las Vegas condominium. Riley glowed, alternating glances between the two men. Sloan was pleased; his father wore a contented smile.

Sloan adjusted the wall-mounted frame that displayed color postcards of some of Las Vegas's demolished casinos—the Dunes, Hacienda, Stardust, Silver Slipper, and the Sands. Mike gestured toward the framed collection of presidential campaign buttons and memorabilia in glass cases on a bookshelf.

"Got any of mine? Got anything from someone that did not ring the brass bell?"

"Everyone I could find," Sloan replied.

Sloan's personal chef placed the evening's first course on the dining room table. Sloan noticed Mike's hand shaking slightly as he poked around with his fork at the salad greens with citrus slices.

"So, Riley," Mike asked, "what's your boyfriend's name?"

"Jett," Riley replied, her smile covering her face from ear to ear.

Mike shook his head, and he asked her to repeat the name.

"Jett. Like an airplane, but with two *t*'s," Riley explained.

Sloan and his father exchanged a bemused expression. Mike decided to change the subject and gestured around the condo. "You own this, the big house close by, a house in Malibu, and an apartment in Paris." Mike turned to Riley. "I worked hard so your father could sing with his band. I gave your dad the freedom to operate."

Sloan expressed his appreciation for his father's assistance but added, "I did this on my own."

"Horse pucky," Mike shot out. "Was it me or Tinker Bell who worked it out so you own your song rights?"

Sloan made an unintelligible response and then told Riley a long-ago story about when his parents took him to church. He had worn a long-sleeved, floral-patterned shirt. His mother had asked him to tuck his shirt in, but Mike had told him to wear a different shirt or stay home. He turned to his father. "You were too concerned about what others would say about how you might lose one vote if someone thought my hair was too long. Truth is, I got you more votes than any endorsement you ever had."

"That shirt was ridiculous," was all Mike would say.

Riley rose from the table with a roll of her eyes. "Great birthday, you two." She headed toward her room. Sloan beckoned Riley back, but she slammed her bedroom door.

"Good job," the men said simultaneously.

Sloan and Mike gazed at each other, then down, then away. Time passed in silence. Sloan knew he needed to act first. He asked Mike for his thoughts about the campaign and if he heard any political gossip about Billy Rogers. Mike leaned forward, appearing pleased to be asked.

"I'd leak and repeat every negative slap he said about Reed when he was stumping for me. Hell, make some up. I'll vouch for you that Rogers said them all."

Mike went on to explain the Democratic Party's fundraising muscle, but that some key hitters were not returning Rogers's calls. He elaborated on how reluctant donors often claimed their partner or the omnipotent and shadowy "board" was required to approve any expenditure. Invariably, that other party was either ill, on vacation, or unreachable.

"If we ever get a poll with you in second," Mike said in a clinical voice, "the political vultures will circle in the sun, and Rogers's contributions will dry up like old bones."

Sloan noted Mike's word choice of *if* and not *when*, but he did not bite on that bait.

"You've got two months from today; that's a lifetime in politics." Mike's voice turned from comfort to a sharper edge. "You're going to get hit on silly stuff. Your song 'Emerald Dream' sounded like it was all about marijuana, maybe harder drugs."

"So what? People don't care if I smoked pot," Sloan scoffed.

"The way to handle it—"

"Handle it?" Sloan interrupted. "There's nothing to handle. Half the country smokes pot."

His father grunted, determined to be heard. "You handle it by saying that, years ago, you smoked pot, it was not smart, and you advise young people never to start."

"The toothpaste is out of that tube."

Riley reentered the room. She gathered herself and spoke with determination. "Papa, you were almost president of the United States." Riley pointed at Mike before whirling in Sloan's direction. "And you're the most famous dad in every school I've been in." She stomped her foot. "Both of you should grow up and grow up now."

"My bad," Sloan quickly replied. "It's one hundred percent my fault."

"No, no," Mike chimed in. "I should know better. I'm responsible."

Sloan explained to Riley how the two men loved each other but had their differences because they operated in "different universes."

"Now you're in the same universe; work together!" Riley commanded.

"We are," Sloan began. "When you were in your room—"

"I was listening; I heard every word," she replied with a smile.

"My little pumpkin." Mike laughed hardily.

Sloan reached out and held his daughter's hand. "When I was eight or nine, your papa bribed me to speak at his campaign event."

"What kind of bribe?" Riley nearly bounced with pleasure.

"Two packs of baseball cards, but I refused. Then he offered four packs of cards; I still said no."

"You love baseball. That must have been tough." Riley was near giddy.

"When we walked to the stage, he whispered to me, right before he was ready to go on, 'One box, son. Twenty-four packs of cards. Just give me one line.' I gave my one line, something about how dad was helping my school. The place went crazy."

"And the cards?" Riley asked, punctuated with a giggle.

"Papa liked my rap so much he bought me two boxes."

"Your bedroom smelled like bubble gum for a week." Mike laughed.

For a moment—for this one moment—the two men were united, both smiling at the memory. Sloan savored this feeling, staring at his father, adding an affectionate wink. Sloan recalled how impressed his grade-school buddies had been when his photo had appeared in the local newspaper. He wondered if Riley would share that joy but was reluctant to push her to join him at a campaign appearance. She was backstage many nights, he smiled with pleasure at the thought of her campaigning beside him but expected pushback from Cindy.

Once Riley went to bed, Mike got up stiffly from his chair, which didn't go unnoticed by Sloan.

"It's been ages, but it still tears me apart," Mike said.

Sloan knew instantly what his father was talking about.

Mike slowly noted that tomorrow was the date that he lost his first son, Sloan's brother. Sloan uncertainly reached out to touch his father's shoulder.

The two exchanged sorrowful stares.

Mike suddenly asked about the campaign. The change in subjects was abrupt. "How's the press treating you?"

Sloan confessed his worry that reporter Ben Davis had questioned his band and backup singers. Davis asked them if Sloan ever joined them in prayer before a performance and had asked if Sloan ever mentioned his religious beliefs.

"Does God decide what song we open with?" Sloan flashed a sardonic smile. "You want prayers in Vegas? Go to a sportsbook."

Mike laughed aloud. "I hope God has enough on his plate without fiddling with the Bears-Vikings game."

Sloan gestured out the window to the neon-blazed Strip. "This city is built on prayers...Please, God, make the dealer bust. Please, God, make Florida State fumble. Please, God, make that roulette wheel stop on twelve, oh please, God..." He paused. "Make sure she's not a hooker."

Mike chuckled again. "People want to know if candidates have *any* beliefs." His voice quickened. "Not counting weddings, have you attended church at least once recently?"

"Not since mom took me...twenty, twenty-plus years. Some people need a crutch. I've got no problems with it."

"That *crutch* line kills you." Mike's expression soured. "You agree there may be a divine being who created this bounty, this beauty, all of this?" He added how God blessed America and how he was not afraid of the eternal peace that awaited him.

Sloan listened patiently and expressed his uncertainty of God, heaven, and an afterlife. "Maybe when you die and Saint Peter greets you, you believe you're in heaven. But what if Saint Peter looks at you with a smile and says you just *left* heaven?"

Mike waved his hand in disgust. Wanting to avoid more problems, Sloan quickly inquired, "How's Michelle?"

"It's nice to have someone to share your life with." Mike paused.

"I'll never marry again, but she's a terrific woman."

"I always said you were entitled to date or marry."

"I never thought I had to ask for your permission," Mike replied curtly.

Sloan allowed the comment to pass. "Your coming here today was good."

"Worked out fine," Mike replied.

Sloan nodded. "You agree?"

"No doubt. Good media for you."

"Next time you come out, I'd like you to meet with our mayor, Elizabeth Javier."

Mike quizzed Sloan for a reason.

"Another good photo op, but this one is for her. If you meet with her, she'll owe me one."

Mike nodded his agreement. "Notice all the cameras on you at the batting cage? Do another athletic event; voters like that energy. Rogers looks pasty, too stocky. He probably hasn't seen a gym since high school. Collins is an ice princess, always dressed as if a Neiman Marcus manikin was stripped bare to clothe her." He waved toward Sloan. "Good night. I've got an early flight tomorrow."

"Dad, there's ten flights a day back to LA. Stick around a couple of days. I've got a few appearances tomorrow. Stay one more night."

"Not a good time. I've got to tidy up some things at home. I'll be back."

"Whoa," Sloan said. "I'll rent a plane, fly back anytime you want."

"No can do." Mike was already walking toward the door. "Not this time."

Sloan was grateful for the day but pondered how their relationship remained distant and how he could close that distance.

TWELVE

June 24, Air Force One

In a light jacket and shiny white tennis shoes, President Bret Reed reclined on a cushiony leather chair. "Best perk in the world," he said and then elaborated, "Best *fucking* perk."

Zimmer sat across from him in the spacious presidential suite at the nose of the plane. He was accustomed to the president's creative use of the f-bomb. Mild swearing demonstrated comfort, while an increase in volume indicated deep concern. Zimmer remained quiet whenever Reed hit the trifecta of profanity, loud volume, and frenetic hand gestures.

Reed spoke in a tour-guide fashion, describing the airplane's three levels, the nearly four thousand square feet of interior space of handcrafted elegance, and a galley that could serve two thousand meals. Zimmer noticed the omnipresent presidential seal on the seat belts, napkins, and on Reed's blue crew jacket with his name embroidered in white. As much as he was enjoying the unique experience, Zimmer reminded himself of his purpose—to marry Reed's interests with Sloan's. Reed's endorsement of Sloan would be a game changer.

"Rogers is not going to win," Zimmer said bluntly. "He won't get within ten points of Collins unless you campaign nonstop for him. I mean, live with the guy."

"That makes *a lot* of sense," Reed said with notable sarcasm.

"The winner is either Tyler or Collins," Zimmer followed up. "That's it."

Reed exhaled before adding, "Billy's not a bad guy, but he's an ideologue. He never challenges an interest group. You'd think every fuckin' group is wrong once."

Zimmer nodded.

"Rogers would spend more money than a drunken Greek finance minister," the president exclaimed. "Now Collins implies I'm a socialist?"

Zimmer had served as California's finance chair for Mike Sloan's presidential campaign but had adroitly pivoted to the same position when Reed won the nomination. Zimmer opened the doors to his entertainment clients, and Reed trusted him to hold his confidences. Grant was an entrenched FOB—Friend of Bret.

Aware of Reed's love of presidential trivia, Zimmer interjected lightly, "FDR was the first president to fly. What was his nickname for the presidential plane?" At Reed's shrug, Zimmer answered, "The Sacred Cow."

Reed swiveled in his chair. From this blue leather chair, he could command the military, negotiate with foreign leaders, and play politics. He shared his respect for Mike Sloan and his appreciation for Sloan's appearances during his reelection with Zimmer, then asked, "How's your campaign?"

"You're the whale in the pond," Zimmer said. "Sloan wins this with one nod from you."

Reed cast a warm smile. "You're not trying to sell me, are you?"

"*Moi?*" Zimmer raised his eyebrows.

"I want to finish my term right," Reed added tightly. "Can Tyler really win this fucker?"

"Give me one month to show you."

"Only two months until the election," Reed said. "*If* I say something"—he exaggerated his words—"you and Martino must time it to maximize the bounce." He paused for effect. "That's *if* I say anything."

Zimmer had been careful not to overinflate Sloan's poll numbers. Now he worried that he'd been too cautious. "You know Martino always errs on the conservative side with numbers."

"Martino, conservative with polls?" Reed laughed aloud. "That big boy is no shrinking violet. What's on tap for the next couple of weeks?"

"Tyler's going to Nevada's rural counties for the first time. Have any thoughts?"

The president began to discuss his latest crime bill and a diplomat's details of China's theft of intellectual property. He stopped in midsentence.

"Forget that—here's what important. The press had a hundred reasons why Mike beat me in the Iowa caucuses. I know it was that damn video of me failing to milk that fuckin' cow. Lord knows it's not a textbook presidential duty. Tyler has to practice, get one good squeeze, and call it a day." He pointed at Zimmer. "Make sure Martino's got that damn cow full of milk. Hell of a note, but that's the best advice I can give you."

* * *

"Gentlemen, you were referred to me by *which* senator?" Martino asked with a glance at his classic Swatch watch. It was nearing eight p.m.; all the staff in Sloan's Las Vegas campaign headquarters had departed.

The two men in dark suits sat on plastic chairs in Martino's windowless office, an office he affectionately termed "the hole." His work there was undisturbed by the daily commotion.

The younger of the two ignored the question and stated bluntly, "We're here to talk about you and the Deer Valley Indian Tribe."

The "suits" were close enough that Martino could reach across his desk and touch them, not that he wanted to. His hackles were rising.

In solemn unison, the men reached inside their coat pockets to remove their badges. The older man spoke first. "Federal Bureau of Investigation. I'm Special Agent Lloyd Shay. This is Agent Kevin Connell."

An involuntarily shudder raced through Martino's body.

"We didn't want to raise any unnecessary concerns, "Agent Shay explained. "If I'd gone to Harvard, I'd call it a little *ruse*." He dangled the last word.

Martino was uncertain if Shay was talented or *too smart* for his own good. Shay was overweight, no doubt an ex–college jock who habitually bored friends with recollections of the last kickoff, last tackle, and game-changing play in his final game. He imagined the agent was saddled with faint memories and arthritic knees, along with his protruding midriff. Martino presumed the baby-faced junior agent Connell was dutiful to his superiors, admired by the bureau's upper echelon as an underling who recognized his place in the hierarchy.

Martino eyed the men cautiously, having no inkling what they knew. "I was a registered lobbyist, and the tribe was a registered client." With a greater conviction than he felt, Martino added, "I disclosed it all."

"Not quite all." Without emotion, Shay summarized the public record: The tribe had submitted a land claim for three thousand acres, seeking sovereign nation status. The Bureau of Indian Affairs had denied tribal recognition, citing the tribe's failure to establish and exist as a distinct community.

"No worries; that's when they brought you in." Shay was firm. "You offered enough *evidence* to convince the Indian Affairs this dozen or so Native Americans with more Irish blood than Connell somehow qualified for recognition."

Martino had a sinking feeling; Shay's facts were in line.

"Congress recognized the tribe, but the first bill in committee prohibited them from engaging in casino gaming. Then you added a senator's son to your team." Shay smiled sardonically. "I just listed all of the qualifications of that inexperienced, uneducated young man."

Shay detailed the sequence: how Martino had acquired options on property adjacent to the tribe's, how the Senate then removed the prohibition on gaming, and how Martino celebrated by flipping the property to a shopping center developer before closing escrow.

"Like an old *Twilight Zone* episode," Connell interjected. "You seemed to know what was going to happen *before* it happened. You and your partners made a tidy twelve million profit."

"Is there a federal law prohibiting real estate sales? Even a lobbyist can make a profit." Martino's pace quickened. He was determined not to play the role of a quivering buck private at military inspection. "If there's nothing else, I'm headed to Charlie Palmer's Steakhouse for a thick steak with grilled onions."

"Final question." Shay cast a chilling gaze at Martino. "Who paid the taxes on your profit?"

The question lingered. Unanswered. The agents sat erect. Their posture was perfect. Their smug expressions were more than grating.

"Mr. Martino, we want to see if we can work out an arrangement."

Martino waited.

"Do you wish to have legal counsel present?" Shay added without inflection or judgment.

"I can listen," Martino replied. His political antenna was on—his mind racing with the doom to Sloan's candidacy if there was any public hint of the FBI and him in an "arrangement."

"The US attorney's got a strong case against you for felony tax evasion," Shay said.

"Damn accountant," Martino muttered, waving his hand as if swatting a fly. "Ya know the tab on the alleged back taxes?"

"*Alleged*?" Shay snickered. "Cute, Mr. Martino, but this isn't an overdue Visa bill. Campaign reporting errors are misdemeanors, but tax fraud carries a max of twenty years."

Martino began to rise from his seat, then returning at Shay's motion.

"The bureau is not focused on your tax problem; we care about a senator introducing legislation that her son profits from," Shay stated. "You help us peel back the onion on Indian gaming, Gala, and the Deer Valley Tribe with some information. Then you pay your taxes, we'll get the penalties and back charges waived, and your tax problem disappears."

Martino hoped he was projecting calm, but his hands were moist as he gripped the chair's armrests to straighten his posture. He prided himself on being able to supply an answer for a candidate in any situation, but he could not fathom an explanation for his own plight. Not now.

"Two options, Mr. Martino," Shay said while leaning forward in his chair. "Cooperate with us, or take your chances at trial. Doesn't mean squat to me which one you choose."

Martino noticed Connell's eyes wandering around the office, either betraying the junior agent's nerves or, as Martino silently dismissed, "a hillbilly idiosyncrasy."

"Zimmer's client Gala is pushing for more Indian gambling." Connell spoke in a smoky barroom pitch. "With you at the helm for Sloan, you can talk to a few elected officials. No, sir, this is not your garden-variety campaign."

"Jail time, boss." Shay was a blunter tool. "Or wear a wire and chat it up with the speaker and the senator. No favored nations here. You play the ponies; you know the odds. It's your call."

The two agents abruptly rose in tandem. Shay removed his business card from his pocket and wrote his cell number on the back. "Call me when you've made up your mind. Take your time, but a call later this week would be the smart play."

After the agents departed, Martino remained seated while pondering his options. He foresaw a parade of horror if word leaked: Sloan's campaign would implode, the White House would never return his phone calls, and he would be persona non grata to anyone seeking a lobbyist.

Martino felt the pulse pounding in his head. His jaw tightened as he grimaced at the thought of luring elected officials with a hidden microphone. He was staring at a lengthy court battle with legal fees that would bleed him dry. Unless the government bungled the case, at his age, a guilty verdict was a death sentence. He propped his elbows on the desk and rested his chin on his palms. He sensed tears welling, but they didn't come.

* * *

Early the next evening, Martino trailed behind Grant Zimmer as the two were escorted to the Pinnacle, a private gaming room at Las Vegas's Gala Hotel. The Pinnacle pried its riches from its green-felt gaming tables. The decor was not his taste, but Martino admired the nouveau Pinnacle's walls, ceilings, and furnishings, awash in cream and gold, its chandeliers and fixtures made of blinding crystal, and the delicate ornamental fans mounted on the walls.

Martino followed Zimmer's purposeful strides, returning nods from the three Asian men seated at an adjacent table. An online profile once noted, "When Grant Zimmer walks into a room, his balls clank louder than the bells at St. Mary's."

A pit boss removed the "Reserved" plaque from the blackjack table.

"I'll sponsor your membership here," Zimmer said as they were seated.

"Like Groucho Marx, I'm suspicious of any club that would have me as a member." Martino chuckled at his joke and then added with disdain, "This city is as real as silicone boobs. It's all a mirage. The girls at the Paris Hotel say *bonjour*, but they don't know if that means 'good morning' or 'let's dance.'"

"All purple," Zimmer said to the blackjack dealer, who acquiesced after the slightest of nods from his superior. Ten thousand dollars in $500 chips were placed on the felt in front of him. Zimmer neatly stacked two $500 chips on the table for the first deal.

"Johnny Romano is frozen with worry about Tyler's chances," Zimmer said softly. "Send him an internal poll, and stamp it 'confidential.' He loves the inside baseball." Zimmer smiled as he turned over his cards—blackjack. "Let's get Senator Jennings to fall back in love with Tyler. Can you say Tyler's remarks were taken out of context?"

"A dozen reporters were in the room. That makes a bad problem worse."

Zimmer's fingers tapped on the table. He cited how Sloan's remarks at the High Noon Club were an affront to Senator Jennings's ego, adding how each of the one hundred senators had egos capable of filling the Capitol's rotunda. "Jennings sees himself in the White House," Zimmer offered.

Martino rolled his eyes. "They ought to erect statues in New Hampshire for all the senators who lost hold of reality."

Zimmer discussed his planned trip to the Capitol and his meeting with Jennings. "I'll take him to the Palm."

The Palm restaurant was Zimmer's favorite. He'd paid for two caricatures of himself mounted on the restaurant's walls. One of him was running up the Capitol steps, the other basking by a pool with the Hollywood sign in the background. The investment paid dividends whenever his clients or elected officials gazed at the sketches. He gently grasped Martino's wrist. "My fiduciary duty is to my client, and that's Tyler. We need to protect him, and everything we do is to benefit him."

"Of course." Martino shrugged. "What are you getting at?"

"Tell your friend at *Politico*—the one who writes the 'Who's Hot, Who's Not' column—that a lot of Jews want Jennings to run for president. I'll tell Jennings what we did; he'll love both of us, and he'll forget his little tiff at Tyler."

"Jews like Jennings?" Martino asked.

Zimmer shrugged with uncertainty. He placed two more purple chips on the table to split the two eights he was dealt. He drew a three on each eight and doubled down. Four thousand dollars were at play on the table. Zimmer smiled at the draw of two consecutive face cards— winning hands. One signal to the dealer, all was well. He whispered to Martino, "Nice sit; nicked them for five grand."

Zimmer rose and slid a black chip to the dealer and handed one to the manager.

As they readied to leave, Martino whispered to Zimmer, "A client might need a little favor with the FBI or the White House."

"No such thing as a little favor from either."

Martino shrugged, assuring Zimmer this was not significant.

"I never call the bureau, and hopefully, they never call me."

Martino paused to gather his thoughts; this was not the comfort he needed. "What if I called—" Martino began.

Zimmer froze in his tracks, gripping Martino's arm. His voice soft, but tight. "Don't call. Any call becomes part of a record, a record you and the campaign don't need or want. Any contact with the bureau could turn toxic for Tyler."

THIRTEEN

June 30, Reno

Three aides were peppering Sloan with advice; the process began on the flight and continued the drive from the airport to the Reno home of Teamsters president Bob Carney.

Sloan was tiring of their thoughts; it was "white noise," blurring indecipherably together. He was also tired of their personas, viewing them as identical computer printouts, well groomed, all hovering in their late twenties or thirties. Their subservient enthusiasm was grating; the educated supplicants were nothing but "paid friends." Pulling the car into Carney's driveway, Sloan instructed the aides to remain in the vehicle.

Sloan soon found himself standing alongside Carney in the labor leader's den. Carney lived in southwest Reno, the city's oldest neighborhood. In autumn, the trees on these streets would be ablaze with color, a western-imprinted New England.

"Roses," Carney waxed with a theatrical wave of his hand toward his outdoor garden. "Delicate in bloom, yet their thorns are like some of our allies: a little prickly sometimes."

Sloan focused on the den's wall-mounted, framed montage of headlines of noteworthy Teamsters victories from newspapers throughout the country. In a corner stood a mannequin wearing a Minneapolis Police

Department uniform, the same uniform worn during a police response that "busted heads" to defuse a Teamsters' strike nearly a century ago. Sloan's focus fixed on the photograph of a young Carney standing next to Governor Mike Sloan.

"Years ago," Carney began, "before my time, the speaker of the California Assembly said, 'Money is the mother's milk of politics.' Your wealth validates that." Apparently sensing Sloan's uncertainty, he added, "It's a compliment."

Sloan accepted the remark with a smile. Long ago, his mother had instructed him that, if there was any doubt, always receive a comment as a positive. "Have you met with Rogers?"

Carney's guttural sound confirmed the meeting. "Billy's as dry as yesterday's toast. I had to round up some guys; no one wanted to meet him. They all asked when you were coming by."

Sloan had done his homework. Now was the time to cash in. "We were born the same year, in the same Santa Monica hospital. Hell, the two of us could be twins!"

Carney laughed aloud. "How did I get the bad genes; you got all the looks and talent."

Sloan reminded Carney of his past support of organized labor, how he had walked the picket line for the Service Employees International Union in their dispute with casino management.

"You stood tall," Carney replied, "but Billy's got a hundred percent voting record with us."

Sloan understood he had to be forceful with Carney. No one raced to support a third-place candidate. "In one week, I'll pass Billy in every poll. Now's the time for you to stand tall and make an endorsement."

Carney plopped himself onto his worn rocking chair. He took a deep breath as he methodically rocked back and forth. "I'm reading the tea leaves. Why is the White House silent on Billy? For God's sake, he's the party's nominee!"

Sloan weighed his answer. He understood mystery was his ally; hints of a backroom deal stirred every politico. "Zimmer doesn't leave fingerprints."

Carney's tongue rolled around in his mouth. He appeared to reflect on the comment. "What's wrong with Rogers?" Carney's voice rose. "He sounded like a black guy at the African American Chamber of Commerce. Saying *y'all* and referring to the crowd as *my brothers and sisters*? My African American VP said she didn't know whether to laugh or cry when Billy said, 'Git down with my campaign.'"

Sloan chuckled. "He's wobbling like a young boy on his first bike ride." Sloan recalled his father's counsel to allow adversaries room to maneuver, but the pressure of time restricted his options. "I'm gonna win this, and the train is leaving the station. You on or off?"

"My guys like you," Carney replied. "I know you've got a shot."

"A shot? If I wanted political handicapping, I'd tune in to *Morning Joe*!"

Carney fidgeted, and Sloan worried he might have pushed too hard, too fast. Sloan allowed a moment to pass. "I remember one labor leader telling me that Billy Rogers was nothing more than a trained monkey."

"True...but he's our monkey."

"Great line, I wish I wrote it." Sloan smiled. "You don't want a trained monkey; the Teamsters need a winner with the political skills to deliver." He walked closer to Carney, now inches away. He intentionally lowered his voice to increase the intrigue. "Read the polls. Billy can't win. You've got two choices: a right-winger elitist who looks down on your members, or me, a guy who's hired Teamsters and will deliver for you. Your choice."

* * *

That night, in the Peppermill Hotel's Tuscany Ballroom in Reno, Sloan stood at the lectern, ready to deliver a short speech before he would introduce the host for the hotel's "Rock around the Clock" Bingo Tournament.

The bingo night room was filled with senior citizens. Sloan grudgingly noted he was closer in age to most of the people in the room than he was to his own aides. He noticed the local news camera crews, presuming they never deemed a local bingo game newsworthy without his presence. Sloan released the microphone from its stand on the podium and moved closer to the audience. He raised his voice, presuming the audience was hard of hearing, but tapping the microphone, he realized it was dead.

He kept his speech short, learning from Reno and incorporating brief remarks at every campaign appearance. He enjoyed blending a policy issue with his celebrity card. He began sharing stories of the celebrities he'd met over the years and wove them into the economic importance of the state's entertainment industry. The cameras focused on his every movement, his every word.

When he mentioned his role in the state's entertainment industry, one throaty voice shouted, "Tony Bennett!"

Sloan smiled, reflecting on his duet with the legendary singer, the experience made even more memorable when Sloan watched his father's pleasure at meeting Bennett.

"With all due respect," a woman said as she rose from her seat, "what experience do you have that qualifies you to be our senator?"

"Fair enough. I've built a large enterprise called blue," Sloan began and went on to detail his firm's role in various industries, its holdings, and partnerships with technology firms. "*blue* is a leader in voice-recognition software."

A wall of blank faces greeted his comments. The room began to stir. To his left, a small group slid their chairs into a circle. They were speaking to each other as if Sloan had ceased to exist. He was puzzled; he was rarely ignored.

"I don't understand, I don't understand," one man loudly stated. "What in God's good graces are you talking about? Let's start the bingo."

"Who cares about blue, green, or yellow?" a woman in the back row shouted. "Why should I vote for you?"

"My granddaughter's favorite color is blue," another elderly woman called out approvingly.

"Get ready!" Sloan shouted with a broad smile, adeptly switching tactics to save the event. "I'm calling the first bingo game." The room stirred. "*Everyone* wins tonight! Sunday brunch is on me...for all!"

Amid the cheers, one woman shouted, "You got my vote!"

"Was that legal?" Sloan whispered to the aide who had moved beside him. "Did I just violate some campaign law?"

"I've been in campaigns all my life, started when I was in high school, still in college when I joined your dad in New Hampshire. Never seen that one before." The aide shrugged. "No clue."

Sloan focused on his opponents' aides, the trackers with cameras ready to instantly disseminate any error into cyberspace. "We'll soon find out," he said softly.

* * *

The next day, Sloan stood in a large exhibit hall at the Douglas County fairgrounds. He alternated smiles, nods, and waves as many in the crowd turned and craned their necks to catch a better view of him.

An aide whispered close to his ear, "No one on the cover of *People* magazine ever crowned Nevada's beef queen."

After his introduction, Sloan walked into the crowd, stopping to chat with a group of children in cowboy hats seated in the front row. After Sloan made some general remarks on agricultural issues, the media shouted its questions.

"I noticed you did not eat any of the beef served at today's barbeque. Are you a vegetarian, Mr. Sloan?" shouted Josh David Mack as Sloan finished answering the previous question.

The room was hushed.

"I vary my diet...but..." The comment failed to quell the crowd's concern.

"All diets need protein, Mr. Sloan," Mack continued in a smug tone that grated on Sloan. "Do you have a problem eating red meat?" the reporter added with a smirk.

The crowd's applause seemed to embolden Mack, and he continued, "One of your former band members told me you once said a cheeseburger was a 'heart attack on a bun.' And that eating a cardboard box was healthier than eating a hot dog. Is that true?"

"Holy Joseph!" one rancher exclaimed.

Rather than challenge the reporter, Sloan gestured slightly toward Mack, his voice dropping to a slight country twang. "What was that boy *smoking* when he told you that?"

A rumble of muttering grew louder. One heavyset man called out, "Ain't good to have a tofu-eating senator!"

Nearly twenty years ago, Sloan had stopped eating beef for health reasons. He had options: he could taste from the nearby platter of freshly sliced beef or reveal his diet and incur their scorn. He smiled to himself. There was always a way out. "Tofu's not on mine or your menu tonight. Let's find that cow I'm going to milk," he shouted playfully.

Mack sputtered, demanding an answer, as Sloan led the entourage to the next hall. He met Bree in the rear of the cavernous building; she was standing near a large black-and-white cow.

"The staff checked her out, her teat, her udder, the whole mooing beast. One guy claims he was raised on a farm," she whispered, covering her hand with her mouth. "The ole gal has more milk than Safeway."

"Tyler Sloan is here to milk my cow," said a local farmer, puffed up with pride, who'd been dubbed the "Cow King." The "King" was north of fifty years old, his build rugged, his blue jeans more than faded. No designer jeans ever rode his ass.

Sloan opened with brief words about touring dairy farms in Central California with his father. He then walked over the strewn hay to the cow.

"Mr. Sloan, the udders are clean, and the teats are dry and plump," the Cow King noted. "Of course, we use milking units, but we appreciate your effort to do it the old-fashioned way. When you milk by hand, you'll better understand our way of life."

Sloan was the "stranger in a strange land." He sat down on a plastic bucket beside the cow's right flank. He had rehearsed this; an expert had briefed him on the cow's possible reactions. He grabbed the cow's teat and turned to his left as the cameras captured him in a series of firm squeezes that resulted in a small stream of milk squirting into the stainless steel bucket.

When Sloan had finished the job, the Cow King raised Sloan's hand in triumph.

"And you thought these hands only held a microphone?" Sloan grinned.

* * *

Sloan and Bree sat side by side on the flight to Vegas. Bree opened her laptop as Sloan instructed her to watch Collins's most recent speech.

"A great President." Collins spoke with a smile. *"The great Ronald Reagan said, 'You can't be for big government, big taxes, and big bureaucracy and be for the little guy.' You know that I know that, but Rogers and Sloan just don't get it."*

"She may quote Reagan, but she's no Reagan," Bree said, closing her laptop when the speech concluded.

The pair moved from a discussion of Collins's positions to his inquiring about Bree's life outside politics.

"My mother was Irish, and my father drank like he was Irish. He was gone a lot."

The more she spoke, the more Sloan's enchantment was growing. He studied her eyes, appearing lively, awake.

Bree explained that because she was the only girl in the family, her mother doted on her. "For a while, my mom called me Murph; she loved that nineties TV show *Murphy Brown*. I take after my mom; she had an edge. I grew up listening to the old stuff, eighties music—lots of Pat Benatar and Joan Jett."

Sloan had grown up listening to eighties music, too, but not because his parents played the "oldies." He asked about her time in college.

Bree explained she'd had little interest in any course that did not further her goal of entering politics or the media. She mentioned her friend's major—women's studies—with palpable disdain. Then she launched into a soliloquy on all the disadvantages women have in competing with men. "But I know how to bat an eyelash while I kick your ass."

Both amused and drawn, Sloan repressed a comment.

"We were not rich; we were not poor," Bree continued. "We were not distant but not affectionate." Bree turned away. "We were fine." She added, "Just fine," but it was not convincing.

Sloan inquired about her father.

"My dad…" Her pause worried Sloan, maybe he was pressing her to disclose something dark that she preferred to remain buried. "Nothing bad, we just don't talk much." She added with a dash of sorrow, "Shakespeare wrote, 'It is a wise father that knows his own child.' My dad doesn't know me."

Before Sloan could express his empathy, she abruptly changed the subject and handed Sloan a printout of the few political figures who endorsed him. "Look here," she commanded.

"They share the same first name: former," Sloan replied without enthusiasm. "Former state representatives, former mayors, and a former general. Who in the hell is Andi Winkler?"

"She's a former congresswoman," Bree replied.

"From God knows where?" Sloan winced, dismissing the importance of the list. He moved to slightly tap Bree's knee…twice.

Bree gave a noticeable pause and gazed down at her knee. Her vision stayed on Sloan's hand, which lingered awkwardly in the air above her knee. His hand quickly returned to rest on his lap.

Her glance at him morphed into a stare. Yet the stare failed to reveal her reaction. He instantly regretted the touch; it was innocent; he rationalized he touched Zimmer the same way, but aware of the razor's edge of limits. This was no backstage dalliance. This was a risk with career-smashing repercussions. One wrong word, one wrong move could unleash an avalanche of doom.

Wayne Avrashow

"Ah…" he stuttered. He quickly asked a series of questions about her victorious campaign in Oregon.

Bree's voice sounded hurried. "We had no money. I hired local volunteers to film our stuff." She appeared flustered. "With your budget, I hired a full staff."

Desperate to keep the conversation moving, he urged her to be candid about how she would run media spots against him if she were hired by one of his opponents.

"I'd scrutinize your past. Painting you as inexperienced could be a plus. I'd portray you as out of the mainstream, reckless, dangerous." She appeared to warm to the task. "I'd dredge up old quotes you made about legalizing drugs. I'd interview your old band members and track down some of your groupies."

"Groupies?" Sloan replied with mock indignation. "Trust me, I didn't need groupies."

Bree playfully tugged on his shirt, almost too playfully. Her hand grazed his elbow. Now Sloan was the one watching her hand. It was her touch that was lingering.

"I'm sure you were not denied your share of *the ladies*," Bree added with amusement.

He relaxed at her show of warmth. "About a year ago, my guitarist and I went to this local bar, kind of a dive bar—"

"You? Tyler Sloan went to a dive bar?" she replied with unfiltered surprise. "Dive bars were my escape during the campaign. Who wants to sit at the Portland Hyatt sterile bar and get hit on by an old guy on a business trip?"

Her smile was enticing. Sloan noticed her smile was not disappearing, still lingering.

"Can't have *old* guys hitting on you," he added lightly.

"Depends on your definition of old." She added a wicked smile.

* * *

Later that night, Sloan released a pent-up sigh and punched in Mike's number, hoping his father could offer some clarity on securing the Teamsters' endorsement or other loose nuggets of political wisdom. He opened with what he presumed was a warm memory for both.

"I still smile every time I think about coming home from school when Mom baked those oatmeal cookies," Sloan opened.

"Quaker Oats, the best product on the shelves," Mike said in appreciation. "Tastes good, and it's good for you. Make it as cereal, cookies, oat bars...whatever you want."

"I'll have Grant cut a deal for you as their new pitchman." Sloan chuckled. He thought he had laid the groundwork and now began to discuss his visit to Carney's home.

Mike ignored the comment about the Teamsters. "I loved when Gladys put in different kinds of raisins and nuts."

"I loved the ones with chocolate chips," Sloan replied. "Let's talk about Carney—"

"She never made them with chocolate chips," Mike sternly disagreed. His tone was battle ready. "Raisins, son. Your mother and my wife of forty-two years made them with raisins."

"You weren't home much. I remember chocolate chips." Sloan met the challenge. He instantly regretted his comment.

"What the hell do you mean I wasn't home much?" Mike charged back. "I signed the papers so you could get your high school classes when you were touring. You didn't eat too many of Mom's cookies on the road, did you?"

Sloan gazed at the ceiling in frustration. He had to get out. "We both loved her; let's just say she made and loved both kinds," Sloan added wearily.

"God rest her soul," Mike replied. "Say, why did you call?"

Sloan's desire to get advice from his father had deflated. He wondered if Mike had purposely avoided his statement about wanting to talk about Carney or if his short-term memory was going. "Ah...just wanted to say hello, see how you're doing," was all he said.

FOURTEEN

July 5, Los Angeles

**Poll: Collins 32%, Rogers 20%,
Sloan 16%, Undecided 32%**

Sitting behind his office desk, Zimmer reached across to overturn the heavy hourglass. He glanced as the sand trickled from top to bottom. The room's only sound was the spinning of Zimmer's silver Montblanc pen on the leather writing pad resting on his glass desk. He forced a smile at Mary Rollins, who sat in a chair across from him. Mary held an environmentalists' cache as the executive director of Balanced Area Growth, a California-based environmental group.

Their differences were distinct, but Zimmer grudgingly accepted their similarities. He alternated between detesting and cherishing her. Although he equated dealing with her with suffering brain damage, he had calculated how to use Mary for his own gain.

The woman's expression was perpetually dour; she doled out smiles as if they were wartime rations. Zimmer chafed at her cause-related jewelry. He forced a "cute" to describe her cat-shaped earrings to signal support of animals' rights.

They had first met when she'd led the opposition to a client's film studio expansion in Century City. Fearful of negative publicity, the board of directors pressured Zimmer to "solve the problem." Zimmer initially attempted to hire a private investigator to find "something" embarrassing on Mary. The investigator cited a conflict of interest and declined—Mary had earlier retained him to investigate Zimmer.

At one stormy public meeting at the studio, she accused his client of various criminal acts. During her outburst, Zimmer whispered to a firm partner that the firm's building should be named after Mary since he would personally have her entombed in the foundation.

Mutual interests led to a rapprochement and a global settlement that both parties honored without the need for written formalities. Twice per year, Zimmer offered his pro bono counsel to Mary and Balanced Area Growth. In return, Zimmer held a "silver bullet": her group would support his clients' efforts or oppose that of his opposition.

Mary had delivered on her side of the bargain with her testimony at a congressional subcommittee on the bill to allow Native American tribes to expand gaming. Zimmer had written her opening line: "Restricting Native Americans is a racist scheme that will shred environmental protection laws."

Zimmer secured a key from his credenza to open a narrow desk drawer to remove an envelope and the annual $50,000 check payable to "The Westside Community Fund." His law firm had created the fund to support "neighborhood improvements" with ten equal payments for ten years. As the organization's sole officer and employee, Zimmer assumed, but never inquired, that Mary was the only recipient of the peace dividend.

"I need more funding if you want more testimony in Washington," Mary said.

Zimmer eyed her unflattering style of parting her natural, graying hair down the middle.

She continued with her usual series of murmurs. Although unable to discern her meaning, he never asked, preferring brevity to knowledge.

"I'm chair of Tyler Sloan's Senate campaign to decide control of the United States Senate." He spoke in a friendly but firm tone as if meting out gentle discipline to a teenage daughter. "Your request may have to take a back seat for a short time."

She frowned and pouted in expression, both pitiful and annoying. "If I'm in the back seat, you can put my testimony right next to it."

Zimmer sighed. "Dear, what type of funding are we talking about?"

* * *

The next morning in Las Vegas, the rumble of the flower trucks and the departing airplanes from nearby McCarran Airport cracked any semblance of morning quiet. Zimmer stood on a dock at the Las Vegas flower wholesaler Stein & Company. He discreetly slipped two folded twenty-dollar bills to a young Latino.

The employee walked away and returned with a cup of steaming espresso in one hand and a vibrant bouquet of pink carnations and purple irises in the other. Signaling his approval, Zimmer wheeled around, leading him toward his car. Zimmer popped the trunk; the young man delicately placed the flowers inside a container.

"Early, Grant, damn early," Jefferson Jackson said as he approached the car.

With a series of exaggerated breaths, Zimmer waved toward the open-air flower stalls, the large docks and trucks being loaded with crates of bright flowers.

"A floral oasis! Breathe deep, my friend." Zimmer inhaled. His voice grew melancholy. "My dear wife, Katie, had a fondness for fresh flowers. God bless her. I often brought home an arrangement from LA's Flower Mart. I think of her smile every time I'm around flowers."

"Did you get my messages? I left three of 'em," Jackson said quickly.

Zimmer noted a slight but insufficient whiff of urgency in Jackson's voice. He silently recalled his line about how "this would be a heck of a business if it weren't for the clients." Zimmer heard impatience in his voice, but he wanted desperation.

"You knew that enviro whack job would demand further studies in Congress on our gaming bill!" Jackson expressed rapidly. "You know that tree-hugging shrew, don't you?"

Zimmer shrugged at Jackson's vent.

"Christ, now the bill is floating in Never-Never Land! The board chewed my ass out!"

Zimmer finally heard pure panic.

"Your firm billed Gala over ten million last year! About that Indian—"

"J. J., my friend," Zimmer interrupted. "I'm a lawyer, not an influence peddler."

"I'm up to my ass in alligators on Indian gaming! It's the showdown at the O.K. Corral!"

Zimmer refrained from critiquing Jackson's creative mix of metaphors.

"We can't have the president veto this bill. Give me an idea of your billable hours."

"No billable hours."

Jackson's eyebrows arched as he asked, obviously puzzled. "Pro bono?"

"No hours. The firm will have to terminate our representation of Gala."

"What in the hell?" Jackson sputtered. "Why?"

"Because you deserve a lawyer you trust, one who you listen to."

Jackson's eyes narrowed. "I know you asked for five, but we ponied up one mil to your friend Romano. That's a lot of cabbage. We're still feeling the effects of the recession."

"Thanks for the economic update, professor."

"I'll give it my best efforts for another mil," Jackson said as his shoulders slumped. "Best efforts? Best goddamn efforts? You want my friends to use their best efforts?" The words barely squeezed through Zimmer's clenched jaw. His face puffed with dramatic flair. "Best efforts? Best efforts will get the House to chew on it for another year and then spit it out."

"No!" Jackson's hand shot forward. The loud response sliced through the constant clatter of pushcarts rolling on the docks. "Gala needs you. One phone call from you, and the White House changes the soup on its menu." He hesitated. "We need your presence public; we need to be transparent."

"No." Zimmer's finger graced his lower lip. "We need to appear to be transparent. Your lobbyist will be the face man and do the public lobbying. I'll work the kitchen door."

Jackson's expression soured. He obviously wanted a more public Zimmer. "Having you stay private would be foolish."

"Foolish? Foolish?" Zimmer's tone sliced, its edge increasing with each repetition. "The last time I was foolish was over a girl in the eighth grade." Zimmer had softened Jackson and now aimed for the jugular. "Johnny Romano needs five mil for a super PAC for Tyler."

"Five mil?" The phrase stuck in Jackson's throat. "Damn bullish, Grant."

"Wake up!" Zimmer's voice pumped louder. "You can put a ribbon and a bow on it or portray it as the noble Geronimo rescuing the tribes with casinos. But more gambling is a medicine that never goes down easy."

Zimmer abruptly went silent, allowing Jackson to worry about filling the dead air space. Power abhorred a vacuum, and Jackson hated silence. Jackson murmured softly, the words unintelligible.

"Don't dick me around on this." Zimmer's eyes drilled ice; his words roared heat. "Gala needs to write a four-million-dollar check to Johnny Romano's committee."

Zimmer shot an intense stare at Jackson before returning to sip his espresso. He casually noted that the espresso lacked the richness of his favorite Italian brand. He had already outlined television ads that Romano's committee could air to boost Sloan or slash his opponents.

Jackson slumped. "Don't know if I can sell it."

"Gala sells losing a paycheck as harmless fun." Zimmer jammed the throttle. "Your marketing wizards can sell condoms to nuns!"

Jackson's forehead glistened with perspiration.

"One question…" Zimmer asked quickly. "Does Gala have a better chance of getting the bill passed and signed with me or without me?"

Jackson leaned close. Closer. Too close, and Zimmer arched his head back. Jackson's hand cupped the side of his mouth. "What's our strategy to get the bill through?"

"There's only one strategy: You deliver four million next week. Johnny's waiting."

* * *

"You own this place?" Martino asked upon meeting Sloan in a parking lot outside a Henderson restaurant. The large neon sign "Louisa's" smacked of classic Las Vegas.

"I own half. *Louisa* runs Louisa's," Sloan replied matter-of-factly.

"*Huevos à la Tyler Sloan*?" Martino chuckled as he read the sign in the window.

Louisa del Mar came out to the parking lot to greet Sloan with two tumblers. "Your favorite, Tyler: watermelon *agua fresca*. No *azucar*— no sugar."

Sloan thanked his partner before she beat a hasty retreat. He eyed Martino, took one healthy sip of the drink. "I officially fired Judson yesterday." He took another sip. "Bree can handle it."

Martino coughed, his drink spilling out; a string of profanities followed. "Hey, man, I thought Bree's work was limited to social media; she's not ready to be the sole media advisor. I'll hammer Judson; he'll turn it around."

Sloan silently shook his head.

"Whoa, getting rid of Judson completely—that's my call!"

Sloan braced himself, ready for the blowback. "Bree's what we need."

"Are you serious?" Martino's arms flailed. "She won one fucking campaign! It's done?"

Sloan wiped his brow at the warming late-morning sun. "Contract signed. Let's discuss the public reason for Miles's departure."

"Reassigned," Martino snapped.

Wayne Avrashow

Reassignments were the preferred explanation. No one was terminated in campaigns unless that act served a public purpose. Martino retreated one step, appearing to calm himself. That calm was short lived; suddenly, his voice shouted like a firing cannon. "Last night Collins had an in-studio interview in town. She messed up her first interview; they gave her a second shot. She got all balled up and said, 'You can't herd cats, and you can't teach an old horse a new trick.'" He paused. "The station edited out her comment."

"It's funny, mixing metaphors, but what did they edit? Where's the story?"

"In the first interview, Chris said how much she loved meeting voters in North Las Vegas. She added, before the campaign, she *never* went there."

Sloan's free palm opened to signal his uncertainty.

"Watch how the Dems will shout racism!" Martino raged on. "They'll claim she insulted black voters in North Las Vegas," referring to the area's sizable African American population.

"*That's* racism?" Sloan questioned. "When does substance factor in?"

Martino repeated *substance* as if the word was Portuguese slang inserted in a *Harvard Law Review* article.

"Some progressives are chewing me out for my comments on school vouchers," Sloan said.

Martino jabbed his finger. "Damn lefty do-gooders. How many jobs do the tree huggers provide? They sip their chardonnay, send their kids to fine private schools, and then cry a river if a poor parent wants a voucher to send their kid to that same school."

A century ago, Martino was the overweight, jolly man in overalls, dispensing candy to small children at the general store. In this incarnation, he lived on an "attack alert," once thanking a reporter who termed him a "slash-and-burn" consultant.

Sloan started toward the restaurant's entrance. "This is the best part of campaigning. I'll go inside, shake a few hands, take some pics…nail a couple dozen votes."

"It's not that easy," Martino replied, his tone uncharacteristically gentle.

"Oh, watch me." Sloan punched the pudgy man's shoulder playfully. "When I'm doing retail campaigning, I feel like Pharrell singing 'Happy.'"

The lyrics were on his lips as he entered the restaurant.

FIFTEEN

July 8, Northern Nevada

"Tyler Sloan!" came a shout as Sloan made his way through the terminal at Reno-Tahoe International Airport. He stopped and looked at the exuberant long-haired rocker and his friends. His two-man security detail moved closer like panthers ready to strike a lone deer. Sloan flashed a "let's see" signal, and his men held their ground.

The young man and his group drew closer. "Meet your younger brother from a different mother! I'm the singer in Ty, the best tribute band out there."

Sloan was aware of the various tribute bands and singers who did more than cover his old songs with Liberty and his solo material; they played it note for note, gesture for gesture.

"We're you, man," the singer added. "But we give a modern sound to your Liberty songs, and play your solo stuff with an edge, little more authentic."

"*More authentic?*" Sloan responded in a bemused tone.

"He's the best Sloan you ever heard," another band member added with pride.

"Where do I rank among the Sloans?" There was amusement in Sloan's voice.

"We do your shit the way it's meant to be done. I hit notes you haven't reached in years." The singer bumped fists with his bandmates. "We're not a sideshow, not like that Hispanic guy who does 'El Sloan.'"

Sloan studied the impersonator with curiosity. He was inches shorter but bore a strong resemblance to Sloan's younger self. His curly long hair was a match for Sloan's youth. The singer's face was unlined, his biceps taut, and his body shifted with relentless energy.

"Have fun, keep playing! You just need one break," Sloan said as he sauntered away, feeling the slight stiffness in his right knee that had recently become bothersome. He turned back. "I presume I've got your votes?"

"Sure!" replied the singer. "It will be like voting for myself!"

* * *

After two public events in Reno earlier that day, Sloan stood on the front edge of the pitching mound to throw out the ceremonial first pitch at Reno's minor league Aces Stadium. He threw a perfect strike, waving to the crowd as he left the mound.

The applause rained down upon him as he walked to the dugout. His walk slowed as the cheers mounted. He stopped to gaze upward at the standing ovation; he turned to his right and then to his left, his fist raised in a salute.

In the corner of the press box, Sloan, Zimmer, and Mike sat together, watching the game.

"You hesitated walking off the mound," Zimmer said, bending down to wipe a slight smudge off his black alligator shoes with a clean cloth.

Sloan returned a sheepish smile. "The old singer still likes applause."

"You're smart to oppose the Indian bill," Mike said with authority.

"Not a hard call," Sloan replied. "It would be political suicide in Nevada."

"But Tyler can tease it," Zimmer added with a touch of defiance. "Hint around with Jackson…spray some perfume in the air—Gala is one of Nevada's biggest employers."

"Show him a little leg?" Mike snapped. "Not on that one."

Sloan leaned closer to Zimmer, his voice muffled but forceful. "Don't get near it."

Turning away, Sloan met the flirtatious gaze of two women staring into the press box. Sloan returned a modest smile, a smile once described by *People* magazine as "engaging." Yesterday Rogers's operatives posted blogs to describe his smile as "phony and devious." A meme was currently circulating around the internet with his face superimposed on the Joker in *Batman*.

"We checked out Rails. He's a retired major in the marine corps," Zimmer said.

"What *exactly* does he do for Collins?" Sloan inquired.

Mike shrugged. "His job is to filet you."

"*Filet?*" Sloan focused on the term. "Filet?" he repeated. He instantly worried how his rock star life could be exploited—that concern was dominant, but the word *filet* made him squeamish.

Mike grabbed an unlit cigar. He shouted out old-school baseball instructions to the manager. "I have something you boys will like, something confidential. It's on a little thumb drive." Mike patted his coat pocket with an unrestrained smile. "You two watch it alone, and I mean *alone*. It's a Collins commercial that never aired."

Sloan pressed Mike for how he had received it.

"My former legislative aide is working for Rogers. She slipped it to me. Use it right, you'll take some points off Collins's lead."

"Why wouldn't Rogers use it?" he asked dubiously.

"My gal intercepted it; she knows Rogers can't win." Mike smirked. "I'm sure she'd appreciate a position with Senator Sloan."

Sloan turned to Zimmer. "Is any of this legal?"

"For God's sake, watch it!" Mike gestured toward Zimmer. "That man can find a way to use it—it's the Hope Diamond."

Zimmer's cell phone chimed. He took the call and cupped his right hand over his ear to hear the caller. When that was unsuccessful, he hurried to a corner of the press box.

Sloan watched intently as Zimmer flashed a thumbs-up gesture.

Zimmer nodded with a series of *Yes, Mr. President*s as he motioned for Sloan to take the phone. Mike popped up and followed his son to the corner.

"Defer, defer, defer," Zimmer said in a hushed voice as he handed Sloan the phone.

Sloan began with a "yes, sir," adding a few more of the phrase, then squeezed in, "It's a two-person race: Collins and me."

"More," Zimmer whispered sharply.

"One good word from you, and it's a dead heat," Sloan added.

"Close it," Mike mouthed fiercely.

"Two good words from you, and we'll celebrate in the Oval Office," Sloan said quickly. A response came, and then he profusely thanked the president before ending the call.

Mike placed his hand forward to seize the moment. "Flood the airwaves with ads in those cow counties outside of Las Vegas and Reno. Then you poll, you'll get a bump in numbers to help you persuade Reed. Then saturate Vegas and Reno and poll again. That'll do it."

"No time for that," Sloan replied. "Reed wants to see me ASAP."

When Mike took a bathroom break, Sloan leaned closer to Zimmer. "Whatever is on this thumb drive, if we're ever asked, *exactly* how did we get this?"

"It was mailed to my firm; no return address." Zimmer wasted no time.

Sloan studied Zimmer, his attorney's response was quick; he presumed the question was not new.

"I need you in Las Vegas," Sloan said suddenly. "I need you when I meet with Collins and that nutcase Rails. We'll get you a suite in the campaign office. Plus, you can keep an eye on my dad."

Zimmer slowly repeated Sloan's last phrase with an ample dose of disbelief.

"Talk to him. Convince him to campaign with me," Sloan added. "I'm in no position to ask him, and not sure he'd listen to me."

Zimmer patted Sloan's hand in acquiescence.

* * *

Wayne Avrashow

As Sloan was holding court with the press corps on the campaign bus to an appearance in Northern Nevada, he noticed an intense stare directed at him by Ben Davis.

The thirtyish Davis was well known in Nevada political circles as the creator of the website the Silver State. The site favored Republican candidates and emphasized religious issues. Critics dismissed the site's political relevance by saying that *God* was its most frequent noun and *pray* the most cited verb.

Sloan's staff had researched Davis. He was a drummer who played in a Christian rock band throughout Nevada and Utah, earning modest paydays but little else. He blogged daily on politics and religion but failed to secure a job at any of the numerous publications he had applied to. Sloan had previously made an off-hand remark to Davis about his love of baseball and Chicago's Wrigley Field.

"Which have you attended more in the last ten years: church or Wrigley Field?" Davis had inquired in an ever-so-polite tone. "When was the last time you attended church?"

"It's been too long." Sloan recognized the insufficient response. "We'll be going back soon, real soon." Then, fully understanding the hint of privilege many people felt when Sloan sang a single verse—many would boast to their family or friends how "Tyler Sloan sang a song for me"—Sloan began to sing "Serve Somebody" in his best Dylan voice.

Smiles appeared on the faces of many of the reporters, but Josh David Mack's expression remained sour behind his wire-framed glasses. "No one asked you to sing," he said, joining the exchange. "The next line in that song is about serving either the devil or the Lord. Maybe you don't serve the devil, Mr. Sloan. But I wonder, are you an atheist?"

Sloan cautiously eyed the scholarly looking reporter as others leaned forward. It was on. He was no longer basking in the comfort of an adoring entertainment media; he was squarely in the crossfire of the two young reporters. He saw Davis nod to Mack, pleased that his media brethren had joined the pursuit.

"Personally, I'm an atheist and think it's cool you are," Mack continued, baiting him, as Davis blanched.

Sloan leaned back to display an air of confidence and patiently shared how often he had accompanied his late mother to church and joined her in her church-related volunteer efforts.

"Nice to hear," Mack replied dryly. The reporter then quoted lyrics from Sloan's songs and interpreted them to indicate Sloan often mocked religion. He cited Sloan's youthful acts to rebel against authority, including his use of drugs, and stated that it was interesting that Mike Sloan was not campaigning for him.

"You got a question there?" Sloan asked to a tittering of laughs.

"Don't tell me how to ask a question," Mack huffed. "I make a statement first; then I ask my question."

Bewildered, Sloan wondered how Mack's technique upheld journalistic integrity.

"How about answering a basic question?" Mack replied. "Do you believe in God?"

It amused Sloan, but only slightly. He was taking hits from this odd couple of journalists. Davis held down the evangelic fort, while Mack had inked his irreverence on his body with an array of tattoos.

The bus exited the freeway, near its destination. One of the savvier of Sloan's aides interrupted. "The questioning is over."

Sloan reached for his bottle of mineral water and took a long sip. He raised the bottle and pressed it against his lips. More time passed. "My mom never pushed her faith, and I'm the same way," he finally said. He detailed the work of blue's foundation and how his company donated millions to the underprivileged, reaching into communities of need. When one reporter mentioned how Sloan's foundation was honored at a chartable event, Sloan returned a modest nod.

Davis rose and moved toward Sloan, keeping his footing even on the moving bus. He seemed incensed by Sloan's verbal dodges. Sloan's aide stood in the aisle, gesturing to the reporters that the session had expired. When that failed, he slid his hand across his throat; this was over. Although Mack and the other reporters returned to their seats, Davis remained standing and loomed above Sloan. "I know you don't have a religious bone in your body."

Sloan gazed upward at Davis, keeping his expression even. "Time to go, man. I've got to prep for the event."

Davis pressed his hand against the back of Sloan's seat. "I have sources on audio. One of your old bandmates said you continuously ridiculed religion."

Sloan's security guards squeezed themselves between Davis and Sloan. "Return to your seat," one commanded, but Davis failed to budge, even as the bus braked in front of the Sparks shopping mall.

Sloan's security aide moved nearer to Davis and said smugly, "Your lady friend from *USA Today* is not as pretty as your wife, but she'll do. You two spent a long time in her room last night. Your room or hers tonight?"

Sloan kept his face straight as Davis glared at him over the security guard's shoulder. "I'm not running," Davis bit out. "You're the man that ran hard with the devil."

As the group made ready to leave the bus, Davis shot Sloan a look of victory.

* * *

The sweat dripped from Sloan's forehead while huffing as Bree's crew filmed his mountain bike ride on Lake Tahoe's Tahoe Rim Trail. This nine-mile ride at Spooner Summit was more than challenging. He cycled past his name on an "Adopt-a-Vista" kiosk that signified his earlier contribution to the trail organization.

"Look, Mr. Sloan! Your name is on the kiosk," a young rider proclaimed.

Sloan half-heartedly waved an acknowledgment, too tired to verbally respond, attempting to conserve each breath.

Another young cyclist asked Sloan to join him on a ride termed "165 Mile Club," which signified one's hiking or biking the entire length of the Rim Trail.

"Sounds great," Sloan warbled. The thought of cycling 165 miles was not enticing.

Sloan appreciated the natural beauty surrounding him. The lake's blue water shimmered, the pine trees rose majestically, the rock formation made for a stunning visual, and the clouds dotted the sky with postcard perfection…but Sloan's thoughts were on the campaign.

Progress and uncertainty were hovering. The poll numbers were inching in his direction; Rogers's campaign was stalling; the president was interested in meeting "as soon as possible"; he was gaining comfort as a candidate; his father was slowly coming around without being "begged." Bree was foremost in his thoughts; her television and social media posts were generating buzz. Zimmer's man still needed to find Denny Morgan and secure the sex tape, and maybe the as-yet-unwatched video his dad had supplied was a beneficial hit on Collins.

A cadre of Bree's youthful assistants wore GoPro cameras mounted on their helmets as they rode in front of, beside, and behind Sloan. One motioned for Sloan to wave. Sloan obliged and forced a smile that he hoped would mask his exhaustion. He worried he would collapse any minute. *How would that visual play?* he wondered.

He silently cursed the staff member who had scheduled this stunt. His legs had begun to cramp when one of the cyclists announced, "Only one more mile!"

SIXTEEN

July 11, Washington, DC

**Poll: Collins 34%, Rogers 22%,
Sloan 17%, Undecided 27%**

Sloan gazed about the Oval Office; the clock read 7:10 a.m. The limousine's dark windows had shielded him from public scrutiny during the short drive from the Hay-Adams Hotel. His entry through the outside gate had been entirely undercover.

President Reed was late for their meeting. Sloan pressed his foot against the plush rug to test its cushion. A Secret Service agent stood silently nearby and glanced at Sloan's hands, which he'd been rubbing fiercely. Aware of the agent's glance, moving his hands apart to normalcy. He was no longer the confident entertainer performing at the president's inaugural ball; this morning, he was a prospective senator. The change was palpable.

He gazed around, seeking to absorb the weight of the historic decisions that were made in this office. He stared at the window where a pensive John Kennedy had stood next to his brother Robert, a photograph impressed in his mind. He focused on Reed's substantial wooden desk, which sat a few feet away, imagining which desk his father would have used had the fates been kinder.

The agent snapped to attention when Reed entered. The president wore a dark-blue warm-up suit and tennis shoes, appearing presidential even with a towel draped around his neck.

"I lost ten pounds and dropped my cholesterol number. I hope Chuck Todd never asks me to explain the good and bad cholesterol."

Zimmer and Martino had offered the same counsel for this meeting: the president leads.

"Remind your dad he has an open dinner invitation." Reed leaned back in his chair. "Do you think he'd like to play a role in the administration?"

Sloan had no clue, unable to discern his father's intentions on his own campaign.

Reed opened his desk drawer and retrieved a large silver-framed photograph of John Kennedy throwing out the first pitch of the 1963 season at Griffith Stadium, former home of the Washington Senators baseball team. The president handed Sloan the framed photograph.

"It's for you. You're a baseball fan." The president smiled. "JFK is firing the pitch, and Johnson is right next to him. It was his last opening day."

Sloan thanked the president for his graciousness.

"Legend has it that Kennedy and Reagan were both great storytellers, both Irishmen with a sense of humor," Reed continued. "I'd like to imagine that, despite their disagreements, they would have enjoyed each other's company."

Sloan's smile was short lived as Reed quickly followed up. "No bullshit. Why are you running? You're famous, financially secure. You've seen how tough this business is, watching your dad."

Sloan worried that the wrong answer could terminate his chance of the president's support. He agreed the stage brought meaning and fulfillment to his life, and joy to his fans. He failed to discern any reaction from Reed. "It sounds trite," he blurted, "but I want to do more. I *can* do more. I want to be in the public arena, not the concert arena."

Reed was silent, pondering Sloan's response. He asked about Sloan's testimony years ago before a US Senate Committee on intellectual property and copyright infringement. Before Sloan could answer, Reed, interjected, "Your testimony was impressive, but I received mixed reports."

"Mixed reports?" Sloan was momentarily shaken.

"I heard some senators did not treat you with respect. True?"

Sloan began to explain the righteousness of that cause.

Reed cut him off. "That's not what I asked."

Sloan had persuaded audiences with a wink and a smile, but this was not his usual audience. When he'd testified, many in the Capitol dismissed him as a mere celebrity. He cited various slights, how senators and their aides snapped photographs, posted tweets, and hoisted cell phones in the air for selfies with him, but few intellectually engaged him. "Only Senator Sidlow took notes," Sloan recalled. "Sidlow wasn't writing a shopping list—he was interested. I was pumped when I saw that." He stole a glance around the office, weighing how much to reveal. "One senator called his wife and then handed me the phone to sing to her as if I were a circus performer."

Reed nodded. "That's what I heard. And that's motivating you to run?"

"No, but after that day, I knew I belonged. I knew I could hold my own in the Senate."

The president rose from his chair and motioned for Sloan to follow as he opened a side door. He explained that he had converted a small office space into an indoor putting green. "The more I play at Bethesda, the more I get criticized, so this is my substitute. Grab a putter," Reed commanded, pointing to a dozen putters stored within a wooden cabinet. "I saw you play in a pro-am tournament. You're good."

Sloan practiced with one putter before taking several practice putts. He nailed his first three putts into the cup recessed into the carpet.

"Got any tips?" the president asked.

"Tips on?" Sloan asked, his tone respectful.

"Putting. I can't sing a lick."

"Your grip is fine, but you want your stroke to be like a pendulum."

The president practiced a couple of swings without a ball. He then aced the next two putts. He gestured toward Sloan. "You're in my next foursome." .

Sloan worried that time was disappearing. "Do you have any advice for me, Mr. President?"

Reed returned a courtly smile. "Show voters your moral compass. I heard you're not comfortable with pronouncements about faith. Try John Wooden or a philosopher."

Sloan gently pressed for something more tangible.

"I saw you on C-SPAN when you went into a store in a small town outside of Reno." Reed pointed meaningfully at him. "*Always* buy something. In New Hampshire, I bought more damn handmade mittens and hats than my staff could ever wear."

Sloan followed as the president turned back toward the Oval Office.

"My nephew talks about being a buddy's 'wingman.' Give me a reason, and give it to me soon, and I'll say something positive about you."

Sloan felt his heart skip. "I'll do that, and I'll be very grateful."

"Have Grant stay in touch. You could actually win this son of a bitch," Reed said, a dash of amazement playing in his voice. He motioned to the Secret Service agent that he was returning upstairs, and Sloan was escorted back to the waiting limo.

* * *

On his return flight to Las Vegas, Sloan called Cindy. He opened with manufactured cheer by inquiring about the latest events with Riley. He frequently talked with his daughter but understood a fourteen-year-old girl might not confide all to her father. The real reason for this call was to confirm that Cindy would be attending a dinner with him in Las Vegas for the charity where they each served on the board of directors. They could go separately, but he wanted the media to believe he had a normal relationship with his ex, the mother of his child. He pondered the idea of a "normal" relationship with an ex; an *abnormal* relationship was likely the norm.

Cindy returned a series of pronounced sighs into the phone. Sloan wondered how many more times she could sigh. Their conversations had developed a pattern: He would offer brief pleasantries, they would exchange operational questions or comments about Riley, he would close with ten seconds of good wishes. He never broke the pattern.

He accepted Cindy's complaint about the media pressuring her for public comment about him; she was uncomfortable speaking in public venues or to the press. She long ago confessed to him while in college that she only selected courses that did not require oral reports. He lightly inquired about her therapy, careful to choose the right word or phrase. She often complained that he was "baiting her." He settled for a general inquiry.

"My therapist thinks group therapy would be beneficial," she replied.

An alarm went off in Sloan's head. "Not group therapy—someone in the group will spill their guts, and yours, to the tabloids for a quick payday. There'll be a photo of you leaving your therapist's office plastered on the internet."

"You're more worried about how it would look during your campaign than you worry about me," she snapped.

He ignored her barb. "I'm concerned about all of us—you, me, and Riley." He followed up with an undisguised bribe. "Would a new Chanel dress work at the Agassi event?"

"And if I'm asked about you?" Cindy asked, her voice perking up.

"I'm a great father—you know that's true—or anything positive would be great. Just be brief. Give them two sentences and then tell them you've got to attend to Riley. My assistant will pick you up Saturday at the airport. You'll be home that night."

"Commercial? No way. Send a plane to Santa Monica."

Sloan held his response. "No problem," he replied pleasantly, priding himself on being able to keep his annoyance out of his voice.

When he clicked off the phone, his smile was laced with a grimace, the usual combination after a call with Cindy. Suddenly he thought of Bree's smile—an *infectious* smile. He smirked at the difficulty of trying to work *infectious* into the lyrics of a song.

It would be another hour before he landed in Las Vegas. He opened his laptop, looking for a diversion. He found himself perusing the Facebook pages of women from his past:

Joan, the too-young UCLA student, now proudly displayed her bridal photographs.

Susie, the receptionist, a sexual gymnast who could only discuss shoes, nails, and hair, had relocated to a small town in Idaho.

His face fell when he saw the "RIP Mommy" post on Lisa's page. She was a few years older during their dalliance, a financial wizard at his first accounting firm. Lisa's photo revealed a lined, but still beautiful face. She was surrounded by her six grandchildren, who were surely now grieving their loss.

Katie was a strong-willed attorney who never compromised, stressing that she was "principled." He'd never understood how her refusal to eat at a sushi bar instead of at the table was principled.

He had pursued Andrea for years, now chilling to see her with a smiling husband and twin girls. Sloan recognized his inability to commit to Andrea. He wondered what turns his life would have taken had he pursued her with the same intensity as his career.

Those women were pages in his life. Cindy was the only chapter, a chapter that did not end well. He had a whole staff of people to make airline, hotel, and restaurant reservations if he wanted to travel, but he had no one—no woman—he wanted to go with.

His cell phone started playing "Start Me Up" by the Rolling Stones; his demeanor brightened when he saw Bree was calling.

"How did it go?" she began.

Sloan rose in his seat, his mood and his posture instantly lifted. "Great! Reed's in play."

The two exchanged strategy ideas before Sloan bemoaned the advice he was receiving from his staff. They had proliferated in number; he could not remember half their names.

"I'm not impressed with any of them," Bree replied bluntly. "If they were the best, they would be with Rogers or Collins."

"You're the first who's had the guts to say that." Sloan recalled one aide's condescending tone. "That guy who looks like Harry Potter lectured me about how I should stand and point during my speeches."

"Those little punks are trying to teach the master how to work a room?"

Sloan was bemused at her audacity.

"Tyler, let's get your handsome face out there. What doofus wants to program you? I'll let you go; get some rest on the plane. I'm slaving away in the office."

"No dive bars tonight?"

"Well…" She paused, voice filled with drama. "Not alone. Call me old-fashioned, but I prefer the right companion."

His head cocked in wonder at her remark; it was tantalizing, yet there was room for interpretation. "The right companion," he began slowly, "one of life's biggest decisions."

SEVENTEEN

July 13, Las Vegas

"How screwed am I?" Martino leaned across the table closer to his friend Marvin Katz. Martino asked the question in a manner that conveyed he was aware of the correct answer, but still…he desperately sought to hear a more comforting analysis.

The two shared a table at the Las Vegas Country Club overlooking the golf course. The club stood across the street from where Elvis made his 1968 return at the International Hotel, which morphed into the Las Vegas Hilton, was reborn as the LVH, and was now the Westgate.

Following the FBI's contact, Martino had asked Katz to quietly research the government's case against him and left unsaid his role in the FBI's sting operation.

"We can twirl the pasta a hundred ways, but…" Martino's voice dropped. "I never paid the taxes."

Martino was grateful Katz did not ask the obvious question of why he failed to pay taxes—there was no right answer.

Katz had achieved a personal injury lawyer's nirvana, earning a third of a multimillion-dollar judgment, and retired to what Martino termed *la dolce vita*—the sweet life. Katz wore a brightly colored Tommy Bahama short-sleeved silk shirt. His thinning hair failed the comb-over test, but his flecked soul patch served its diversionary purpose. Martino braced against the scent of his well-dabbed cologne.

The attorney flexed his biceps and detailed his in-home gym, tanning bed, and personal trainer. "I turned forty; got to keep fit when you date the young ones. I went with one to an aerobics class. Crazy chick didn't tell me it was *advanced* aerobics. Damn near killed me!" Katz pointed at Martino. "Don't *ever* mention the word *Pilates* to me."

Martino was quickly tiring of tales of Katz's dating adventures. He laid out his defense strategy of attacking the US attorneys as partisans seeking a political vendetta.

Martino continued, trying to gauge Katz's reaction. At each pause, Katz was waving his hand for more. Martino elaborated on how he could make the rounds of talk shows and dismiss it all as a Republican plot. At Katz's scowl, Martino discarded using that approach.

Katz acknowledged that Martino's press conference defense might influence public opinion but calmly questioned its impact on a jury's deliberations.

Martino halted, understanding the frailties in his defense.

"Clever, but it still makes me queasy." Katz sat with arms crossed.

"Give it to me straight, Marv."

Katz's gaze reflected mild disappointment. "When the naked, damning facts are laid out in court, your political skills are worth nada, zip, *bupkes*, zero. Assume the case is tried; what would most jurors conclude?"

Martino bit his lip as he absorbed his attorney's analysis. He gazed down at his yellow legal tablet of bullet points, desperate, but unable to extract a winning defense.

Katz explained that the US attorney had an unblemished conviction rate prosecuting white-collar crime and was on the short list of nominees to the federal bench if the next president was Republican.

"You know politics is all about relationships, and that attorney wants to hang your Demo scalp on the wall," Katz added.

Martino softly noted his relationships with a few Republican officeholders.

"They don't seat senators in the jury box." Katz's tone was firm. "Your case has…difficulties."

Martino inhaled, held his breath, and then exhaled deeply. Glancing outward to the golf course, he sought tranquility but failed to locate it in the manufactured greens.

* * *

Later, Martino sat on the hard beige bench seats as the Las Vegas Monorail car sped south to its last stop at the MGM Grand.

"Anyone ride this boondoggle?" Speaker of the House Bernard Pinkerton asked him. The speaker was in Las Vegas on what his office described as a "fact-finding mission" to review public transportation. Pinkerton's aides sat dutifully in the rear of the sparsely populated car. Las Vegas Monorail was the city's sop to rapid transit, an elevated dual-track system that failed every ridership and financial projection.

Martino eyed his watch, knowing the monorail trip would consume fourteen minutes. He had tested his MP3 recorder, concealed in his briefcase, to ensure a fail-safe technological performance. Another recording device was hooked to his coat pocket as a backup; his cell phone was recording Pinkerton—he was not taking any chances.

The speaker vented his displeasure of the constant fundraising required to assemble a financial war chest to maintain his speakership. The monorail slowed at the upcoming Bally's stop. "This system is a loser. It doesn't come close to the airport." Pinkerton waved his hand as if to shoo away an annoying fly.

Martino nodded in silent agreement, without interest in the city's transit system. His only mission was for Pinkerton to spew damning remarks.

"Sloan's campaign is sputtering," the speaker said.

"What will you say if we win it in August?" Martino replied without missing a beat.

"Congratulations." His dry tone revealed he presumed he would never utter the word. Pinkerton detailed his fundraising meetings with

Nevada casino executives before casually, too casually, mentioning Martino's former client, the Deer Valley Tribe.

"You've been a good friend for that tribe," Martino cooed. "And now you want…"

The slightly built Pinkerton leaned forward, unknowingly closer to Martino's wired system. He complained about how the tribe never supported him or his political committees.

"What's next?" Martino asked casually, laying the bait.

Pinkerton's face squeezed in the agony of being the child not invited to the party. "I saved their scalps on your bill. How much will they make if Congress approves their right to partner up with Gala and the others?"

Pinkerton rocked back and forth on his bench seat. With the smattering of fading freckles on his face and his crossed legs, he resembled a wayward schoolboy who was aware of his bad behavior but was oblivious to any adult scolding. "My victory fund is five hundred large short of its goal," he said crisply. "Pocket change to the tribe. I'm sure they want their bill to move faster than this old thing."

The subway train slowed as it approached the MGM station.

"Where and when do you want to meet with them?"

"I just did," Pinkerton replied as he rose. "Make it happen."

* * *

A few minutes after midnight, Sloan and Collins stood on a large concrete pad the length of a football field at Hoover Dam, flanked by Zimmer and Rails. The night sky was speckled with stars, the desert air pure as a modest warm wind blew across the terrain. Godforsaken and God blessed.

The dam was forty minutes southeast of Las Vegas. Its construction in 1928 was a bloody undertaking with lives lost battling hazardous construction, desert heat, and winter winds. Rented women and gambling halls were welcome diversions.

"I've never shared our past—except..." She nodded toward Rails. Collins had an unmistakably sharp snap to her voice. Her lips were tight, her expression even more locked.

Sloan read from her expression and tone that she was more worried than irritated. He shared her concern regarding the political fallout if the video Morgan held was aired. Back in the day, society's double standard would allow a man more leeway than a woman in a messy affair; but he had no desire to test results in today's climate.

The soft moonlight illuminated and flattered Collins. Yet when she moved a couple of steps under the bright industrial lighting outside of the dam, her camouflage of powdering, patting, and puffing failed to disguise the realities of aging.

"Rails told me your team may use that *doctored* video," she said with an edge.

Sloan allowed himself a near smile. "It's not doctored, doesn't need to be doctored."

Collins returned a dismissive grunt.

"The three of us were walking away from the camera like an old *Crazy Girls* billboard," Sloan said, referring to the long-running Strip adult show that featured a bevy of naked, well-shaped derrieres.

"Rails is a military man," Collins said. "His reports are that it's been enhanced. It was dark, indoors; it can't be clear."

Rails nodded in affirmation.

"We're not that old," Sloan replied. "It was the eighties, not the fifties. The camera had a light for indoor filming."

Rails answered his cell phone. He spoke in a style evocative of a firing machine gun. "Major Rails, unsecured line, identify." He terminated the call with equal force.

Sloan discreetly raised his eyebrows toward Zimmer. "You called the meeting, Chris." Sloan was intentionally circumspect, assuming Rails was covertly recording the conversation.

"In the campaign, we're each peeling back the onion on each other," she replied. "That's fair game, but I thought it best to have an understanding."

"Both sides play it straight," Rails added with velocity.

Sloan stared out at the dry, barren distance. Cactus and brush dotted the landscape. He was uncertain if Rails was merely a harmless eccentric or an overzealous campaign kook who could implode or explode in any direction.

"Sex, drugs, and rock and roll equal a scandal. If that video airs, Rogers wins, and we both look like fools," Collins added.

Sloan prided himself on his skill to discern the intent of all the promoters, agents, record-label executives, publicists, and sycophants who genuflected to him. He hastily glanced at Zimmer. Tonight's headline read, Collins Does Not Have Video.

"You might air it to shame me and think you'll be perceived as some macho dude," Collins inserted. "But trust me, you air it, and Rogers wins."

"We'll unleash our nuke if we hear a whisper you're airing it," Rails blurted as if each word was a lethal capsule being immediately expelled from his mouth. "A preemptive strike."

"A nuke?" Sloan mocked. "Find some hidden meanings in my lyrics?"

"Hef with a microphone." Rails nearly smiled. "There's some fruit in that grove."

"Dig around, Colonel Klink." Sloan glared at Rails. "Let's call it a night." He turned to Zimmer and motioned for him to follow; the meeting had ended.

Minutes later, Sloan's head bounced off the headrest in Zimmer's Mercedes. "That guy's a whack job. The big takeaway is they don't have the video—they think *we* have it."

"Either Denny Morgan sold it to Rogers, or he's holding out to increase the bidding."

"Did your guy find him or not?" Sloan pressed.

Zimmer was uncharacteristically soft in his response. "Yes…and no."

Sloan frowned.

"He's back from Hawaii, which is where he's been since you met with him, but he has not been back at his apartment. He can't stay undercover forever. My guy's close."

Could Morgan be on a drug binge? Sloan wondered. *Did he sell the video to Rogers to finance his Hawaiian vacation? Is he clever enough to negotiate for more?*

"Find the bastard already," he snapped.

EIGHTEEN

July 16, Las Vegas

The sun sweetly kissed the eight a.m. morning, but soon the desert would bestow its sweltering impact. Sloan studied Bree as they walked alongside the lake behind the gates of his Lake Las Vegas community.

The custom-home community was unique among the numbing sameness of Las Vegas's typical tract housing, where rows of three-floor plans and three alternating exteriors equaled a neighborhood. He spent most of his time here, as opposed to his condo; it was only thirty minutes from the Strip. However, those thirty minutes bestowed upon the location a sense of being a world apart from the neon blazes of his daily life. It was here he found tranquility.

Today he was sharing that tranquility with Bree. He silently noted, amused, and admiring, that as she spoke, her facial expressions were far from subtle, her pleasure instant and visible, her annoyances pronounced. "In politics, the fresh face always has an edge," she was saying, layering the compliment on him with her next words. "And you're the freshest face in the game."

"I was in Washington last year." He was gesturing toward the lake. "An older congressman told me that when he first got elected, voters would interrupt his breakfast at a local coffee shop to praise his work. Now, at the park with his grandchildren, people yell at the kids, 'Grandpa is a crook.'"

The two exchanged smiles. Nearing the water, he noticed her gaze resting comfortably on him. He indulged, glancing back as the lake's reflection cast a radiant glow upon her. Bree's fair skin was illuminated in a satiny aura. A mild wind swirled, her crimson hair slightly ruffled.

"You're engaged?" he asked, well aware of the answer.

"He's a solid guy, a real solid guy. He's got his pluses…" Her voice drifted.

Sloan took note of her measured words and seeming lack of emotion.

"His mom is awesome," she added with detachment.

"Sounds like a perfect match."

The warm wind kicked again. Her smile nearly cried for his touch. He had to be disciplined, thrusting hands in his pockets, shielding himself from any temptation.

"He can be tough," Bree muttered. "It's not an easy relationship."

Sloan hesitated, uncertain of what he wanted to say.

As the two moved down a pathway and saw a few of his neighbors walking in the distance, a solitary woman walked toward them and shouted, "Tyler Sloan!"

He anticipated that the woman would tell him how one of his songs was playing when her husband first asked her to dance or when they shared their first kiss as his music played softly in the background.

The woman whirled to face Bree with an outstretched hand and introduced herself. "I'm Diane." She glanced approvingly at Bree. "I read that you had a lovely daughter, Mr. Sloan."

Bree responded with a nervous smile. The woman flashed disjointed smiles between a series of quick and unrelated questions about Wall Street, nuclear power, and terrorists.

"Call Susan at my campaign office," Sloan replied. "Or check her out, our positions out on Facebook, follow us on Twitter."

"Can I just talk to someone?" the woman asked with a razor's edge.

Diane's words skipped haphazardly with disjointed emphasis. "Immigrants are pouring into Nevada. Abdul and five turban heads can stuff a bomb inside my purse and destroy the Strip. I want you to stop the crazies, or we will all be blown to smithereens."

"I'll call you personally," Sloan added gingerly. "Write down your name and number."

"*Personally* call," she exploded. "What the heck does that mean? Do you have a card?"

Sloan shook his head. "I don't have one, but here's how to contact the campaign." He handed her a card with the campaign's information.

Diane stared at him, convinced he was the eccentric one. Sloan watched with subdued amusement as she walked away with one of his songs on her lips.

"Let's go before she asks me to name the prime minister of Uganda." He motioned for her to follow him home. "I've got to show you something."

"Hang on," Bree said with annoyance. Her earring had become dislodged. She removed her pearl earring and touched around her ear. She was busy, fiddling with earring pieces, complaining about the clip-on earrings. "Check my earring to see if it looks right."

Sloan leaned into and lightly touched Bree's shoulder as he examined her ear. He knew he was closer than needed. He tried to be discreet as he inhaled, her perfume intoxicating.

Minutes later, the pair sat in Sloan's living room. He inserted the thumb drive from his father into his laptop and played the unaired Collins commercial, which he and Zimmer had watched previously. In the first clip, Collins was walking up the steps of Nevada's Capitol building in Carson City. In the next, she was speaking at a state senate hearing as the announcer's deep voice intoned.

"Chris Collins testified at our state's Capitol against storing nuclear waste in Nevada and preventing a catastrophe. But one public official refused to protect Nevada."

The camera focused on an empty chair at the hearings.

"State senator Billy Rogers was silent on this critical issue at this critical time. Where was Billy Rogers when Nevada's safety was at stake?"

The video showed an unflattering photograph of Rogers standing on the beach, wearing an island shirt, a silly smile, and a half-tilted straw hat while holding a drink in one hand and a pink umbrella in the other. Men and women in similar poses surrounded him.

"Where was Billy?" The announcer added gravely. "Billy Rogers was partying with lobbyists instead of protecting Nevada."

The image closed in on a photo of Rogers looking smashed. The video momentarily went black and then returned with Collins joined by members of the camera crew.

"That's a good hit on Billy," Collins said as an aide readied to remove her microphone. "Ply a couple of shots of tequila into some of Tyler's groupies and get those tramps talking. Then let song boy and freckle face defend it."

"Very sincere, Chris, very sincere," the same off-camera voice responded.

She chuckled. "It *should* look sincere. I took enough acting lessons."

"Well, little freckle face?" Sloan said when the video ended. "Give the tramps tequila? Acting lessons? This is a godsend."

Bree wore a stern expression. "How did you get this? Did you get it legally?"

"An old friend gave it to me—an old friend I trust. I've been a punching bag in the campaign. We're too damn soft; we're playing it too nice. Let's air this and put Collins on the defensive. It's her turn."

* * *

As preplanned, Sloan and Cindy entered the ballroom in the MGM Hotel to greet Las Vegas's A-list at the annual Andre Agassi Grand Slam Charity Ball. They stopped to view the offerings in the silent auction. Cindy praised the chandelier resting on a large table, which was flanked by security guards ensuring its safety.

"It's a Chihuly; bidding starts at two hundred thousand," Sloan noted and then added with sarcasm, "something every home needs."

Cindy's eyes drank it up greedily. "Look at how it casts sparkles on my gown, Tyler. I could dance in these lights."

Sloan began to reply but was interrupted by a well-suited, ruggedly handsome executive of a casino group that owned properties throughout Nevada. "I was here when you sang at the first Agassi event," the executive said in a voice two degrees above polite. "On the way home that night, my wife told me she was leaving me."

Sloan remained mum at the instantly awkward moment; Cindy was blatant in her ogling the man.

"Hope you're not singing tonight." The man laughed loudly. "I can't afford another divorce."

Sloan forced a smile, cringing at being the passive punch line. Cindy giggled.

The man leaned into Sloan, his voice muffled. "My board doesn't see you winning."

To this man and his brethren, the outcome was all that mattered. The casino industry *never* gambled. They were political pragmatists with partners and shareholders who stacked the odds on their side at the gaming tables and cashed their chips by supporting winning politicians.

"Ninety percent of what's going to happen hasn't happened," Sloan said firmly, but he read doubt on the man's face.

"Cut the crap. How-can-you-win?" he asked forcefully.

Sloan gripped the man's shoulder. Tighter. "Don't support those two losers. I'm gonna win, and I always remember my friends." He dropped his hand. "Excuse us," he said and steered Cindy in the direction of *Las Vegas Review-Journal* publisher Randolph Whitman and his wife.

Randolph Whitman resembled a silver-haired model in an upscale-clothing catalog. Sloan could imagine Randolph standing grandly on a yacht, sipping a martini with the family insignia on a winter-white sport coat, generations of Whitmans genuflecting to him in blond respect. His wife would sit stiffly on a lounge chair, admiring her diamond bracelet. Sloan's mission was to secure their favor, the first step in gaining the newspaper's endorsement.

Sloan skillfully dispensed saccharine pleasantries to Mrs. Whitman, the helmet-haired grand dame. She wore a fixed and uncertain smile, holding a full champagne flute, drowning in a monochromatic sea of beige hair, clothes, skin, and drink.

Cindy smiled and nodded, interjecting murmurs, most appropriate. Then, excusing herself, Cindy drifted away to join a group of women off to the side.

Randolph, the editorial board's dominant force, pointedly asked Sloan how an independent could make an impact in the Senate. Sloan employed the "political canoe theory." He began steering the canoe to the right with calls for fiscal discipline, then dipping the oars in the water steering to the left, the Senate's division granting him leverage to guarantee Nevada would be on the receiving end of its fair share of federal funding. His vague phrases accelerated his journey to dry land from this Gucci-imprimatur vise.

Sloan held his smile at the Whitmans' collective nods of approval—this was too easy.

* * *

A while later, as Sloan neared the men's room, it occurred to him that he had lost sight of Cindy. He scanned the sea of faces for his ex-wife, hoping she was still behaving herself. She had handled herself well so far, but his pleasure was momentary. He spied her next to the bar. His eyes widened in horror when he unmistakably saw her pop a pill in her mouth and follow it up with a chaser, he presumed a vodka on the rocks with a lemon twist, her favorite drink. He quickly made his way toward her.

When he reached the bar, Cindy's eyes settled on someone behind him, and he felt a pat on the back.

"Hello, stranger," reporter Tammy Keller greeted him when he turned.

Awash in radiance, Tammy's figure was magnificently displayed in a clinging V-neck black dress. She cast a quick glance toward Cindy as if to fulfill the mandatory obligation of acknowledging another woman's presence.

"All polls show you're moving." Tammy's vision fixed on Sloan with a seductive smile. "Appear on my show, and you'll get a real bounce."

"Good night," Cindy interrupted and walked away, heading toward the exit.

Sloan sputtered a goodbye to Tammy and followed Cindy, moving briskly before consciously slowing himself to avoid drawing unwanted attention.

When he reached her, he gently grasped her arm. "What the hell was that all about?"

"Sleep with her, but I'm not holding your coat." Her words slurred.

"I talk to reporters. I don't sleep with them."

She recoiled at Sloan's gentle touch. "Don't touch me."

Sloan instantly regretted the arrangement to attend the event together. She was a powder keg ready to explode—and, in fact, he was prepared to explode, but differently. He gestured to the men's room. "Wait here, Cindy," he implored. "We'll work this out."

He bolted into the men's room and unzipped his pants in front of the urinal. His shock nearly stopped nature's act when he realized that Cindy was standing next to him.

"What the hell?" He looked around to confirm they were alone.

He finished, zipped up his pants, and hastily washed his hands. She stood next to him, examining herself in the mirror and rummaging around in her purse for lipstick.

"We gotta get outta here," he urged and tried to take her by the arm.

When she pulled away, her purse snapped utterly open, and its contents bounced onto the tile floor. A full container of Xanax rolled the length of the room to rest under the row of sinks, and the second container rested at their feet.

Both jumped with a start when Ted Richman entered the bathroom with the Four Tops' "Baby I Need Your Loving" on his lips. His words trailed off, his eyes widened when he saw Cindy on her knees, scrambling to get her belongings back in her small purse.

Sloan's stomach tightened, fearing tomorrow's headline: Ex-wife, Pills, and Booze in the Men's Room.

"Come here often, Mrs. Sloan?" the reporter asked.

"Ted, I'm sure you understand…" Sloan began.

Richman took a moment to study Cindy as she closed her purse and got to her feet. Then he gave Sloan a hard look. "I didn't see this," he said with a hint of pity in his voice. Turning to Cindy, he added, "Get a hold of yourself."

Cindy looked down demurely as if the gravity of the situation had somehow worked its way through the haze. She permitted Sloan to steer her from the room by her arm. As they left, Sloan gestured to the reporter to acknowledge that he owed him one.

* * *

The estranged couple stood on the tarmac for Cindy's late-night return flight to Los Angeles. The ride in the limousine's back seat had been blanketed in silence.

A week from today would have been their wedding anniversary. Sloan reflected it would have been their fourteenth. At their last anniversary together, the relationship was so frayed that, after they watched a videotape of Riley's first birthday party, they retreated to separate quarters. When first married, the couple enjoyed Saturday matinees of foreign movies, both enjoying exchanging reviews of the movie—moments now so distant that Sloan questioned if they actually shared that joy or if he was conveniently replacing fact with a fantasized fiction.

Noticing the tears in her eyes, Sloan caressed her hand to comfort her. His voice was soft. "I care about you. You can't drink *and* take pills. OK?"

Cindy dabbed at her tears with a tissue and composed herself with a series of breaths as the airport's lights shined upon them.

"I know it's tough to stop," he said, his tone gentle. "I've had my share of problems. I understand the urges, but you've *got* to stop. Think of Riley," he added gingerly.

"Riley?" Cindy sprang back, her tone fierce. "You're not exactly father of the year. You asked her if she wanted to campaign with you without asking or telling me first? You want to use our child as a prop? Like your dad *used* you?"

Sloan was silent for the remainder of their wait. He stood with regrets at *ever* confiding in Cindy; it was not worth the words, but he'd never thought his father *used* him during campaigns. In politics, the candidate's family made appearances even if the spouse and children were terrified; it was a warm family photo. Sloan got it. Every candidate followed that script. No, Mike did not use him. Actually, those moments forged a bond between them, he hoped to do the same with Riley. He had issues of far greater substance with his dad.

A glance at Cindy, no upside in pursuing the matter, not tonight.

NINETEEN

July 18, Boulder City/Las Vegas

"Now, this is an omelet." Richman smiled like a carnivore ready to pounce on fresh meat as he poked into the bacon-and-cheese Downtown Omelet.

Sloan thanked the waitress when she placed his more diet-conscious egg-white omelet before him. The two sat in the corner of one of the rooms of Boulder City's Coffee Cup. Sloan's security duo sat sipping coffee a few tables away.

Boulder City's mainstay was where Sloan and the *Review-Journal's* Ted Richman would commence their Saturday together. Thirty minutes outside of Las Vegas, locals and Las Vegas refugees sat amid a quirky decor, with walls adorned with skateboards, snowboards, and surfboards. Prominently placed among the wall's clutter was a chummy photograph of the café's owner and Sloan.

Sloan leaned across the table closer to Richman. "Know anything about Chris and her husband, Creighton, abusing their duties as trustees?" Seeing Richman's hesitation, he added, "Off the record."

"Nothing's off the record." Richman smirked. "Hell, we'll start that after breakfast." He continued with the guilty pleasure of betraying a vignette that would never return to haunt him. "Bottom line—

Creighton screwed his dead partner's children. I was at the *Times*. We almost ran it, but it got a little hinky when Creighton told our editor the paper better have the second-best libel lawyer in LA because he's got the best and he's ready to file. Strange rivers run through that man's mind."

Sloan probed if the *Review-Journal* would have an interest in reviving the story.

Richman returned a plaintive "don't bother me" moan. His tone reflected his weariness of a half century of chasing leads, phone calls, and doors slammed in his face. Richman vented that he was one tap on the shoulder away from being told his services were no longer needed.

"Punk editors are demanding more and paying less. I'm the oldest guy in every meeting at the paper. My boss calls me T. Rex, thinks it's funny. My wife tells me, don't worry; if they fire me, they get an age *and* race discrimination claim. But that's not my style. I need something, give me an angle, I need to survive the next round of job cuts."

Sloan again shared his appreciation that Richman "looked the other way with Cindy."

The reporter nodded in acknowledgment. "I owed you one for tipping me off on your announcement. I'll tell you this: Bree Baker was a good hire; she's tough. Miles Judson was a jerk. In the three weeks he worked for you, he never returned my calls."

While the media allowed campaigns license with the truth, probation was never granted for the capital crime of failing to return a press call. Sloan chuckled; then the men finished their omelets in hungry silence.

After breakfast, they stood outside on Nevada Way, a six-foot-tall ice cream cone advertising the adjacent ice cream shop towering over them. Richman was popping two pieces of chewing gum in his mouth.

"I hope this gum angle works." Richman began to chew. Confirming they were still off the record, Richman explained his own family member's battles with addiction problems. He spoke with his usual pauses, now with sympathy, when he asked about Sloan's public admission of substance abuse. "Was it cocaine?"

Sloan returned a blank stare, trying not to blink.

Richman shrugged in acceptance of the nonresponse. "Some in the media are grumbling for you to answer. There's a couple of wagers on which substance it was."

"Comforting to know they're focused on the real issues," Sloan added with obvious sarcasm.

Richman hesitantly touched Sloan's arm, causing him to brace. The act seemed unusually warm for the gruff reporter.

"I heard…" Richman's voice was low. "I heard the FBI is snooping around town, around your campaign, around Washington."

"My campaign?" Sloan blurted, moving closer. "You don't mean me; you mean someone close to me? Right? What about?"

"Indian gambling," Richman replied curtly. "The current bill and past shenanigans in DC."

"Details for the slower students," Sloan joked, nervousness cracking his voice. "I played Boston but only drove by MIT."

"Check your staff…rumor is at least one may know something."

"Talk to me." Sloan moved within inches of Richman's face now. Feelings of dread weighed on him. Any FBI investigation was fraught with peril.

"That's all I got."

Sloan accepted the response, but a pit had settled in his stomach.

Next on the agenda for the pair was a Sloan speech before Friends of the Planet at a Spanish Trails home in Las Vegas belonging to one of the group's board of directors.

Sloan stood on the deck in the spacious backyard. Cynics snickered that a person could locate more escorts than environmentalists in Las Vegas. Still, this organization's leadership included the usual suspects to lead the battle on environmental issues that affected Nevada.

The first questioner offered a mini-speech on "environmental justice" before demanding that Sloan sign a pledge to reduce greenhouse gases.

"I'm not signing any pledges."

"You don't see a problem with greenhouse emissions?" the man retorted.

"Sure, there's a problem, but signing a pledge is a political gimmick, not an answer."

"Billy Rogers signed that pledge," the event's host gently inserted. "He also signed our pledge to reduce the state's carbon footprint."

Sloan bubbled with irritation. He thought his credentials were beyond reproach and that pledges were but worthless paper commitments. Signing one pledge would deluge him with requests across the political spectrum; he hoped intellectual thinking would prevail over the political gimmick.

"I've acted responsibly," Sloan replied. "I'm not paving paradise to put up a parking lot. You want me to be honest—not just tell you what you want to hear." Sloan surveyed those gathered. At the lack of any reaction, he gingerly asked, "Right?"

The muted reaction reminded him that political courage was an admirable theory, but to a den of true believers, moderation equated to political treason.

* * *

Throughout the day, Richman accompanied Sloan as he crisscrossed Las Vegas to address groups in North Las Vegas, Summerlin, and Green Valley. In the early evening, Sloan's security men drove the reporter and Senate hopeful through the neighborhood between the Strip and downtown, amid pawnshops, wedding chapels, and meth addicts. They drove on East Fremont Street, past the midcentury Bonanza Motel's roof-mounted wagon and the Travelers Motel's sign that proclaimed, Your best bet in LV since 1936. The car stopped at a red light in front of the Roulette Motel, upon which sat a large sign bearing a roulette table and wheel. The car in front of them, an older Honda Civic, had bumper stickers that read Go Vegan, Say No to Pesticides, Recycle Now! and Save Nevada's Deserts.

Sloan gestured toward the beaten-down car. "I'll make a wild wager and bet that driver is not a Republican." Sloan immediately worried how that or any other flippant remark could backfire on him when spoken to a reporter. He changed the subject to ask Richman for his take on Rogers's latest verbal faux pas.

"Rogers said, 'Vehicle traffic on the Strip is an alligator around our necks.' Even when a reporter corrected him—'*Albatross* is the word you're looking for,' Rogers was oblivious. His response was, 'I never went to Harvard and damn proud of it.'"

"He receives a loud ovation," Richman said, chuckling, "whenever he retells that story."

Sloan found it puzzling but let it pass as Richman switched the conversation to Collins. He volunteered that while she appeared to him as a choreographed display, many voters had succumbed to her charms.

"Every one of her remarks sounds like it has been vetted by a focus group," Sloan pushed. "Ask her some follow-up questions; check her depth."

Soon, the men entered downtown's Golden Gate Hotel, which was once named the Sal Sagev, *Las Vegas* spelled backward. Old photographs of San Francisco and Las Vegas adorned the dark wood wall panels, revealing a time and place when men wore suits and women wore dresses to a casino to gamble.

"Now you walk through these joints, some bozos are wearing muscle T-shirts and drinking margaritas from a quart plastic glass," Richman sneered. "No class."

A piano player singing American standards caught their attention. Sloan suddenly felt the urge to sing. With the piano player's blessing, he began to sing one song from the American Standards songbook. Several patrons moved closer. He ad-libbed when he forgot the words, singing about "sad, glad, had to be you." With the song over, he took a theatrical bow to hoots of approval, then placed a hundred-dollar bill in the pianist's glass bowl.

Next, Sloan and Richman found themselves in the hotel's Bay City Diner. The room's photographs were of tourists of a bygone era. One image reminded Sloan of a photograph on the living room mantel of his childhood home. His parents were at the Copa Room at the long-ago-demolished Sands Hotel. His father wore a rakish smile, and his mother leaned back in demure glamour. A friend had once asked Sloan the identity of the two "Hollywood stars" in the picture.

Richman offered a weary sigh. "I'm glad you cited the city's history when you met with the civil rights group. Could you imagine Sammy Davis and those great entertainers being booked to *play* at the hotels but not being able to *stay* in the hotels?"

After being seated in a corner booth, Richman buttered a large piece of sourdough bread with great deliberation, methodically spreading the butter into every nook and cranny. "What's the story with your ex?" he asked casually, too casually for Sloan's comfort.

Richman eyed Sloan, then took a bite of the bread.

Sloan slowly sipped from his water glass. Apparently, Richman's commitment to not report on Cindy had a shelf life. He now seemed bent on a closer examination.

"Has she taken the medication long?" the reporter queried nonchalantly, studying his bread.

Sloan swallowed hard, able to feel each membrane in his throat. Richman or any other reporter or blogger could manufacture a nexus of Sloan's lifestyle to Cindy's dependency on prescription drugs. The question hung like a dark, foreboding cloud. Sloan allowed moments of silence to pass. "I thought you were looking the other way on that," he finally said.

"We're still good. Just a friendly reminder she's got to be careful combining Xanax and booze."

Sloan was scanning the room, looking looked upward at the ceiling. His eyes then locked on the reporter, but neither spoke. "Off the record for a personal matter?"

Richman turned off his recorder.

"Obviously, she has a problem. It just started recently—or at least I've just become aware of it recently. She always liked a drink, but now it's gotten worse."

The reporter nodded sympathetically. He turned the recorder back on and asked about Mike Sloan's role in the campaign, how often they spoke, and when Mike would be making campaign appearances for Sloan.

Sloan pointed to the photograph on the wall of Candlestick Park, former home of the San Francisco Giants. "That's where the Beatles had their last concert. My dad and I went to a Dodger-Giant game there. Man, it was windy. Great name for a park, but worst location."

"Mike called me last week; he sounded great." Richman chirped.

Sloan cast a worried glance across the table; he'd been unaware of the call.

Richman sipped from his scotch on the rocks, eyeing Sloan with every sip. He carefully placed the glass on the table. "How often do you guys talk?"

"Whenever I need good advice. He's my ace, my go-to guy."

Richman retrieved another piece of the sourdough bread and repeated his spreading ritual, which Sloan was finding maddening. "Mike asked me a lot of questions about the campaign." Richman held the well-buttered bread in the air and went mute as the waiter brought the dinner entrées. Once the waiter left, he added in his usual deliberate style, "It sounded like he wasn't fully briefed on the campaign."

Sloan was taken aback. He had been keeping his father informed in a roundabout way through Martino and Zimmer, but Mike might still be irritated by the sting of his surprise announcement—and the fact his son was not begging him to campaign at his side. "Maybe he just wanted to chat with a reporter, an old friend he respects," Sloan suggested, masking his insecurities as to whether Mike would either critique the campaign to Richman or share why he had limited his time in Nevada.

Richman took a long sip from his scotch. "Don't think that was it."

TWENTY

July 20, Primm

**Poll: Collins 36%, Rogers 22%,
Sloan 18%, Undecided 24%**

Primm, Nevada, was an instant city, almost an illusion magically elevating from the desert on the Nevada-California border with three casinos and a shopping outlet mall. The Back Country Conference held at Primm's Whiskey Pete's Hotel was created to lure tourists to Nevada's cow counties, those vast masses on Nevada's map mostly ignored.

Several attendees at the conference turned to shoot glances at Sloan as he conversed with Bree in the rear of the ballroom; fame was his constant hole card.

"This speech the aides drafted is recycled gruel," Sloan muttered as he skimmed the bullet points of a speech listed on a series of index cards. "Do you think I need this?"

Bree responded with a silent shrug.

"No shrugs. Talk to me. You weren't hired to shrug or nod."

She leaned closer to him and covered her mouth with her hand.

"Martino had me give these to you. My view? It's beyond this stack of cards; this staff is draining the life out of you. I'd give you one card with a few points and let you wing it. Look at them; half of this crowd is staring back at you. You know what they want."

Sloan smiled at the obvious—this group wanted Tyler Sloan. "I've got it." He handed the briefing cards to Bree. "Put your sweet lips on these and kiss them goodbye."

Sloan walked to the stage, fueled by the game's speedball rush of adrenaline. He likened it to emerging from backstage to start a concert. He grinned broadly at the adulation.

"Use me!" Sloan opened with a suddenness that appeared to jolt the audience. "I'm visiting each of Nevada's seventeen counties. I can handle a mountain bike, done a little river rafting, and love to hike. I'll do it, you post those photos, link your social media to mine, and together we'll spread the word about all of Nevada!"

Many in the crowd stood and clapped appreciatively.

"Do you really think the Democrats, Republicans, and their special interests care about Ely?" he asked in a mocking tone. "Have they ever set foot in Fallon?"

The response was loud. "Nooo!"

"Have the Democrats or Republicans and their special interests stimulated the economy in your town?" Sloan was thriving in the give-and-take. "I can't imagine you want *more* needless, senseless, big-government regulations hamstringing your businesses."

Others joined those already standing to shout their agreement. The applause dial was spinning madly.

"Let's take it back!" Sloan shouted. "Let's take our government back!"

Sloan visualized the crowd's energy in his palm. He gave it a gentle squeeze by raising his voice. "The two parties think they're too good to waste their precious time on you! They think they're too good for rural Nevada! Not me! We're united! Let's take it back!"

"Take it back!" Several voices rang out. "Take it back! Take it back!"

"Take it back," Sloan commanded with a full smile. "You've got true grit—let's show it! The two parties have no clue! Let's take it back! Take it back!"

"Take it back! Take it back!" the room echoed.

Sloan concluded his speech and nearly dove into the crowd, exchanging high-fives, hugs, and handshakes. He looked among the faces for Bree, and his eyes settled on her. She was mouthing, "Viral."

* * *

The next morning in Las Vegas, Martino, Gala CEO Jefferson Jackson, and Senator Victoria Singleton huddled at Sinatra's restaurant at the Encore Hotel. The voice of Billie Holiday was softly piped into the room.

Martino had advanced this meeting. The burnt-orange banquettes allowed his briefcase, which contained a listening device, to rest comfortably. The ballpoint pen clipped to his shirt pocket included a microscopic camera to film the proceedings. He was tech-ready to solicit criminally damaging remarks about past dealings with the Native Americans. He planned to feed the FBI a morsel but needed to time it to prevent any leaks; any publicity could humiliate him and, of course, end Sloan's candidacy.

The senator's skin was a snug fit. A YouTube video mocked her repeated surgical procedure with images of various "before" and "after" photographs of her as the disco classic "Tighten Up" played in the background.

"This place is dying," Jackson said. "There's no one here." His ubiquitous jewelry and constant grin recalled a caricature of a casino executive flaunting his wealth.

"They're closed for breakfast," Martino said with pride. "They opened for me so we would not be disturbed."

Martino watched Singleton's nod of admiration. The senator gazed around the room and lingered on the room's "touches." She spoke in detail about the dragonflies embroidered on the elegant cream linen napkins and the meticulously designed adjacent garden.

Descriptions of the senator could be used in a seminar on the creative use of adjectives. To her allies, *powerful* and *strong-willed* preceded her name. To her detractors, *ruthless* and *vindictive* were high praise. Martino once noted, "Hers has teeth in it." He leaned forward, his posture conveying a severe message was imminent. "We have a problem. A reporter is snooping around."

"Problem?" Jackson's voice dropped despite the absence of other diners. His grin disappeared just as quickly as it had arrived.

Martino detailed how a reporter contacted a White House aide to probe about the Deer Valley Tribe's senate approval. Singleton appeared nonplused, shooing away any inference of culpability.

Martino ignored his vibrating phone when he saw that FBI agent Kevin Connell was calling. He returned his glance toward the senator. He mentioned that the administration's aide was a friend, and the reporter had cited an email from Singleton asking the Interior secretary to view the issue with a set of fresh eyes.

"Fresh eyes?" Jackson slammed his fist in his palm. "No story if a senator wants a cabinet member to look at something. Don't go limp on us, Tony." He glanced at Singleton. "Sorry, Senator, poor choice of words."

Singleton exhaled as if this conversation was an unnecessary bother. "I'm speaking at a rally for Billy in an hour. I don't want to be rude, but why are we here?"

Martino added that the reporter mentioned the senator's son, Danny.

"So? I have a son." The senator's voice ticked weaker.

Jackson pressed for more. He clearly sensed the story's potential impact more than the senator's blasé reaction indicated.

For Martino to receive his get-out-of-jail card, he needed someone at the table, right here and now, to recall how Singleton had insisted her son would participate in Martino's land flip.

"Danny is a licensed real estate broker," she said with modest conviction.

"He's a grown man, and you're not aware of his daily business," Jackson added.

Martino innocently asked how he and Jackson were introduced to Danny.

The senator glanced at her glistening fingernails before turning to Jackson. Jackson's palms turned upward. "I never met him before."

Singleton focused on Martino. He avoided that stare as he turned to view the life-size photograph of Sinatra hanging in the bar area.

As the waiter brought the plates of breakfast, Singleton asked harshly, "What is this?"

The waiter meekly described the calorie-laden egg-and-sausage dish.

"I'd die if I ate this," Singleton snapped. "Check my order. Scrambled egg whites, English muffin dry, and orange juice. That's it."

The quivering waiter shuffled backward before disappearing.

When the senator was adamant, she did not arrange the introduction of her son; all others squirmed in mental anguish to forge together a plausible story.

Singleton adjusted the single orchid that was encased in a glass bowl on the table. She blurted aloud, "Susan McCarthy. Susan introduced one of you to Danny."

"Best not to add anyone else," Jackson commanded. "Who knows what she'll say?"

The senator glowed with smug confidence. "Susan died last spring. It's a clean slate."

Jackson's lips puckered before a slight smile graced his broad face.

Martino had long grown weary of Singleton's demands, both during Reed's campaign and the tribe machinations. He had little regard for ideological warriors of any stripe. While she cast a "holier than thou" public front, she was pleased to write legislation to benefit her marginally functional son.

Martino had witnessed other legislators' careers fade to black by power's intoxicating fumes. Everyone in public life was but one story from disgrace. A former colleague of Martino's was convicted for violating campaign-reporting laws and now was a political blogger in the *Foothill Press*. Martino had no clue where those foothills were located.

"Don't call me anymore on this," Singleton snapped as she rose. "You two iron out the details. I'm going out to resurrect my candidate—

the one this guy"—she pointed at Martino—"keeps burying." She cast a wicked stepmother's smile at Martino. "Sloan would have been our nominee and the next senator, but he's got so many issues with Mike that he couldn't be a Democrat. Now he's slicing away votes from Billy; the man could hand the seat to Collins."

"He's going to win, and you're going to need him," Martino replied respectfully.

Singleton returned an expression as if she had just taken a bite of fresh lemon.

TWENTY-ONE

July 22, Las Vegas

**Poll: Collins 38%, Rogers 22%,
Sloan 18%, Undecided 22%**

Sloan faced the film crew on a high plateau in the Red Rock Canyon as Bree barked instructions. He wore a blue chambray shirt, khaki pants, and hiking shoes. Walking toward the camera, gesturing toward the crimson rocks, the cliffs where mountain climbers trod and hawks soared above.

"I'm Tyler Sloan. My daughter, Riley, and I love hiking here at Red Rock. In Nevada, we have a special bond with nature. The outdoors are part of our culture, part of our soul. I'll protect this rugged oasis. I'll protect our open space." He smiled at Riley, standing beside him, and put his arm around her. "It's our responsibility to be good stewards and protect our environment for our children and future generations."

"I'm in." Riley gestured to a nearby incline. "Let's hike over there."

Bree and the film director signaled their approval, and the crew readied themselves for a break.

"You're a natural." Sloan bent down and kissed Riley. "Let's get you onstage."

"I'm ready for my close-up." Riley laughed, turning to exchange a high-five with Bree.

Someone pressed a cup of coffee into Sloan's hand; he took a grateful sip. The eighteen-hour days were draining and his sleep restless as he was awakened each morning with thoughts of conflicting strategies and too many moments of "what ifs" and "I should have said X."

His coffee was half-finished as his team was regrouping. The break was short, too short.

"We have a script," chimed Heather, Sloan's press secretary.

"No scripts," Bree said firmly, before turning her attention to Sloan. "Just walk and talk; you know what we want."

"But we wrote a great script." Heather approached a full pout.

Sloan ignored her and nodded his readiness. Riley gave him the thumbs-up; he was doing this segment alone. Walking near a red-tinged rock formation, Sloan was intent on capturing the "right look" of an earnest gaze at the picturesque setting Bree had staked out.

"I'm not demonizing my opponents." Sloan was walking while being filmed. "Nevada's issues are not going to be solved by eager-to-please politicians. Republicans and Democrats each have their club, but I'm not joining those special interest clubs, not taking their money or their influence." His right index finger pointed at the camera. "I'm not bound by any political party. I'm knocking down every barrier; let all in Nevada rise. That's my fight; join me. Let's take on the corrupt special interests."

"Perfect." Bree turned to her cameraman, who nodded approval.

"You ad-libbed that?" Heather asked with admiration.

Sloan exhaled and walked closer to Riley so that the two could share a private moment. "You know my aide you said looks like Harry Potter?"

His daughter giggled. "He may look like Harry, but he's evil like Lord Voldemort."

Sloan smiled at his daughter. "He's not evil—just the speeches he writes. They are *way* too long…still want to say a few words for me at an event?"

"Do I?" Riley bounded with enthusiasm. "Um, yeah!" With that, she gave him a quick kiss goodbye and went to join a couple of her father's aides for a hike.

One of Sloan's remaining aides, flanked by a couple others, approached him with some unsolicited advice on how to handle the press, citing instances where Sloan could improve.

"Did you see me on *Sixty Minutes*?" Sloan's voice rose in exasperation. "You know how often I've been interviewed? Don't worry; I can handle the media."

Seemingly oblivious to Sloan's agitation, another aide chimed in, "When you meet a voter, it's a good idea to—"

"I sang at Dodger Stadium with fifty thousand people screaming my name. Believe me; I get this."

The two female aides walked away, accepting, or at least quiet in their objection. Two young men on his staff remained, pestering Sloan, repeating their pleas to take their advice.

"Between us, guys." Sloan lowered his voice. "Either one of you ever open your mail and find a thong, a phone number, and a photo?"

The two exchanged nervous glances, near frozen, until one whispered, "I wish."

Sloan dismissed them with a wave of his hand as Bree was approaching.

"What's your take on Richman's latest?" Sloan asked.

Bree repeated the gist of Richman's column: "Sloan's opponents are flawed, worn like an old sofa." She added with assurance, "Ted's calling the race wide open."

Bree's auburn hair was a spark of fire. Sloan glanced at her blue jeans, white blouse, and rings of red earrings—how often did he notice a woman's earrings? *Never* was the obvious answer. Cindy once complained he failed to comment when she dyed her hair black.

"Do we need another spot?" Heather chimed in, determined to leave her imprint.

"We're covered," Bree replied. "My new video of Tyler has him at a park surrounded by women. You can feel the tingle."

Heather gave Bree a cringe-worthy glare.

* * *

Sloan stood behind Martino in the campaign office, leaning over a laptop to view Rogers's latest ad. It opened with a video of Sloan bounding up the stairs of a private plane surrounded by his entourage. An image of Rogers filled the screen. "Unlike my opponents, I was born and raised in Nevada. I don't own a private plane." His voice rose as if to amplify the issue's importance. "I fly commercial!"

"Voters don't want a hardware store clerk as their senator," Sloan said, dismissing the ad.

Martino shut the laptop and informed Sloan that Collins and Rogers filed joint motions in court to deny Sloan's own legal motions for inclusion in the one scheduled debate. The two opponents had banded together, seeking to relegate him to the alternative debate.

"The *alternative* debate?" Sloan said with a bite. He worried his manager had grown soft, irritated by Martino's apparent lack of pushback. "I'm not debating with the gal who dances in a bikini in front of the state Capitol...It's a myth how my band Liberty got its name." Sloan watched the puzzlement on Martino at his out-of-context remark. "It was not about some esoteric fighting for freedom. I saw a movie on television when I was a kid, *The Man Who Shot Liberty Valance*. I heard Gene Pitney's voice singing the title song. I just liked the name Liberty."

"Why are you telling me this? Put it in your memoirs," Martino barked.

"I'm trusting you with that personal nugget, and I'm trusting you to get me in that damn debate. Spare me the details if it's messy, but I've got to be in it."

"I'm trying; believe me," Martino nearly whimpered.

"Try harder." Sloan punched Martino's shoulder, this punch harder than friendly. He had rehearsed his next question, waiting for the perfect time to ask. Without sharing what Richman had told him about the FBI, he asked, "Have you noticed any of our staff being distracted?"

Martino asked for specifics.

"Any staff taking days off or just missing for hours? Any making a lot of personal calls?"

"Not that I've noticed, but I hunker down here. I hire good staff, discuss the day, and let them do their jobs. Why?"

Sloan ignored the question. "Did any of our staff lobby on matters with you? Either before or after Reed's campaign?"

Martino paused. "Our press secretary, Heather, I contracted out with her for a couple of clients, different matters. She's talented."

Sloan avoided asking about the Deer Valley Tribe.

"Why are you asking about this? Why now?"

Sloan aired his grievances with the talents of several staff members.

"Before we dismiss some, I respect you—do you have some history with them?"

"I worked with a few in Reed's campaign, but you tell me which ones need an ass kicking, and I'll do it."

"Did Heather work with you on that matter with the Native Americans?" Sloan eyed Martino; he appeared not to flinch.

"No, she helped on a contract matter in Illinois." He paused to try to recall her other efforts. "She was with me lobbying Congress for an agricultural group. If it means anything, J. J. Jackson was involved in Deer Valley, but you knew that."

Sloan nodded. "Let's move on. What else is going on?"

Martino confirmed the authenticity of the Collins video Sloan had given him days before. "I'll have Bree look at it to cut a spot. If done surgically, it's the mother lode."

"Bree's already seen it."

"What?" Martino exploded. "Before me? I figured you wanted Grant to see it for his legal take, but Bree?" He was beyond flustered as he rose from his chair. He turned toward Sloan with a tortured expression. "Hey, you can't…" He began to push back and then stopped.

"What did your team uncover with the opp research?" Sloan asked.

"Rogers is a Boy Scout," Martino said, still visibly upset by the slight. "Even the sucker's 401k is heavy in bonds. He donates money to his local church *and* synagogue. The press—you know, the typical suspects with the progressives—they have his back."

"We paying you for that bit of news?"

Martino's tight expression underscored that he would not be the target of any humor. "I need to ask—your relationship with Bree." Martino regained his footing.

"Media consultant," Sloan replied and stopped. "She's my media consultant."

"Go on," Martino added with his usual bluntness.

"I've got enough on my plate without this nonsense," Sloan said, opening and closing his fists. Then he flexed each finger to rid himself of the tension.

Knowledge was power, and a single morsel of Sloan's thoughts would forever empower Martino. Political loyalty was trumped when advisors wrote postelection memoirs disclosing private conversations. Sloan's fame guaranteed a book from a campaign insider would earn a publisher's attention, especially if the manuscript was a kiss-and-tell for the winning candidate.

"The staff is asking me questions," Martino continued. "Heather is suspicious."

"Cut Heather loose. Hell, cut 'em all loose." Sloan waved his hand in the air. "I only need you, Bree, those techies…maybe a handful of others."

Martino hesitated, obviously pained. "The two of you were seen strolling by the lake."

"You trailing me? *My team* is trailing me?" Sloan rose from his seat. "What's wrong with you? You're way off track."

"She was in your house with the blinds closed for over an hour."

"I met with my media advisor to show her the Collins video."

"Did anyone see you? Talk to you?"

"One woman," Sloan stated in a matter-of-fact tone. "One *crazy* woman." He rose and walked to the window. He cast his gaze northeast of downtown into the city's rubble of older brown and gray buildings.

Martino rolled out a stream of nightmarish "what ifs" regarding Bree's fiancé and the "crazy woman." Sloan was pleased when Zimmer and Bree entered the room to ban further interrogation.

Bree immediately darkened the lights and downloaded Sloan's latest commercials to show on the big-screen television. The first ad included photographs of Sloan and President Reed when Sloan appeared at an event for the president. A voice-over stated with authority that Sloan's experience was "broad and far reaching."

"I remember Reed was raving about the White House chef," Sloan said lightly. "Some chicken dish he loved."

The last commercial was an updated biographical spot with a black-and-white image of Sloan and his father standing together. Sloan bit down on his lip as he studied the photograph. He was sixteen, standing at attention in front of the Capitol dome as his father gripped his shoulder. As he aged, the resemblance to his father was more pronounced.

Sloan clapped his hands together. "How and when do we use the Collins video? She comes across like a spoiled princess."

"My spot is ready," Bree replied. "The needle jumps in every focus group. Let's air it."

Sloan wanted advisors to fight with him until "the last dog died." But if he lost, Bree would gear up for the next campaign, Martino would retire to San Francisco, Zimmer would return to his law practice, and his "paid friends" would scatter; there was always a new campaign or lobbying firm. He had to avoid a backlash that could batter and bruise his reputation; the risk to his legacy was paramount.

Zimmer rose from his chair with fists clenched. He mused aloud about the debate's impact on the election. "Presume Tyler's in and shines in the debate." He turned to Martino. "In your best judgment, is that enough? Do we win or lose?"

Sloan had sliced Collins's lead, but the gap was increasingly stubborn to close. Martino's only prediction was that Rogers would not win.

Sloan grabbed a football from the corner of the room, passing the ball between his hands. "We're losing; that video is the Hail Mary pass we need."

"It's very close to the line, maybe too close," Martino noted.

"That's why there's a line," Zimmer snapped. "We dance close, but never over the line."

Sloan smiled at Zimmer's love of the battle.

"It could cause blowback," Martino insisted.

"Don't go wobbly on us!" Zimmer thundered.

"How do we answer the question of how we got the video?" Martino said with mounting exasperation, unable to snare an ally to his side. "It could drag your dad and his source into it."

"Check your cup, buddy." Sloan tightened his grip on the football. "When you've got nothing, you've got nothing to lose. To me, running second is nothing." He whistled the football to Martino. "We're airing it."

* * *

Sloan was scheduled to speak that afternoon at the Cosmopolitan Hotel. As Sloan, Bree, and a handful of his aides boarded the elevator, two women in their late twenties squeezed in with them. Upon recognizing Sloan, the petite, dark-haired Asian woman squealed, and Sloan obliged her request for a selfie. The other, a shapely Hispanic woman wearing a Dallas Cowboys football jersey, said, "I'm a huge fan; can you sign my jersey?"

Sloan whirled to an aide for a Sharpie marker, which every aide carried for such an occasion; the woman lifted her jersey, revealing her bare breasts. "Hit the high notes," she purred.

"No!" Bree blurted.

The elevator bell rang, and the woman hastily pulled her jersey down. Sloan was left holding the Sharpie as the doors slid open. The two women hung on each other in fits of giggles as they departed the elevator.

"Let me guess," Bree said with a conspiratorial smile. "You're going to tell me that's never happened before."

"First time for everything." Sloan winked as they headed toward the meeting room.

* * *

"Dodgers won again tonight," Mike Sloan announced over the phone.

"It's nine fifteen. I thought the rule was I never call you after nine," Sloan replied.

"Read the rule, son." Mike chuckled. "You can't call me, but I can call you."

Mike detailed his phone call from Senator Buddy Jennings. The senator wanted Sloan to caucus with the Republicans, and in exchange, he would be named chairman of a subcommittee.

"He's got a few ex-senators ready to fly out to endorse you," Mike added. "Bob Russell, Bill Best, and Marjorie Garvey."

"Garvey? Wasn't her husband indicted?" Sloan asked.

"But she wasn't."

"Russell? Who in Nevada ever heard of the guy? What state was he from?" Sloan asked.

"Vermont. He only served one term; Jennings told me he's a terrific guy."

"Best was defeated in the primary. So, two were booted out, and one resigned because the feds were closing in," Sloan continued. "Tell Jennings to keep them—don't need or want 'em."

"Jennings asked if you could sing at his holiday party."

Sloan's arm pushed the phone out as he shouted profanities. "That jerk wants me to sing at his Christmas party?"

"Well, a holiday party—his wife is Jewish."

"Tell Jennings to get a monkey in a powder-blue suit to sing 'Jingle Fucking Bells.'"

"Whoa, I'm just the messenger." After a moment, Mike added, "Was I right on that Collins video?"

Sloan affirmed its brilliance, adding they were "working on" when to air it.

"Working on it?" Mike commanded. "The election is in a month. Air it now so it has time to percolate. The mail-in and absentee ballots are going out this week."

Sloan expressed Martino's concern that the ad could have a counterproductive effect.

"Hogwash. Air it next week. Trust me on this."

Sloan's thoughts began to whirl. His father had just called Martino's strategy "hogwash." Who on his staff seemed the most distracted? *Martino*. That's when it dawned on him that his manager could be a target, suspect, or whatever euphemism the FBI liked to use.

"I trust your judgment," Sloan replied. "We'll air it as soon as we can."

TWENTY-TWO

July 24, Northern Nevada

The Meet Tyler Sloan event at the American Legion Hall in Ely, an hour's drive from Reno, filled the room to its capacity. The media and their camera crews lined the rear of the room. The air-conditioning wheezed noisily but without a chilling effect. Sloan rolled up his sleeves for relief.

A row of Legionnaires sat behind him on the stage. The older men proudly wore American Legion hats. War was never fought with young men or women from Malibu Beach or Manhattan's high-rises, but wars destroyed the young lives of brave soldiers from the Carson Valley.

The current president of the Nevada Legionnaires was the designated emcee of the event. He introduced himself and told jocular stories of how his ownership of a local auto dealership related to that of a politician. Sloan smiled at the corny jokes. Following his introduction, he gave a brief stump speech before concluding, "Thank you all for coming out here today. I'm going to win this; I can feel it."

"You can *feel* it?" The Legionnaire president was mocking from the side of the stage. "I'm glad you *feel* it, but you'd probably be a lot happier if the polls *showed* it." The president laughed but soon became aware he was the only one laughing. With a flustered expression, he called for questions.

The first came from a handsome young man wearing a crisp white western shirt and black-brimmed hat. "Mr. Sloan, we've had family ranches sold to developers, and now they're called *ranchettes*." The last word spat out of his mouth with the taste of bile. "Please sign our pledge to protect the family farmer."

"I'm sorry; I don't sign any pledges." Sloan was exasperated at another request to sign a pledge.

"You haven't read it," the man replied impatiently. "Billy Rogers signed it. It's short and sweet: support farm prices and the federal loan guarantees to family farmers."

"First," an older woman roared, "damn government needs to quit taking our money and giving welfare to every barefoot, teenage, illiterate, pregnant Mexican coming across the border."

Sloan's pressed his palms downward to dampen the verbal fire. "Hold on," he said firmly. "Hold on. We can do all of the above: secure the borders, have a humane immigration policy, and assist the family farmer."

"What do you think about cattle, Mr. Sloan?" Another man was leaning against the wall near the exit door. He resembled the well-weathered, stereotypical rancher of the age-old Marlboro Man. The visual was perfected; he was holding a cigarette outside the open door. He sneaked a drag on the cigarette, the smoke swirling upward in dissipating white wisps as he amused himself by blowing smoke rings as he tapped his finger against his cheek.

Sloan pondered the question, silently repeating it. *What do I think about cattle?* He almost smiled, asked countless questions, but this was a new one. "I think a lot about cattle—"

Sloan was grateful a young woman interrupted. She requested he sign her petition to prevent children from viewing porn on the web. She balanced a toddler in one arm and bounced a stroller containing a fussy infant with her free hand. When Sloan didn't respond quick enough, she added curtly, "I didn't have to beg Chris Collins to sign it."

"You don't want candidates to genuflect before you," Sloan said, immediately aware his choice of words garnered blank stares.

"You support porn?" the woman exploded.

Suddenly, shouts were being fired at Sloan from every direction. He raised his arms to call a cease-fire. He held no natural bond with this crowd. He could have the audience view him as a without-a-clue-pampered-rock-star; had to avoid the squishy political middle. A famous Texas politician once described the middle of the road as the place where "armadillos go to die."

"Why am I running?" Sloan was avoiding the squishy middle, changing the topic with a rhetorical question. Brief success, the audience was silenced. He flashed his smile. "Why in the heck am I running? I don't need a job. I don't need to hear applause or get a paycheck. I was pretty well paid at my last job."

Laughter rolled across the room; their hostility tempered. This crowd worked hard and played by the rules but perceived that the game was rigged for others. He understood the game, doling out promises and staying nimble without committing. Yet he was not risking his fame, fortune, and legacy to merely *play* the game. He was shaking the body politic to *win* the game.

"I'm not an expert on ranching, but this city boy understands that your life is not easy. I saw that with my dad in California's Central Valley when he was governor. You may have to educate me on the details, but not on the righteousness of your cause. This city boy understands that the two parties only give you platitudes."

A few hands clapped. The cheers began modestly but increased steadily; he made headway.

As he walked out the door, his path drew him inches from the tattooed reporter, Josh David Mack. He thought of all the cheap shots Mack had fired at him. Sloan looked around to ensure that his gesture would not be seen by others; he drew his lips together in a pucker at Mack and kissed the air.

* * *

"So, how were my hands today?" Sloan asked.

Bree's smile confirmed the out-of-context question was far from innocuous, the question recalling their first meeting. "I presume you're not asking about your manicure?"

The two sat alone in the rear seat of the campaign SUV on the drive to Ely's private airport. His security detail followed close behind; his staff rode in another car. Rather than spend four hours driving Highway 50 to Fallon, a chartered plane would have the crew at their destination in less than an hour. Sloan was scheduled to speak at Fallon's Barkley Theater.

Sloan was staring out the vehicle's window, riffing on how he went back for the umpteenth time to watch the Reno speech. He pounded the armrest in frustration.

"It's not that important," she mildly protested. "You've corrected it."

"I mastered the entertainment media. A local reporter would ask how I liked their city. A talk show host would ask for an anecdote about the tour. No need to prep for those interviews. I'd appear at an award show, pose for photos, engage in mindless chat with a reporter, easiest gigs known to man." He smiled. "My assistant brings me a gift bag filled with designer accessories and cool tech gadgets, just for showing up." A meaningful look at her. "TMZ *never* stumped me. I have ideas on combating terrorists, how to fix the economy, provide incentives for companies to hire, but no one wants to hear details. They only want the sound bite."

"You're nailing every question. The *Wall Street Journal* editorial writer didn't stump you. You're—"

"You were right on Reno. Why did I grip the lectern so hard? I almost shattered it in pieces? Ya think it was a little insecurity?" he asked with a smile.

She appeared in no hurry to answer that question.

"When I started out as a teenager, I would always hold the mic on the first song, maybe a little too tight, just to get my bearings. Now… I don't hold a mic for comfort…but I guess I needed something to grab on to for that first big speech."

Bree's gaze darted from side to side before landing directly on Sloan. "Maybe you're a little too hard on yourself. Maybe Tyler Sloan is too tough a crowd…for Tyler Sloan."

He exhaled deeply. His gaze slowly moved upward, then down, before resting on Bree. "Maybe I am."

TWENTY-THREE

July 26, Las Vegas

**Poll: Collins 38%, Rogers 21%,
Sloan 21%, Undecided 20%**

***Shielded by a* Daily Racing Form,** Martino jotted cryptic notes to his attorney, Marvin Katz. He sat alone in the corner of a sportsbook in downtown Las Vegas. Bettors in the small room were scattered, reflecting the unwritten rule that each respected the other's privacy.

FBI agent Kevin Connell startled Martino as he took the seat next to him. Only a small Formica desk divider separated them. Connell pointed at Martino's *Daily Racing Form.* "Nail a pick-six today and cover your fine." The agent smiled at his reference to the exceedingly tricky wager of selecting the winner of six straight races.

This sportsbook was light-years from the skyboxes in the sportsbook at the MGM Grand; far darker than the well-lit Mandalay Bay, and its chairs bore no resemblance to Bellagio's supple leather, which bespoke an elegant country club.

On an early Tuesday morning, bettors wagered on East Coast racetracks. It was action. Action was the drug of choice.

"I never heard of these tracks. But then again, some people would bet on cockroaches with numbers," Connell said.

"Great seeing you, pal. You were numero uno on today's call list." Martino forced a dose of sincerity. "Each race is a little puzzle. I bet a couple of races to clear my mind before I slay the political dragons. No lawbreakers here, Agent Do-Right."

Connell acknowledged the barb with a barely there smile. His bemused expression revealed a conqueror's pleasure. "Decision time, Mr. Martino. You're a little too cute returning my calls after hours to my office. I gave you my cell line, man."

"Here's the deal," Martino stated with authority in his voice despite his hushed tone. His package was total confidentiality; he would wear a wire and receive full immunity. "That's my framework."

"Framework? Framework?" Connell laughed aloud. "Wake up, hoss. You're not negotiating with a stack of blue chips. You're a little porky when it comes to leverage. It's your call, but Sloan doesn't need any leaks in the press about it."

Martino was a little surprised Connell was not more circumspect with his threat, but Martino dismissed it. He glanced down and noticed the detailed stitched handiwork on Connell's shiny black western boots. Martino silently mocked that the agent would pay a week's salary for bragging rights to custom boots.

"Two elected officials will keep you out of prison," Connell added. "I'll bring by your equipment."

Martino stole a glance at the television screens that showed the flashing tote board with the odds of the upcoming race. He only had to delay the FBI for one month, just until election day. "Total confidentiality, one official, and I don't testify."

"Bull," Connell stated firmly. "No testimony, no deal. I'll unleash the legal suits."

"Hold on. I got something for you—" Martino began.

"Let's take it outside." Connell nodded toward the door.

Once inside Connell's white Dodge Charger, Martino retrieved his iPod, where he had transferred the Pinkerton audio file.

"Listen up, Kev," Martino instructed.

Connell raised his index finger, obviously pondering the implications while listening. His lower lip rolled back inside his mouth; he was without expression as Pinkerton discussed the Deer Valley Tribe. The audio ended as Pinkerton exited the Las Vegas Monorail car.

"Always thought Pinky was a straight arrow," Connell muttered.

"Never trust the self-righteous ones," Martino added knowingly.

The agent suddenly pierced Martino with a stare. "This is too short. Where's the entire file, *kemosabe*?"

Martino explained that he would deliver the unedited version after their final agreement.

"Edited version?" Connell fumed. "We can't move on an edited audio file. You're no fucking recording engineer remastering old basement cassette tapes. A first-year law student gets his client off with edited *shit*. Don't play with me!"

"Finalize our deal; then you'll get it all, the full monty."

Connell wore a twisted, deadly smile. "I'll get a search warrant in a few hours for your place at Turnberry," Connell said, referring to Martino's rented Las Vegas high-rise residence at Turnberry Estates. "But why wait? Some off-duty boys could drop by right now."

The pair exchanged hard and silent stares.

"I want the entire…fucking…unedited file!" Connell's face contorted with anger.

"Get a subpoena!" Martino shouted louder than Connell would ever dare. Noticing Connell's jaw clench, Martino lowered his voice. "I got you the speaker of the house."

"Our deal is *three* names." Connell was unfazed.

Martino only knew one poem, and if there ever was a moment to recite a poem, this was it. "The poet Tennyson. 'The path of duty was the way to glory.' This case is your glory."

Connell was obviously puzzled and irritated. "Tennessee?"

"Tennyson, he was a poet." Martino was pleased someone knew less than he about poetry. "This case is your glory."

"Fuck you! Every word that bastard Pinkerton muttered, the same of your meet with Jackson and Singleton. I want the tape with every fucking word at our next meet," Connell huffed.

The statement stung. Martino was angry at his own naivete; no surprise, the bureau was tracking all his movements. They apparently staked out the Jackson-Singleton breakfast. He now worried that his phone and apartment were bugged.

"I'll be by your place tomorrow morning at eight," Connell charged.

"You'll love the recording with Pinky, but listen carefully, listen between the lines."

"Thanks for the etiquette lesson, Ms. Vanderbilt."

Martino asked for more time to "nail down" Singleton and Jackson. His focus now was on delay—for him and for Sloan.

"Did a mule kick you in the head?" Connell protested. "You haven't delivered squat. I'm your only friend at the bureau, and my bosses are like wolves ready to howl."

Martino raised a finger. "One week."

"One week. One fucking week is all you got."

* * *

Sloan stared around the office in his campaign suite, his eyes rested upon a beaming Grant Zimmer sitting behind the same desk Zimmer used in his Los Angeles office.

"You brought every chair, desk, table, and photo?" Sloan laughed with amazement. "Even your Steuben glass pieces?"

"I work best when I'm comfortable. My billing clock is taking a little holiday."

Zimmer's assistant from Los Angeles greeted Sloan. With the same efficiency Sloan had seen for years, she placed a silver tray on the circular meeting table filled with minimuffins, fresh fruit, and juice.

Zimmer motioned for her to adjust the tray "a smidge closer."

"A civilized way to start the day," Zimmer noted. "Your preference, Tyler?" He waved as if the king's feast was served before him. Zimmer gestured to the table at the latest edition of *Vanity Fair* magazine, which had a profile on Zimmer, describing him as one of the nation's most influential lawyers. He repeated one line from the article: "'His gentleman's glow disappears behind his gunfighter's soul.' Love it! The best business development is an article calling me a son of a bitch."

Sloan gestured to an oversize, framed photograph mounted on the wall and asked what year it was taken.

"Downtown LA, the fifties, back in the day," Zimmer said. "My dad kept this photograph in his office for motivation. He dreamed of practicing law at the biggest firm in town, O'Toole & Morton, right there on Spring Street." He pointed to a multistoried building in a grainy section of the photograph. "He had two strikes on him. Jews rarely got in that door, and his book of business was not what the blue bloods wanted. He represented black entertainers and what they called 'Negro businesses.' Of course, one of those was the largest black-owned insurance firm in the nation. My dad opened the door for me at Warner Brothers, so fuck 'em all; I've done all right."

Zimmer turned melancholy as he glanced at the framed photograph of his deceased wife, Katie, on his desk. He explained that they both realized her health was failing at their last anniversary dinner together. He recalled with pride how she held his hand and said her supreme life's pleasure was being Grant Zimmer's wife.

Zimmer turned his head away from Sloan, seemingly to guard his emotions. He reached to sip his espresso from a royal-blue demi cup. Zimmer examined the cup, explaining that he and Katie purchased a set when they were in Milan. He mused aloud about Tuscany, the village of Montepulciano, and how they visited wine cellars from the fourteenth century.

Sloan respectfully allowed Zimmer his moment. When he felt enough time had passed, he asked, "If the Teamsters are pumping funds to an independent committee for Billy or Chris, which group would they use?"

"For Reed, they used the Fairness Fund," Zimmer replied.

"I thought that was the AFL-CIO?"

"No, they have the Freedom Fund."

Zimmer had worked over, under, sideways, and down the legal membranes of countless campaign committees. The independent committees were legal blurs, forming for one campaign and then dissolving postelection akin to a 1930s carny tent in an Oklahoma dust bowl.

"I thought that one was funded by religious groups," Sloan said.

"The evangelicals have their own fund." Zimmer paused, unable to recall the name of the fund. "The teachers have…"

"Who's got Keep America Free?"

Zimmer spoke in a melodic rhythm. "The chamber of commerce has the Nevada First Fund, and another group has Nevada's Future. Money in politics is like rain falling down the side of a mountain. It veers right, veers left, under boulders, or down a river. Eventually, water finds a route, and eventually, political money finds a path home."

"You can make a couple of haikus out of that." Sloan laughed.

Sloan sought Zimmer's counsel on airing a contrast ad that would include Collins's failure to vote for twenty years. He was determined, allowing how Martino's focus group was not swayed. "I don't buy his numbers. A Senate candidate not voting for twenty years is a legitimate beef. What I did twenty years ago is important; why not her?"

Sloan opened his laptop to air the previous evening's *In the Office* show. "Listen to this."

"How about the students boycotting UNLV and Reno until the price of tuition is cut?"

"Let 'em boycott," the host growled. "Make room for the serious students."

"Anything new on the campaign?" the caller asked.

"My sources tell me," Dr. D. replied with a flourish, "Sloan has a new campaign strategy. He's everywhere. Retail politics, my friends. You might be bowling next to him at your favorite alley or see him when you're teeing off at a driving range."

"Can he win? Can he really win?" The caller's voice quickened.

"My sources tell me..." The host's tone was sincere, conspiratorial. "Sloan may hit Collins on something close to home, close to her home. That's a headline from the *Office*."

"Who's leaking our stuff?" Sloan asked Zimmer.

Zimmer sat silent, his hand raised in the air to request silence. Sloan wondered aloud if Martino could be the leak.

Zimmer appeared surprised. "He's an old pro." A look of worry creased his face, his voice uncharacteristically soft. "I'll tell him something, I'll make it up, and we'll see if it leaks."

"Both parties amended their motions in court, barring me from the debate." Sloan's voice hurried as he rose and paced. "Get me in that damn debate."

Zimmer flashed a smile at the skullduggery. He tapped the intercom and told his assistant to reach the president's aide on Judicial Affairs. "There's always a friendly judge." Zimmer beamed toward Sloan. "Start prepping—I'll get you in that debate."

* * *

Later that evening, Sloan watched Riley standing near the swimming pool's concrete edge. Riley had begged both of her parents to allow her to spend more time in Nevada during the campaign's final month.

He recalled her as a toddler who bounced on his lap, the little girl who rode "horsey" on his back or when he would gently "fly" her across the room. He had tried to create a second home for her in Las Vegas, decorating her bedroom in bright pink and purple, but she rarely spent time there.

At times she remained "Daddy's Little Girl" who thrilled him with an unrequested kiss. Yet her independence was blossoming. He thought with feigned horror that he would soon meet her boyfriend. Decades of recording and touring had caused him to miss too many of Riley's dance recitals, school plays, choir performances, and softball games. When he'd divorced Cindy five years earlier, he'd dedicated himself to spending more time with Riley.

Sloan submerged himself in the spa's hot, bubbly water, and Riley placed her feet in the water. Her music played from the outdoor speakers, and she sang along with the young male singer: "Moan all night. Scream all night."

"What's this junk you're listening to?" he asked gruffly, then decided to ease off. He had to pick his battles.

He playfully "pulled" on her toes, recalling how he used to recite the story of the three little pigs before his fingertips danced up to her knee as the three pigs "ran all the way home."

"I remember you changed the final verse." She chuckled. "One pig sang at the Hollywood Bowl, another pig at Madison Square Garden, and the other ate pizza."

"Did you miss me when I was on the road?"

"Got used to it," she replied in a stinging matter-of-fact tone.

"I'm glad you're here, sweetie. Your presence helps me; helps the campaign."

"How?" she asked and then answered her own question. "More media?" Riley kicked her feet in the water. "Let's go shopping, maybe a pet store to look at puppies?"

"Papa would be so proud of you." Sloan smiled.

* * *

Sloan awoke at five a.m. after a restless night. A few minutes later, he was sitting with a cup of coffee at his dining room table. He opened his laptop to watch a national public affairs show that aired the night before. The show included an analysis of the Nevada Senate election. The show's host introduced the guest Mark Morris, the director of a volunteer organization with ties to Republican and religious groups.

An American flag pin adorned Morris's lapel. In his mid-forties, his boyish smile, full cheeks, and rosy complexion stamped him as a nonthreatening, middle-aged choirboy.

The political right supported Morris in his self-described "mission to preserve and protect the family." Doubters whispered that his fondness for female companionship would lead to a moral misstep and land him preaching at tent revivals in small Southern towns. Sloan wondered if anyone was opposed to preserving the family?

"Chris Collins is a fighter," Morris gushed, "with a soft Mother Teresa quality."

"Mother Teresa?" Sloan muttered in distaste. He sipped from his coffee.

"Every candidate has a weakness. What is Sloan's Achilles' heel?" the host asked.

"His Achilles' *high heel* is more accurate." Morris's eyes twinkled in a sinister departure from his usual preacher's soft sincerity.

"Bastard," Sloan muttered as the credits ran.

The night before, he had dreamed about his late brother and his parents. He walked to his den to retrieve the flash drive that held old family movies. He watched as he sipped his coffee, amused as his eight-year-old self mugged for the camera. Mike crept up behind him to tightly grasp his son and rough up his hair.

The video continued with his father standing between his two sons, Tyler and Mike Jr., or J.R. Mike's left hand rested lovingly upon J.R.'s shoulder, while his right hand lay to his side, not touching Sloan.

Sloan recalled when he was left behind as his brother and father flew to San Diego for meetings that preceded a trip to the border to meet with Mexican leaders. A meeting in Mexico had intrigued the young Sloan. Yet his father had informed him there were no more seats available on the plane. Sloan had been mystified how a governor could not find a place for his own son.

Sloan stared at the laptop, which now aired a bright screen saver. He thought of Riley sleeping down the hall. He would have found a seat for her.

Wayne Avrashow

TWENTY-FOUR

July 29, Las Vegas

"This paper publishes a diagram of the polyp on the governor's colon but has no space to detail my energy policy?" Sloan muttered in frustration.

Martino shrugged in response from his seat beside Sloan. They were on their way to Sloan's appointment with the editorial board of the *Las Vegas Review-Journal.*

Sloan again recited the main points he would make during his presentation to the board. The *Review-Journal* had convened seven board members to decide endorsements, but Martino stressed that publisher Randolph Whitman was the paper's benevolent dictator. "Focus on Whitman; he's the big dog."

"We're good with Whitman." Sloan recalled meeting the scion to the newspaper's founding family at a charity event.

Martino moved on to another topic. He praised Collins's latest commercial, which criticized Rogers for an extravagant public expense in refurbishing the bathrooms in the state Capitol when he was president of the state Senate. "Damn good tagline, mocking the million-dollar price tag as 'The Royal Flush.'"

Sloan chuckled as the car stopped in front of the *Review-Journal* building. With security in tow, he strode boldly from the vehicle to the front doors of the newspaper headquarters.

A few feet from the entrance, an elderly woman, slightly hunched over, called softly, "Mr. Tyler Sloan?"

Sloan grasped the well-dressed woman's hand with care when she offered it. Her smile held a grandmotherly sweetness that could easily grace an organic cookie label.

"Mr. Sloan, your mother was a dear." She held the papers in her hands tightly as a warm wind blew. "Gladys and I met at church. We volunteered together at the Shriner's hospital. She was always helping the less fortunate. She was a good Christian woman."

Most of his father's friendships had been born from exchanges of professional favors. His mother's friends, on the other hand, were often "strays." He remembered telling her once that one of her friends— a woman who sported hats adorned with plastic fruit—seemed "lost in space." Gladys had cheerfully replied that her fruit-wearing friend was only temporarily in orbit.

"Do you need a taxi?" Sloan asked, looking around to see if she was alone.

The woman pointed to a waiting car and assured him that her son would be driving her home. She stuffed her papers into her small woven purse and pulled out a folded hundred-dollar bill. "Take this for your campaign. I loved Gladys so."

Sloan surmised that his mother would now be close to this woman's age if she were still alive. He envisioned her with the same gray hair and a slight stoop. He held his gaze upon his mother's old friend, the encounter felt surreal. Her friend had appeared as if dropped from the heavens as a reminder of his mom.

"You're very generous." Sloan bent down to her eye level. "Instead, donate in my mom's name at the church. That would be perfect."

The smile she beamed at him provoked tears, which welled in the corner of his eye.

"I've told all my friends to vote for you," she said with a wag of her finger, her voice fierce but cracking.

Sloan thanked her for her support as he escorted her gently by the elbow to the waiting automobile. Onlookers glanced approvingly at the pair. Before he opened the passenger door, he kissed the woman's forehead. With the door open, he leaned to see her son. The man smiled in appreciation.

"Take good care of your mom," Sloan said and blew a kiss to the woman.

* * *

Shortly after that, Sloan and Martino entered the room commonly called the "Masters" for its many works of art that hung on the walls to meet the *Review-Journal* editorial board. Randolph Whitman sat at the head of the eighteen-foot rosewood conference table. In his mid-sixties, he was the aging preppy in his blue blazer, yellow shirt, and striped tie. Sloan sat at the opposite end of the table; Martino took an empty chair along the side with the others.

When one board member teed up a soft question on Sloan's views on the local economy, Sloan analogized that the city had slid all its chips on one industry, equating it to a roulette table's reds and blacks—but the ball had landed on the green. He added that his company, blue, had spurred investment downtown with the renovation of older motels in the darkest times of the city's recession. Although several of the board members nodded in appreciation, audible murmurs arose from Ivan Brodsky, a retired university economics professor. His murmurs grew louder to indicate his displeasure.

Martino had briefed Sloan that Professor Brodsky was the board's most progressive member. "He's left of everyone you've ever met. Meet Brodsky, think Leon Trotsky."

"Your solutions at blue were worse than the problem." Brodsky's tone was foreboding. "New businesses in a neighborhood can trigger a rent increase, and established businesses that can't pay those inflated amounts are forced to flee."

"Gentrification has proven to be good for the economy," Sloan said, softening his tone to avoid a heated confrontation. He glanced around the room, hoping for a friendly voice, but grew disappointed when the board members returned a Mount Rushmore–esque array of stony stares.

Brodsky held strong. "Do you want a juice bar on every corner?"

Whitman firmly tapped the table. His expression soured; no patience for Brodsky's class warfare. Sloan pitied the person who'd convinced Whitman to include the professor on the board.

Whitman began to praise Sloan's years of entertaining and the generosity of his blue foundation. Then the hammer hit: "I'm concerned about your history. It's no longer a disqualified that you inhaled."

"I presume I'm not the only one in this room who inhaled." Sloan returned a smile.

"Your life sounds like more than mere youthful indiscretions," a board member noted.

"I led a rock star's life." He had used the line before; it had intrigued anyone on the receiving end. "People ask me about my songs or my experience with other entertainers. No one cares what I did after the concert."

"If you gain our endorsement"—the chairman leaned forward in utter seriousness—"we want assurance that your campaign will not be pure mudslinging."

"We're not tying your hands." Whitman's younger brother, Chad, sniffed. "Criticize your opponent's positions, but Creighton Collins's legal affairs are *not* relevant in this campaign."

Sloan froze internally. He looked hard at Chad, determined not to flinch, but this comment confirmed there was a leak in his campaign.

"Do we have your commitment to conduct a positive campaign?" Chad followed up.

Sloan's commercial with the Collins video was ready to be aired, delayed only to maximize its effect. If he blatantly refused to make this commitment, he could kiss away any chance of the paper's endorsement. Acceding to their request might earn him their endorsement, but that would be tantamount to surrender.

His father had charmed state legislators and members of Congress; one memory was seared. A group of California legislators arrived at his Sacramento home to see the governor. Young Tyler was charged with the duty of bringing the legislators soft drinks and beers while they gathered on the backyard patio. Before his father joined them, Sloan overheard a couple of the legislators whispering plans to "play" the governor. He stayed inside, the blinds partially drawn, the screen door cracked open while surreptitiously monitoring the meeting.

Mike arrived and listened, asking probing questions, nodding often. Then, Mike leaned forward in his chair and reminded all of what he needed. His hands outstretched as he asked one question: "What do you need? Don't tell me what you *want*; tell me what you *need*." The remainder of that meeting was light and jovial; his father reduced their needs, made a deal, outwitting the legislators.

Now, Sloan held his gaze squarely on Whitman. He understood that the publisher's inherited wealth equated to a man hungry for the praise of his own accomplishments; insecurity ran through his veins.

"Mr. Whitman, you were on the Cal debate team, same as my father." Sloan gestured across the table. "Berkeley debates were vigorous, and you won awards on that Cal team." He added as if in secret, "Don't tell my dad I said so, but you won more than he did."

Whitman expressed false modesty, but his "aw shucks" smile confirmed his pleasure.

"Mr. Whitman was a tough debater, and representing our great state in the Senate is not a job for a choirboy. I'm not rolling over for attacks from my opponents." Sloan spread his hands outward in a magnanimous gesture of peace. "But rest assured, you have my commitment that I'm not going to bring Creighton Collins's *legal affairs* into the mix."

Randolph Whitman nodded approval, and his brother seemed appeased. The stone statues even smiled, mollified; the pack was at bay.

* * *

"Boss," Bree stated gravely as she slid into the booth across from Sloan in a private room at Louisa's restaurant where he was having a late dinner. "We've got a situation." Her voice quickened; her face stamped with worry. "Hell, we've got a *big* problem."

"Situation?" Sloan asked cautiously as he took a handful of tortilla chips from the basket in front of him. He nibbled on one nervously.

"A buddy of mine from the bureau tipped me off—*Martino* is wearing a wire."

The words stabbed like an ice pick. His body jerked back before thrusting forward, smacking into the bowl of chips on the table. "A wire?" Sloan repeated. "I don't believe it. There must be some mistake."

Bree's words were sharp and precise. "Tax fraud."

Sloan waved away the waiter who hovered nearby as disbelief washed over him. He pressed his hands to his forehead. "Why? Why? Why?"

"Didn't pay Uncle Sam all his due," Bree responded coolly.

"When?" Before she could answer, he asked again, "Damn it, when?"

"A few years back when he represented the Native Americans." She went on to summarize the various allegations against Martino and what the FBI and US Attorney's Office expected from Sloan's manager.

"How do you know this?" Sloan pressed. "Spill it. Tell me every detail."

Bree exhaled. Then exhaled again in an apparent attempt to clear her thoughts. She'd gone on a date—she emphasized *one date*—with an FBI agent back in Oregon. "I know, I know, not my type. Anyhow, he was in Las Vegas last night and wanted to meet for a drink. We met. He knew my connection to you and Martino's involvement in the campaign; maybe he was trying to impress me—OK, maybe he was trying to get in my pants. He told me he was running background on Martino. That word threw me. Background? Background for what?

He gave me a peek at an email detailing plans for Martino to wear a wire…" She emitted a series of deep and quick sighs. "It's beyond anything I've dealt with."

Sloan pounded the table with a grimace on his face. He silently recalled every conversation with Martino that could be used against him. Nothing was illegal, but there were flippant remarks about Rogers, Collins, and members of the media. He had discussed details of his time in rehab, his relationship with his father, the number of women in his life—any of it could be twisted, mangled, or misinterpreted. In a best-case scenario, it would embarrass him. In the worst case, it could defeat him.

"The agent shared all this with you? That doesn't sound right."

"I have to tell you? How men do stupid things when they're trying to get some."

Sloan accepted it with a nod, as she quickly added that the evening ended without event.

"What do you think triggered this?" he asked.

Bree shrugged. "No clue. I've heard Martino talking about betting baseball games. Maybe he's got a gambling problem. The agent told me they got 'em dead to rights."

The tension in Sloan's head threatened to implode his skull. Martino was now the screaming suspect for the leaks. A rush of betrayal filled Sloan.

"Desperate men do desperate things," he said finally, his voice trailing. "Don't let him suspect you know anything." He eyed Bree piercingly, pointing at her. "This stays between us."

* * *

"Did you forget the rule about calling after nine?" Mike asked when Sloan called him at 9:30 that evening. "Well, go on, it must be important."

"How well do you know Martino?" he asked bluntly.

"Why?"

Sloan politely but pointedly repeated the question.

Mike went through the litany of campaigns in which Martino worked for him and various other candidates. He cited multiple campaign victories and defeats.

Sloan cut him off. "Anything personal you know about him?"

Mike coughed loudly. "Give me a clue what you're concerned about."

"I don't want to color your thinking. What's his personal life like?"

"All I know is the man lives and breathes politics—well, that and food, the man never misses a meal," Mike replied with a chuckle, although the concern was still evident in his voice.

"Anything personal? Ever seen him with a woman…or a guy?"

"Can't help you there. I've never been to his house, he was over to mine, but he's not really a personal bud. We've had a hell of a lot of meetings, phone calls over the years. No card games, not much on a personal basis. What's this about, son?"

"He's not engaged in the campaign. He's distracted."

"Odd, he's usually on top of his game. Heck, my body was still warm when he jumped to Reed after the primaries," Mike complained, then coughed again. "I heard he needed the paycheck."

"Money?" Sloan weighed the comment. "I thought he would be set after all these years. He lives in a great house—maybe a little unkempt— but it's a sweet neighborhood."

"Talk to me. What exactly happened?" Mike pressed.

Sloan feared admitting failure. He worried that he could be blamed for not seeing Martino's character flaws—but he wouldn't have been the only one. Neither Mike nor President Reed had sent up a red flag. Sloan hesitated and then blurted it all out. "He didn't pay his taxes, and the FBI wired him to gather incriminating evidence. Don't worry; I never said anything to him about private matters."

"Damn!" his father shouted. "That son of a bitch, that bastard!"

A long pause followed. Sloan was painfully aware, if Martino were to be publicly named by the FBI, his campaign would likely be buried by a scandal that had absolutely nothing to do with him.

"Two things," Mike said abruptly. "First, fire him, and fire him now. You cannot have the story leak while he's your manager. Second, what do you need from me?"

"How many debates have you done?" Sloan asked.

Mike yawned. "What's the relevancy of the number?"

"Eight debates with Reed during the primaries? Ten?" Sloan conjectured.

"Twelve, but I've done over fifty in my life."

"Fifty? My number is zero." Sloan gazed upward, maybe to summon courage. "I need you out here."

Sloan braced himself for his father's reply.

"Soon, I'll be there soon enough," Mike replied.

Sloan allowed less than a nanosecond to pass. "Dad, soon enough is not good enough. You're right, I've got to fire Martino. That means I need you, really need you, for debate prep."

"I'm fighting a damn cold, or I'd come out there tomorrow."

Sloan failed to detect Mike's voice being "off" but decided not to press.

"Have Grant call me," Mike added. "I'll go over the debate with him. Then, you can call me, and I'll give you a final prep."

"I'm counting on you," Sloan said wanly. His stare at the phone was with more hope than certainty.

TWENTY-FIVE

August 1, Las Vegas

**Poll: Collins 38%, Rogers 22%,
Sloan 22%, Undecided 18%**

Zimmer pulled a lens-cleaning tissue from his coat pocket to methodically remove dust from his titanium-framed reading glasses. He dismissed people who would pay thousands of dollars for expensive glasses and then ruin the lens with a coarse fabric. "J. J. keeps coming around," he said in an airy tone. "He's calling me every day."

"Jackson is a ticking time bomb," Sloan replied quickly. "A congressman told me his first hearing was a noncontroversial bill in committee that Gala was supporting. J. J. came into the legislator's office a week later and peeled off ten one-hundred-dollar bills, saying that Gala appreciated the vote. The legislator was stunned, kept his hands in his pockets, and told him he voted for the bill on its merits." Sloan elaborated that the freshman legislator assumed Jackson's actions were a test, akin to a corrupt cop testing the rookie to see if he bit on an illegal scam. If the rookie acquiesced, the veteran then owned a piece of him; return favors were expected.

Zimmer muttered his apologies for mentioning Jackson in the first place. "You had something urgent."

Sloan paused and deeply exhaled. "I need your counsel." He hesitated. "This is huge."

The words seized Zimmer's attention. He placed his espresso cup on the campaign office's table, which separated the two. His hands extended, his palms out; he was primed.

"I'm ready to fire Martino," Sloan said crisply.

"For God's sake, why now?"

Sloan rapidly strung the phrases together in a chain of damning actions: "He's wearing a wire, he didn't pay his taxes, and he's involved in an FBI sting."

Zimmer's hand shot upward, a signal he needed to absorb this blast. The news jarred even the most senior of senior counsels. He asked a series of questions as to the how, why, when, and where. Sloan elaborated on how Bree had obtained the information.

"You're right. He has to go." Zimmer's tone was cold, but no one questioned the efficiency of executioners. "You cannot betray the king, and this is a betrayal. He has to go." Zimmer gave Sloan a quick history of another political scandal. "This can't leak on your watch."

* * *

That evening, the Las Vegas Strip's sui generis skyline and its cacophony of lights and videos failed to soothe Sloan. His mental pendulum was swinging wildly. He stood at the living room window of his condominium, burdened by the implications of the bombshell on Martino. Adding to his worry was Zimmer's failure to pin down Denny Morgan, which Sloan surmised meant that Denny had already sold the ménage à trois video to Rogers. He feared a nuclear fallout if Rogers unleashed the video. He was gripped by a sinking and novel feeling— events were out of his control.

Bree sat at the dining room table, busy on her laptop. She read aloud from an article from the latest issue of *Rolling Stone*. "Do you know the musician Bobby B.?"

He confirmed the guitarist had played on a Springsteen tribute album with him.

"He just had a knee replaced, but the dude's still going on tour next week," Bree said.

"Next week? Is he touring in a wheelchair?"

She ignored the rhetorical question. "You know the singer from the band White Heat?"

Sloan stretched his arms behind his back to release the tension. "I like his voice, a nice raspy edge."

"Sorry," Bree said evenly. "He's got throat cancer."

The news rendered him mute.

"How about that soul singer, Baby G? This article said she sang a duet with you."

Sloan braced himself. "What's wrong with Baby G?"

"She's in the hospital, recovering from a stroke."

"Jesus! G's about my age. Is *Rolling Stone* publishing hospital bulletins now?"

Sloan waved his hand to forestall further comments and motioned for Bree to follow him to his bookshelves. They were filled with books and political memorabilia in display cases. He called the political pocketknives, matchbooks, and bottle caps "pleasing anachronisms" and offered Bree an impromptu political history lesson.

"The pieces speak to me. I think about that World War II vet who really liked Ike when he put these 'I Like Ike' matches in his pocket. Did someone use this Teddy Roosevelt pocketknife? Why did a 1975 Los Angeles City Council campaign hand out bottle caps?" He gestured at a couple of books before adding that he could tell a lot about a person by the titles on their bookshelf. "No need to skim a Facebook page." One smirk and a pause. "I must sound like some old guy rambling on."

"I don't hold that against you." She returned a sufficient smile.

Sloan studied Bree's rapidly changing expression, one moment pensive, an instant later gleeful. Her hands busy to emphasize her points; she was defying a debutante's tip on femininity. Bree had the rare gift, an ability to be coy and sultry in a singular expression. He silently mused how much passion she could deliver to the right man at the right moment.

"Martino told me to hold off on buying time for that Collins video," she said.

"Post it now; gauge the pushback—if it goes right, air it on TV and run Facebook ads." He thrust his index finger forward like a Colt .45. "Do it! Buy time now."

Her fist clenched, her enthusiasm pronounced. "That's the take-charge guy I want. The take-charge guy we need." She added softly, "The guy *I* need." Her last words lingered.

He cast his first real smile of the night, but it mirrored his uncertainty about her.

Her voice dropped. "Would you rather talk about Martino?"

Sloan had little clue about what she wanted from him and even less what he wanted from her. Lately, she was scattering hints of her failing relationship with her fiancé. He thought of his flawed marriage, his string of one-night stands, and how he had failed at meaningful romantic relationships. He studied her, eying her from her auburn hair to her crimson shoes. "Let's call it a night. I'm meeting him in an hour. Let's talk tomorrow."

* * *

As it neared midnight, Sloan waited alone for Martino in the Neon Boneyard with his security detail standing nearby. The outdoor salvage yard and its six gated acres housed dozens of neon signs from the city's golden era. Many had been restored; others lay in various conditions of rehabilitation. Casinos instinctively focused on the next Hold 'Em tournament—there was no winning "vig" in protecting the city's history.

The Boneyard's large sign proclaiming Silver Slipper Gambling Hall Entrance was framed in a neon bow of lights. The silver high-heel slipper was a feminine dab amid that era's neon cowboys, horses, and sultans. Legend held that Howard Hughes bought the Silver Slipper Casino, in an evil act, dimming the sign to ensure his rest at the adjacent Desert Inn Hotel.

As a child, on a family vacation in Las Vegas, Sloan had walked with his mother and his brother from the Silver Slipper to the adjacent Last Frontier Village and the faux Russ Miller's Saloon. The saloon was the facade for an arcade with rows of child-friendly pinball machines located on a frontier-style dusty road with a wooden hitching post that never met a horse. Slot machines generated a higher ROI, and the Village was demolished decades ago.

Martino arrived and followed Sloan as they walked past the grand sign for the Stardust Hotel. The majestic, discarded signs were displays of Las Vegas's eccentric kitsch and glamour.

"What's new, Tony?" Sloan uncharacteristically used Martino's first name.

When Martino cited various staff issues and the pending debate, Sloan firmly grabbed his shoulder. "Not business—I'm talking about your troubles, bud."

A moment of silence passed.

"Meaning?" Martino replied with noticeable uneasiness.

"You know damn well what I mean. You wired up?" Sloan pressed. "You wired now?"

Martino's head dipped slowly. Chastised. Shamed. Agony filled his expression. He began to speak and then abruptly halted. "No...of course not." His voice soft. "How? Who told you?"

"And that matters?" Sloan spewed.

Martino's confession was a long and winding road as he told of how agents from the FBI and the US Attorney Office "tag teamed" him to ensure his assistance. While his dark eyes often burned with a furnace-like intensity, those eyes now reflected blank resignation. He was no longer a citadel of strength. Martino sighed. "All because I didn't pay some taxes."

"People don't wear wires for not paying their taxes. There must be more."

"Tax fraud. They're alleging tax fraud."

"And?" Sloan stretched the word for emphasis.

Martino bit down on his lip. Sloan noticed the man was near tears.

"Why do you ask questions if you know the answers?" Martino asked.

Sloan impatiently waved for more.

"Years ago, I was involved with the tribes on some land deals. The new gaming bill has brought attention to that…the attention that haunts me."

"How does all this affect my campaign?" Sloan pushed.

Martino's voice was barely audible. "I never recorded you, never wore a wire with you. I never harmed you…no, not at all."

Sloan chafed at Martino's manner, contrite to a point, no apology, no explanation.

Martino's fingers were tightly interlocked as if he could wring out a rationale, but any defense was futile. He had fulfilled his promise to the FBI by delivering audio files with Speaker Pinkerton, Jefferson Jackson, and Senator Victoria Singleton. He expected a grand jury indictment for all three on charges ranging from undue influence, attempted bribery, and accepting bribes.

"Pinky was a snap." Martino spoke without the rancid odor of shame.

Sloan muttered obscenities, frustration spewing into the warm night. He recognized his fatigue was filtering all his decisions. Yet no explanation could obliterate this betrayal.

"Why?" Sloan asked. "Why did you do it?"

Martino stared past Sloan with a sorrowful gaze. "I was hurting financially." Martino expelled his breath. "I was leveraged in real estate deals, even a couple in this wasteland. Prices fell; offices went vacant. The deals were upside down. Like a fool, I gave personal guarantees, and when the banks called some loans, it was musical chairs—the music stopped. A sudden stop and I couldn't find a chair. The Indian payday cured all my ills."

Sloan listened, seeking in vain for Martino to express a hint of remorse.

"I'm too damn old to make another fortune," Martino added offhandedly.

Sloan moved closer. "Think about the media coverage I'd get if it leaks that the FBI is probing you. Collins and Rogers—hell, the DNC and RNC—would unleash ads; I'd be buried. They'd tie me in to this."

Martino slightly shook his head. "You're innocent."

"Damn it, you know the drill. "News reports, their ads would be filled with photos of the two of us, with headlines about you and the FBI. What would you do if Collins's manager got indicted?"

"I'm not indicted," Martino protested.

Sloan waved off the technical correction. "I know you're leaking stuff." Sloan's irritation bubbled. "No bullshit, tell me why."

"Leaking?" Martino was suddenly indignant. "I haven't leaked one item—someone *is* leaking, but it's not me."

Sloan viewed Martino with less than zero credibility, but somehow his outburst rang true. In politics, trust is the coin of the realm. Martino's trust was once secure with Mike Sloan, yet faith had to be earned, not inherited. Poof—Sloan's confidence in Martino vanished as if it was a prop in a David Copperfield show on the Strip.

Martino looked pained, his shoulders slumped. "Every time I see 'Breaking News,' I almost pee in my pants." He kicked the dirt with his sneaker tip and offered a pained mea culpa. "I didn't hurt anyone."

Sloan held up his hand, his patience exhausted. "We need to cut and cut cleanly. Leave now," he said quickly. "We'll announce that your doctors advised you to immediately reduce your stress. We'll issue a statement; you'll wish me well. Don't do any interviews. Go dark; go underground."

Martino eyed Sloan with a wounded gaze and offered his services covertly in a last-attempt plea. He was spilling out reasons how Sloan needed his debate prep expertise, even on a sub-rosa basis.

The debate was in four days. For a moment, Sloan surmised that if Martino were a traitor, at least he would be the most valuable traitor in the debate prep room. Yet he also knew that even if their public relationship looked the same, he could never look at Martino the same way. The taste was too vile. The man had risked Sloan's political future, and being aligned with him in any way screamed danger. "Return home," Sloan said wearily, too spent to argue. "Bree and those overpaid wonder kids will do the debate prep. I'll beg my dad; maybe he'll lend a hand."

"Mike would be great, but I briefed presidents when that *girl* you put in charge was still in diapers."

Sloan bit his lip and shook his head. He was done.

"What is your public reaction to my leaving?" Martino asked, defeated.

"I'll be respectful."

"Respectful?" he snapped. "Screw that sanctimonious drivel."

Sloan placed his hand on Martino's shoulder as a measure of comfort. "You and my dad go back a long way. I hope you know I appreciate that." Sloan was in full damage control and sought to soften the blow.

Martino muttered softly that this was but a "transitional" moment in his career. Sloan knew different—this was Martino's last political hurrah.

Sloan started out of the Boneyard, but then he returned to Martino. "Call Grant if you think of something that can help," he said, offering a subtle hint not to call him. He lightly patted his former manager's puffy cheek and strode away.

TWENTY-SIX

August 4, Las Vegas

Zimmer carefully untied the ribbon atop the gold box. With a surgeon's care, he removed the lid and carefully slid the small box toward the Teamsters' national president. Bob Carney rose from his chair to examine each of the chocolate delicacies, each with various shapes and colors nestled in the tissue.

The attorney offered a connoisseur's review of each piece. First, the rich flavor of the dark chocolate piece overlaid with a single almond slice, the texture of cookie crumbs buried within the creamy milk chocolate, lingering with pleasure on how the sweet taste of caramel with pink sea salt compared to that of his first kiss. He boasted that the executive pastry chef at Bellagio Hotel designed each confection; each was worthy of an entry in the Guggenheim.

Zimmer removed a Henckels knife from his desk drawer and sliced in half the seashell-shaped chocolate speckled with coconut flakes. He handed half to Carney and lovingly placed the other half under his tongue. Leaning back in his chair, he mouthed a long sigh of pleasure.

"Mouthwatering," Carney replied the moment the chocolate melted in his mouth. "Whiskey would be a nice chaser."

"Sounds like a plan." Zimmer motioned for Carney to follow him to the minibar.

The descending sun's orange glow dominated the desert portrait, which was perfectly framed by the windows of Zimmer's corner office in the Howard Hughes Center. For security purposes, the campaign occupied two entire floors.

Zimmer poured bourbon into two ice-filled glasses. He hesitated a moment before splashing water in his own drink, a small concession to the acid reflux that plagued him.

The men exchanged political gossip before Carney strolled in the direction of the large leather sofa. Zimmer rushed to place a GZ-monogrammed black coaster on the rosewood coffee table before Carney could rest his glass.

"This is a small-batch bourbon, Cyrus Noble, aged in Kentucky, distilled in California." Zimmer took a sip as he sat across from Carney.

Carney methodically stirred his drink in the GZ-monogrammed tumbler. "We'd like more enthusiasm from Sloan on the collective bargaining bill."

"Enthusiasm?" Zimmer blurted. "You want enthusiasm when getting a blowjob, not to endorse a senator. You can deal with Tyler. Rogers may be a loyal puppy, but he can't win."

"Exactly which voters make up Sloan's base? Menopausal gals and gray dudes trying to turn back the clock?" Carney leaned forward. "We'd appreciate it if you spoke to the president on that trade bill."

The trade bill was riddled with controversy. Congressional approval would be drawing an inside straight, and Carney had just confirmed the Teamsters were one card shy. Zimmer pressed if the Teamsters were ready to endorse Sloan.

"The board would have to consider that," Carney replied evenly.

"You're a lawyer, Bob; know the call of the question." Zimmer had perfected the art of covertly insulting his opponent. Although Carney had graduated from law school, Zimmer knew he had failed the Nevada bar exam. He raised his voice before halting with sudden silence to assess if his burst of anger met with strength or if adversaries shuffled meekly in retreat.

"Sloan's different…" Carney proceeded carefully.

Zimmer waved his hand. "Cut to the chase. You won't offend me."

"My wife doesn't follow politics, wouldn't know the vice president if he kissed her, but she's pounding on me to endorse Sloan."

Zimmer smiled smugly, explaining that was the exact reason why Sloan would win.

Carney added that he was comfortable dealing with both Democrats and Republicans, but the uncertainty was if Sloan held power, the power of the determining vote in a divided Senate.

"Coffee at my DC law office is a congressional alumni event of both parties," Zimmer said crisply. "Add my relationship with Sloan, and you're covered."

Zimmer noticed Carney's glance at the framed photograph of him with President Reed on the golf course, which had been strategically placed on the end table. Carney squinted to read the inscription. "Grant, a trusted advisor, and dear friend. Our next tee time? Bret."

A measure of the depth of a political relationship was disclosed by the setting and inscriptions on any photograph. Two stiff smiles at a political dinner without an autograph was a standard gift, while a personal dedication divulged a closer bond. Candid snapshots coupled with an intimate note signaled friendship—a rare commodity in politics.

Zimmer sensed Carney's pulse kick up a notch as he invited Carney to join him on Air Force One with the president the following week. The president had given conflicting nods to both proponents and opponents on a bill that the Teamsters were pushing.

"Best place on the planet to discuss your bill," Zimmer added easily. "Rumor has it that your super PAC's coffers are bulging with unspent millions."

"We're saving it for a rainy day."

"Rainy day? The storm is threatening your bill right now. Five million in the last week in this state would unleash enough thunder and lightning to tip the election to Sloan." He eyed Carney. "You can be the kingmaker."

Zimmer returned to his bourbon, the ice resting on his lips in the oversize glass he termed "a bucket." His stare at Carney was more persuasive than any raised voice. "Bob, some people call me the gatekeeper to the president."

"Don't sell yourself short. My friends call you the gate."

* * *

Sloan's phone buzzed, and he was startled to see Martino's name on the caller ID. He slipped the phone back in his pocket. He had purposefully told Martino to call Zimmer. He wasn't interested in answering a potentially tapped call.

He opened the debate prep meeting by commiserating with over a dozen of his staff members about his former manager's health. He gave his rehearsed line of hope for Martino's speedy recovery, his voice reverberating in the gray, nondescript warehouse.

There was no shortage of vacant industrial parks in Southern Nevada. This warehouse was large, furnished to mirror the debate environment. Sloan would stand at a lectern and gaze into identical lighting. At the same time, members of his staff would portray panel members; they were inhaling the intoxicating air of youth, advanced degrees, and proximity to power.

The questions were fired, and he was delivering crisp answers. As soon as he finished answering a question on terrorism, a pair of staff members began to argue over his response. In moments, the voices turned to shouts. The stockier of the two was nearly spitting in the other's face, shouting that Sloan needed a more aggressive foreign policy. In contrast, the other argued for a greater emphasis on diplomacy. They jabbed their fingers into each other's chests, and it was only a matter of time before a physical fight would ensue.

The inmates have seized control, Sloan thought with anger, nearly leaping from his stool to pull them apart. He sent them to separate corners to restore order. "I fired an amazing guitarist in my band because he was a pain in the ass," he told the group. "At the next outburst, I *will* fire all of you—talented or not."

The aides were hushed. Several glanced at each other as if to accuse them of provoking Sloan, and a few dipped their heads in shame, but none dared challenge Sloan's authority.

Sloan gestured toward the mock candidates who were serving as Rogers and Collins. "Let's go through a dry run."

"You need more prep time," Heather, his press secretary, disagreed, offering her advice in a soft, respectful tone to ensure that she didn't cross the line to "pain in the ass." "Billy Rogers has lived and breathed politics for twenty years, and Collins's career was on the tube. She's a pro. They're both pros."

"And I sang in my kindergarten play." Sloan clapped his hands. "Let's roll."

"Are you a role model?" the stand-in for Rogers asked Sloan. "You are an admitted drug user who cannot even approximate the number of women you slept with."

"Let's talk about real issues," Sloan replied. "Let's discuss reforming health care and defending our homeland against terrorists."

The woman portraying Collins expertly matched the politician's speaking style. She was skilled in adopting her mannerism of expressing disapproval with a slight shake of her hair while wrinkling her nose. "There you go again, not answering direct questions," the Collins stand-in scolded. "Character is important to Nevada's sisters, daughters, and mothers."

The debate moderator began with a dramatic effect. "Mr. Sloan, on the website Beliefs.net, you were the only candidate to receive an F on religious issues. Care to respond?"

Sloan raised his finger toward the moderator but then dropped his hand to his side; that gesture was too harsh. He responded with his standard answer about private beliefs and the largess of the blue foundation. A sudden stop; that response sounded to *him* like a dodge. He recalled Reed's advice on saying *something* to demonstrate he had a moral compass.

"Let me work on something," Sloan said, breaking the rhythm of the rehearsal.

Bree instructed a pair of staff members to review and gather quotes from the Bible and from various philosophers' views on morality.

While Bree spoke, Sloan was rummaging through his memory for relevant song lyrics. "Has to be genuine, no sound bites from someone I don't know." He paused to summon ideas. He raised his hand; he tried it out.

"'The most important thing in the world is family and love.' The great basketball coach John Wooden said that, and I've been incredibly fortunate to have both. My mom was a nurse. She had a kind soul, attended church regularly, and cared for those who are less fortunate. My dad always supported me. My daughter, Riley, is a marvel, smart, and loving. She'll campaign with me; you'll meet her."

Several aides applauded; shouts of "bravo" rang out. The remainder of the session continued without any more disagreements or breaks in character. As the preparation concluded, one of the aides handed Sloan a large briefing notebook. He glanced through a lengthy draft of his closing speech. "This close is programmed for some Manchurian candidate."

"There's drama in those remarks," the aide replied defiantly. "Moving drama."

"It's not my drama," Sloan hastily replied.

The aide's silence confirmed his acquiescence.

Sloan clapped his hands and thanked his staff before huddling privately with Bree. "I need a break. Let's blow this pop stand."

He told his security team they could follow him, but he planned to take an Uber with Bree. The comment prompted a puzzled look from her.

"Fun stuff happens whenever I do this—just watch."

* * *

Bree and Sloan slid into the back seat of the unfamiliar car and exchanged pleasantries with the driver.

"So what brought you to Las Vegas?" he asked the driver.

"Not tall enough to be a showgirl, not stupid enough to be a stripper," she responded. She went on to explain that she sometimes sang in shows, but her real passion was songwriting. She added with excitement that her first real gig was as an opening act the following month at the Orleans Hotel. If the stars were aligned, that one week would allow her to "kiss Uber goodbye."

"Man, you look familiar," the driver said, glancing in the rearview mirror. "You...you look a lot like Tyler Sloan—rocker gone politician. Anyone ever mention that?"

"He's heard that before," Bree assured the driver, repressing her smile.

"Dude, you could be his twin."

Sloan leaned forward from the back seat. "I *am* Tyler Sloan."

The car screeched to a halt. The driver whipped around to stare in disbelief. "Why am *I* driving you? Why aren't you in a limo? You're running for the Senate!"

"Taking a short break," Sloan replied. "How many Uber violations would there be if I drove my media wizard home, and you sat in the back seat and sang me one of your songs? A singer always has to be ready for their cue."

"Violations? I won't tell if you don't." The driver was snappy in her reply.

They switched places, and Sloan took the wheel. Bree slipped into the front passenger seat. As Sloan began to drive, the woman started singing, a slight country twang coming through in her words. "I'm waiting, waiting for you," she sang, which to Sloan's ears didn't sound half-bad. "I'm staying, staying for you," she concluded, as he pulled into the driveway of Bree's building.

Both Sloan and Bree clapped.

"I liked it," Sloan replied. "You have the hook, a woman or man can sing it, the song conveys emotion. If you want, send an audio file to my attorney, Grant Zimmer, in Los Angeles." He wrote a short note on Bree's business card and handed it to her. It read: *Grant, listen to this, Tyler.*

The woman was staring at the card, overflowing with disbelief and good fortune. She carefully placed the card in her wallet. The driver handed Bree her phone to take photos of her and Sloan; he accepted, but had Bree shoot a video while they did a duet. Placing his arm around the woman's shoulder, he and the driver sang a verse from her song.

* * *

Later that night, Sloan glanced at his cell phone. His earlier calls to his father had not been answered. It was nearing seven in the evening. He called again. "The Collins ad is working," he said with enthusiasm when Mike answered.

Airing of the "Collins video" had created a blistering political maelstrom. Conventional wisdom whispered that the commercial was an act of desperation, but it wounded Collins. Methods were damned; supporters shared a singular goal: toasting the winner on election night.

Sloan detailed for his father how Collins and her surrogates were staying on message—Sloan used stolen property, but none denied the video's damning lines.

Mike was quick with praise. "One talking head said that your explanation of an anonymous mailing to the campaign office requires a leap of faith greater than Mother Mary's virgin birth." He chuckled.

"We bought more time for the ad; we're turning up the flame," Sloan replied. "Those ads reveal another side of Chris. It's like finding out that your neighbor owns fifty cats and doesn't clean the litter boxes."

"And who delivered that little gem to you?" Mike asked, with a bounce in his voice.

"You aced it, Dad." Sloan's voice dropped, "Look, I really need help on the debate. Are you feeling well enough to fly out here? Some face-to-face time would be great." When Mike evaded that question, he changed tactics. "What if I'm asked a question I know nothing about? Some federal law or proposed bill I've never heard of?"

"Dance and keep dancing. Don't ad-lib an answer; keep talking about anything related to the question. The moderator has to move on."

"Not good enough. What if it's something I know drop-dead nothing about? Do I support the Winkler bill or more aid to Kirkistan?"

"Where?" Mike asked sharply.

"I made up Kirkistan. But what if it's something totally foreign to me?"

Sloan worried at Mike's pause, evidence that he had never met a candidate for a significant office without a vague knowledge of a subject matter.

"Not even a clue?" Mike probed.

"Not a glimmer. I don't want to give Rogers an opening to spew about his experience, governing is not on-the-job-training, and yadda, yadda, yadda."

"Pause, nod, and discuss anything related to the subject."

"You're not getting it," Sloan said with exasperation.

"*I'm* not getting it?" Mike barked. "You called me because *you're* not getting it."

Sloan did not respond. The argument was too reminiscent of past decades.

"Here you go." Mike's voice softened. "Amplify on an earlier question. Get into it quickly. Tell them that subject is so important you need to finish your remarks. Keep talking; don't you dare let them interrupt you."

"Bottom line—how do I win the debate?"

"Don't get bogged down in the weeds. Remember, you're the only one on that stage that people ever paid to see. Collins is a washed-up newscaster, and listening to Billy is like downing an Ambien with a martini chaser."

"Did Martino call you after I fired him? It will be public knowledge right after the debate."

The line went silent.

"Son." There was a long and more-than-pregnant pause. "He called. He wanted me to convince you to let him back in. I told him that Tyler is in charge; you're making all the calls."

Sloan expressed his appreciation. "What was his mood?"

"Depressed, but he's not seeking revenge. He told me about the FBI, and I assured him I'd help him any way I can. That seemed to please him."

"Good work. Keep a lid on Martino. I've got enough on my plate to worry about."

* * *

The next evening, Bree listened patiently as Sloan vented about Collins's latest campaign ploys. "Collins is working day jobs to show she's connected to voters? She's dealing blackjack in Lake Tahoe, baling hay outside of Ely, and sitting in a Reno hotel customer-call center? People buy that?"

Bree noticed Sloan's yawns of fatigue. "You OK?" she asked with warmth as he walked to the edge of his living room window.

He waved his hand with a theatric gesture at the city's skyline. "It's *Blade Runner* painted by Edward Hopper," he said, mixing movies, artists, and centuries.

"Come." She patted the sofa. "Come sit with me."

Sloan sat down at a comfortable distance. She seemed pleased by the modest victory and especially so when he gurgled his appreciation for her. "You really care about me."

Bree looked struck by his tone of surprise. His response begged the question: How many people did he think cared for him?

"Of course I do." Her answer quick, nothing more revealed. Sloan knew that look, and he hoped this wasn't just a schoolgirl's crush on a rock star.

"Try to understand me, not as a candidate, but as a man. It's essential."

Bree reached across the sofa far enough that their fingertips grazed. At that moment, Sloan fantasized that they were a couple; he wondered if she ever did the same.

The touch was at once comforting yet propelled him off the sofa. His rise abrupt, walking behind the couch, more anxious than nervous. Standing behind her, a slight graze to her back, a touch on her neck, brief, yet tender. He was cautious; the touch hinted at intimacy.

"I don't fear losing the election. I've made records that got panned. One album was termed 'banal and bland.' No five stars with that one."

Bree reached back and held his hand as it rested on her shoulder. "Talk to me."

Her response soothing, prompting a tighter squeeze of her shoulder. "I get bored in a comfort zone."

"You know how many guys want what you have?"

"I've been dealt a great hand. My father was not rich but famous; his fame opened a lot of doors." Sloan fondly recalled the pride at seeing a poster for his band to appear at a small local club; the poster was tacked to neighborhood telephone poles. He detested that the sign proclaimed the band's lead singer was "The Congressman's Son." He moved around the couch to face her. "When I told our drummer how much I didn't want that, the dude laughed and told me he didn't care—we got booked, and we'd get paid. He was right; that one gig gave us the chance to show we were the real deal—and we did."

"It's one thing to be dealt a great hand," Bree interjected, "but you've played the hell out of those cards."

Sloan casually accepted the compliment with a nod. "Dylan was the greatest songwriter; loved his line about picking either fortune or fame." He smiled. "Both are pretty damn good." Sloan paused, silent moments passed.

Bree finally broke the silence. "And?" she probed.

"Fame in politics is a hell of a lot harder than fame in my last gig." Sloan gauged how much deeper he could go, should go in revealing personal emotions. Taking a chance, he was plunging deeper.

Six months earlier, the night before his fiftieth birthday, he was alone, alone by choice, reflecting on his life. He took great pride in Riley, acknowledging without ego he was an international star with fame and financial security. Yet, no meaningful relationships with women beyond his failed marriage. He fell short in measuring his success against his father; Mike's legal and political battles enriched lives.

"I could have stayed onstage. It's a great life. I don't have any recent hits, but"—he extended his arms out with a smile—"in this town, I don't need them."

The young woman stared up at him, her piercing stare unexpected. Sloan recalled her comment that he was nearly the same age as her father, but from the way she was looking at him, she was not seeing a father figure. The generational differences were disintegrating.

She seemed hesitant to say more, then asked innocently, "I like to quote Shakespeare, but do you want a better line?"

"Go for it."

"Anaïs Nin," she replied. "'And the day came when the risk to remain closed in a bud became more painful than the risk it would take to blossom.'"

Sloan smiled. "I wish I wrote that." He walked away, appearing uncertain where to land. He stood only a few feet away, yet reluctant to rejoin her on the couch. "It's not just Collins and Rogers. I'm battling against all the media doubters." He bit his lower lip. "And don't forget my dad."

She looked puzzled. "Go on," she said, her voice light.

Sloan reached down and grasped her hand, feeling the engagement ring on her finger. She returned a squeeze.

"Facing my dad after a loss would be a cold morning, a cold morning coming down."

Her brows furrowed.

Sloan smiled reassuringly. Their hands remained locked. "Let's call it a night, Bree…but, if you're game"—he was uncertain how to deliver each word—"love to do it again."

TWENTY-SEVEN

August 7, Carson City

**Poll: Collins 38%, Sloan 24%,
Rogers 21%, Undecided 17%**

Sloan greeted Chris Collins at the center of the debate stage with a firm grip in their handshake. The ends of her lips slightly puckered as she gazed past him.

Billy Rogers's expression dampened in dysphoria. His drawn appearance matched his latest poll numbers. His makeup powder obscured the dark shadows and bags that had formed under his eyes. The lines Mike termed "Mondale-esque."

Candidates instinctively knew when their dream was transforming into a nightmare. Media cameras mercifully never memorialized that exact moment, but Rogers grasped his fate. In an attempt to recover, Rogers downed an energy shot. His palm was noticeably moist as he grasped Sloan's hand.

By the luck of the draw, Sloan stood at the middle lectern. He received a dab of powder from a makeup assistant. The director announced that three minutes remained until airtime.

Thick black cable lay on the floor of the Bob Boldrick Theater in Carson City. Strung above were countless bright lights mounted on platforms for the statewide, televised debate. The glare from the banks of lights prohibited candidates from seeing clearly beyond the first rows.

Two of Collins's aides served as bookend drill sergeants, barking hushed commands. Her campaign manager urged the director to use the camera angle that captured Collins's left profile.

Sloan camouflaged his apprehension—this was his first debate.

"Two minutes!" was shouted from behind the cameras.

Sloan had boiled down his debate points to one index card for his questions to Collins and another for questions to Rogers. He scanned each card before placing them on the lectern.

All campaign staff hurried to exit the stage when "one minute" was called.

Rogers stood alone, vigorously nodding as if listening to an imaginary pep talk. He retrieved from his pocket another energy shot bottle. He made short work of the container.

Sloan impishly winked at Collins. She appeared visibly annoyed by the gesture.

An assistant director shouted down the final ten seconds.

"Good evening, I'm Tammy Keller, moderator for tonight's debate between the three candidates to represent the State of Nevada in the United States Senate."

In a booming voice, Rogers delivered an opening statement citing his years of government experience. Sloan dismissed his clenched fist as a prop for the leadership he could not summon.

Sloan began with a mix of his business and life experiences. He delicately sliced his opponents. "Vote for one of my opponents if you think we're on the right track. If you're not satisfied, rest assured I'll shake things up. I'm not change dreamed up by political consultants. We'll end excessive regulations that strangle businesses; we'll get people back to work and drive down health care costs by transforming insurance companies into nonprofits."

Collins's rhetoric was a sledgehammer verbally slamming Sloan: "We need a steady and *experienced* voice in the Senate."

A gust of partisan excitement swept through the hall as she turned to Rogers. "Mr. Rogers is not shy about grabbing more of your money, more and more taxes, or as he calls it"—she curled her lips—"*enhanced revenue.*"

The debate panelists performed on their own stages, each desiring to ask the noteworthy question that would dominate the following morning's conversation when journalists and political junkies converged at the water cooler.

Sloan's staff had compiled each panelist's tendencies. Moderator Tammy Keller would pose complex questions to prove her bona fides. Mary Marcus, the young director of an online political website, would ask questions in keeping with her crown as the self-appointed spokesperson of millennials. The *New York Times* national political correspondent, Alan Newcombe, had a well-documented career of ripping body parts to ensure a headline.

Sloan recalled Martino's parting counsel to be aggressive but not angry, avoid smirks, sighs, or sarcasm. Above all, Sloan had to be himself—nary a contradiction.

The debate's first half hour passed uneventfully as the candidates wrestled with the standard laundry list of issues. No surprises.

"Mr. Sloan, convince the voters of Nevada you're qualified." Mary Marcus appeared to take delight in her question. "Name the leaders of Iran, Israel, and Libya."

"My, oh my," Sloan began as the audience tittered. "A third grader with a smartphone could answer those questions. Senators need clear judgment; let's avoid snap quizzes and gotcha questions." Sloan held a satisfied smile. All was well.

Newcombe's smile could be judged as either sympathetic or snide as he asked Collins about Sloan's airing of the commercial-in-a-commercial of her.

"Batten down the hatches," Collins said forcefully. "Tyler Sloan's attack machine has geared up by airing distorted and stolen videos—moments taken out of context. Unfortunately, expect more smear attacks against my family and me. Mr. Sloan refuses to answer how he received that stolen property."

The Collins faithful applauded before being reprimanded, "Hold all applause until the debate's conclusion."

Sloan seized the hanging thread in Newcombe's question. "Chris Collins's own unedited words reveal her disdain for the voters."

"How dare Ms. Collins," Rogers said suddenly, jolting the room with his incongruous charge. "How dare she question my patriotism and mock my service in the National Guard. We should examine *her* personal conduct."

The outburst jolted Sloan. Was Rogers preparing to drop the news on the Sloan-Collins coupling?

Before the debate, Sloan had drawn sips from his blended olive oil, honey, and herb shooter to coat his throat. He ignored the tall glass of water provided to each candidate. He limited his liquid intake in fear of reliving his father's tale of a New York Senate candidate who drank too much water and was hopping back and forth throughout a debate.

Mary Marcus's question was directed to Collins. "Are questions of personal conduct appropriate in a political campaign?"

Collins seized her moment with a dramatic pause. Her hesitation degrees too sly for an issue that would never endanger the safety of the republic. "I rely on my faith to guide me," Collins's voice modulated, searching for sincerity.

Newcombe slowly stroked his gray beard, a tactic the reporter employed before posing questions akin to flying shrapnel. He asked all three candidates, "Have you or any member of your immediate family ever received treatment for any addiction or a mental disorder?"

The question was a projectile discharged from a stun gun. Newcombe's smugness seeped as the three candidates exchanged quizzical glances.

Sloan wondered if an ex-wife counted as an immediate family. Would he be unchivalrous if he referred to her in any context? Would a nonanswer to treatment be equated to defining the meaning of the word *is*? Silence on Cindy's years of therapy might steer him to the hellhole where false denials of insignificant questions mushroomed into allegations of dishonesty.

Sloan flashed a smile. "The emotional health of our grandmothers is not relevant. What's next? Do we line up tonight for full-body scans?"

"Ha!" Rogers interjected sharply. "Whose sanity is being questioned?"

Tammy Keller asked the only question that mattered to many voters—how Washington could improve Nevada's economy. The problem was impossible to answer within the one-minute time frame. A thoughtful discourse would propel viewers to refrigerators and journalists to dismiss a candidate's inability to summarize solutions.

Collins literally and figuratively pivoted toward Sloan. "I have a real plan to create jobs, not like Mr. Sloan's flimsy scheme."

"Cute response"—Sloan joined the battle—"saying you have a plan, and I have a scheme, but that's no answer."

"Using a word like *cute* is patronizing and sexist," Collins protested.

"Don't jump on every word to determine if it's politically correct." Sloan's voice rose.

Rogers lifted his microphone from his lectern stand, his face flushed as he marched toward Sloan, moving as quickly as a guided missile. His facial makeup was now infused with perspiration, his everyman persona vanishing in a near-demonic shadow.

"Tyler Sloan." Rogers's voice was sharp and loud. "Tyler Sloan." One hand waved in the air. "You can't *sing* your way to the Senate."

"Mr. Rogers," Tammy Keller stammered. "Please return to your lectern."

Sloan eyed Rogers; his opponent kept moving closer. "What's going on, Billy?" Sloan placed his palms up in a signal of peace.

"Don't put your hand out at me." Rogers's head was bobbing as he moved closer to Sloan, appearing ready to charge. "You think you can *buy* this election?" Rogers now wagging his index finger inches from Sloan. His eyes darted dangerously between Sloan and Collins.

"Billy, Billy, we're going to work this out." Sloan held his ground. "Go back to your spot and finish whatever you want to say."

Rogers reached upward and grabbed Sloan's shoulder. "People are hurting. They want *solutions*, not *songs*."

Collins held her lectern tightly—a white-knuckle flyer terrified that she was the next target.

Rogers was glancing at the two uniformed security officers who appeared off camera in the stage wings. Rogers nodded toward them before returning to his lectern. The audience murmured with uncertainty and a collective nervous giggle.

"Ms. Collins," Tammy Keller stated, "by a flip of the coin, you're first to ask Mr. Sloan a question."

"Mr. Sloan's *show* has indoor fireworks; he likes to sing about freedom. But our country needs real protection against terrorism. Mr. Sloan, do you support Senate Bill 232?" Collins asked.

Sloan's fears had materialized. He had no inkling of SB 232 other than Collins's word of terrorism. He thought of voicing his support— didn't everyone support a bill that fought terrorism? Yet messy details lurked in every measure. His hands moved into a pyramid shape as he spoke, slowly parting in graceful gestures, conveying control while avoiding sharp movements that smacked of panic. Yet there was no victory in prevailing in a miming contest.

"Let's get serious about terrorism," Sloan responded, ready to pivot to another topic.

"Yes, let's get serious," Rogers suddenly weighed in and then just as abruptly halted.

At a brief pause, Collins reached inside her lectern to retrieve her purse. She removed two pieces of an automatic weapon and snapped the pieces together to ready the gun.

Newcombe slid back from his chair, ready to duck beneath the moderator's table.

Collins held the gun upright as the audience audibly gasped. "Don't worry; it's not loaded. Both of my opponents oppose the Second Amendment's right to bear arms."

Sloan eyed Collins, aware of the power of YouTube dramatics.

"The National Rifle Association supports your candidacy because of stunts like this," Sloan retorted. "We don't need a weatherman to tell us which way the wind blows, and we know that waving that gun means nothing if you don't have the guts to take on the NRA. Join with me to eliminate the nightmare of automatic weapons in the hands of deranged killers."

"Nonsense!" Collins hastily replied. "The NRA—"

"Ms. Collins," Tammy Keller interrupted, "the rules do not allow a second rebuttal."

"I have to respond, have to respond," Collins whined to the audience's muffled laughter.

Sloan was relieved when it was Rogers's turn to ask Collins a question.

Rogers began quickly, with a determination that would be impossible to stop. "My question is not for Ms. Collins, but for Mr. Sloan." Despite Keller's objection, Rogers was a freight train that could not be slowed. "Mr. Sloan, the people of Nevada have a right to know," he fired rapidly. "What was the cause of your addiction? Why were you admitted to Betty Ford? Was it cocaine?"

The room was hushed. Keller muttered apologies. Her control of the debate was now a distant memory. She glanced at Sloan with a silent plea for forgiveness. Sloan ignored the lump in his throat, had to show command. Avoiding the topic was not an option. Ducking this question would be followed by streams of media questions and internet innuendoes.

"We all make mistakes in life. I made more than my share. My life had too many temptations...I was weak and succumbed. Tonight, I ask for forgiveness from the good people of Nevada. Gandhi spoke that forgiveness is the attribute of the strong; many biblical verses speak to the human act of forgiveness. I'm asking for forgiveness." The audience remained still. "When I was young, I tried cocaine; I battled cocaine, and cocaine won. I was stupid and wrong. I needed help, and I got it. I am a stronger man because I overcame that problem."

The audience remained fixated on his words. "I know the power of addiction." He leaned on the lectern, his tone conversational, not confrontational. "I know some watching tonight have their own demons—alcohol, tobacco, gambling, or drugs." He was now the counselor-in-chief. "Be honest. Be proud of your strengths, but be strong enough to admit your weaknesses. If you need help, get help. If I hadn't reached out, if I hadn't had family and friends who cared... I might not be here tonight."

The audience's applause was mounting despite Keller's half-hearted attempts to quell the outburst.

Tammy Keller thanked the panelists and signaled for closing statements.

"Day one," Rogers boomed. "I have the experience from day one." He shifted into an impromptu economics seminar analyzing the nation's economy. He rambled on, drowning in a statistical sea, sounding more like a candidate for treasurer of a national notary association.

Sloan began to smoothly recite his achievements, still uncertain of the audience's sympathies. Was he worthy of forgiveness, or merely a rock star dilettante? "My father, Mike Sloan, was a great governor of California, a principled man. When he was a lawyer, he argued to defeat antiquated laws that suppressed voting turnout in minority communities." His speech was slowed by emotion. "My father never quit. Never."

Sloan rested his hands on the lectern, gazing to the farthest reaches of the hall. "Look beyond my opponents' fear tactics and personal attacks. Here's the truth—my opponents cannot change Washington. They're more of the same tired, drab nonsense. Tonight, there was nothing new from my opponents. Why? Because they have nothing new. Real change cannot come from beating our heads against the wall with party A or party B. The two parties are poisoned by bribes disguised as campaign contributions. I have the guts and skills to challenge the status quo. It's our government; let's take it back!"

Sloan sensed a victory when ever-so-slight smiles formed on the faces of the debate panelists. He held his cell phone aloft and read his number aloud. "Call me. Let's keep the dialogue going."

Following Collins's warmly received closing statement, the debate concluded, and the three candidates parted ways without engaging one another. Aides surrounded their respective candidates, but Tammy Keller managed to make her way to Sloan's side. She motioned for him to join her to the side. They found a corner.

"You just did the impossible; admitted using cocaine and gained votes," she whispered. "Quite a combination. Collins's team is haranguing me about you and some young woman, and Rogers's gang told me there's a bombshell about you and Collins coming. Get ready."

Sloan held his smile despite the bracing news.

* * *

After midnight Sloan turned off his computer; he'd read all the debate analysis he could find. Tonight recalled those endless nights on the road when he bunkered down in a hotel room after a concert. The rush was gone, and loneliness engulfed him.

When he was young, after a concert, he'd often partake in room-service companionship. One nod to his staff, and the blonde in the low-cut blouse or the two brunettes with enticing smiles in the front row provided gratification on demand. A harsh reminder of time's passing was when one of his companions told him the morning after that her *mother* would be "so jealous."

He had no urge to call the real estate agent who habitually forgot to wear her thong but always remembered to ask which of his friends needed a "condominium with a view." His mood mirrored one of his songs of romantic regret. He thought of Bree.

He looked down at his cell phone and noticed there was a voice mail. He scanned his recent phone calls and saw that his father had called about thirty minutes after the debate.

Sloan listened to the message: "Son, that was the best debate by any man named Sloan. You made an old man proud."

A spontaneous smile. His eyes grew watery. He listened to the message again. Then he repeated the last part aloud: "You made an old man proud."

He raised his fist in triumph.

TWENTY-EIGHT

August 8, Las Vegas

**Poll: Collins 37%, Sloan 27%,
Rogers 20%, Undecided 16%**

"How could FOX call the debate a draw?" Sloan snapped at Bree. "The overnights have us moving; we didn't cut four points off from Collins's lead with a draw."

The plane increased speed as it hurtled down the runway at McCarran Airport.

"MSNBC called Rogers the winner?" Bree replied with puzzled irritation.

"Billy? The only thing he won was the meltdown derby."

"They said he was the aggressor, full of fire," Bree replied.

"Full of fire? How about an IV full of caffeine?" Sloan snapped.

Sloan wondered about the comment from Rogers about Collins's personal conduct but held his thoughts. Rogers's sinking poll numbers and desperation could lead him to air the sex video, blow the race up, and pray he would be the last one standing.

Sloan glanced at Bree. He was tempted to confide in her about the video but still cautious; there was an exponential danger in having more people know. He would wait.

Today's *New York Times'* coverage included debate analysis by two university professors in a column entitled "Who Won?" One professor chaired NYU's Mass Communications Department; the other was a senior member of Georgetown's Political Science Department.

Blaring across the top of *The Times'* page was a large color photograph of Chris Collins's "tough-sheriff" wave of a gun in the air. Sloan and Rogers were in separate nondemonstrative pictures below. The professors cited Sloan's honesty in "coming clean on his addiction," Rogers's knowledge of government, and Collins as "a great communicator."

"Intellectual masturbation for two nerds," Bree snapped.

"Richman got liquored up at a retirement party last week for a fellow reporter," she added with a mischievous smile. "He was dancing hard with his pal Johnnie Walker. He got on a roll and questioned the sexual preference of his editor. Then he shouted at some young reporters about them not doing enough *shoe leather*, whatever that means." She grazed Sloan's arm. "Whitman told Ted he's got two strikes, and the next pitch is a low curve."

"He's hungry to return to his boss's good graces, feed him something," Sloan said.

"I want to be blunt." Bree waited for his nod before continuing. "Is your ex all right?"

"Who's asking?"

"Me. Riley made some comment that day at Red Rocks that concerned me—something about her mom always falling asleep before she does, and 'she needs pills to sleep.' No one else heard her. Riley knows something is amiss. That question at the debate about family members and addictions got me thinking. I had to ask."

Sloan explained that Cindy had been in an auto accident a few years ago and started taking pills for the pain. He also mentioned the Xanax Cindy took for her anxiety. "Then she mixes meds with booze." He continued about how he hoped it was only a temporary phase but added his own worry. "It's not good for her or for Riley. I had someone covertly notify her friends, hoping they'll intercede. It's manageable now, but I hope they do an intervention."

"Can your ex damage us?" Bree asked.

Sloan silently recalled all the confidences he or any spouse shared. "Nothing is damning, but twisted the right way, everything is damming. The good news is we have a civil relationship; the bad news is Cindy's got a vindictive streak and a creative imagination."

"We need to keep her under wraps in the final stretch," Bree replied.

"I'll talk to Grant again."

* * *

Sloan and Zimmer rode to the Palms Hotel for the opening of the CineVegas Film Festival, a coupling of Hollywood's film industry with Las Vegas. On the way, he insisted that Zimmer press Mike again to join him for campaign events. Before Zimmer could reply, Sloan wistfully began to reflect on his childhood, speaking in bursts and fragments.

Long ago, he was awarded a platinum album at a record label party...a room filled with suits and women...he was young, and Mike was absent...campaigning for reelection...Sloan kept glancing around the room...just in case. Mike's victory was inevitable, but he wanted a landslide to satisfy the swirling presidential buzz...won by twenty points...but no appearance with his son.

Zimmer listened politely.

Without prompting, he said, "I also have some good memories." Sloan began explaining how Mike battled the record label to secure Sloan's future...how Mike told him after he left his boyhood home in Nebraska and the magic of first witnessing palm trees and the Pacific in

Santa Monica…how his dad calmed him, in dealing with critics…his charge when every teacher knew his father; many admired him.

"It made me feel special. I had the special dad." Sloan abruptly stopped his trip down memory lane and asked for news on President Reed.

"Reed's staff is frozen with indecision," Zimmer said apologetically.

"You ever hear how I got my first record played?" Sloan asked rhetorically. "My buddies inundated the old LA radio station KHJ with phone calls, demanding the playing of 'No Time.' It's the same with Reed. Start something spontaneous."

The two arrived at the Palms Hotel, where an event hostess greeted them effusively. "This year the theme for the charity event is 'Feed the People—End World Hunger.'" She was placing a multicolored ribbon on Sloan's lapel. The hostess explained its significance. "The industry's run out of single-colored ribbons. These red, blue, and green ribbons signify our fight to defeat world hunger."

Zimmer asked the woman if Rogers or Collins were attending.

"Rogers, yes." The host added with a sneer, "Not Collins. When the industry hears *Republican*, they think *Nazi*."

The two approached the festival entrance into a roped area near a large tent outside a manufactured sound stage. A group of young women dressed in tight jungle-print dresses with strategic tears across their bouncing chests shouted their greetings in unison: "Feed the People! Feed the People!"

Inside the tent, Sloan met an actress who, in her last movie, portrayed a journalist who discovered a cover-up of Wall Street insider trading.

"Don't let them do it." The actress's dark eyes and passion paled beside her political intensity. She tightly grabbed Sloan's wrist. "They've rigged the financial system. Next week, I'm testifying before the Senate Banking Committee. I'll set them straight."

Sloan returned a smile as Zimmer discreetly rolled his eyes behind his spectacles.

The young actor Nichols Denton approached wearing dark sunglasses despite the indoor venue. He was speaking loudly on his phone, blithely discussing various deal points. Denton flashed the bright smile that earned him multimillion-dollar movie guarantees.

"I ripped off one of your quotes," Denton whispered to Sloan. "The one about 'I'm the canvas for women to paint their dreams.'"

"No problem." Sloan shot a quick wink at Zimmer. "I ripped it off Rudolph Valentino." He continued past Denton's puzzled gaze. "Rudy sang lead in a big-hair eighties band."

Sloan and Zimmer continued inside the studio toward the three areas that were designated as regions. Each region represented a different level of world hunger. The first was "Famine." Sloan stared at the manufactured scene of thatched huts, bamboo trees with heat lamps, humidifiers, and several burly armed guards dressed in green fatigues. A prop man released a batch of buzzing flies.

The hostess cheerfully explained, "Each region reflects hunger with a different food theme, but all relate to quesadillas. The first region has a rice flour tortilla but no filling. The second region is called 'Poverty,' and that area has cheese quesadillas."

The second region housed a modestly improved environment. Large burlap sacks of beans were stacked upon a mule-driven cart. "Power to the People" was spray-painted on a tattered mid-1970s Chevrolet as two children in beggar's clothes were holding out a paper cup.

Sloan walked closer to notice a Guess label hanging from one child's shirt. He thought of Alice staring through the looking glass.

Sloan and Zimmer entered the third region. An American flag graced the area termed "Greed and Opulence."

A card described the quesadilla: "Organic blue-corn tortilla, brie cheese, seedless red grapes, New Mexican roasted Hatch chilies, and a dash of Himalayan sea salt."

Sloan leaned into Zimmer, his voice laced with sarcasm. "The *perfect* quesadilla to remind us about world hunger."

A reporter from *US Magazine* asked Sloan to pose with a well-known country singer. The singer said to the reporter, "Country music relates to spiritual souls across the globe. My songs, like those of Tyler

Sloan, strike the human chords of love and hope for our fellow man."

As the singer walked away, he whispered to Sloan, "Hope you had your boots on."

One of the paparazzi shouted, "This same 'All You Need Is Love' guy took a swing at me last night at Pure for taking a photo of him and his new girlfriend!"

The hostess was escorting Sloan and Zimmer to a final area, introducing them to a "water sommelier." The man was beaming behind a table with bottles of water and a banner proclaiming, Water Tasting-Five Waters-Five Continents.

"May I pair your water to match your food?" The sommelier gestured to a water bottle from Australia. "This water complements vegan diets."

Sloan raised a bottle of water from Poland. "Could you pair this water with chicken?"

The sommelier shook his head. "The minerals in that water enhance a beef entrée."

Sloan gestured to a bottle of water from Fuji.

The sommelier answered knowingly. "Keep that one neat."

Sloan winked at Zimmer, who wore an expression of disbelief. They were greeted by a young woman, fully tatted; various rings were attached to her nose, lips, and ears. She explained the jewelry was all turquoise, as "my link to the Native American suffering."

"This movement is about people working together with people who care about people who share a kinship with mankind," she holistically gushed.

The pair was ready to make a speedy exit, but they were interrupted by a couple in their path wearing big smiles and a booming greeting: "There he is, my main man!"

Sloan could not recall the man's name or where they'd met, and he certainly didn't know the man's young wife. He shot a glance at Zimmer, a cue for the attorney to introduce himself to get the man to offer his name.

Zimmer extended his hand. "Grant Zimmer."

"Good to meet you; I'm George," came the hoped-for reply.

"My, George, your hand is cold," Zimmer said, following their handshake.

"To match his heart." The wife smirked.

George was unperturbed as he praised Sloan's entertainment career.

Sloan recalled George as a producer of casino hotel shows; he congratulated the couple on their recent marriage. This wife was younger, blonder, and thinner than her predecessor.

"Let's meet in September after the election when you've got some free time." George winked. "Let's map out a Cirque-style show based on your songs and your campaign."

George epitomized all the doubters who dismissed his chances, and Sloan glared ice at him before delivering a firm "I'll be too busy in DC."

"Well." George was slow in his reply.

"Too busy to meet."

"Uh, but of course," the producer stuttered. A quick removal of his business card from his jacket, he held it out. "But just in case—"

Sloan let the card dangle. "There is no *just in case*." He leaned in, grazing George, able to whiff his cologne. "I'm winning this damn thing."

Minutes later, Sloan and Zimmer were climbing into the back of the car for the drive back to the campaign office.

"What in the hell was that about?" Sloan sputtered. "Not that fool George, but the whole event?"

"A little too pretentious for you?" Zimmer's smile was revealing.

"Who knew the importance of quesadillas?"

"Maybe next year—it's all about pizza." Zimmer shook his head, a look of pity on his face. "I almost cried when you asked the water boy about pairing water."

"If hypocrisy were a religion," Sloan said, "that event would be the altar."

TWENTY-NINE

August 10, Beverly Hills

Zimmer stood in a corner where he had a clear view of the seating areas in the Polo Lounge at the Beverly Hills Hotel. He eyed the elusive Denny Morgan sitting at a corner table on the outdoor patio, precisely where Zimmer had been informed he'd be.

He allowed time for the singer to get comfortable amid Morgan's contented smile and gazes at the abundant trees shading the famed patio. There was a distance between the tables, the space favored by celebrities the lounge had been attracting for decades. The hotel was dubbed the "Pink Palace"—its bedrooms used and abused to shield Hollywood affairs for over a century.

"Denny Morgan," Zimmer said merrily as he approached the table.

Morgan rose and smiled with an outstretched hand to greet Zimmer. He enthusiastically bubbled details from what his manager was told: Morgan had the opportunity to appear on a tour of classic rock bands. "Love the hotel!" He was gushing admiration for the hotel's image on the Eagles' *Hotel California* album. He was pumped. "Just saw Katy Perry walk by."

Taking his seat, Morgan gestured for Zimmer to take the empty one across from him. "Perfect place, a launching pad to mount my comeback." He smacked his hands together in a celebratory gesture.

"Denny, there's no tour." Zimmer stared hard at Morgan. "Your career is over." His voice dropped with firmness. "I'm Grant Zimmer, Tyler Sloan's attorney. Let's talk about the video."

As if he'd just been rear-ended, Morgan jolted forward and then back. His mouth fell open; his expression froze. When he began to rise from his chair, Zimmer motioned for him to sit. "The four gentlemen standing in the corners prefer you sit."

Morgan paused in midrise. He turned to eye the four muscular, suited men in sunglasses in each corner of the restaurant.

"I have a few more in plain clothes stationed at every exit. A couple of men are by your car right now. I hope they're not needed."

"Son of a bitch," Morgan muttered as he sat down.

Zimmer eyed Morgan as a hunter would his prey. His laser-like stare beamed across the table, contrasting with Morgan's eyes darting around the room.

"You sold the video to Rogers." Zimmer's harshness startled Morgan.

Morgan took a breath, then another, still another. He rubbed his temples, the artist melting down, suddenly aging.

"You blew it," Zimmer continued. "Tyler helping you with your songs was worth more than a hundred K. He even offered to match the amount."

"Tyler knew that story was all bullshit. He never wrote a word of those songs."

"What's wrong with you? Piggies get slaughtered. You had a great deal, but you went piggie on us."

Morgan glanced at the monogrammed cuffs peeking out from his beige summer suit. "Rogers paid me two hundred K." His voice weak. "I wasn't greedy; it was that extra hundred thou."

"Denny, today is your lucky day. I'm making you an offer. Don't fuck it up."

"An offer I can't refuse?" Morgan asked nervously. "But Rogers already has the video."

Zimmer leaned forward, his teeth bared like a Doberman ready to attack an intruder. "How did Rogers pay you? Cash or check?"

"They wired the money to my account."

"The video. How many copies did you make?"

"You're certain"—Morgan paused—"I made copies?"

"Where are they?" Zimmer asked tautly.

"Two more." Morgan's voice dropped. "Both in a safe deposit box at my bank."

Morgan's leg was banging the table so hard the water glasses rattled. The tightness around the singer's eyes had to be derived from the needle of a dermatologist. He was clinging to a thread of youth.

Zimmer removed his Montblanc pen from his inner pocket and spun it on the table. His voice was methodical and menacing. He detailed how his firm could file a lawsuit against him, citing various counts of action. He vowed to seize every penny Morgan had or would ever have.

"We'll leak to TMZ; you've had a relapse—drugs and drinking." Zimmer was too rapid for Morgan to interrupt. "Every promoter in every town will know. We'll garnish your wages if anyone dares to hire you, every fucking penny. Every time you sing 'Get Up,' you'll get a chill thinking of my sweet face. This *punim*." Zimmer gestured at his face. "You double-crossed Tyler, and I take that personally."

"I can't start over. I'm not the cat I used to be," Morgan moaned. "That's the offer?"

"You're a lucky man. I have one last, best, and final offer. A couple of the men standing around us will accompany you to your bank. You'll give them both copies, and they will give you a prepared statement." Zimmer pointed at Morgan. "You'll sign it, and when we tell you, you'll read the statement exactly as written at a press conference. *Exactly* as written. You will tell the media you sold the video to Rogers, who promised you he was going to air it and destroy Tyler Sloan and Chris Collins."

Zimmer gauged Morgan's reaction—the singer was pale with fright. "Did someone from Rogers's campaign call you on your cell?"

Morgan nodded, appearing almost afraid to speak.

"Call them today," Zimmer commanded. "I want a record of a series of calls between you and his people. Call them every day. Make up some bullshit reason."

When Morgan pled ignorance on what to say, Zimmer snarled. "I'll spoon-feed you. In the first call, you'll thank them; in the next call, press them to name which aide viewed the video. Tell them you might have another video. Ask when they plan to air it. Ask some girl out. Ask the goddamn weather in Vegas." He spat the final words. "Make fucking phone calls." Zimmer suddenly smiled—his "madman" persona, capable of any action. In one sentence, he was a crazy friend of Sloan who would avenge the double cross; the next moment, he was a comforting counselor.

"When you're at the bank, get a copy of your statement that shows the transfer. Your new best friends will drive you home. Go on your computer, print out your phone records of all calls to and from Rogers's campaign. Give the transfer statement and the phone records to my men."

"I'm tempted to tell you to go fuck yourself," Morgan said neatly.

"Instead of that"—Zimmer's tone stayed friendly—"Tell me where you want to retire."

Morgan licked his lips. "Is this my last wish?"

Zimmer said calmly, "No, I want you to live a long and happy life."

"Ah…Cabo San Lucas. I can scrape by on my money there."

"Mexico. Nice. Do exactly as you're told, and three hundred large—" Zimmer paused. "Three hundred thousand dollars will be wired into your account when you hit the beach in Cabo. With Rogers's payment, you'll have a half a million to sit on the beach, get drunk, and chase señoritas." It was Zimmer's turn to smile. "Not a bad life."

Morgan wiped the tears from his eyes.

"Read the statement, stand up, and leave the press conference. Not one new word." Zimmer added with a tight smile, "There'll be two snipers on the roof after you exit just in case you decide to ad-lib."

Morgan's mouth fell open, his eyes enlarged.

"Do not pass go; do not answer one question," Zimmer said. "Your bags will be packed before the presser. You exit the room; security drives you to the airport, where a private plane will fly you to Cabo. You will never talk about me, this lunch, Tyler, or the video. Got it?"

Zimmer pulled on his earlobe to signal it was time for the security team to escort Morgan out of the restaurant.

"Yes, sir, yes, sir," Morgan said, nearly sobbing. "I'm glad we met."

"We never met."

THIRTY

August 12, Las Vegas,
10 Days to the Election

Poll: Collins 38%, Sloan 28%,
Rogers 20%, Undecided 14%

Sloan stopped walking. He sublimated his concern at seeing Ted Richman lurking beyond the lobby entrance outside of his condominium. Richman leaned against a potted plant, smoking a cigarette.

"On a stakeout?" Sloan asked lightly.

"Anyone live in this ghost town?" Richman gestured above at the high-rise as he moved deliberately toward Sloan.

Sloan noticed the white stubble of a beard. "You growing a soul patch?"

"I've got soul, don't need no damn patch. I was running late and didn't shave. I'm a millennial today."

"I thought you quit smoking." Sloan stood a few feet to the side of the entry.

"I've quit five fucking times since we last saw each other." The reporter grunted. "Why did Martino bail?"

"You heard him—he's ill. His doctor was adamant."

Richman flicked the cigarette butt to the pavement. "Let's connect the dots." Richman retrieved a notepad from his coat pocket. "You flew to San Fran and begged your dad's buddy to manage the campaign, but now he's too sick to even advise you over the phone? Smells like Martino has troubles. Legal? Personal? Financial? Maybe you don't want those troubles near you. Not now."

Richman flipped the notepad's pages. "Indians and gambling. Zimmer represents Gala, and Martino was their lobbyist. Now Martino ducks out? Did he really bail on you? Or did you shove him out after you discovered something?" Holding out a hand to cut off a response from Sloan, Richman continued, "Martino was out and about in San Francisco last week. He wasn't a sick man at Golden Gate Fields quaffing a couple of brews with a buddy while playing the ponies."

Sloan wiped his brow; his mounting worry matched Richman's increasing agitation. "Did you share your three-shooters-on-a-grassy-knoll theory with Martino?"

"He clammed up, rattling off excuses about being cooped up, enjoying a nice day at the track."

"You're off base." Sloan's forceful response momentarily froze the reporter. "Did your friend take Martino's blood pressure? Did Martino pee in a cup? Maybe he's really sick."

"That tonnage he carries can't be good, but no presser? A press conference would have got you some sympathy. Wake up, rock star. I don't believe Martino, and I don't believe your story about how your team got the Collins video."

Sloan stood silent.

"Fundraising is always murky business, but your super PAC committees have more byzantine relationships than a Persian wedding."

The assertion provoked a pause; then Sloan was waving it off.

"Come on, man." Sloan was answering, but not directly. "No problems here."

"Your dad is here for one day to watch you hit baseballs, then you guys go to Reno for a minor league game, and now he's back in Cali?

What's up with you two? You're in the homestretch, and you guys are barnstorming on a baseball tour?"

"He'll be back soon, real soon," Sloan said with false assurance.

"Soon? The election is in ten days. Hope he doesn't wait until Christmas to see his son." Richman glanced around. There was no one within one hundred yards, yet he motioned Sloan closer. "I'm this close"—his fingers were barely apart—"this close from getting my ass kicked to the curb by that damn boy editor. I've fed you some damn tasty morsels; feed me something. Remember the old Temptations' song 'Ain't Too Proud to Beg?' Well, I ain't too proud."

"Tell me what you're fishing for."

"I've been deluged with internal emails between Rogers's campaign staff. The rats are jumping ship. The emails were *lifted*—I guess that's the right word—*lifted* from Rogers. A couple had ideas, novel ways the campaign could screw Collins. One said it won't be the first time she's been screwed by an opponent." The reporter's smile was casual. "Are you in that equation?"

Sloan shrugged off the innuendo.

Richman cleared his throat. He shuffled closer, his breath laced with tobacco and cocktails.

Sloan recalled his father's counsel about Richman: "A Pulitzer-winning journalist sober, a terrific reporter after one drink, a pain in the ass after two, but a mean bastard after three."

"In one email," the reporter began, "there was a reference that you and Collins once dated, and the word *dated* was in quotes."

"You won a Pulitzer; now you're asking me if I ever *dated* Collins?" Before Sloan could continue, he abruptly halted, hastily smiling at being recognized by an approaching young couple. He stopped and posed for an impromptu selfie before entering the lobby doors and moving toward the elevator as Richman fell close behind.

"You're not searching for a story; you're searching for a conspiracy." Sloan's voice was crisp. "You think I'm conducting the whole band?"

The two stood together in front of the bank of elevators.

"Quincy Jones, Jay Z, both could produce," Richman replied quickly. "Onstage, Tyler Sloan orchestrated every beat in the band, every strobe light, even each word of your introduction."

"I'm not that smart to have figured it all out, and I'm not that dumb to have tried. Sell the screen rights to Oliver Stone—he'd appreciate all your angles."

Sloan entered the elevator. Alone, he emitted a grave, body-shuddering shake. Richman was piecing together a damaging puzzle. One headline could deliver him to the United States Senate; another drop him off the cliff of political oblivion. Instead of hitting the penthouse button, Sloan hit the open arrows. He rushed outside toward Richman, who was nearing his car.

"Ted!" he called, and the reporter turned. "Sorry, I got a little hot there." He was huffing as he reached him. A quick confirmation, this conversation was off the record.

Sloan placed his hand on Richman's shoulder with a comforting squeeze. "You're right; my turn to give you one." Sloan began to tell Richman about Collins's appearance on Tammy Keller's FOX News show, but Richman waved his hand to dismiss the news. "I got that press release yesterday."

Sloan wore a gentle smile. "Who's the special guest?"

"The president. Old news. I got that one yesterday too."

"If you were in college, you'd get a gentlemen's C. You're looking at the *extraordinary* guest. It's a birthday surprise for Chris. I'm walking on after a couple of minutes."

Richman nodded with a congratulatory smile. "What's your game plan?"

"Still figuring it out; probably hit her contributions from special interests."

"Demand another debate," Richman said quickly. "I'll write it, keep it ready, and send it out the second you walk off stage."

The reporter cracked a smile before his expression changed to a disturbing seriousness. "Ah…" he started and then stopped.

Sloan could not discern if Richman's unbroken stare was one of pity or sympathy. "Tell me," Sloan said softly, attempting to mask his worry.

"Not sure when and not sure how, but someone is going to ask you, just bluntly ask you"—Richman paused—"about your brother's car crash." Richman glanced upward as if to summon courage. "It's terrible to pry into a death in the family. It'll hurt your pop. One reporter asked me if the *Times* ever looked into the cause of the crash."

Sloan's pulse raced. His jaw locked; he could not speak.

Richman's words were slow. The reporter was obviously pained.

Sloan motioned for more.

"One reporter asked if I was aware, had suspicious if you met with the county coroner, or if an autopsy was done. The *Times* never looked, never asked."

Sloan pulsated with mixed emotions, anger, and sorrow colliding in his gut. He steadied himself. When Richman explained that was all he knew, Sloan lightly bumped fists with the reporter and turned away.

* * *

Sloan was sipping from his wineglass, mulling over Richman's last comment. Noticing Bree's nearly empty glass, would he be a gentleman or a scoundrel to pour her one more? A pause, uncertain of her reaction. It was well past nine o'clock; he'd be pushing the envelope to go much later.

Her denim jeans were snug, titillating. She placed one hand on her hip, an alluring statement of strength and sex. She stood at the window, viewing the Strip from his condominium. She sang a song's chorus, "Dance, summer, dance."

"That song fits a night like this," she said, turning to him.

"Glad you like it." He walked toward the window, closer to her.

She smiled. "Not as good as your stuff, but catchy."

"It was catchy when I wrote it twenty-five years ago. The song you know is a cover."

"My bad." She covered her mouth in an exaggerated display of horror. "Really?"

"Really." He returned a nod, intent on not being smug.

He gave a short riff on his style and method of songwriting. He recalled with pride how one critic compared his lyrics when he was young, which were typical boy-girl romance, praising the depth of his songs as they evolved into reflecting loneliness, despair, mysterious women, and questioning authority. "I don't write a lot now, just fool around a little at the piano."

"You've got a hundred different playlists. Do you really need more?"

He admired how Bree could be an intellectual gladiator, analyzing methods to eviscerate his opponents, but a moment later, she was a nurturing soul. Filled with an urge to share more of himself, he was rambling about family memories and the antics he and his brother shared with their parents.

"It's nice, satisfying to look back at memories," she said.

"No, it's never the past. All of those little snippets are you, right now in the present," Sloan continued, then stopped, giving more at her urging. "I recently rummaged through a box of family videos and letters. My mom found some pot in my closet and told my dad. He was back in DC; he called and chewed me out." He was still tentative. "Fair enough. Then I got a letter from Washington telling me to straighten up, to follow my brother's lead." Sloan wanly smiled. "He had no clue J.R. sold me the stuff. My brother was always the chosen one, until he wasn't."

"You…" Her voice was comforting but uncertain. "You kept that letter?"

He understood it was an odd memory to share, disjointed to the moment. In a different time and place, he would move to touch her, hold her, run his fingers through her hair. He inched closer, ostensibly to the window to share the view. He was ready. He believed she was ready, but…"How's Mr. Solid?" Sloan asked in a not-so-oblique reference to her fiancé.

"Josh will be in town tomorrow for a couple of days." Her voice was devoid of enthusiasm as she detailed a litany of the problems in their relationship. She stammered, "I'm telling him tomorrow that it's over."

He steadied himself to not reveal any reaction. They were distant enough that he could use the panoramic view as a subterfuge. He noticed the top button of her blouse was unbuttoned, uncertain when or how that occurred. More important was whether the button accidentally was loose, or not. His hand momentarily drifted out, close to touching her, but then he drew it back. Her reaction could dart in too many directions.

"Nice shoes," he said casually as he gazed down at her high heels. He mentally slapped himself for the silly comment.

"There are moments when stilettos"—she wore a delicious smile— "are comfort shoes."

Their eyes locked. Neither budged. A quick gesture for her to follow down the hallway. Once arrived, he opened the room's double doors with a flourish.

"Wow," Bree exclaimed in awe of the large white piano that dominated the room.

Sloan sat at the piano's bench and began to play. He sang scattered verses. "The King wore the mask; I'm fighting through, up to the task."

After a silent moment, Bree said, "In that song, you're searching, you're struggling." She snapped her fingers. "It's about you and your dad."

Sloan allowed a smile. "Not a bad guess."

She moved to sit on the bench next to him, then scooted closer. Her mere presence sparked a tingling rush. She gestured to the adjacent master bedroom. "Is this the pit stop to the bedroom?" She grazed her fingers on the piano's hard rock maple wood. She tapped a couple of keys, marveling at the piano's clarity.

"Great pianos respond, almost anticipate my every desire," Sloan breathed.

"Better than a woman?" Bree grazed his fingers as they rested on the piano.

Sloan rested his hand on her fingers. "What do you want?" His words were safe but leading.

"It's time for the choice." Her voice was seductive.

Sloan held his smile.

"Another glass of wine," she continued, "or we call it a night."

She was close enough that he could touch her anywhere he desired.

Her head was tilted, her lips enticing. "You know the Beyoncé song?"—her words flowing with innuendo—"the song about whether baby wants to slow it down?'"

His body was surging with teenage testosterone, yet he checked himself. Danger was looming above his next words.

"I don't think this baby"—she pointed to herself in a coquettish manner a debutante would envy, then looked at Sloan—"or this baby wants to slow it down."

"Bree." He reached out his fingers lightly, grazing her cheek. He caressed her face; then his fingertips rested upon her full lips. Their lips met, tenderly, gently. Their kisses turned passionate. Deeper. His fingers slid to lightly brush the outline of her breasts. Sloan's passion was burning; he imagined their bodies entwined—yet he slightly disengaged.

"What's wrong?" she asked with obvious worry.

"Nothing. You're a vision, you're smart, you're beautiful..."

She appeared hurt. "There's a *but* there."

Sloan described how much he wanted to take her in the other room. Now. Right now.

"But?"

He responded with a litany of "should haves" and "should not haves" with various women in his life. "You're the right woman, but it's the wrong time." He kissed her lips. "I'm giving you a rain check. We'll go to Paris after the election. I'll make it special for you."

Bree did not respond. He was unable to gauge her reaction. Was she thrilled at the invite or irritated with him for turning her down? Far too much silence filled the room. The still was broken as her cell phone rang in the next room. She looked at him, gestured with one finger as if she welcomed the break to determine her response. She rose silently from the piano bench and left the room. When she returned, she appeared shaken. He knew there was more at play here than what had just transpired.

"I never thought he'd be covering you...and not be such a jerk," Bree stated, desperation in her voice. "No, he's a real prick."

Sloan stood, his palms open. "No clue what you're talking about."

Bree muttered scattered phrases: "I should have told you, but I never imagined."

"You're not making sense. Slow down. What should you have told me?"

"Josh doesn't like you, but you knew that." Bree closed the distance between them.

"How do I know that? I've never met the guy."

"My fiancé is a reporter, the guy who fires cheap shots at you—Josh David Mack. That was him on the phone just now. He was asking me if I was 'getting cozy with that loser rocker.'"

"What?" Sloan shouted. "Your fiancé is *that* Josh? When in the hell were you going to tell me? Jesus, Bree…" He walked away from her; a Kafkaesque nightmare was threatening. "Damn it, Bree! Don't you think you owed me that? Right now," he commanded. "Tell me exactly what he knows about the campaign. And…how does he know you're here? How in the hell does he know?"

Sloan took two steps toward her, dumbfounded at the whirl of events.

"Nothing. He knows nothing." She was clearly rattled, her words rapid. She was not aware Mack would be at DC's High Noon Club until after that meeting. She assumed that would be Mack's only contact, but then he was assigned to cover Sloan during the last month.

"When was the last time you slept with him?" Sloan snapped.

"It's not what you think." She moved closer to Sloan. "Please trust me on this."

"When?"

"We spent a weekend together in San Francisco before you first contacted me. After that weekend, I knew it was over."

Sloan retreated. He mentally kicked himself; a tragic misread. "You should leave. I need time, time alone," he said evenly, checking his temper.

Bree nodded; her expression soured. She kept her distance, muttering goodbyes, and left.

Fifteen minutes later, Sloan's phone rang.

"We have to talk," Bree said with disturbing urgency.

"It's late."

Bree sobbed. "Please don't hang up."

"I'm listening."

"Josh was downstairs waiting for me. He's following me home right now."

Sloan pushed his voice to calm; he could not panic her.

"He confronted me outside your condo. He accused us of having an affair. I denied it. Said we're working late, but…he didn't believe me—especially after I lied to him about where I was."

"How did he know you were here?"

Her voice cracked. "He hired a private detective."

Sloan heard sobs and labored breaths. He urged her to relax.

"I'm OK. Josh insists on seeing you." Her voice quivered. "He said if you refuse, he'll release photos on his web page."

"Photos?" Sloan scanned his memory for any recent damaging photos. "Photos of what?"

"The fucking creep has photos of me leaving your condo and others of the two of us near your home. They're all date and time stamped."

"But we didn't do anything."

"He's nuts." Her voice composed, instantly switching to consultant mode. "Meet him and defuse this. If any photos leak, we'll be playing defense until the election."

Sloan exhaled deeply. A spurned lover inside the press corps was far from nirvana. "I'll meet him." He let a moment pass. "Look, we'll be fine; we'll figure it out. Give me a couple of days."

"I'll set something up."

When Sloan went to bed, sleep did not come easily. His feelings for Bree had morphed—the morning before, he was singing in the shower, the old standard about how she made him feel so young, but now his anger was self-directed. How foolish to expose his feelings to her. Was he blind to the age difference? Should he have avoided a personal relationship?

"That fucking Mack," he muttered.

THIRTY-ONE

August 13, Los Angeles,
9 Days to the Election

**Poll: Collins 37%, Sloan 30%,
Rogers 21%, Undecided 12%**

Sloan tiptoed up the stairs of Cindy's Malibu home; Zimmer and Mike Sloan waited in the living room. He quietly opened the double doors to the master bedroom. Pausing to scan the room, a momentary lapse recalling pleasant times, cherishing its ocean view. He mentally slapped himself—no time for a stroll down memory lane. He moved toward the master bathroom and opened Cindy's medicine cabinet. Her absence was the perfect opportunity to do some digging.

His eyes raced to scan the various medicines. He turned the bottles to read the labels for sleep aids, pain relievers, and anxiety meds. All the prescriptions were recent, and none of the containers were full. Cindy had two primary doctors; Dr. Goldman, in Brentwood, prescribed the bulk of the medications. He lined up the containers and took a photo of each on his phone: Percodan, Xanax, Ambien, Vicodin, and Darvon. *My God,* he thought, *she's got a damn pharmacy in here.*

He tiptoed out of the bedroom and hastily made his way back downstairs to await Riley, who was visiting with a friend on the front lawn. Upon Riley's return to the house, they walked together to her bedroom.

"I didn't do anything wrong." Sloan's words were soft. Riley's body stiffened, her eyes narrowed as they sat on her bed. Her room was filled with photographs she had taken, including a series of photos of Sloan she had recast as a Warhol-style montage canvas on the wall.

Riley was no longer the gleeful toddler who'd played so often with Sloan at the local park that she called it "Daddy's Park." That little girl was beyond his command.

Sloan was gripped in a role reversal, feeling the unease of a wayward child pleading innocence to his parents. Events were swirling; he needed to cushion Riley from a pending media storm. As he held her hand, his voice was calm. "I'm human; I made mistakes." He moved to discuss his past use of cocaine. He did not qualify or try to explain it away, and he was grateful she did not ask many questions.

"That's OK, Daddy; I know you're good now." She reached over to give him a hug.

He decided to be preemptive, telling her Bree's fiancé was a reporter who was mad at Bree for ending their relationship. The reporter was angry and jealous of Sloan. "He might say some things or post some things that are not true. There were some old videotapes when I was a young guy; some might be embarrassing."

Sloan watched her, still holding her hand, cursing himself for past errors he could not erase with time or words.

She appeared puzzled. He was unable to discern if she wanted to hear more, or the whole idea repulsed her. He calculated each of Riley's reactions, bothered that her shoulders slumped, appearing more vulnerable, struggling to assimilate each tidbit.

"I like Bree, and maybe one day we'll date, but right now we're just working together. I'll let you know if that ever changes."

"Bree's cool," she said quickly, her smile reassuring.

"You're right about that." Sloan matched her smile.

He once measured Riley's growth by her choice of Halloween costumes. When she was barely walking, she wore a bunny costume and held tight to Daddy's hand, frightened by older children in costumes of pirates, witches, and ghouls. A couple of years later, she was a little princess. For the last two Halloweens, she had had no desire to be with either parent, a small but understandable rite of passage.

"You wrote a lot of songs about women, but you don't have much luck with them," Riley said sympathetically.

He glanced behind her at the photograph of the dimpled kindergarten girl with Cindy, both wearing dresses and pearls. Behind that frame was a black-and-white picture Riley took of him huddled in a jacket on an overcast morning amid the antiquities of Rome's Forum; that image graced *Star* magazine. It was Riley's first payday.

She smiled when they discussed her joining him for the campaign's final days. He kissed her good night and assured her he'd be there until her mother returned home from her "appointment." Then he gestured to the photograph. "Remember when we went to the Coliseum? Now we're the campaign gladiators."

"We'll kick the lion's ass," she said with animation before enveloping him in a warm embrace.

* * *

While Sloan was upstairs, Zimmer and Mike viewed the latest Collins ad on Zimmer's laptop. The first image was of a long-haired young man in a courtroom, standing awkwardly in a one-size-too-small suit, leaning down, and whispering to his client. "Just passed the bar; today's my first trial." The ad continued with a young woman in surgical scrubs, a nervous smile, and raised hands: "My first open-heart surgery."

An elevator door opened at a Las Vegas high-rise building. A gruff young man in a worker's uniform rolled a cart filled with tools out of the elevator. "Try it…I think it's working." The announcer added solemnly, "The United States Senate is not *American Idol.* Senator Sloan?" A series of laughs closed the ad.

"It's a good sign." Mike nodded. "This ad is a good sign." His voice was low to ensure Sloan could not overhear them. "She's going after Tyler. Her polls show her it's either her or Tyler—Rogers is history."

Zimmer sought confirmation that Mike would return to Nevada for the final week. As Mike appeared to reflect on the request, Zimmer wondered how this father-son relationship had become so entangled that he was the one who had to ask; he was the designated closer of the deal.

Mike's words were slow to form. He questioned how his son could achieve political fame so quickly. He restated his own thirty-plus years in politics, how he had knocked on doors when he first ran for the state assembly, his years in Congress, followed by two terms as governor of California. Mike was puzzled by how his son could step off the stage and, in ninety days, establish himself in a campaign for the US Senate.

"Tyler was a long-haired kid who smoked pot, chased girls, and sang. His brother was the one who always wanted to attend the rallies, sit in the governor's chair. Tyler barely came by the Capitol. Now… I should meddle in his business?"

Zimmer patted Mike's hand. "Governor…"

"Please," Mike said kindly, "it's Mike, not Governor."

"Mike, I don't have a son, and my dad and I had our ups and downs. Yet we always knew we could count on each other."

"Why didn't Tyler's campaign seek and use every list and contact I had?" he asked with annoyance. "Damn it, I won the Nevada primary six years ago, not *sixty* years ago. He's running away from everything I built. He thinks I'm a damn cooler."

Mike was referring to the old gambling term for a down-on-his-luck guy who the casino would direct to stand near a player on a hot winning streak to cool the winning roll.

Zimmer slowed his voice. "Trust me. Tyler needs and wants you. Come to Nevada and saddle up, ol' cowboy—with your skills in the last week, we can win this."

Mike nodded at Zimmer's urging. "What else is going on?"

"I took a meeting with Morgan in LA."

"You *took* a meeting?" Mike queried. "You met with him?"

Zimmer explained he *convinced* Morgan to deliver two copies of the video, but unfortunately, Rogers had a copy. He detailed his plan to weave Morgan and Rogers together and have the video released. "I've seen the video." He smiled. "Collins had a great ass…and so does Tyler."

"He's got good genes. What do you think? Let's play out the politics."

"If it airs, Collins may gain some sympathy votes, but it diminishes her. She looks like a drunken tramp. If we play it right, Rogers will be the scumbag who released it. Tyler will get votes after women turn on Rogers. Morgan is prepped. When should he hold his presser?"

"Let me noodle on it," Mike said. He stared away to gather his thoughts. He rose and walked in a circle, starting to speak and then halting. "The whole thing is a Faustian bargain, and Morgan sounds like an unsteady vessel," Mike spoke clinically, the medical professor lecturing students on dissecting a body in medical school.

Zimmer added that the results of the video were consistent in every poll and focus group—the candidate who leaked the tape would have blood on their hands. He recalled one woman in a focus group wanted to "castrate a candidate who would air that video."

"On a scale of one to ten, how certain are you that Rogers will lose votes?"

"Eleven. He'll be the scumbag and Collins the tramp. I don't *think* Tyler would be hurt, at least not much."

"Not with his past—he'll be viewed as a lovable, incorrigible rascal." Mike smiled, perhaps in admiration. "A rascal always beats a scumbag and a tramp. Rogers looked desperate at the debate, like a rubber-legged boxer answering the bell for the final round."

"When does Morgan do his presser?" Zimmer asked again.

"Friday morning," Mike barked with certainty. "It'll dominate the media. Tyler goes on the tube Saturday as the victim. Rogers sputters his denial, but he'll look sleazy. Poor Collins, the woman wearing the scarlet letter." His smile grew to a magnificent glow. "That's a hell of a ticket to punch to the Senate."

"When do we run it by Tyler?" Zimmer asked. "We have to run it by him…don't we?"

Mike shook his head. "After the election. He'll thank us, but I don't want him to veto this. Act now and ask for forgiveness later."

"Maybe I hint with him? Test his reaction?"

"No." Mike smiled. "Like the old TV show, on this one, *Father Knows Best*."

When Sloan rejoined the men, he suggested his father go upstairs to say good night to Riley. Alone with Zimmer, he showed his attorney the photos from his cell phone. With Zimmer's nod of approval, he sent Zimmer a copy; the photo captured each medication Cindy was taking. Cindy was still seeing the same doctor since they were married. He asked Zimmer again for his plan.

Zimmer nonchalantly raised his hand, his signal that there was no need for worry.

"It can't be traced back to me," Sloan said, keeping his voice low but urgent. "You're sure you know someone who knows this doctor? You sure you have a guy?"

"Tyler," Zimmer replied with a confident smile, "there's *always* a guy."

THIRTY-TWO

August 14, Las Vegas,
8 Days to the Election

Poll: Collins 38%, Sloan 30%, Rogers 22%, Undecided 10%

"Our long-distance romance is not working," Sloan said the moment his father came on the line. He could no longer delegate this to Zimmer. It was an early-morning call, assuming correctly that Mike was home. "We started to talk about this last night in LA but got distracted. Look, I need you here. It's your choice: stay at the house or condo. I'll have a driver for you." He was irritated at his vulnerability when asking for his father's help. He felt like a child asking for one more scoop of ice cream.

"Martino called me," Mike said.

Following a pregnant pause, Sloan asked, "And?"

Mike summarized the story. Martino had been sitting in the waiting room at his dentist's office in San Francisco when the FBI agents

Martino had negotiated with made additional demands. "Martino pushed back," Mike continued. "He told them he'd already given them the audio files they wanted, and he'd done his part."

"Was my name mentioned?" Sloan asked, his voice low but rapid.

"Not a word about you. Martino assured me of that," Mike said, easing his fears.

"So, is he out of the woods?"

"The agents demanded that he testify." Mike chuckled. "He told them to go fuck themselves. He's back. That's the Martino I know. He told them he was done, or they could see the man in the black robes."

"Do *you* think it's over?"

"Can't say for certain, but he's lawyered up and sounded positive."

Sloan pondered it all. The hostility he'd felt toward Martino had diminished, but not the fear of the repercussions if Martino was publicly named. He had hoped to speak to his father in person, but Mike had deftly avoided responding to his request to join him, so he decided now would have to do. "Dad," he began slowly, biting down on his lip, the words difficult for him, presuming they would shock his father, "Richman tipped me off: a reporter is investigating J.R.'s death."

"Why?" Mike blurted.

"You know the story is often in the cover-up."

"Is there no shame?" Mike snapped. "Damn, damn, damn." His voice trailed… "I'm still devastated."

"Me too."

Sloan and Mike rarely discussed J.R. Sloan had learned years before that the subject was too raw for each of them.

"Richman wanted to prepare me, and I wanted you to be prepared." A moment passed while Sloan allowed Mike to fully absorb the news. Then he began again with as much encouragement as he could muster. "Dad, my campaign needs the master's touch." He instantly worried that was too much sugar.

Again, Mike didn't respond to the request and instead cautioned Sloan on what could transpire in a campaign's final week. "Do you remember on the eve of the Iowa caucuses, my press secretary was arrested for lewd and lascivious conduct in a park bathroom…with another guy? How about that idiot staffer who used my campaign app to send out nasty rumors about other candidates? Son, expect the unexpected."

"I've only watched the Weather Channel, but you've been in the eye of the hurricane." Unsure how to fill the ensuing dead air, Sloan continued, his voice skipping along, "The campaign winds are blowing wild and free; the political waves are crashing against the rocks."

"Good lyrics for a song, but what the hell does that mean?"

"It means I need your help," Sloan replied meaningfully.

The sounds of silence engulfed the conversation. Sloan's pride was bruised, but he'd had little choice. It was now or never.

"Ah…" Mike began and then halted with a pronounced sigh. "I wasn't around enough for you when you were young, but Tyler, I believe in you. I *always* have…I just didn't know how to express it. You were always independent, not like your brother. I knew where I stood with J.R. I knew I had to help J.R. With you, I never could figure it out; but I knew you were the strong one, the one I didn't have to worry about." After a moment, he said, "I was right about that."

Sloan slowly shook his head at how wrong his father had been. He'd always needed Mike. This was a time for truth now: sharing his own instincts recognizing his older brother's weaknesses, J.R.'s inability to relate to others, his few friends. Life came naturally to him. The roles had been reversed The younger brother was the mentor, hiring J.R., loaning him money that both knew would never be repaid, and finally, protecting him after his passing. It was a burden often too heavy to discuss; some things were best unsaid.

"Dad, that's all past, it's—"

"No," Mike said firmly. "I should have told you how proud I was of you. I should have expressed my feelings. You deserved that. Look at you. You're an admirable man, a *great* man."

Sloan's eyes closed, head bowed, unaccustomed to his father's affirmation. Mike elaborated on his feelings, citing his own shortcomings, his inability to express his pride in his son, his failure to reveal his emotions. His voice finally trailed off, and then he added quickly, "I'm flying in tomorrow. I'll call you when the eagle lands."

* * *

Tyler Sloan stole and deceptively edited Chris Collins's personal property. That's a new low in political campaigns…and that's saying a lot. Mr. Sloan has exited from the political high road and landed in a muddy swamp.

Sloan read the online *Reno Gazette*. The newspaper had switched from a "no endorsement" to endorse Collins. The editorial cited her "innovative ideas" and, in a pretzel twist of logic, praised her flippant remarks that aired in his commercials and showered Sloan in a firestorm of condemnation. Sloan's analysis of the endorsement's impact was interrupted when Bree rushed into his campaign office.

"Your security team just told me," Bree sputtered. "There's a GPS on your car…and mine."

"What?" Sloan exclaimed, rising from his desk chair.

Bree walked in a circle. Her every word was riddled with anger and confusion. She explained that the GPS was "military issued."

"Military?" Sloan asked. "Collins's man, Rails? Those bastards knew where we were every minute. Every fucking minute."

Bree waved her hands in the air, clearly agitated, seemingly confused. "This must be connected to Josh. When he said he'd hired a private detective, I should've known that was ridiculous. He doesn't have any money. He's working with Collins's campaign. That's how he was keeping such close track."

"Have my security team sweep my house and condo—and your apartment too."

"I'm on it," she assured him. "And you have an appointment with Josh in an hour."

Sloan held a steady gaze on Bree. He silently cursed the damn luck of finding himself caught in a lover's triangle with Bree and the reporter.

Fighting his feelings of being foolish, believing he had matured past this nonsense. Jealousy was never a quality that gripped him, but now he realized its hold on him. "I'm ready for the bastard."

* * *

At the scheduled time, Sloan plastered a smile on his face, ready to mount a charm offensive as Josh David Mack entered the office. The men shook hands, and Sloan pointed out his sports memorabilia and entertainment posters mounted on the walls, attempting to elicit casual conversation from the reporter. Mack appeared bored by the niceties, and Sloan signaled for him to join him at the more inviting couch and seating area. Every time Sloan attempted to build a comfort factor, Mack returned a hard stare.

"Seen any shows in town?" he gently inquired.

"No time."

"How long have you been a reporter?"

"Long enough."

"Where are you from?"

"I was a Cub Scout, but I'm not here to talk about my merit badges."

Sloan observed the obvious as irritating smugness crept across Mack's face. The young man wore the look of a handsome, anger-filled geek.

"If you agree," Mack said, "nothing we say goes beyond this room, and the photos of you and that red-haired mistake I made, they'll never hit the internet."

Sloan forced a casual smile as he reclined on the black leather sofa. Mack sat across from him with a body language capable of compacting steel.

"Bree is my aide," Sloan said quickly. "There's no romance between us."

"Two a.m.," Mack said, and then repeated it with more menace. "*Two a.m.* My people watched your condo for weeks—everyone left early, but my *fiancée* stayed until *two a.m.* Think I'm stupid? Don't bullshit me."

Mack leaned forward, and Sloan braced himself. The reporter had gone through a body scan before he entered the suite, and the security cameras were watching his every move, but with a character like him, Sloan guessed anything was possible. He relaxed when Mack shifted his weight back from him.

"You said 'my people'?" Sloan stated. "Who paid for the private detective?" Mack's gaze darted away from Sloan in response.

"You're being used," Sloan said simply, pushing without pressing.

Mack scowled.

"You know she keeps odd hours," Sloan went on. "Sure, one night, it was late, but I'm an old singer. I'm on Vegas time—we end late; we start late." He stretched out his hands to convey comfort. "There's no problem here."

"I said no bullshit," Mack snapped. "A hot girl like Bree leaves your place at two, and nothing happened? I read that girls used to stalk you, and this campaign hasn't slowed you down."

"I'm not the reason for your breakup," Sloan advised in a tone akin to a friendly uncle's. "I've been there, every guy has. Go back to school. Live well—that's the best revenge."

"You're in the Rock and Roll Hall of Fame, and the best you got is, 'Live well is the best revenge'?"

Mack flashed him a psychotic grin. Sloan was ready to signal at the camera, the one signal that would summon security.

Mack's voice was sharp and loud. "Don't fuck with me!"

Sloan did his best to muster a stoic expression.

"You want a photo of you two partying late at night going viral?" Mack's voice quickened. "Maybe someone even starts a rumor you're back on the powder."

The two men exchanged measuring glances.

"Let's reach an understanding, and have this thing disappear," Mack said more calmly.

Sloan's stomach clenched, trying to remain calm despite the ring of fire from a spurned lover.

"Wire one million dollars to my account, and you'll get the chip with all the photos." Sloan scrutinized the reporter. The mere posting of late-night photos of him with Bree—even if they were simply standing side by side—would divert media attention and place him on the defensive in the final days of the campaign. With his history, images of him with a beautiful woman half his age could be interpreted to mean he was more "player" than a senator.

"Deal or no deal?" Mack demanded.

Sloan held his stare, noticing the slight shaking of Mack's hand.

"Twenty-four hours." Mack was licking his lips. "Your opponents want to mess you up. When they're done, you'll be like that washed-up guy in your movie singing for dollar tips." He grinned with pleasure. "Those dudes have so much shit on you."

"Out!" Sloan's shout startled the young reporter. He pointed to the door. "Screw you! Out! Leave in the next five seconds, or my security team will have your nuts rolling down the hallway in opposite directions."

Mack's eyebrows popped high; he nearly jumped off the sofa. As he hurried to the door, he shouted without turning back, "Twenty-four hours!"

"Out!" Sloan commanded.

The moment the door slammed behind Mack, Sloan heard his security team talking to the reporter. He worried about him posting the photos, but any transfer of funds would be succumbing to blackmail. Either scenario could be political death. He needed to stall the spurned lover. His mind raced with ideas, some in conflict, some solid. His first thought was to have Bree contact Mack, tell him he had reconsidered and would wire the funds—he needed to buy a week.

* * *

Later that day, Sloan met backstage with Tammy Keller in her dressing room. The room's largess rivaled the dressing rooms he had frequented while performing. Keller had a private shower in the bathroom, a large walk-in closet lined with designer outfits, a long counter with abundant cosmetics, gels, powders, and hair-styling apparatus— all surrounded by seemingly never-ending mirrors and lights.

Minutes before her television show would air, Keller's eyes were closed as the makeup artist dabbed her forehead with a powder puff. Tonight, her one-hour, prime-time news-magazine show was being broadcast live from FOX News' Las Vegas affiliate.

The show's ratings had plummeted into a near-death abyss before the producer hired Keller as the host, airing a live broadcast and narrowing the show's focus to entertainment, soft news, and politics. The marriage of celebrities and politicians was an equal-opportunity venue for tearstained mea culpas for wayward behavior.

After Keller exited, Sloan remained behind in her room, along with his security detail. This is where he would watch the beginning of the show. Sitting in a living-room-style setting, Keller opened with her standard two-minute commentary on whatever event of the day had piqued her interest. She flashed her smile, turning her gaze to the camera to welcome President Reed, who appeared via satellite from the White House.

Reed was projecting strength from moment one. No matter the setting, his preternatural calm demonstrated a president in command. The camera selectively bestowed its gifts, and Reed instinctively understood how to use those gifts.

Keller floated mandatory softball questions before shifting her intensity. "Is the Nevada Senate election a referendum on your legacy?"

"My friends in Nevada have a clear choice." Reed deferred a direct answer.

"How do you define the choice, Mr. President?"

"Ms. Collins's tax scheme would punish the middle class and strip our military's readiness. That will not happen on my watch."

"And Mr. Rogers?" she asked in a tantalizing tone.

Sloan braced with hope and anxiety at Reed's forthcoming answer.

"My concerns about Mr. Rogers are with his economic views." The president was firm but friendly. "There are limits on government spending; only so many cookies in the jar."

"Where does that leave you, Mr. President?" She was oozing with respect.

"I'm more focused on the country than a political party."

Sloan smiled in anticipation. Reed had dissed both of his opponents.

Reed's earnest midwestern calm was on full display. "Tyler Sloan is certainly qualified to serve in the United States Senate. He would serve Nevada and this nation well." The president paused for a moment. "He would be an outstanding senator."

"Yes," Sloan said aloud, thrusting his fist upward.

His two security guards rarely expressed their emotions, but they both gave him flashing smiles, and one repeatedly pumped his fist in the air.

Keller paused with a slight smile. Fair and balanced were annoying gnats compared to the controversy of Reed's failure to embrace Rogers. The interview concluded as Keller gazed into the camera. "We'll have Chris Collins in our studio after this break."

Zimmer had secured a "meringue-layered agreement" with Keller's producer. Reed was the foundational bottom, and Sloan was the icing.

Sloan left the dressing room, standing undetected in the wings. From that vantage point, he was able to study Collins and her Rose Bowl Queen smile as she sat across from Keller. Keller's first questions floated like fluffy chiffon puffs. Collins had survived more robust interviews on her own infomercials.

"Voters are questioning Tyler Sloan's ambition," Collins said, delving into attack mode. "He wants his first job off the stage to seize control of the United States Senate?"

As Collins delivered a monologue of criticism of the "wannabe" senator, Sloan made his way onto the stage with long, confident strides. "I thought I heard my name," he announced, wearing his signature smile. Collins's voice died away, and Sloan extended his hand forward for a shake, receiving a limp response. He took a seat on Keller's right. His mere appearance pushed the high-speed button on the political blender.

Collins instinctively returned to the camera as her comfort food. She shifted in her chair, shaken by Sloan's appearance. "Here's your chance, Tyler. Tell Nevada voters which taxes you want to raise."

Prepared, he flashed a warm smile. "To quote a president from your own party, 'There you go again.'"

"That's no answer," Collins charged. "No doubt you're skilled deflecting straightforward questions, but the people of Nevada deserve answers. That's what they're looking for in their senator."

Appearing to be enjoying the political cage match, Tammy asked, "Mr. Sloan, *exactly* how did your campaign obtain Ms. Collins's commercial?"

"As I said, it was delivered anonymously. That video was *not* stolen, nor was it edited." Sloan was calm. "The video is authentic; those were her words, not mine."

When they first met, back in the day, Sloan appreciated Collins's intuitive skills to slither, twirl, and coo. Now her stare into the camera confirming her skill set was transformed. One smile signaled her intentions were to slice Sloan with a soundbite.

"Mr. Sloan excels at diversion; he's a charlatan," Collins said quickly. "He claims to not be raising funds from special interests, but he has his independent committees raising millions."

"I've restricted contributions to one hundred dollars or less, raised more small donations than anyone in a Senate campaign." One smile softened his next comment. "In contrast, your campaign has been propped up by over fifty million dollars from outside special interests and Washington lobbyists. Let's compare contributions."

Keller's smile grew broad at the skyrocketing ratings-palooza.

"Mr. Sloan, is your character a legitimate issue?" Keller asked.

The director waved a finger in the air.

"I'll match my character against Ms. Collins and her Wall Street special interests and Washington lobbyists." He turned to Collins. "Chris, let's agree right now to one final debate. You pick the time and place."

Off camera the director waved for a wrap-up and cut to a commercial.

"We'll be back," Keller announced, leaning forward in her chair as if she were as excited as the audience to hear Collins's reply.

The makeup artist descended on the interviewer, and Sloan stood with a direct look at his opponent. She hopped up from her seat and quickly closed the distance between them.

"You think you can get by on your charm and good looks?" she spat out, her voice no louder than a whisper. "You're going down. Tell me, did you and that young girl—uh, what's her name, *Bree?*—enjoy your little rendezvous around the lake and all those late nights in your condo?" She moved inches from Sloan's face, her voice curt. "Don't be so damn smug. We've got a couple of guys from your old band lined up to tell your adoring public how you guys snorted coke off groupies' tits."

Sloan returned her iron gaze. She was close enough to kiss him but angry enough to bite his lips off. "You've got a past, too, Chris."

"Debate you? If it snows on the Strip next week, we'll debate. If not...fuck you," Collins fumed. Her lips trembled with anger. "I'll rip your heart out if that video ever airs." Her voice was deadly, menacing.

"If it airs, it won't have anything to do with me," Sloan whispered back. "Rogers has it—he'll probably air it; his only chance is to blow this race up."

Collins's face drained of color. She stammered incoherently before spinning on one heel and retaking her seat.

THIRTY-THREE

Tuesday, August 15, Las Vegas,
7 Days to the Election

Poll: Collins 38%, Sloan 30%,
Rogers 23%, Undecided 9%

The caller ID flashed "Mike Sloan," and Sloan switched over to take the call.

"You're late," Mike said bluntly. "I'm in the parking lot, in a black Audi."

Sloan directed the driver of the campaign SUV to park next to the Audi that was only a short distance away.

"These housing activists," Mike said quickly, as he slid into the back seat beside Sloan.

"These groups are always begging for more. They want the government to rob Peter to pay Paul. And, remember, the world is filled with more Pauls than Petes."

Sloan raised an eyebrow.

Shortly after that, the two men—surrounded by security guards and a bevy of cameras—walked the short distance to a newly constructed low-income housing apartment building in North Las Vegas.

The sun blazed as a group of youngsters kicked around a soccer ball on a small patch of grass adjacent to the building. The young Latino boys froze in play when Sloan joined them. Mike watched off to the side adjacent to the camera crew.

Sloan dribbled the ball from foot to foot and then slammed it into the net. The group of boys cheered. "Goal! Goal! Goal!" one shouted in his best announcer's voice.

Sloan smiled—shameless media hype, but the boys enjoyed it. His entourage made their way into the building and was escorted into the meeting room. His entry met with cheers and whispers from mostly minority constituents; Mike's presence clearly startled several of the attendees.

After Sloan's opening remarks, Alice Wesson, the executive director of Southern Nevada's Community Core, posed the first question. Her granny dress resembled a Woodstock-era artifact taken hostage from a 1965 tie-dyed time warp. She voiced displeasure that Sloan had failed to support community nonprofit groups.

Sloan was filled with patience, reminding her that the blue foundation bestowed a grant upon the Senior Housing Group, who built eighty apartment units the previous year in Reno.

"The Senior Housing Group is a *regional* group—not a *community* group, Mr. Sloan. They don't represent the community." Alice's tone rebuffed any sense of irony.

Sloan was indifferent to the distinction, responding in supple phrases within a smoky haze. He gauged the reaction; almost everyone listening was smiling with a warm glow. Success in political math was to add, not subtract, votes. He noticed his father's admiring gaze on him.

The room buzzed with side conversations, and one man, weighing three hundred pounds on his best day, hushed the audience to silence: "Respect for a great entertainer!"

Sloan seized the moment to introduce Mike. "The man himself is here, my dad. *Mi padre*, Governor Mike Sloan." Despite the scorching heat, Mike's beige suit remained perfectly pressed. Sloan was aware his father prided himself on his appearance, once described as "debonair." No rumpled suits for this man.

With his father at his side, he spoke extemporaneously, his voice slowing as he announced, "*La magia de esta comunidad es encontrada en su gente, en sus familias.*" He translated for the reporters: "The magic of this community is found in its people, in your families."

A sea of smiles emerged, and a few reporters shot surprised glances at one another. Aside from belting out a few verses of "La Bamba" on one occasion, Sloan had never publicly spoken in Spanish.

He gestured toward a young family and flashed his smile. "*Su sonrisa me recuerda ha la de mi hija.*" He repeated in English. "Her smile reminds me of my daughter." Then, his voice spiked sharply, "*Mi hermanas, mi hermanos.* I will not abandon you. *Yo no te abandonaré.* I will never abandon this fight. *Yo nunca te abandonaré en esta batalla.*"

At the hearty round of applause, Sloan felt confident he had won the day. That confidence was chilled as two well-dressed women began circulating throughout the room, distributing a newspaper reprint to the media and the seated activists. Sloan scanned the copy an aide handed to him.

A reporter from the local NBC affiliate held the reprint from the *LA Journal* up. "Is this true, Mr. Sloan: When asked about religion, you said that you find heaven between your girlfriend's thighs? And did you say that religion is a crutch strong people don't need?"

Sloan held one hand aloft, ostensibly signaling for additional time to finish reading the handout while scrambling to craft an answer. His gut fluttered, and he smiled, knowing how to avoid the "deer in the headlights look." He kept his eyes away from Mike, fearing even the most innocuous of glances could be its own separate story of needing "Daddy's help." This story was an easy-to-digest morsel to feed the media beast's voracious appetite in the campaign's final days.

"It's a defunct newspaper and an ancient story," Sloan said firmly, looking up, determined to project strength. "I was in my early twenties, and I hadn't had a chance to fully experience the joys and gifts of life. Like most young guys, I said stupid things. But the people who distributed this nonsense—my opponents—this is politics at its worst." He looked at the paper with a scowl. "Voters are wise to these political dirty tricks."

"*Which* opponent?" a local reporter called out.

Two reporters exchanged knowing glances.

"Who else would distribute an article older than half the people in this room?" Sloan held steady, running through former and current news anchors who would not stoop this low. "Neither Rachel Maddow nor Laura Ingraham would run with this drivel."

"Why did you single out *those* two reporters?" a female reporter asked harshly. "Exactly what are you implying about female journalists?"

"I'm not making any distinction between male and female," he responded, needed to dampen his frustration at the questioner's implication. "There are two of the many respected journalists who would not trump up thirty-year-old nonsense. My youthful ignorance is not a story."

"I have a more serious question," Alan Newcombe of the *New York Times* said from his seat in the front row. "And I apologize if this causes you grief, but…" He went on to summarize the death of Mike Sloan Jr.—J.R.—who died twenty years earlier at the age of thirty-two.

Sloan stole a quick glance at his father, whose lips were glued together in anger.

The reporter explained that the diary of the Los Angeles County coroner had been uncovered by a writer working on a tell-all on the deaths of various celebrities.

The coroner in question had earned himself the moniker "Coroner to the Stars" by critics due to his penchant for holding press conferences following a celebrity's death. The governor's son qualified for the status of his celebrity "clients."

Newcombe said that the diary detailed a meeting between the coroner and Grant Zimmer the day following the death of Mike Sloan Jr. "Mr. Sloan, did you or your father direct your counsel to meet with the coroner?"

"I did," Sloan replied without hesitation. "My attorney is not just my legal counsel. He is also a very close family friend. I trusted him to act on my behalf when I couldn't be there." An edge returned to his tone. "I hope you appreciate that this remains an excruciatingly painful subject for my father and me. I cannot fathom why you would raise these questions."

Newcombe popped out one more apology but detailed the string of events. J.R. died in a one-car automobile crash on Pacific Coast Highway at two in the morning. Two days after, Zimmer met with the coroner, who performed an autopsy that disclosed a blood alcohol level reflecting a small consumption, equal to one or two beers. No drugs were found in his system. The body was buried the following day, even before formal funeral services.

Sloan braced for the damning innuendos, and Newcombe promptly obliged. "Numerous eyewitness accounts placed Mike Sloan Jr. at a Malibu party that evening. Those same eyewitnesses reported to the county sheriff that he had been drinking alcohol, smoking pot, and snorting cocaine."

Sloan acknowledged that he had heard the same rumors. "However, I personally spoke with my brother's girlfriend, Amanda, who was at that party with him—a woman I trusted. She told me Mike had only two beers that night—that was it. My brother's crash and subsequent death were a tragedy—nothing more. He simply lost control of his car." Sloan paused. "Amanda would certainly corroborate these statements."

"She died a year later," Newcombe replied. "But, I believe you knew that." The reporter's voice was laced with the certainty of a trial lawyer building his case. He added that the coroner retired a month after Mike Jr.'s death, and two months later, he was driving a Mercedes S Class along the streets of Maui. "Do you think it's odd, Mr. Sloan, that a public servant who had lived in a modest suburban home and drove a county-issued Ford would suddenly splurge on a hundred-thousand-dollar car and a beachfront condominium?"

"I never met the man," he replied curtly. "I have no clue about his retirement plans. Only the coroner could answer why he chose Maui or why he traded in his Ford for a Mercedes."

"The coroner has Alzheimer's disease, Mr. Sloan, and I suspect you knew that as well." Newcombe was causing a stir. "So, his memory is not reliable."

"How hard did you question him, Mr. Newcombe?" Sloan returned the thrust, seeking to wound the reporter.

"I was respectful, Mr. Sloan," the reporter replied, as the tension mounted between the two. He glanced around the room. "I assure you and my colleagues of that."

The media was hanging on Newcombe's every word as he stitched together a potential scandal.

"Mr. Sloan," the reporter asked again, "did you have any knowledge of the coroner's home or car purchase?"

"How could I? I told you I never met the man. I had no direct dealings with him, and I was not privy to his personal life. Maybe he splurged in retirement. Who knows? What are you getting at?"

"With your success, you could have chartered a jet to rush to the hospital the night of your brother's death. Why didn't you do that? Why send your attorney to meet with the coroner on such a personal matter?" Newcombe pressed.

"I've already told you. My attorney is a close friend of the fam—"

"Get out of here with those questions!" Mike yelled. "Son, don't answer this crap."

All eyes turned at once to Mike, then back to Sloan.

Sloan raised his hand. He was prepared, but he could not appear too prepared. "My brother had just died, Mr. Newcombe. I could barely function from the emotional distress of losing my *only* brother. The fact that I didn't meet personally with the coroner is a nonissue. I hope you are not criticizing me for how I handled my grief?" A short pause, "Everyone grieves in their own manner."

The audience was nodding, appearing sympathetic to Sloan.

"Did your brother have a substance abuse problem?" Newcombe asked, his voice firm.

"I saw my brother drink too much on occasion." Sloan kept his tone even.

Sloan felt the media's delight—it was more than a parry and thrust between the two; it was an exchange of body blows.

Newcombe held a pause that was miles past meaningful. "Did you ever do drugs with your brother?"

Sloan glanced away from the reporter. His real audience was outside of this room. Every reporter craned forward, anxious to hear his response or watch him sink into a hole of sputtering admissions or disingenuous explanations.

His voice dropped. "We shared a beer or two—most brothers do. The pain is that I can never see my brother again. If you've never lost a close family member, you can't imagine the sorrow—you can't imagine the agony of a parent who has lost a child. I saw the agony on my parents' faces, and I see it now on my father's face." He stared at Newcombe. "Enough." He was calm but firm. "This story is old and closed. Your questions are inflicting needless pain on my family"—he turned to stare at Mike—"and they are irrelevant to this campaign."

* * *

Sitting at the breakfast table, gripped by fatigue, Sloan stared into the mirror. He was struggling to comprehend the blur of campaign events. He sat at the table with a pad and paper, engaging in his preferred ritual of jotting down the pluses and minuses.

The minuses were a series of bullet points: photographic innuendos of an affair with Bree, Martino's issues with the FBI, his admission of cocaine addiction, the ménage-à-trois video, and now Newcombe suggesting a cover-up surrounding his brother's death and autopsy report.

He recalled a quote from Ian Fleming's 007 series about how James Bond judged a string of peculiar events: "Once is happenstance. Twice is a coincidence. Three times is enemy action." He smiled wanly; he had crossed the threshold beyond enemy action.

Mike entered the dining room, cursing aloud about his lack of sleep, his arthritis, and a series of other maladies. He cursed again as he slid a chair closer to the dining table.

Sloan poured freshly squeezed organic orange juice into a glass and handed it to his father. "Nothing like freshly squeezed oranges to start the morning," he said with more cheer than he felt.

Mike took a sip of the juice. "Anything wrong with Minute Maid?" he asked gruffly, though it seemed he was enjoying the fresh beverage.

After a moment passed, Sloan reached out and gently grasped his father's forearm. "We have a problem, Bree and I…"

"Damn it!" Mike blurted, then stopped himself from going on, appearing to recognize that this was neither the time nor the place for a parental reprimand.

Sloan explained that nothing untoward had occurred, but that her ex-fiancé—a reporter—was blackmailing him over photos that hinted at an affair. He followed that up with a string of muttered profanities. "I haven't seen the photos, but nothing happened between us, so there's no way they can reveal anything salacious. Maybe just us walking side by side or her leaving my place after midnight. Still, the mere suggestion of an affair could be damning."

"You're Tyler Sloan." Mike shrugged, citing various elected officials with scandals who emerged unscathed. "We can turn this to your advantage. Remember, you're Tyler Sloan."

"Dad." Sloan's patience was not obscuring his fears. "Don't keep saying I'm Tyler Sloan."

"You're no hypocritical preacher with his secretary in a parking lot. Go on the offensive. 'I'm single; she's single.' Blast the media for diverting voters from the real issues."

"Be straight with me. Would the average guy think I slept with Bree?"

"A photo of her leaving after midnight?" Mike began. "Pretty young thing, red hair, angelic little face, good fig—"

"You're not judging Miss America. What do you think?"

Mike's pause was meaningful. "Every man would make goo-goo eyes at her."

"Are *goo-goo eyes* good or bad?" Sloan chuckled. "Sounds good."

"Look, you're a disciplined guy. You used to hole up in the recording studio for weeks. But even a disciplined marine may stray, but don't worry, you're not a standard-issue candidate."

Sloan patted his father's hand and then went to retrieve his tablet. Upon returning, he played the previous night's broadcast of *The Office*.

The talk show host loudly greeted the caller, "Dr. D. is taking calls. Who's 'In the Office'?"

The caller immediately pounced. "You want a senator who can't keep his pants zipped? A senator who'd rather do drugs than attend church? That's your man?"

"Nevada's schools are failing; he's got ideas."

"You think a guy with a kid at a private school in Malibu can help?"

"You're satisfied with the status quo?"

"No, but..." The caller's enthusiasm was diminishing.

"The last week is the test for Sloan—let's see if he can take a punch, or two, or three. Does the singer have a glass jaw? That commercial with Collins was smart."

"It was stolen property," the caller protested.

"Politics is a contact sport. No wimps allowed." The host dropped the call. "Who's 'In the Office'?"

Mike methodically took a sip of his juice. He sipped again. His words appeared to pain him. "If I had beat Reed, you'd win this seat easy. My failure put you in this predicament."

Sloan rarely witnessed this level of personal reflection on his father's part. He motioned to the four large Rolodex organizers Mike had left on the counter to bring to the campaign office. "How many cards in that golden Rolodex?" he asked.

Mike shrugged with faux indifference as if mentioning any number would belittle its importance.

"Let's talk for a minute about the ménage-à-trois video," Sloan suggested, immediately noticing how his father recoiled. "It's an ace in the hole for Rogers."

"He'll never air it," Mike said with certainty, before steering the conversation to what really plagued both men. "Let's talk about your brother—God bless him." He began to reminisce with tenderness about all the time he'd spent grooming J.R. to follow in his footsteps. It was clear his father idolized his memory; it was clear the memories pained him.

Sloan kept his thoughts private. He had been suspicious when he heard about J.R.'s crash. Contrary to what he'd told the media, he had seen his brother ingest drinks and drugs with reckless abandon. Following Sloan's graduation from rehab, his brother had continued to bring vials of white powder backstage until Sloan finally ordered his security team to revoke J.R.'s pass. Outside of the Osmond family, banning drugs backstage at a rock concert in the eighties was blasphemy, yet Sloan had to stop the madness.

"I have a right to know," Mike said in a tone that Sloan could not dodge or duck. "Was that reporter, right? Did J.R. have a problem with booze and drugs?"

Sloan paused. One look away from his father, his glance shifting before returning with a pronounced exhale. His eyes were resting on his father. "Maybe some things are best left unsaid."

"I have a right to know," Mike insisted.

Mike appeared vulnerable. Sloan once had excuses at the ready if this conversation was raised, but years had passed; he thought the topic was closed. There were no answers to satisfy his father. "Why put ourselves through it?"

"For the last fucking time, I have a right to know."

Sloan began slowly, pausing often. He explained that he'd immediately conferred with Zimmer upon hearing the news. His marching orders to Zimmer were to contact the Los Angeles County coroner. Sloan made it clear; he did not want details of how, why, or what it took, but Zimmer agreed to shield the family from further pain. Sloan was blunt—he was relieved when the coroner's autopsy omitted any sign of cocaine and gracefully altered the alcohol content in J.R.'s blood. "Grant told me he put a blanket over it."

Mike sat motionless, absorbing the news. His shoulders slumped; his face twisted into a pained expression. He began to ramble, admitting he was aware of his elder son's erratic behavior but hoped it was not indicative of a more significant problem. "Your mother and I," Mike began softly, "we wondered if J.R. might have an attention-deficit problem, or maybe he was trying too hard to please me."

Mike was slow with his words, wearing the knife-stabbing-in-your-heart pain of a parent's loss. "I deluded myself, maybe to protect your mom...maybe to protect me." Mike sat still, seeming to need time. "Did Zimmer buy the coroner a car? You must know that. An attorney doesn't front that kind of green, no matter how great the client is."

"I knew after the fact. Grant billed me the amount over the next year for various conferences and generated a report I had no use for. We covered our tracks."

"No, you didn't. There's no proof you paid, but why in hell would Grant Zimmer buy the coroner a car?"

"There's no payment from Grant." Sloan acknowledged he never understood Zimmer's exact actions but was assured the payment could not be traced. As a founder of a local bank, Zimmer had access to records and knew what actions would trigger the attention of bank examiners. "The bank collapsed a long time ago; there are no records."

Sloan remained steadfast that his actions were necessary to protect his parents.

"I saw Mom's pain. And..."—Sloan hesitated before delivering—"this was months before your toughest reelection to Congress. It could have derailed all your dreams. I saw Mom crying gut-wrenching tears, tears that tore her apart."

"You did the right thing," Mike said quickly before pausing, a pause to seemingly weigh all the consequences. "You did it for the right reasons," he added wearily. "Yes, you did."

Mike stood; the two men embraced.

Sloan felt emotionally relieved. They had been united in their grief for J.R., but his parents' loss was more haunting. Now they were joined in sharing a secret that had burdened Sloan for too many years. He detected an intimacy growing between them, unaccustomed but welcomed.

* * *

Sloan sat alone in his bed, working his laptop to google every story about his brother's death. There was nothing new, easing the pit in his stomach.

He grimaced when other searches revealed images of Bree and him walking around Lake Las Vegas posted on the Political Fool website. One photograph captured Sloan with his hand on Bree's shoulder. Another had her hand resting on his elbow, gazing at him with admiration. Another image, a more damning one, showed the two in a sticky embrace that suggested intimacy. The worst was one of Bree leaving his condominium with a time stamp of 1:55 a.m. Her clothing could be interpreted as disheveled. The caption read: "Bed head?"

The Political Fool dished the dirt without fear of retribution, its authors unknown and unclaimed. "Tyler Sloan's campaign is hotter than the Las Vegas summer…reports of his latest squeeze are sizzling…a Sloan coupling is never breaking news…but this lover is his media advisor, Bree Baker…despite their generational age gap and Baker's engagement…we wish them well…any polls on how cuckolds are leaning?"

The wicked combination of politics, drugs, and sex was slammed into a higher gear. Winning candidates defined issues on their terms. Effective political spin was immediate and marginally visible—delays heightened speculation, implying the responses were crafted in a Chappaquiddick laboratory with threadbare excuses and marginal credibility.

Sloan rose from his bed, startled to notice, for the first time, a framed photograph of Bree on his bedroom dresser. He walked closer. She was wearing cyclist's gear, standing aside her bike, presumably in front of her Oregon home. The photograph was probably two years old. He smiled at her audacity.

"Cute," he said aloud. He mentally reflected on how and when Bree had surreptitiously placed the art deco frame in his bedroom. He had not described a grown woman as "cute" in more years than he wanted to confess. She'd made her move; it was his turn.

THIRTY-FOUR

Wednesday, August 16, Las Vegas,
6 Days to the Election

Poll: Collins 38%, Sloan 31%,
Rogers 23%, Undecided 8%

The furnace blast of the day's heat lingered into the early evening. Accompanied by Riley, Sloan walked through Las Vegas's Town Square, an outdoor retail complex that lightly smacked of European avenues.

Before he was scheduled to meet the media for the photo opp, he motioned to Riley to follow him; his security team was following close behind. They detoured into the Coffee Bean in the Town Square.

There were ritualistic moments wherever he appeared in public. He derived pleasure, accepting some might term it *perverse pleasure*. A typical routine would develop when entering a grocery market, shopping at a store, or today, visiting the Coffee Bean. Inevitably, someone would stare in uncertain recognition—unimaginable that Tyler Sloan could be here.

He gently stroked Riley's hair as they stood in line. The turning stares commenced; one woman blew a kiss in his direction. He returned smiles and waves. The silence broke when the barista laughed a hearty "Hey" and pointed at him. The woman standing in front of them turned back to glance. She shook her head vigorously as if to snap her back to reality. She remained silent, but her mental gymnastics were at play. *Was it him? Is it really him?*

"How ya doing?" Sloan stuck out his hand and asked for her name. The woman was flustered; he introduced Riley.

Sloan would likely forget this thirty-second interaction, but the woman and others he spoke to would remember it for the rest of *their* lives. A cell phone image would memorialize and instantly inform the social media worlds of this chance encounter.

After leaving the Coffee Bean, Sloan saw and greeted Billy Rogers, who was making his own media push through the outdoor mall. The two exchanged forced pleasantries as the cameras captured the "twofer." Politics was a short-attention-span theater. Press conferences on policy generated scant media coverage, but his public appearances were magnets for fifteen-second videos.

A posse of twentysomething-ish men nudged one another. The surrounding media crushed around Sloan—the tell that he was the alpha male. The men gingerly approached Sloan.

"I grew up listening to your stuff," a young tattooed man said enthusiastically.

"They still work for you?" Sloan asked, instantly regretting the question. If the response was sour, the media would record a rebuke.

"Sure, you're cool," another replied.

"Cool?" Rogers mocked the word while turning to the cameras. "That's what's important?"

"What you sayin', dude?" one of the men snapped, moving toward Rogers.

The other man tapped Rogers on the back. "Chill out, little man."

Sloan instinctively moved to stand in front of Riley to protect her in case this situation turned ugly. The female member of Sloan's security team grabbed Riley's hand and walked her to a safe distance.

Rogers whirled to confront the buff young man in a muscle shirt and thrust his index finger in his chest. *"Little man? I've worked hard for you."*

All media cameras and cell phones focused on Rogers and the muscle shirt as the distance closed between them.

"Wimp," the guy snorted.

Rogers grabbed him, swiftly placing him in a headlock. *"Wimp? Who's the wimp now?"*

Several security officers inserted themselves between the men before the confrontation could escalate further. Sloan stood off to the side, pitying his opponent. Rogers was melting, succumbing to the pressure. Each day he was slipping toward a near-certain loss, but the debate and this exchange degraded him to ridicule.

Shooing his aides aside, Rogers briskly walked to approach Sloan.

Rogers was speaking with his mouth partially shielded, but the words emerged. "The election doesn't go to the candidate who fornicates with the most women."

Fornicates? Sloan thought incredulously. Uncertain if he should say more, Sloan simply patted Rogers on the shoulder and wished him well. He motioned for Riley to return to his side as they continued their walk through the mall.

"Look, Dad!" Riley exclaimed. "Girl Scouts! Let's go there!" She bounded toward the large group of energetic girls—Daisies, Brownies, and Juniors—and their parents.

Sloan followed, amused by his daughter's exuberance.

The scout leader introduced Sloan, who quickly introduced Riley as a former Girl Scout of Cadettes rank.

As if on cue, Riley announced, "I had fun being a Girl Scout. We camped under the stars, performed in plays, and even went surfing."

Sloan placed his hand on Riley's shoulder and smiled.

Riley told the girls, "Taylor Swift used to be a Girl Scout. She even signed my sash."

The young girls collectively gushed, and Sloan felt momentarily stunned by how quickly his daughter had assumed control. Only a couple of years older than most of the girls, she was suddenly their mentor.

One of the scouts stepped forward and stated authoritatively, "My dad told me that sometimes you're not really singing—it's just a recording of you singing when you were younger."

Sloan bent down slightly to meet the girl's eyes. "No, I always sing in real time."

"My dad doesn't lie," the girl responded.

The Scout leader placed her hand on the girl's shoulder as if to caution the girl not to push it.

"Of course not," Sloan hastily replied. "I'm sure your dad is a great man, but I *always* sing."

"Who won when the brontosaurus fought the pterodactyl?" one of the scouts asked.

"I'm not really sure. Dinosaurs, right?" Sloan stammered.

"You don't know, and you want to be the president?!"

Giggles followed.

"I'm running for the Senate," he corrected with a smile. "But I'll study the brontosaurus-pterodactyl issue." He turned to Riley. "Can you look into that?"

"Will do!" she said and took out her cell phone and gave instructions to Siri.

Sloan wore a beaming smile, sharing the media's attention with Riley.

"If you really sing all your own songs, sing us a song!" another Scout called out.

Cheers followed.

Sloan gestured toward the American flag propped up on a pole behind them and belted out, "Oh say can you see, by the dawn's—"

"*Anyone* can sing that song." The girl shook her head.

"There's a reason we all sing that song," Sloan replied. "This is a great country—worth singing about."

With that, he waved goodbye to the gaggle of girls and led Riley farther into the mall. The media and crowd were following. Suddenly questions were shouted. The shouts grew louder as if higher volume would provoke honesty.

He stopped when he heard Richman's voice slice through. "Where's Bree? Have you spoken to her fiancé? How long have you two been an item?"

Sloan instantly regretted Riley's presence. With a glance at his security guard, the woman seized Riley's hand and walked her out of the media's fire.

Later that evening, Richman's brain cells would be floating on waves of Johnnie Walker, but in this precocktail hour, he was tough, lucid, and persistent. He repeated his questions.

Sloan surveyed the press corps, confident they were all punching above their weight. "*That's* what's important to you?" He gauged their temperature. "Questions about my assistant are snide, silly, and sophomoric."

A bellowing voice emerged from behind, and the crowd instinctively parted. "Treat me nice, Sloan!" Standing before him, a fortysomething Elvis impersonator with his "sausage filling" stuffed into a white jumpsuit casing. He assumed a "karate chop" pose à la Elvis circa mid-seventies and looked at Sloan expectantly.

"Love the King," Sloan said with a tightening smile as "Elvis" drew closer, the smell of alcohol prominent in the man's sweat.

Sloan's security man wedged between them.

"I had Priscilla, and you have Bree. TCB, baby!" the man slurred as he was led away by the mall's security detail.

"Vegas heat bakes a crazy soufflé," Sloan whispered to an aide, before turning away and finding himself face to face with Alan Newcombe.

"Let's talk about your brother," the reporter said sharply. "You said you had no idea how the coroner purchased his car. Does that remain your position?"

"It's not a *position*," Sloan replied. "I'm telling you what I know."

The reporter's presence was no surprise, but this confrontation held no upside.

Newcombe appeared to draw strength, surrounded by his media colleagues. His questions were rapid, nearly stepping on Sloan's response: "Why was Grant Zimmer at the Beverly Hills Mercedes dealer the day after he met with the coroner?"

"Is there a headline when an LA attorney goes to a Mercedes dealer?" Sloan was keeping it light.

A titter of laughter followed, appearing to annoy Newcombe. The reporter was blessed with a voice that demanded attention; he was booming, undeterred. "But *Zimmer* did not buy a car. The *coroner* bought one the next day."

Sloan shrugged. He needed to get out and get out now.

"The current manager at the Mercedes dealer is certain in his memory. He was a new salesman, swore the coroner bought a car, not Zimmer." The reporter's tone confirmed that he'd heard too many dodges in his career. "Zimmer is *not* returning my phone calls."

"I'll ask Grant to call you," Sloan offered with assurance. "In the meantime, I'm here to answer any questions about the campaign." He looked past Newcombe. "Anyone? Questions?"

* * *

"Mrs. Sloan," Dr. Goldman announced upon entering the exam room in Brentwood, Los Angeles. "Your ex-husband's candidacy is exciting. He could really win."

Cindy strained to imagine any excitement emanating from the staid doctor, who peered over his glasses at his tablet.

"Still experiencing migraines?"

"This morning, the pain hit me like a bolt," she said quickly.

"It's been quite some time since your auto accident."

"The pain comes and goes, worse at night." Cindy was adjusting her paper gown.

"You've been taking medication for a long time," the doctor said cautiously, "more than one. I'm not comfortable with that."

Cindy had rehearsed her response, expecting this for several months. "But sometimes the pain is excruciating. You don't have to worry. I just need it to help me sleep."

Dr. Goldman was rallying to stem the middle-age softness apparent in his loose jowls. Because he was dating a girlfriend of hers, Cindy was aware of his recent hair transplant. She tried not to be noticeable, casting repeated glances at his hairline.

"Dr. Goldman, look at me. I'm financially set for life with a beautiful child. I have more men wanting to date me than a reality show." Her voice was charming and flirtatious. "Am I the kind of person who gets addicted to drugs?"

The doctor paused. He turned to his nurse, who handed him an iPad with her history.

"No more medications," the doctor said firmly but professionally. "You need counseling. I fear you are or could become addicted to the pain meds." He handed Cindy the brochures. "These are three outstanding rehab centers in Southern California. And here's a prescription for that treatment. That's the best medical advice I can give you."

"What?" Cindy nearly screamed. She had already located two other doctors to prescribe her favored medicines. "I don't have a problem. My *ex* had a problem. Not me."

"Mrs. Sloan, I cannot prescribe you any more medications," he said firmly. "I want to help you, and these centers are the best way for me to do that."

THIRTY-FIVE

Thursday, August 17, Las Vegas,
5 Days to the Election

Poll: Collins 38%, Sloan 30%, Rogers 24%, Undecided 8%

"*I used to leave places* like this at dawn," Sloan said with a sigh, looking around at the deserted Mix Lounge on the fifty-fourth floor of Mandalay Bay. The Mix would not open to the public until nine p.m., and the cleaning crews had just finished preparing for the raucous night ahead.

He sat beside Bree, overlooking the city below through the large windows. They'd been deep in conversation about the campaign. Sloan dismissed the idea of Bree holding a press conference to answer questions about Mack. He knew any public statement she made could open the proverbial floodgates, pressing for details about her visits to his residence. He envisioned her being eviscerated by vultures with press credentials.

Sloan explained that his security team had vetted Mack's background. "Did you know he was kicked off his college's newspaper?"

"No, but I ignored one blaring sign," she said. "His dad had a heart attack and died after we started dating. I thought he was having a hard time coping, figured it was due to his dad, but it didn't stop—anger management issues. I worry," she said, her voice so soft that Sloan strained to hear her. "I worry about us."

The word *us* was new, never uttered. Sloan smiled and placed his hand on hers and patted it tenderly. He sang, "Don't worry, baby."

"Do you trust me?" she asked.

He nodded.

"Tell me what that one song means, the song with the lyric 'Anticipate the memory.' How would you *anticipate* a memory?"

Sloan patiently explained his rule to never reveal the meaning of his lyrics.

"There's an exception to every rule," she replied with a cajoling smile.

He was stirred by her flirtatious response. His refusal to explain his lyrics created an air of mystery, forced the listener to reflect. Maybe it was pretentious, but he wanted his words to be appreciated as art, interpreted in the manner his audience desired, yet Bree was not a mere audience.

"Stay in the present," Sloan explained. "But if your mind drifts, then focus on how sweet this time, this memory will be."

Bree returned a satisfied smile. Sloan had passed her test. Her smile reflected the joy of sharing, the meaning of the lyrics irrelevant. He turned from her as Zimmer announced his presence with an exaggerated throat clearing that demanded attention.

"You said it's heaven here from November to May. It's not November now, Toto. It's one hundred and ten fucking degrees." Zimmer wiped his brow with a white handkerchief. "It took real chutzpah for that Spaniard to name Las Vegas the Meadows."

Sloan's shrug signaled he had no interest in a vent on the weather. "It's seventy-two degrees in here," he said, using his usual line about the Las Vegas summer.

"My bad," Zimmer said, taking a seat, and then began machine-gunning a series of questions about potential fallout from the Sloan-Bree photographs.

"There's no money shot of the two of us because we never did anything," Sloan said, referring to the images on Political Fool.

Zimmer shot a quick glance at Bree. "It's the optics." His eyes stayed on Bree. "The optics of your late-night departure are damning. It's a damning perception."

"She left my condo late. What's that crime called? Hard work in a campaign?"

Zimmer asked for and received confirmation from Bree that she had booked all four networks for Sloan to deliver a prime-time statewide speech Saturday night. He turned to Sloan, reminding him of his earlier counsel. "Don't get defensive in your speech. No one's electing a saint. Abe Lincoln said, 'Show me a man without vices, and I'll show you a man without virtue.'"

"Ol' Abe didn't have cable news, the internet, and talk radio riding his ass," Sloan replied lightly. "MSNBC keeps airing that one speech when I garbled my words, but the bastards never ran the clip of Rogers grabbing that kid in a headlock. FOX has a body-language expert explaining how I hold my hands when I speak; somehow that reveals deep insecurity. Give me a break."

Sloan outlined Saturday's speech for Zimmer. "Still tweaking the details. I'll hit back a little, then go on the offensive." He cast a knowing smile. "If I do it right, it's like the old Russian saying 'I'll come out of the water dry.'"

Zimmer glanced at Bree; his tone held no apology. "I need time alone with my client."

Bree cast a perturbed glance at Sloan before complying.

Zimmer's vision followed the young woman as she walked away. "Let's talk—Rogers and the video."

A pang tore through Sloan's gut, even though he knew this topic was still on the table.

Zimmer leaned forward. "Presume an independent group hired and polled focus groups to gauge their reaction to a similar situation—"

"There's no similar situation," Sloan interrupted him.

"It's a hypothetical. How would voters react if Rogers airs the video?" Zimmer eyed Sloan; he was confident. "You *gain* votes if it airs."

"*Maybe*," Sloan said softly, not convinced. Knowing Zimmer, he assumed the question was not merely a hypothetical. "I presume you, or someone we know, hired a focus group."

"We need to be prepared if it airs. I wanted reassurance; I didn't think you'd lose votes."

Sloan initially played along but then replied, "All right, but..." He ran through other political controversies. "Others survived sexual scandals, but I wanted to win based on merits, my skills, not some damn sex tape."

Sloan sighed loudly, the frustration and pressure omnipresent. "We have more pressing concerns than a tape that might never see the light of day. Is it possible for any records to be uncovered from the dealership or bank regarding the coroner's Mercedes?"

Zimmer took his time, explaining he routed funds from an offshore account into the coroner's account at a bank that he cofounded. That bank wired funds to the Mercedes dealership. The bank failed two years later.

"Aren't records kept? Even on a closed bank?" Sloan queried. He locked and unlocked his fingers, ceasing only when he became aware of Zimmer's penetrating stare.

"Records were kept for five years. I *personally* watched the bank documents being shredded. The only thread is that the dealer has a record of funds being wired from a defunct bank from a limited liability company that later dissolved. Per state records, the coroner was the LLC's only member. The LLC wired the funds; they're the buyer." He added firmly. "Case closed."

Sloan rose and stared past the Strip, his vision resting on the farthest mountain range. He turned to Zimmer. "Worst case. Give me the worst case."

"There's no worst case. I'll blast Newcombe on Saturday. The Sunday talk shows will eat it up. My media friends will protect me; they hate that tight-ass Newcombe." He paused. "I occasionally drop tidbits on them."

"Every attorney in my life has told me," Sloan said with a weary tone before gesturing at Zimmer, "including my attorney for the past twenty years, there are no slam dunks. There's got to be something that could go wrong. We need a plan B."

"I covered our tracks," Zimmer boasted. He explained that he leased a car from the dealership the day after his first visit to establish a valid reason for being there.

"Smart," Sloan replied, still not at ease with the sequence of events.

"Yesterday, my secretary retrieved all the records. I kept *everything*. On Saturday, I'm releasing copies of my lease, and I'll demand an apology from Newcombe and the *Times*." He paused. "I may threaten them with a libel suit unless they apologize."

"Whoa, demand the apology but no threats about filing a suit. We don't need a fight with the *New York Times*."

* * *

"Here's where *The Prince* holds court," said attorney Edward G. Prince with a theatric wave of his hand as Mike and Zimmer were entering his office on Valley View Boulevard.

Prince often referred to himself as "The Prince." Billboards plastered across Las Vegas blared, Injured—Car or Workplace—Call The Prince. Poster boards bearing the same message graced bus shelters around the city.

The attorney's hair and body were thick and full. The sleeves of his custom shirt—displaying a small prince-like crown on his chest pocket—were rolled up; his taut forearms were on full display.

Mike shielded his eyes from the sheen of the suit coat hanging on the hook of the closed office door. By design, he would defer to Zimmer for this meeting. Both agreed that they needed third-party distance to intercede with Denny Morgan. Since Zimmer had referred local cases to Prince, Zimmer would use his firm to retain Prince to obscure any payment.

Prince outlined a new case he was handling for a local casino group. "We're going to install video blackjack devices in every casino restroom. It's a wasted opportunity if nature's call interrupts your gaming."

Zimmer glanced at the engraved nameplate on Prince's desk. His mere name was insufficient; the nameplate announced, *This Prince fights for the little guy.*

Prince detailed how much money he had raised for Mike's Nevada primary campaign six years earlier. He appeared wounded when Mike returned only a mild nod of appreciation.

"You did a good job sealing those court records," Zimmer interjected, referring to an earlier case Prince had worked on for Zimmer.

"When I seal cases, I seal them with Gempler's," Prince replied. When he saw no hint of recognition, he added, "It's the sealant the military uses to bulletproof their tires."

Mike flashed Zimmer a gaze for his cue that read "enough of this BS."

"Let's cut to the chase. Is Morgan ready?" Zimmer quizzed.

Prince took charge; he'd had numerous contacts with Morgan, all conversations were on disposable cell phones. "Morgan knows his script. Had to coach up the old hippie." He waited a moment before adding, "Gentlemen, I'd like to speak bluntly."

"Have you ever held back?" Zimmer replied with a dash of mischief.

"Who is my client? *How* and *when* will I be paid?"

"Morgan is your client. The fifty thousand will be wired to your account upon your return from LA," Zimmer replied.

"I thought about it; fifty K for this migraine is a little light," Prince complained. He turned to Mike, overflowing with how it was his "honor" to assist him.

"Let's call it a contingency case." Mike turned to Zimmer. "Wire fifty K to the Prince's trust account after the press conference, and presumably all goes well, fifty K more, two months later after he sends you a bill." He smiled benevolently at Prince. "We take care of our friends."

* * *

That same evening, Sloan was ready to conclude a series of drop-ins at a string of old-school Las Vegas restaurants—Casa di Amore, the Peppermill Fireside Lounge, and the Golden Steer steak house. His final stop was the Italian American Club on Sahara Boulevard, two miles east of the Strip, self-dubbed as the "Swankiest Club on the Planet."

Sloan entered the vast circa-1960s restaurant that featured live music performances. He quickly counted the house—over four hundred were jammed into the room for a wedding reception for a Sloan campaign volunteer.

The wedding band abruptly halted as Sloan entered. The bride shouted with joy as the room cheered his arrival.

Sloan enjoyed the respite from his worries, basking in the chants of his name and shouts of encouragement. He walked with the groom, being introduced to the entire wedding party and many guests. "Keep shooting!" the bride demanded of the video camerawoman and photographer. Dozens of guests were lining up for a quick photo with Sloan.

Sloan eyed the five-piece band, the two guitarists, saxophone player, organist, and drummer that filled the small stage. A full vibrant-red curtain hung behind them. *The oldest of the old school,* he thought. He motioned to the band to continue playing the Italian folk music his presence had interrupted. The guests resumed their traditional dance.

"It's too lame," an aide whispered near his ear. "Whatever you do, do *not* dance—there are cameras here, and it's just not cool."

"I'm not dancing." Sloan mocked the aide's advice. "I'm upping the stakes."

Following the bandleader's introduction, Sloan approached the stage with gusto. A young pup with this band of Italian men, he stood with a microphone in hand, basking in the adulation.

He surveyed the room. His mere presence had pumped the reception with unfiltered joy. No one here cared a wit about who he dated. The bride and groom would tell their grandchildren about how

Tyler Sloan had attended their wedding. He had broken one vow he'd made to himself today with Bree—now he would shatter another.

"*Chi mangia solo crepa solo,*" Sloan said, startling the audience with his fractured Italian. "Forgive my *Italiano*; I think that means, 'Who eats alone dies alone.' Well, I'm not eating alone tonight!" His hands waved across the room. "I'm eating with my friends tonight!"

The crowd cheered; Sloan realized a wedding party filled with wine would cheer anything. "Before I join you, I'm singing for my supper."

The cheers mounted.

"What do you think? Should we do one?"

The reception erupted, a mad scramble for cell phones to hit record—instant viral.

He knew one singer was perfect for this crowd; one name would stir *every* soul in the room. "Tell me, was there anyone greater than Francis Albert Sinatra?" One pause at the sustained roar. He stole a glance over his shoulder, "You boys know 'Under My Skin'?"

The music began as Sloan gave a Sinatra-like shout, "Kick it!"

THIRTY-SIX

Friday, August 18, Las Vegas,
4 Days to the Election

**Poll: Collins 38%, Sloan 30%,
Rogers 24%, Undecided 8%**

"Governor," Bree began politely. "With all due respect, Tyler's got a team of volunteers who could drive you. Why did you insist on me?"

"It's a sensitive assignment. Be honored I asked you."

"Sensitive? Tyler's security team has a woman who worked for the Secret Service and a guy that was a Navy SEAL."

"Exactly." Mike waved that comment off. "I didn't want this outing to be a chapter of a book one of them would write."

Bree began uncertainly. "Are you concerned about Rogers airing the sex tape?"

"Hell no," Mike scoffed. "If anyone airs it, Tyler gains. Trust me."

Bree had the destination's address in her GPS but asked who they were going to see.

During the drive, he filled Bree in on Pedro Abreau, tracing the man's family history back to pre-Castro Cuba. During the Castro regime, the Abreau family had worked backdoor channels to position themselves for a slice of the billions the Soviets pumped in. Now, with the Castros out, Abreau needed to wedge his family back into the booming tourism industry.

As Bree turned into a residential neighborhood in southwest Las Vegas, from his position in the back seat, Mike gestured toward the car in the driveway of a one-story residence. "Pedro doesn't own a car; he leases a new Cadillac every year."

After they exited the car, Mike took an exaggerated breath. "It's like that scene in *Apocalypse Now*. Nothing beats the smell of campaigning, especially for my son."

Bree smirked. "Not my type of movie, but I've heard the *napalm* line."

Mike and Bree approached the screen door, where they received a chilly greeting from a buxom blonde holding a small dog.

"Cute poodle," Bree said.

"No." Mike was patient in his correction. "This little darling is a Bichon Frise."

The blonde smiled and placed her hand out. Mike bent down to kiss it, which she accepted with a showgirl's confidence. She was beautiful, and she knew it.

Bree muttered her apologies with an inconspicuous roll of her eyes. She and Mike entered the modest home. The blonde's tight bodice moved seductively as she led Mike farther into the house while Bree motioned that she would wait in the living room.

Mike followed her to a darkened den where Pedro Abreu sat on a cloth chair.

"You met my niece?" Abreu opened.

"I'll bring in the sandwiches," the blonde said, kissing Abreu's forehead.

Abreu clicked the remote control to decrease the volume of Celia Cruz, a famed Cuban singer of the last century.

"Nice neighborhood, very stable, not one for-sale sign," Mike said.

"I buy them as soon as I see a sign," Abreau replied. "I like to know my neighbors."

Before Mike would ask for the check for the political action committee he and Zimmer had established for his son, he retrieved an envelope from his navy suit pocket and handed it to Abreau. He explained that the letter was from the president.

Abreau closed his eyes. He caressed the envelope, tracing the raised presidential seal on the envelope's upper-left corner and slightly rubbing the soft, textured stationery between his thumb and right index finger. He kissed the letter before returning it. He requested that Mike read the letter aloud.

Mike had called in a chit with the president. Reed's chief of staff was quick to agree but puzzled this letter was Mike's only request. The administration had delivered.

"Dear Mr. Abreau: My dear friend Governor Mike Sloan has personally communicated to me your willingness to serve America and Cuba. Please keep Governor Sloan advised of how you may be of assistance as we embark on a new journey between our two countries. Best Wishes, Bret Reed."

Abreau dabbed tears from his eyes. He nodded in reverence toward Mike.

The blonde returned with two small plates; on each rested a tuna sandwich on toasted wheat bread with corn chips indiscriminately scattered on each plate.

"Great tuna fish," Mike said with enthusiasm after taking a bite.

"Dried cranberries," Abreau replied with a knowing smile.

Mike finished the sandwich and nibbled on a few corn chips before he rose.

"Governor Sloan," Abreau said with reverence, "one day I hope to call you *Ambassador* Sloan. Will you be the ambassador to Cuba?"

Mike's smile would serve as sufficient affirmation for Abreau. He continued the smile as he eyed the five-million-dollar check payable to the Committee for Nevada's Future.

* * *

"Desolate, barren, or sparse—pick your adjective, Bree," Mike said as he reclined in the Town Car's back seat as the day continued.

The landscape was pure desert as Bree sped west on Highway 160 to Pahrump, a town whose fame arose as the home of legalized prostitution only one hour from Las Vegas.

As instructed, Bree turned into the gravel driveway, a sign proclaiming their arrival at Babette's Ranch. On the faded-pink stucco building, a wrought iron sign was emblazoned with a caricature of a French maid.

"No way," Bree exclaimed loudly. "I'm not going to a whorehouse."

"Brothel. It's legal in this county. I'm picking up a check, not a girl."

"Nope. I'm not going in." Her hands gripped the steering wheel. "No, no, no."

"Fine," Mike replied with annoyance. He instructed Bree to start honking in thirty minutes. He added that if he did not come out, she had to go in.

"I'll honk, give you five minutes, and then I'll knock." Bree held a stare of disbelief at the front door. "Come out when I knock. Please, Governor, come out when I knock."

Mike rang the bell and, upon entering, noticed a motley crew of customers seated at the elaborate bar. Despite the sure-thing odds, each man was downing another shot of courage. He felt a pang of pity, sympathizing with their loneliness. He had no a desire to join them but understood their plight.

Mike was escorted to the center of the room as a lineup formed. Eight, ten, now twelve women scurried to join the lineup. One woman hustled in late as she carried outlandishly high-heel pumps in her hand.

One young man rang the doorbell. He walked in, gazed at the bevy of scantily clad women, and flashed the grin of a Powerball grand-prize winner.

The women were all young and mostly nubile, peaking in their erotic quotient. They were uniformly decked out in lingerie, midriffs, bikini tops, and thigh-high-cut dresses.

Wayne Avrashow

Babette's owner, Robert Jacowski, offered a series of respectful nods to Mike. He was wearing a yachting cap with a woman clinging to each arm.

"Good to see you, Bob," Mike said.

"Call me Captain; everyone else does." The owner extended his hand. "I'm the captain of this pleasure cruise." He gestured to the women as if they were the main course on that evening's menu.

Mike winked to the ladies. He turned to Jacowski. "Business before pleasure."

He followed the captain into his office and took a seat. His eyes fell on the man's watch.

Jacowski extended his arm. "A Patek Philippe, but I don't have to tell you that."

"Exquisite," Mike murmured. "I've never seen one like it."

"You never will. It's one of a kind."

Captain Robert explained that he had acquired the watch at a Sotheby's auction before detailing the watch's attributes—a casing in twenty-four-carat white gold, a crème-colored face that revealed gold applied Arabic numerals, and a dozen perfectly placed gemstones.

"Seems you're more interested in this watch than the women." Bob chuckled.

"It's a timepiece, not a watch," Mike said softly.

Mike dwelled on the captain's ever-present smile. The man had worn a perpetual grin since the moment he arrived. Of course, for many, being surrounded by willing women and having sufficient wealth to buy a Patek Philippe at an auction was reason to smile. But it was more than material or female contacts; most of Mike's political friends were type-A men and women in professional and prodigious occupations. Most were racked with stress, pressure, and ailments too numerous to mention.

"Bob, er...Captain," Mike began, "to be honest, I had some trepidations coming out here. But your enthusiasm is contagious; I feel good being around you."

"Maybe all those hotties have something to do with that," Robert said with a laugh. He reached across the table to hand Mike the promised check of one million dollars payable to the same independent committee Abreau had donated to.

Mike understood that the game was riddled with unspoken quid pro quos. In Mike's world, there was always a reason, yet his host was not seeking legislation or an appointment. The lack of motive puzzled Mike; he was compelled to ask without specifics, "We're good?"

"Honor to meet you. Honored to help you son."

Mike eyed his companion. "Any request? I'm used to people wanting something."

"Dinner with your son," came a reply without hesitation. "I'd be very pleased if you joined us."

"OK." Mike was soft.

The captain stood and waved for Mike to follow him into another room.

Upon entering, Mike gasped. The room was a shrine to Tyler Sloan. A series of autographed photos of Sloan dominated the room. The walls were dotted with framed Sloan records of differing vintage, the antiquated 45s, albums, posters, concert tickets, and backstage passes. The shelves were neatly aligned with tape cassettes.

"None are replicas. All originals," Robert confirmed with pride.

Embarrassed at how his knowledge of his son was surpassed by Jacowski, Mike listened as his host rattled off trivia about each record, where it was recorded, and the length and cities on each tour. Then he slid the watch off his wrist and placed it in Mike's palm. "It's yours."

"No, no." Mike was flummoxed.

Robert stuck his hands behind his back. "Don't embarrass me by declining my generosity. There are more than a few men buried in the desert who have committed lesser crimes."

Mike glanced at the Patek Philippe, then back to Robert, who wore a satisfied grin. He worried if he was being played by a celebrity-stalking Rupert Pupkin. He removed his own watch and affixed the Patek Philippe onto his wrist.

"How much does it cost for one woman for one hour?" he asked and then added with designed nonchalance, "Just wondering."

"No charge, and I'll throw in a little blue pill from my private stash. But trust me, go for two girls; you won't regret it."

* * *

Bree was sending emails on her phone when Mike opened the driver's side of the car. "I'll drive back," he said. "You'll be the navigator."

Bree stayed behind the wheel. "When was the last time you drove?"

"It's been a while, probably before I was governor."

Bree calculated that it had been at least ten years and shook her head. "Relax in the back seat. I'll play the latest *In the Office* for you."

She started the car when she saw that he was safely in the back seat. The car chimed out a tone, and she said, "Play audio."

"Suzanne from the dazzling lights of Las Vegas, you're 'In the Office.' Talk to me about the Senate race," Dr. D. was snappy with his usual command.

"What can you tell me about Sloan's father?" Suzanne asked.

"A little louder," Mike instructed Bree.

"The office bestows a little history." The host described Mike Sloan's long, loping strides through the state Capitol's corridors, which inspired allies and intimidated adversaries. "The man was an equal-opportunity tough guy. One year the state legislature was late in passing the budget. As the deadline approached, ol' Governor Sloan had one of his aides stop the clocks in the legislature…literally, they stopped the clocks."

"Was that legal?" the caller asked.

"The legislators screamed, but a budget was passed the next day. The budget was on time if you honor the broken clock."

"Were the clocks your handiwork?" Bree asked with a smirk as the segment concluded.

"An electronic malfunction." Mike chuckled. "That's our story, and we're sticking to it."

The car began its return drive to Las Vegas on Highway 160, and Mike sang aloud. "It's a good day for singing a song. It's a good day from morning to night."

* * *

At the Hollywood Roosevelt Hotel on Hollywood Boulevard, Denny Morgan sat down to face the most substantial media presence he had encountered in decades. Turnout was spiked by the leak that the rocker Morgan would be dropping a "video bombshell" about the Nevada Senate campaign and Tyler Sloan. The media were crammed into the hotel's Blossom Room, the site of the first Academy Awards. Pages of Hollywood's history could be written with stories from this hotel and room.

A group of publicists hurriedly distributed Morgan's written statement.

"I will read a brief statement," Morgan said solemnly.

Morgan was infatuated with Hollywood's history. He'd pled with Zimmer to grant him, as the dying man was allowed, his wish to hold his press conference at the Roosevelt Hotel. The renovation in the 1927 vintage hotel lobby retained its dim lighting, paneled ceilings, and chandeliers. The hotel was rife with salacious tales from its occupants from the last century, Marilyn Monroe, Charlie Chaplin, and Clark Gable. Historical photographs of Marilyn lounging and modeling by the hotel's pool were plastered in Morgan's apartment.

Prince stood in the rear of the room watching Morgan. The singer began, then paused to gaze about the Blossom Room, appearing to appreciate his "final curtain call." The singer flawlessly read his two-minute statement. At the critical moment, he raised his eyes to meet the camera lens. He announced he had personally handed Billy Rogers the videotape of Sloan and Collins and that $200,000 had been wired to his bank account that day.

"Billy Rogers paid me two hundred thousand dollars for this video," Morgan repeated. "He told me he wanted to destroy Tyler Sloan and Chris Collins. That was sick. I have to stand tall to defend the integrity of a good man like Tyler Sloan."

With Prince's nod to an assistant, the ménage-à-trois video aired on the LED board that had been rented for the occasion. Black stripes had been strategically placed across private parts, but Sloan's and Collins's faces were clear. The other woman's face was blurred.

A collective gasp filled the room, but no eyes turned away.

When the thirty-second clip ended, Prince discreetly raised one finger to signal to the chief publicist it was time to escort Morgan from the room. The singer gave one final wave before a hasty retreat. Prince smirked at Morgan's audacity in portraying his actions as heroic. The singer had received $200,000 to double-cross his friend and then pocketed another $300,000 to publicly denounce that act.

Prince thought: *If this old rocker can snare half a million to air an edited thirty seconds of a decades-old sex tape, The Prince is in the wrong business.*

* * *

"Damn it! Damn it!" Sloan shouted. "This could kill me."

He and Bree had just watched a live feed of the press conference on the laptop in the back seat of the Ford Explorer Hybrid.

Bree grasped his hand, attempting to add comfort. "Your dad was very confident you would gain votes if the video ever aired."

"Damn, Morgan," Sloan shouted. "Did he do it to help me or fuck me as payback for that tour years ago?" He thought of Riley. "What will Riley think? Will her friends tease her?" He muttered expletives and slammed his fist on the armrest, blaming himself for "messing with his daughter's mind."

He thought of calling Cindy, but then realized he needed to call Riley directly. He blurted random thoughts about the impact the video might have on the campaign. Would Collins lose or gain votes in sympathy? What would Rogers do? What should he say?

He held out his hand to forestall Bree's comments. A moment passed, now drawing a slight smile. His thoughts swirling, reassessing his initial outburst. His words slow. "It's more than an odd coincidence. Zimmer ran a focus group and was certain it would benefit me. He told me the same thing my dad told you. I didn't ask Zimmer; he volunteered it."

"Mike was confident," Bree replied. "And he said if *anyone* airs it. What does *anyone* mean?" She appeared to weigh the enormity of Sloan's statement. "What are you getting at? What's going on?"

Sloan maintained his glance out the car's window as they sped along the freeway. He sought clarity, finding solace in the barren desert. He knew how his father operated. He recalled aloud how Zimmer told him how he negotiated deals without involving his clients "for their own good." Both his father and Zimmer shared the same belief system—they knew best.

"They each said too much," Sloan said slowly. "They each knew too much." He paused. "Grant's too clever for his own good. His fingerprints...and maybe my dad's, are all over this."

THIRTY-SEVEN

Saturday, August 19, Las Vegas,
3 Days to the Election

Poll: Collins 37%, Sloan 30%, Rogers 22%, Undecided 11%

"Have you explained these incidents to your daughter?" a reporter pressed as soon as Sloan and Zimmer exited his Lake Las Vegas home.

Although tempted to ask, "What incidents?" Sloan held a slight smile and kept walking. He would not display weakness. The media accepted distrust, but weak candidates were juicy prey to be devoured.

A cacophony of additional questions rose from the press corps gathered in his driveway. The two men, surrounded by his security detail, slowly made their way to the SUV. It was a manageable drive for him to deliver his statewide address from his office in blue.

"Mr. Sloan, understand I really don't want to ask, but—" another reporter began.

"Then don't," Zimmer snapped.

Sloan recognized Zimmer's error. Flippant responses evolved into prominent features on evening broadcasts where "experts" concluded that stress had seized the campaign. Sloan returned to the reporter and asked him to state his question.

"Your reaction to the Morgan press conference and the airing of a snippet of the video?"

"I was shocked by Denny Morgan in releasing it, but more disappointed by Billy Rogers. Billy's conduct is the real story...Watch me tonight; I'll address everything."

Sloan quickened his pace to reach the door of the SUV. He climbed into the back seat, and Zimmer slid in the seat next to him. Sloan had been around Zimmer long enough to discern when his smile was but a mask. Today, that smile was flash-frozen with anxiety. After a couple of silent moments passed, Sloan noticed Zimmer's edge was palpable.

"Anything you want to tell me?" Sloan asked with calculated innocence.

"No, you're prepped, you're ready."

"Not about tonight, about anything else? Anything on Morgan?"

Zimmer licked his lips; his voice was soft. "Focus on tonight—we'll talk after."

The noncomment was sufficient to confirm Sloan's suspicions. "After the polls close, the three of us are going to have a little chat. Bookmark that, for now. Where are we with the president?"

Zimmer simply said he needed to call the White House.

Sloan interpreted this nonresponse to mean that Reed would watch tonight's speech to gauge his political pulse. A steady pulse could presage a Reed *nod* toward Sloan; a weak performance would silence Reed—or worse, secure an endorsement for Rogers.

"Just to be clear," Zimmer began slowly, "tonight you're dancing around rumors. The first rumor, you're sleeping with an engaged staffer who is half your age. Second rumor, all the allegations of covering up your brother's death. Then, you want to top it off by ripping into Rogers for releasing a video of you getting ready to do the nasty with Collins?"

"Well." Sloan cast a modest smile. "I'd say it differently, but you nailed it." He stared straight ahead, his voice firm. "I'm in the arena, bloodied and bowed, but I'm in the arena."

Zimmer stared at Sloan with a connoisseur's appreciation. His smile slowly unfolded and turned into a chuckle that was followed by a series of guttural laughs. The hearty laughter was contagious. Sloan laughed so hard his eyes filled with tears.

"Tonight's a little political rope-a-dope," Sloan said when he caught his breath. "I'll take some hits but land some punches."

"Brass *cojones*, my man, brass *cojones*," Zimmer said admiringly.

* * *

Sloan's office had a modern decor, an abundance of glass, brushed aluminum, and bleached wood. A US flag was mounted in a cylinder behind his desk.

After greeting the camera crew, he walked closer to his bookshelf. He drew inspiration from the row of separately encased Jackie Robinson baseball cards, realizing any of his problems were trivial compared to the torrents of prejudice and hate Robinson encountered. The set spanned the player's legendary career—from the 1947 rookie card to the final 1956 card that showed Robinson sliding boldly into home plate amid the swirling dust, wearing his Brooklyn Dodger blue *B* cap.

Sloan studied the framed black-and-white photograph of his father dressed in his usual dark suit, striped tie, white shirt, and matching handkerchief. His father's dress code was direct: "A man always looks good in a freshly pressed white shirt."

In the photograph, Mike's temples were gray; his jaw jutted. Sloan was ten years old in the photo as the two sat on a train somewhere in California. In that photograph, Mike was younger than Sloan was now, but to Sloan, his father appeared wiser. His thoughts drifted to Mike's alleged actions with Morgan, but he mentally pushed that aside;

it would not take up space in his mind right now.

He moved to his desk and closed his eyes to visualize cheering crowds as he stood onstage. He then read aloud his speech as it rolled down the teleprompter. Aware of his tendency to speak too rapidly, he asked the technician to slightly decrease its speed. After a moment, he sipped a brew of honey and oil to soothe his dry throat. He was ready. He watched the director count down. Twenty seconds until he was live.

"I'm Tyler Sloan." He opened with a satisfied smile, awash with unexpected serenity. "During the campaign, I've stated my vision to move Nevada, our nation, forward. My focus is outside of any bitter, poisoning partisanship."

He gave a light brush over policies, a moratorium on business regulations, fiscal stimulus to create jobs, measures to benefit Nevada's inner cities and rural communities—but this was not a political science salon. Tonight had its own pulse.

"Years ago, I was offered a spot judging talent on a TV show," Sloan said. "It sounded like fun, the pay was great, but that's not me...look!" he raised his voice to seize the viewer's attention. "Behind me are stacks of the federal tax code." He gestured to the volumes that stood perfectly aligned behind him on a credenza. "The code has seventy-five thousand pages and four million words. You need to be in the weight room to lift it and have an advanced degree to understand it."

His hands rested comfortably on the desk. "Conventional political wisdom was right; the two parties would join against me. Nevada voters have been besieged with internet rumors, half-truths, innuendos, and a private thirty-year-old video that embarrassed Ms. Collins." A half smile to cushion him against further damage. "With Photoshop, you may see distorted images of me kissing Marilyn Monroe or Jennifer Lawrence—maybe both.

"Why did I run?" His tone demanded an answer. "Not for fame or fortune, but to make a difference. I'm running against the special interests that have shackled Nevada with corrupt political cronyism."

Sloan shook his head as if to chastise Collins and Rogers. "My opponents have no solutions, so they point fingers and giggle about my dating life. You kidding me?" His voice rose. "That's not important; you deserve better."

The Teleprompter suddenly halted, sputtered, and froze; its words no longer tumbling forward. He had to improvise—no different from improvising on the stage.

"People ask me about my faith or how often I attend church. I'm not a student of the Bible like my mother was. She said, 'God blesses those whose hearts are pure.' I've made my share of mistakes, but I like to think that my heart is pure."

Sloan rose and urged the cameraman to follow him. He touched lightly on his celebrity, slowing as the camera was filming the walls dotted with mounted and framed posters of rock shows. The posters autographed to him ran the gamut from Chuck Berry to the Who and more recent Las Vegas appearances by Britney Spears and Céline Dion.

He gestured around his office. "My company employs more than a thousand people; half reside in Nevada. The two parties are bogged down in petty partisanship, fighting against each other. I'll change that. I'll fight for you."

He stood still, his hands outstretched, palms open. "Nevada knows Lady Luck. Lobbyists and special interests say voting for me is a roll of the dice, but *I'm* not the gamble. The real gamble is continuing the same path, same people, the same stale ideas. That risk is a losing roll of the dice."

The camera clicked off; the light dimmed.

Sloan looked over at Zimmer, who held a "thumbs-up" signal. Sloan raised his clenched fist in victory.

* * *

Palm Memorial Park was the final resting place for entertainers, gangsters, and politicians. Sloan's mother's will directed she would be interred in Nevada alongside her family. It was well past closing when Sloan arrived at the Las Vegas cemetery. He gained access with his time-tested bribe—a photo of him and the security guard on the guard's smartphone.

He strolled along the path between grave sites. He stopped at a stone that read, He did the best he could. Each grave marker allowed him to calculate life spans, determining those who were cheated and those who outlived the odds. He walked on and stopped at his brother's grave. J.R. had been cheated.

Sloan had secured a position at blue for J.R. when the firm was founded, but his brother chafed against any structure, preferring to play the role of an unofficial jester. While others were annoyed at the routine, Sloan grudgingly accepted his brother's idiosyncrasies, referring to him as the "Jokerman." One day, J.R. shouted how much he resented that title and quit abruptly.

His brother's memory stirred a cauldron of emotions. He remembered when they were at Hollywood Park racetrack, and J.R. had a violent outburst after a losing race. He recalled when his brother went to Las Vegas but cashed in his return airline ticket for one last run at the tables. Their mother had to wire money for bus fare for his return.

He wistfully recalled how the two brothers painted their street manhole cover green to serve as home plate for their "over-the-line" games; and when their father took out a baseball bat to hit tennis ball fungos over their heads, in front of them, behind them, anywhere but right at them.

Sloan recalled the exact moment when he received the dark phone call that his brother was gone. His eyes welled with tears. J.R. never found inner peace, and now his weaknesses could be exposed in controversy. He placed a rose on his brother's grave site; J.R. had done the best he could.

He still clutched a small bouquet of flowers for his mother, who was buried near the lake. He cast a wan smile at the dozen fresh red roses that were placed in front of her headstone. He knelt and touched the inscription of his mother's name, "Gladys Sloan," before putting his bouquet beside the roses.

Growing up, he had ignored friends who dismissed time spent with their mothers as a burden. He grimaced when others ridiculed the obligation of gifting their mom perfume or flowers on Mother's Day. Soon after his mother's death, a family friend told him that she was taken because God needed her. He never accepted how God needed his mother more than he did.

Sloan thought of one moment, his game-winning catch at a Little League baseball game. While running off the field to the cheers of parents and friends, the public address system announced, "Great catch by Tyler Sloan!" His mother yelled to the announcer, "Who caught it? Who caught it?" The announcer cheerfully replied, "Mrs. Sloan, that catch was by Tyler Sloan!"

Tonight, he ached for her presence. If only she could have attended one more Sloan campaign rally—*his* campaign rally. He regretted that she never saw Riley and that his daughter's only grasp of her grandmother was gleaned from photographs and his vignettes.

He knelt on one knee, kissing his fingertips before brushing them against the tombstone's raised lettering. Emulating how she had signed notes with only her initial, he delicately traced the *G* of his mother's name. With eyes closed and tears welling, he lifted his fingertips from the tombstone to graze across the grass.

With a heavy heart, he returned to his car. At the cemetery exit, he stopped the car and leaned through the window to thank the security guard once again. "The flowers on my mom's grave," he said. "Any chance you know who placed them?"

"Governor Sloan was here just about an hour ago," the security guard replied. "You gentlemen use the same routine."

"Routine?" Sloan quizzed.

"The governor begged me to let him in. I told him I was sorry about his wife, that I voted for him, and that it was an honor to meet him, but it was past visiting hours. He was very kind, but he insisted he needed to see his wife. He pulled out his business card, signed it, and told me if my family ever has any legal problems, he is our pro bono lawyer. Then we took a photo of the two of us." The guard playfully wagged his finger. "The apple did not fall far from the tree."

* * *

Late that night, Sloan sat alone at home reading Ted Richman's op-ed article entitled "Trust Your Gut?" that would be published in tomorrow's newspaper.

My first impression of Sloan was of a man who offered a refreshing change to politics. Then his campaign soured; his campaign manager resigned; commercials were questionably aired; illicit actions have been hinted at, although never proven; and an old video threatened to turn his campaign into a reality show. I'm stubborn. I hold to my initial impression—Sloan is an inspirational man with unorthodox views who can make a difference. He relates equally well to casino executives, blackjack dealers, and the disadvantaged. While you may chafe at some of his personal faux pas, frankly, Scarlett, I do not give a damn. Last night Sloan answered the fundamental question—the singer is ready for the Senate. Tyler Sloan is the real deal.

Sloan placed a throat lozenge in his mouth. Richman's praise was meaningful; the reporter had covered multiple presidents and more campaigns than Sloan could recall. He also reported on Mike Sloan. Earning his kudos was confirmation Sloan could play the game—and play it well.

THIRTY-EIGHT

Sunday, August 20, Reno,
2 Days to the Election

Poll: Collins 36%, Sloan 33%,
Rogers 22%, Undecided 9%

"You nailed it son." Mike was filled with pride. "Last night was a home run."

Sloan and his father were being driven to a Sunday service at Reno's most significant African American church. They drove past the Bethel AME church, a small, A-frame house constructed in 1910. A cross rested proudly atop Reno's first black church.

"Black churches are where the votes are," Mike added. "Like the old bank robber Willie Sutton said when someone asked him why he robbed banks: because that's where the money is." Mike paused. "We can't do my old habit of having dinner election night at Chasen's." He referred to the legendary and long-demolished Beverly Hills restaurant. "Remember how the maître d' was always decked out in a tux? That cheese toast was the best appetizer." Mike smacked his lips.

"Any thoughts on Morgan?" Sloan gave a gentle probe, no interest in Mike's reminiscing.

"See the overnight polls? That scumbag did you a favor."

"I'm not as confident as you and Grant," Sloan said casually. Mike stiffened when Sloan patted his father's knee. "We'll talk more about it after Tuesday."

Mike squirmed in his seat, glancing out the side window.

As they walked near the church together, Mike motioned for Sloan to walk ahead of him. "It's your name on the ballot, not mine."

Sloan grinned and gripped hands with the parishioners walking toward the stage to greet Reverend Reginald Biggins. The Reverend dipped his head toward Mike as a sign of respect.

Reverend Biggins held an unquestioned stature; the community leader cast a powerful aura. His large frame was enhanced by a flowing black robe, white shirt, and red tie. Sloan liked the sound of his voice, terming it "a bear-like growl coated with honey."

The reverend shook his head in disgust while citing the "racism that poisons our society." He said, "We *must* rise above prejudice and peacefully confront ignorance. We *must* find common ground with those who share our struggle."

Biggins paused to blot moisture from his large, round face. "We know all lives matter, but since this country's founding, we were told black lives do not matter. That must be corrected. This morning, we're blessed to have two men who know our struggles and who share our hopes. Tyler Sloan is here. I know what you're thinking." He stretched the word across the length and breadth of the church. "I knooow what you're thinking. Why place our hopes with a singer, a rock 'n' roll star?"

Biggins raised his hands to muffle the mild laughter. "Tyler Sloan's foundation has pumped resources and hope into our community. But before we hear from him, we are honored"—the reverend's voice rose—

"*honored* to have with us a legend, his father, the great governor of California. Mike Sloan spoke in my father's church in Los Angeles." His voice slowed. "Governor Sloan risked his career to battle against apartheid in South Africa. He rebuffed the misguided souls who sought to invest hundreds of millions of dollars of public pension funds in that country. His exact words were, 'Over my dead body will the State of California supports racism, apartheid, or inequality.'"

The church rang with *amens*. Mike rose and greeted the reverend with his signature greeting, cupping Biggins's right hand within both of his hands. The two men embraced.

"I used to be Mike Sloan." He smiled at the responding laughter. "I'm here this morning motivated by my love for you, the reverend, and my son."

Sloan studied Mike's nuances; each gesture had a purpose. With one wave of his hand, he cavalierly dismissed Collins and Rogers. His clenched fist communicated strength, and when he opened his hands, he was caressing the parishioners.

"My son has a lifetime commitment to equality. My son demanded that African Americans have the same opportunity in the music industry's corporate offices as others have been granted onstage."

A columnist once compared Mike's deep voice to a foghorn in a tunnel. Now that voice occasionally cracked but remained potent. Sloan noticed his father's hand gripping the pulpit, aware of the slight tremble. Mike appeared to realize this and seized a tighter grip.

"Stay with my family," Mike roared. "Stay with my son. We will not forget you, I never have, and my son never will. God bless you. God bless each one of you."

Biggins embraced Mike and again dabbed the sweat from his forehead with a bright-red handkerchief. His eyes scanned the heavens, his words jumping with sharp spikes of inflection. He ran Sloan's first and last names together as one. "TylerSloan, TylerSloan." Biggins slammed the pulpit with his fist. "TylerSloan did more than write songs for our brothers and sisters. TylerSloan is committed to securing federal grants to help our church's nonprofit organization build housing right here in Reno."

Sloan fixed his smile on Biggins, unaware of the housing grant.

Biggins's receding hairline and large face gave his forehead an unusual prominence. His thundering voice nearly rattled the stained-glass windows, threatening and mocking those who would disobey his counsel. "TylerSloan is our next senator! TylerSloan! TylerSloan!"

Applause resounded as Sloan bounded to the pulpit. The reverend's broad smile and embrace were the visual seals of his support. Standing at the pulpit, Sloan praised his father and the reverend, dishing equal doses of politics and sermon. His voice spiking with emphasis and falling with drama. "God is not finished with me. I'm still on my journey. My father stood with your parents and grandparents in the struggle for voting rights and opportunities. I stand together with you in our unfinished struggle. We know the fight for justice and equality continues."

Sloan removed the microphone from the lectern stand and moved across the stage. He recited a series of "hopes and dreams" as the congregation responded with nods, amens, and shouts of agreement. Pacing across the stage, a boxer bouncing on his feet, challenging all comers. The congregation surged with currents of electricity. He returned to the pulpit, but his energy couldn't be harnessed.

"We can do it! We can do it!" Sloan thundered. The amens grew louder, rolling through the faithful, mounting in a crescendo; he was speaking with gut-wrenching force: "We will not falter! We will not fail!" Sloan abruptly raised his arms for silence. The chapel hushed still, his arms raised. His head bowed, chin down, eyes closed. He bit his lip before asking for their forgiveness and their prayers. "Stay with me; pray with me." His head remained bowed.

Slowly, almost imperceptibly, Sloan's chin tilted upward, his smile now a touch defiant. His gaze began in the first pew and methodically touched on each row until he reached the stained-glass windows that lined the rear of the church.

"There is no justice when a child recognizes the sound of an AK-47 automatic weapon before they recognize the sounds of your church choir," Sloan added humbly. He turned to face Reverend Biggins. "Reverend, I don't want to merely *hear* your choir. May I sing one hymn with that heavenly choir? May I?"

The congregation tittered with excitement as the reverend nodded his approval.

"'Amazing Grace' was written by an Englishman over a century ago," Sloan began. "The song's writer, John Newton, was not a religious man, but when the storms were rocking his British navy boat, and his life was endangered, young John called out to God. The boat was saved, and John began his spiritual journey. He quit as a slave trader and began religious studies."

Sloan nodded to the church's organist and began to sing "Amazing Grace."

The choir filled the chapel in voices rising and falling in rhythm with Sloan. When he'd sung the last note, he stepped from the pulpit to the reverend's open arms. Every eye in the church was fixed upon the two. Sloan whispered, "About that nonprofit housing…"

Reverend Biggins's large hand wrapped around Sloan's shoulder, his voice deep but soft. "Son, the Lord knows your needs even before you do."

* * *

Sloan had lost track if this was the day's sixth or seventh speech. He had forgotten the school's name but surmised it was a community college based on the size of the gymnasium.

Standing at the lectern at the Carson City school for the day's last event, he amused himself by finding one person in the crowd to share a common element. He noticed an elderly woman in the front row. "Your lovely smile reminds me of my dear mother." He thanked the teacher who introduced him and added, "I have the exact same shirt."

The audience was overwhelmingly white, yet Biggins's church remained on Sloan's mind. "Too many people, rural and urban, people of all races and ethnic groups, are trapped by a web of circumstances. We have a moral obligation to assist those who are trapped." Sloan paused. "As Dr. Martin Luther King Jr. said, 'We either all rise together or stay down together.' Join me to lift all of Nevada to new greatness."

At that moment, the confetti-filled balloons were accidentally released from the auditorium's ceiling to blanket Sloan in a deluge of silver, blue, and white shreds. The crowd appeared startled, yet Sloan smiled through it all—he had encountered more obstacles this week than harmless balloons.

His voice reflecting weariness, modestly stronger than a sandpaper whisper. Resting one hand on the lectern, he offered a brief riff through policy issues. He asked for questions. Audience members with questions stood obediently at a microphone in the front of the gym.

"I have a serious question," stated a man dressed in a worker's uniform and jacket.

Sloan asked for his name, but it wasn't given.

"Who appointed you to take away our Second Amendment right to bear arms?"

Sloan again asked for the man's name.

"Answer my question. Why are you taking away my rights?"

Sloan's vision suddenly blurred. He leaned against the lectern to steady himself. He could feel his pulse throbbing in his temples and felt sweat break out on his forehead. "I have not taken away any of your constitutional rights and will not do so. I want to protect our children and our families with reasonable waiting periods and background checks."

Determination was seared upon the man's gaunt face. His wayward straw hair frayed upward and outward. "I'm a hunter, a sportsman," the man said, each word sounding more menacing than his last. "I'm not building a nuclear weapon in my backyard. I ask again, why do you want to take away my constitutional rights?"

Sloan felt light headed; the crowd was dissolving in swirling fog, their faces melting like a Dali painting. Sloan studied the man. He appeared to be in his mid-thirties, wearing a worker's uniform, a jacket puzzling with the room's stifling humidity. Sloan was massaging his temples, seeking clarity, the crowd appearing in a haze.

"You have rights, but everyone has a right…to be free from violence." He drew a weary breath. "Hunters don't need assault weapons and machine guns."

The host of the event finally intervened to remind all those with questions to be respectful. "Thank you, sir, for your question," he said. "And now, let's hear from another." He invited the next person in line to step forward.

Sloan appreciated the save, seeking distance from the questioner. He was unable to thank the host for interceding. He had forgotten if his name was Sandy, Andy, or Randy.

The young man took one step in retreat from the microphone but then turned abruptly and flashed a disjointed smile. "Don't mess with my baby!" he shouted with startling intensity. "Don't touch a mother's baby and don't touch a man's gun. My gun is my baby!"

With that, he whipped a Glock pistol from inside his jacket pocket. The crowd dispersed in screams and whimpers, rushing to find cover or the nearest exit as one shot rang out, another bang, another shot.

Sloan momentarily froze on stage, a moment before feeling an intense burning sensation in his shoulder; the bullet had grazed him. The pain caused him to drop to one knee. His teeth clenched, his shoulder felt numb. His mind dizzy, unable to steady himself. *Damn, I've been shot*, was his only thought.

Local police and security guards converged from all angles and wrestled the shooter to the floor while Sloan's security team stormed onto the stage and surrounded him. His team whipped out their weapons, turning away from Sloan, scanning the crowd, running to the shooter.

A woman rushed to the stage, announcing, "I'm a doctor, I'm a doctor."

Sloan's shirt was torn, and the doctor quickly examined him. Her voice fortified him. "One bullet grazed you—it doesn't look like any arteries were hit." She barked out her command, "Let's get him to ER."

Sloan clenched his teeth at the burning pain.

* * *

After being examined and bandaged, Sloan was assisted onto the jet for the return flight to Las Vegas. His left arm was in a sling. Medication had dimmed the pain, his thoughts muddy. Bree had called Riley, Mike, Zimmer, and Cindy to assure them that he was fine.

His aide Heather held on to his uninjured arm to steady him as he was eased into his seat. Bree was lightly dabbing his forehead with a damp washcloth. Her eyes were tight with worry. Sloan slumped in his seat and took a series of calming breaths.

Bree handed him his cell phone to talk to Riley. "Sweetie, Daddy's fine."

He listened to his daughter sob; then he heard her tears flow. Amid the cries, she explained that she'd seen the news while surfing the internet. "I thought you died," Riley said with a pain he had never heard from her. It was a gut-wrenching sadness.

"I'm hurting, but I'm OK; the bullet just grazed me." He tried to find humor. "Lost a good shirt and suit, but angel, I'm fine, expect to be campaigning tomorrow. Why don't you ask Mom if you can fly in and join me for the last two days? This was one nut case; there's nothing to worry about."

The pilot stood across from Sloan. His thick arms lay across his chest. "The doctor said you were fine, but we can get to a hotel a few minutes from here and fly out tomorrow, or we can sit here awhile. No hurries, no worries, take your time."

"I'm…" He cast a tired smile. "I'm tired. Need to go home." Sloan turned to Bree. "How did that psycho get past security?"

Bree explained that the shooter worked at the school and stored a Glock subcompact gun and ammunition in his locker.

Heather stood and leaned closer to Sloan. "Do you want some good news?"

Sloan was almost too tired to nod as she added, "The president said Nevada will be in good hands if you're elected. His exact words, 'in good hands.'" Sloan summoned a weak smile as she added, "Rasmussen's latest poll? Dead heat with Collins."

Sloan rested his head on the pillow, pondering what had just occurred. Tomorrow's first event was in eight short hours. What possessed the man to shoot him? What drove one human being to try to kill another? He thought of John Lennon, the school children, all the tragedies and lives lost to senseless gun violence. He felt a fatigue light-years beyond tired, ready to sleep for days. Yet he had to finish. He had to close.

THIRTY-NINE

*Monday, August 21, Southern Nevada,
1 Day to the Election*

**Poll: Collins 36%, Sloan 35%,
Rogers 22%, Undecided 7%**

Sloan moved slowly as he strode onstage before a capacity crowd at the Thomas & Mack Center, the off-campus home to the basketball team of the University of Nevada, Las Vegas. His movements were restrained as he performed the candidate's kabuki theater of smiles and nods. His left arm rested in a sling, his shoulder bandaged; he gestured with his right hand.

He masked his displeasure at seeing a sign that read, Honk if You've Slept with Tyler Sloan. Seeking to avoid any embarrassment, he'd avoided heavy medication, relying on Advil and grit. His speech was brief. A campaign video that presaged his entrance had pumped up the crowd.

Sloan placed his right hand on the lectern. "Last night was a little rough; getting shot at takes a lot of the fun out of a campaign rally." The crowd hesitated before cheering. "Some people say electing me would cause chaos in Washington. Chaos in Washington? Talk about redundancy." He leaned forward on the lectern. "Your grandparents will recall how Elvis was chaos; your parents would cite the Beatles or Muhammed Ali as chaos; you may say that rap, hip-hop, and electronic music are chaos." He partially raised his right hand, forcing a smile past the now striking pain. "What's wrong with a little chaos?"

* * *

"Richman wants a few minutes," Bree said, approaching Sloan and Zimmer on the campaign bus.

Sloan popped two more Advils.

"I'm whipped," he declined. "You two see the ol' dog."

"He said you *need* to hear him," Bree replied. "It's all off the record. Besides, the ol' dog will cover you in the Senate."

The polls would open in thirty-four hours. Sloan rubbed his temples to combat a mild but persistent headache. He smiled when Bree adjusted the pillow under his left arm. He instructed her to bring his father in to join the meeting with Richman.

"He's sleeping," Bree replied in a maternal tone.

"Let him rest," Sloan replied. "Bring Richman back; let's hope the ol' dog's not growling. If he is, Grant deals with him."

Richman entered the private section at the back of the bus. "You're going to shake the political world tomorrow," Richman said gruffly as he took the seat across from him. "I hope it was fun for you."

"More fun than when I was sixteen with April in the back seat of my Mustang." Sloan was laced with sarcasm. He shot an apologetic glance at Bree. "That was off the record, Ted."

Richman waved acceptance.

"What was an opponent's best ad?" the reporter queried.

"That old barber who cut my hair during a campaign swing in rural Nevada. I laughed when I saw it." Sloan impersonated the cranky barber from Ely: "I cut his hair, but I need to cover his views; oooh… that boy ought to keep singing."

Richman vented. "I asked this guy for directions on one of your stops outside of Fallon. He told me, 'Left at the filling station, right at the Dairy Queen.' That's how people live?"

"Collins ran some great spots," Bree added without inflection, like a technician reviewing x-rays. Consultants viewed winning political campaigns as museum-quality masterpieces while losing efforts were relegated as garage-sale art.

"I was on her campaign plane when Morgan held his presser." Richman's grin widened. "She screamed, 'Oh my God!' five frickin' times and then described you and Rogers in pretty creative terms. Hell, she should have been that original during the campaign."

Sloan leaned into Richman. "Who writes the website the Political Fool?"

"Honest?" Richman's eyes squinted in his response.

"We'd prefer it," Zimmer replied, winking at Sloan.

Richman prefaced his answer with how he would deny any knowledge of this conversation. The website was a joint effort of two reporters from the *Huffington Post* and *Politico.com*. He paused. "Oh, yeah, that kid Josh…whatever-his-middle-name-is Mack, he contributes sometimes."

Sloan's gut tightened, but he was careful to keep his expression stoic. He avoided even a glance at Bree.

Richman eyed Bree. "The Collins romp was a long time ago, and this smart gal is no thong-snapping intern. Neither hurt you."

"Let's not go there," Bree snapped.

Richman grunted an apology. He looked hard at Sloan as if seeking to detect a reaction. "Collins doesn't know how, but she blames you for the video's release."

"Did you hear Morgan?" Zimmer interjected. "A pity Rogers sunk so low."

Richman's smug expression signaled his suspicions. "Morgan vanished. There's a report that two of you were yucking it up at the Orleans Hotel in May at his old-timer's event."

Sloan acknowledged the meeting and their long relationship.

"Exactly." Richman was quick to respond. "Why would an old friend throw you under the bus and sell the video to Rogers?"

"The power of the purse—money talks," Sloan replied.

"Maybe Morgan dropped his nuke to help you, to hit Collins." Richman's voice was measured; he had given thought to his words; these were not spontaneous musings. "Maybe Rogers thought the video was too hot to air. Morgan leaks it, blames Rogers, and drops off the face of the earth. A boatload of intrigue, buckets of mystery."

Sloan was content to listen.

"I solved one mystery," Richman said as he opened a large manila envelope he had brought on the bus. He removed numerous letters printed on plain paper. He explained that all the letters were unsigned, sent via the postal service's overnight mail, all addressed to: "Ted Richman, the *Review-Journal.*" None had a return address.

"Each letter revealed your campaign strategies, press conferences, and television spots days before they aired." Richman's voice was flat, nonjudgmental.

Sloan's posture turned instantly erect; he stared uncertainly at Richman.

"We also received emails from a random email account. We tried but couldn't trace it." The reporter was clinical, a voice without inflection, while giving Sloan printed copies of the emails. Sloan read them before passing them on to Zimmer, then to Bree.

"The info was always reliable except for two referred to Creighton Collins and a trust matter, but you never raised that. One email early in the campaign gave me the exact dates you were in rehab and that it was cocaine. I knew it well before you went public. The emails had a ton of personal info, but that's not my style."

Sloan recoiled as he shuffled through the letters. The information slammed against him like a series of debilitating body blows. His jaw locked as he attempted to display a veneer of coolness while shivers shot down his spine. He forced himself to project composure.

"The letters never mentioned the sex tape," Richman added, pausing meaningfully as if taking Sloan's measure.

Sloan bit down on his lip to avoid a primal scream.

He scanned his memory. Who in the campaign knew about Creighton Collins and the trust? Martino and the FBI? Did Bree confide in Mack? The first tip on cocaine was the tell—a secret he only disclosed to Zimmer when news broke that the electronic files at the Betty Ford Clinic were hacked. But there was no reason for his attorney to sell him out. If he was elected, Zimmer's influence would skyrocket.

Richman broke the ensuing silence with a loud clearing of his throat. "At least someone still uses the post office. Bottom line, you had a fifth column feeding me."

"Thoughts? Who do you think it was?" Sloan asked sharply. "You must have an idea."

Richman's vision darted between Sloan, Bree, and Zimmer.

"An inkling. I have an inkling," Richman replied with detached coolness.

"Damn it—out with it," Sloan said firmly.

"Years ago, we had a bomb scare at the paper. It's not public, but we starting recording all incoming calls until we're certain they're legit. When we started getting these packages, our lawyers gave us a longer leash. We feared we were being set up for God knows what. Your caller used a device you can buy online to disguise your voice from male to female. The voice was analyzed, and the mailings fingerprinted."

Richman fixed a hard stare at the three. He appeared to summon courage as he blurted, "Creighton Collins called, and your ex-wife sent the letters. She most likely was sending the emails—too much personal info for anyone else to know."

"Damn it," Sloan blurted. When his head snapped back, he shouted aloud from the pain in his shoulder.

Sloan's mind was a swirling dervish of thoughts. Cindy knew almost nothing about the campaign but could have skillfully pumped Riley for information. Years before, Cindy had surreptitiously accessed his emails and could have done so again. Silently cursing, he recalled on their honeymoon confessing details of the reason for his stay at Betty Ford. Those details were part of the marital bargain, confide in spouses.

"By the way, how are you feeling?" Richman asked suddenly.

"How do I feel?" Sloan snapped loudly. "What the fuck, Ted? Yesterday I was shot, and today you tell me my ex-wife tried to sabotage me." He breathed deeply to temper his anger. His voice was not close to being calm. His words slow: "How-in-the-hell-do-you-think-I-feel?"

"Sorry, very sorry." Richman was chastised. "My bad, that one's on me."

Sloan nodded to the reporter. "We're good. I owe you one."

Richman appeared in no hurry to leave. "I covered your dad in the Florida primary when it was humid as hell, mosquitoes the size of pigeons. He never even wiped his brow. Another time we were in a blizzard in New Hampshire. Mike never complained. He told me how his dad, your grandfather, was a poor kid in Lincoln, Nebraska, and stood in the snow selling newspapers for two cents." He pointed at Sloan. "You got those genes; you never complained."

Sloan mouthed a silent "thank you" as he grazed Richman's hand. After the reporter exited the private cabin, Sloan motioned for Zimmer to draw the sliding door to ensure their privacy. He placed his finger on his lip to signal for quiet until he was confident Richman was no longer within the listening range. "My ex-wife?" Sloan was laced with anger. He muttered aloud about her drug dependency, how an addict's actions were never logical. He repeated the word *addict*—the first time he'd described her that bluntly. Her Judas kiss had erased any empathy for her.

Sloan thumbed through a stack of emails and letters Richman left. The writing style resembled Cindy's. He sighed in a cathartic release, attempting to grasp the enormity of her actions. He linked dates and activities with the staff person who had knowledge of each event. Creighton Collins needed an inside source, and Cindy could not possibly be aware of every detail.

"Martino knew it all," Zimmer said tightly. "Maybe he cracked for a cash fix."

Sloan slumped in his seat. He went through a retrospective vetting of each campaign staff member's possible motives. What they knew and when they knew it. No one appeared to possess all the details contained in each letter.

"General Rails. Major Rails. Whatever he was, was he doing covert operations to bug our office?" Bree said, mocking Rails's penchant for utilizing military phrases.

Sloan gripped the stack of letters and spoke in a stream of consciousness. Martino held all the keys to the campaign kingdom. His legal troubles remained an ominous dark cloud, and the notes to Richman could be part of a deal with the FBI. Alternatively, a low-level volunteer could have seen memos or overheard conversations. A campaign mercenary could have flipped when Sloan's chances were dim. Rails was an obvious choice for a role as a conduit or more.

Sloan adjusted the pillow under his arm in a futile attempt to find comfort. "I'm not keeping any of that hired-gun staff. If I wanted to find the culprit, I'd have to give lie detector tests to twenty people. I'd be dubbed the paranoid senator. I'm moving on, got to move on."

* * *

Hours later, sitting alone in the rear of the campaign bus, Sloan listened to a live airing of *In the Office*.

"Sloan gave a good speech, but who forced him to cheat with another man's fiancée?" the caller asked with dripping sarcasm. "He and Chris Collins were an item? Billy Rogers is trash for buying that video. I feel bad for Collins; it's an unfair double standard for women. But, feel sorry for Sloan, questions about his dead brother. Honestly, I'm confused about who to vote for."

"Hold your thoughts," the host replied. "My editorial is on after these commercials."

Sloan recalled his success at his surprise appearance on Tammy Keller's show. One more surprise appearance—he hastily called the station. The screener quickly proclaimed, "You're on next."

When the show returned, Dr. D. proudly announced, "Good evening to Tyler Sloan. Great to have you join us 'In the Office.' Any final thoughts on the campaign?"

"I've enjoyed every minute of it. Sometimes I've felt like a juggler with chain saws. The good news is I've sparked a few calls to 'the Office,' and I'm glad to help the doctor's ratings."

"Always grateful for the assist." *The host* chuckled. "Mr. Sloan, I sincerely hope you're feeling well. You're in the executive suite tonight. Go ahead and make your case."

"Let's look at the last week." Sloan was at ease. "I've called for reasonable controls on the sale of guns and ammunition, for tax incentives for business to start and prosper. I've incurred the wrath of the teacher's union when I demand greater accountability in our schools. I'm proud to be an equal opportunity irritant to the special interests."

"I admire your guts, but is character a legitimate issue?"

"Sure, but my opponents mistake true character. There's no character in trading your votes for campaign contributions. There's no character in bowing to the special interests."

"These personal controversies about you…are they important?"

"It's hard to imagine who I dated thirty years ago or last week is important. A decent person would not subject my father or any parent to recalling details of their son's death, my dear brother. Nevada voters are focused on the now. They're focused on my plans to create jobs, educate our children, and mobilize our country against acts of aggression by China, Russia, or North Korea. We must be prepared, threats from multiple sources. That's what's important."

"Thank you, Mr. Sloan." Dr. D. abruptly clicked off Sloan and continued without a pause. "The good doctor has kept his piehole shut until tonight. Here's my editorial. First, we salute Chris Collins as a patriot, but she's too beholden to the status quo. Billy Rogers's beliefs?

Totally out of step with Nevada; increasing taxes and regulations is never a winning prescription. Sloan's dating life, what he and Collins did when they were young, does not matter to me one whit, but yes, Rogers knows better than to buy a purloined video.

"I've always been a fan of the entertainer Tyler Sloan. I studied him during the campaign; he's more than a fortunate son with God-given talent. The man has achieved on his own merits, his talents, and his intellect. Tyler Sloan is clever...and that's a compliment—he gets it; he gets Nevada."

The host added forcefully, "Forget your litmus tests—Sloan is tough and smart. Politics is Darwinism, the survival of the fittest. Sloan is the fittest. Sloan is Nevada's best choice."

"Yes!" Sloan yelled. He laughed aloud; he laughed alone. These were wild swing:; from third, twenty points behind Collins, to now, where cynical radio talk show hosts were shouting his praises. "Yes!" he shouted again.

FORTY

Election Day, Tuesday,
August 22, Las Vegas

Sloan carefully retrieved the envelope from his coat pocket. He had a minute before the workers would arrive at Caesar's Palace employee-entry gate. He was surrounded by dozens of volunteers waving Sloan for Senate signs and a hearty media corps that stood with him at six a.m.

He turned his back to the cameras, asking his aide to open the envelope addressed to "Daddy." He read the smudged note on pink stationery, dotted with red hearts. Riley had drawn the US Capitol Riley "Senator Sloan" hovering above the dome.

Despite his body aching from the shoulder wound, despite his mental state, he was a muddy mix of adrenaline and fatigue—he was ready.

A regular stream of workers sought his autograph on T-shirts, scraps of paper, and dollar bills. Even with his right hand, any signature drove his pain; his staff was encouraging cell phone photos.

"Bree and Chris, both look fine," one burly man whispered to Sloan.

Four young, shirtless men stood nearby, enthusiastically waving Sloan for Senate signs. Each of the four had a letter scrawled in red on his chest: *S, L, O,* and *A*. Sloan asked lightly, "Where's the *N*?"

"He slept in—last night was a killer!" one of the men shouted back.

Mike approached and greeted his son. "A little toasty for seven a.m., but this beats Iowa in January. It was so cold my ears were stinging, and my nose froze."

* * *

On the flight north, Sloan squeezed in telephone calls to voters who'd responded to his debate close in which he'd urged Nevada voters to call him.

"Mr. Jose Garcia? This is Tyler Sloan. You called me last night?"

Garcia asked Sloan to summarize his immigration stance and then shouted, "Go!"

Sloan blanched at the volume. "Immigration is like a complex issue." He attempted levity. "It's like a multilayered cake; you have to eat a full slice to grasp all of the flavors."

"A cake?" Garcia loudly mocked the analogy. "You're going dooooooooooown!"

Sloan held the phone aloft. "Mark him down as undecided."

* * *

A string of impersonators sang "Viva Las Vegas" as Sloan stood on an outdoor stage in downtown Las Vegas. He was surrounded by the neon visual blast of the Fremont Street Experience.

"Only in America can someone like me run for office, and only in Las Vegas could"—he pointed toward the row of impersonators lining the front row—"Marilyn Monroe, Mike Tyson, and Lady Gaga sing my praises."

Sloan felt a pang in his shoulder and noticeably winced. The audience responded with a sympathetic moan. Suddenly, cheers, then sustained applause as if the audience sought to rally him.

"You're tough!" A shout rang out.

"Me? No, let me tell you about political toughness." Sloan was feeling loose; he was telling stories. "One hundred years ago, Teddy Roosevelt was running for president on the Bull Moose political party ticket. Teddy got shot at a rally. Teddy fell, got up, and finished his speech. He said, 'It takes more than a bullet to stop a bull moose.'" He waited for the cheers. "I might be tough, but I'm not Teddy tough."

The famed "Howdy Partner" sign with "Vegas Vic" was glowing with kitsch and promise. Sloan appreciated the odds—this could be his final political speech.

"I've traveled all around the globe; there's no city like Las Vegas! Great to be home! I've fought for you." His voice cracked. "And you've been there for me. Today Nevada will elect a fighter to the United States Senate." He paused to take it all in. "*Vaya con Dios.*"

* * *

"Is my lip gloss on straight?" Riley asked her father as she viewed her compact mirror for a last-minute touch-up.

It was 9:00 election night, and from the back seat, Sloan studied a hotel under construction; the site was the former home of the Rivera Hotel. At its 1954 groundbreaking, casino executives proudly displayed nine fingers to signify that its nine-story "skyscraper" would be the city's tallest. The hotel's final years resembled an aging dame smothered in lipstick and cream but unable to mask her wrinkles. The "Riv's" sixty-year run of hot dice ended with the city's spectator sport: a televised hotel implosion.

After arriving at the Mandalay Bay Hotel for the election night festivities, Sloan and Riley were escorted to a hotel suite. Access was restricted to his inner circle. Sloan eyed his father, the raconteur, surrounded by a coterie of staff.

Sloan stood in the corner of the suite, bouncing from one foot to another, his jaw tightening when one aide announced the first results were overdue.

Mike came close to Sloan and lightly grasped his shoulder. "We have this one."

Sloan gobbled mints from the glass dish. He noticed Zimmer pacing incessantly. He hoped his own wayward nerves were more discreet.

"*Schpilkis?*" Zimmer asked, using the Yiddish expression of visible nervousness.

CNN's anchor announced that their exit polls had the race as too close to call between Collins and Sloan; Rogers was projected to finish third.

The moment that report ended, another anchor read breathlessly, "The first count of absentee ballots shows Chris Collins with thirty-eight percent, Tyler Sloan thirty-four percent, and Billy Rogers with twenty-eight percent."

Riley looked uncertainly at her father as he slowly walked her into the suite's bedroom. Her eyes began to tear; her lip quivered. He forced a minimalist smile that belied his fears. He caressed her hand. His facade was strong, yet he braced himself for the worst. He would not allow Riley to bear witness to his surrender.

Mike joined the two in the corner of the suite. "We have this one."

Sloan softly cursed, irritated at the flippant remark. The mere thought of delivering a concession speech caused him to reach into his pocket to grab a handful of pink antacid tablets. As he walked, the pain from the wound stabbed again, and he slugged down two Advils.

"You OK, Daddy?" Riley asked, the tears now beginning to trickle down her face.

He bent down to kiss away her tears.

Sloan stood alone at the sliding glass door, gazing into the Strip's neon. He wondered if the national media would dismiss him as a freak candidate or a courageous challenger? How would he answer the questions asked of all defeated candidates: "What would you have done differently?" and "Will you run again?" Psychic probes into shattered hopes.

The fog of war was always damp in campaigns, only clearing in postmortems where talking heads explained with dogged certainty what they failed to grasp twenty-four hours earlier.

"It's not even all the absentees," Mike said with conviction. "The fat lady's not singing. Hell, she's not even in the room."

Sloan maintained a blank stare outside the window. "It's over. We had to hold even in the vote-by-mail. My hardcore fans figured to vote early."

"Tomorrow they'll call you senator," Mike said with assurance.

Sloan sought to grasp a glimmer of hope, yet the numbers never lied.

"Trust me," Mike said emphatically. He explained that the voters who'd mailed in ballots were not aware of the president's supportive comments, did not hear Morgan's press conference or view Sloan's speech on Saturday.

A loud knock on the door prefaced Heather's entrance into the room. "Mr. Sloan, NBC has reported all the absentees; we're only down by one, but they're not projecting a winner."

Before Sloan could respond, the Harry Potter doppelgänger entered and thundered, "ABC announced you won the first three live precincts reporting from Carson City."

"Good news, Daddy?" Riley asked in near desperation.

Sloan lightly caressed her shoulder. "Could be, sweetheart."

The initial dark cloud in the living room had dissipated as Sloan, Riley, and Mike returned to join the crowd. The room burst into cheers as one network anchor stated, "It promises to be a long night, but a Sloan upset is a real possibility."

Standing with Zimmer in an unoccupied corner of the living room, Sloan patted his right coat pocket. "Here's my victory speech." He then patted his left coat pocket. "The concession speech. In my pants pocket is my Gore speech—we'll keep fighting."

"Don't forget which speech is in which pocket," Zimmer cracked.

At eleven p.m., the suite was riddled with anxiety amid thin reeds of hope. Sloan drew his father and Zimmer together. He expressed his deepening worry that the two political parties could band together in an unholy alliance to deny his election. He asked if Jennings could locate an arcane Senate rule to not seat him. If there was no senator in the seat,

Jennings could protect his majority, each party would have a "do-over" in fifteen months at next November's election.

At Zimmer's blank stare, Sloan's uncertainty grew. The answer man was mute.

Mike motioned for Bree to come to his side. "Get us Senator Jennings on a secure line. We'll take it in the bedroom."

* * *

"Senator, we should work together," Sloan opened with a wispy political cliché that he instantly regretted.

"Gotta count all the votes," Senator Buddy Jennings said and then repeated, "*all* the votes."

Sloan grimaced at the pointed emphasis of *all*.

"You gave me your word, Buddy"—Mike spoke loudly into the speakerphone—"that as majority leader, you would support the results, whatever they may be."

"It's Nevada." Jennings's reply held a flourish resembling that of a keynote speaker at a national political convention. "Chris's people are not cashing in their chips. It's still tight, boys."

Sloan glanced at his phone. His lead remained tenuous; his margin held at nearly two thousand votes with a third of the votes counted. "Let's not waste each other's time. If you push me out now, I'm caucusing with the Dems."

"Now, now, now." Jennings's voice of artificial sweetness did not soothe. His tone moved to a level of southern hospitality, the tone either charmed or annoyed depending upon which side of the Mason-Dixon Line your ancestors were raised on, "I'm not pushing you anywhere. As the leader of my caucus, I have to abide by the will of my caucus."

If Sloan won, he would be courted by both parties dangling plum committee assignments as enticements to join their caucus and vote for their leader as the majority leader. The current minority leader was holding on his other phone line, and two other senators who were expected to seek ascension to leadership had left messages in the past twenty minutes.

"Tyllllerrrr." Jennings stretched the word like a Confederate rubber band. "I have to wait until Chris concedes. Your daddy knows this. Give me a day to sort this out."

"The president's aboard," Sloan stated firmly. "You heard him yesterday."

"I've been threatened by too many presidents," Jennings bellowed. "God bless the president, but I've committed to Chris and my party."

Sloan was respectful before he cranked the heat. "Senator, one day, Grant and I are going to be asked to help fund your next opponent. How should I answer?"

"Son, you're jumpier than a long-tailed cat in a room full of rocking chairs," Jennings replied. "Mike, call me tomorrow, let's keep the dialogue open."

In the next instant, Zimmer was punching the White House phone number on the speakerphone.

Zimmer spoke in hushed tones. He assured the president that only he, Sloan, and Mike were parties to the conversation.

"Hell of a campaign, Tyler, a hell of a campaign," the president replied, his words slightly slurred. "Mike, glad you reached out to my staff, glad to help with that Cuba letter."

"Bret," Mike paused and then corrected himself to utter the phrase that still carried a foul taste. "Mr. President...our party had its shot with Billy."

"Well, he's beating the Green Party gal," the president stated merrily.

Zimmer's hand motion reflected a man drinking from a glass.

"That was one motherfucker of a campaign," Reed said. "Nothing comes close."

The hour was late, and Reed had enjoyed a cocktail...or two...or three.

Zimmer expressed his concerns that a federal judge would pay heed to a united front of Republican and Democratic senators alleging election fraud. Only the power of the presidency could rebut that effort.

"It smacks of a coup if Jennings dicks around with it," Reed said pointedly.

"Mr. President, I'll be in the foxhole with you," Sloan said in a tone that masked his anxiety. "An early statement from you may stop any legal shenanigans."

"Grant," Reed began slowly, "call my counsel in the morning and work with him on a statement from me. We honor the Constitution, and no one is stealing this damn election."

The moment that call ended, Sloan contacted the campaign's legal counsel. His lead had diminished to twelve hundred votes.

It was after two a.m. in Washington, DC; the counsel requested a minute to "clear her head." Sloan cited a run of possibilities. She was measured in her responses, listing an array of legal issues and challenges if the Senate refused to seat Sloan.

"I'm not paying you for a Constitutional Law seminar," Sloan snapped. "What the hell will happen?"

"You *should* win in court." Her tone was calm. "But as the governor knows, that does not mean you *will* win in court. We cannot depend on fairness."

"Fairness in an election?" Mike replied. "The ultimate oxymoron."

* * *

Sloan and his entourage exited the suite to meet with his supporters downstairs. In an elevator crammed with staff, Bree whispered, "It's a good night, sweet prince."

In one move, Sloan discreetly grazed Bree's shoulder and leaned into her. "I hope I'm not catching you on the rebound."

"No rebound, but get ready for a hell of a bounce back." She gently grazed his good shoulder.

Moments before the elevator door opened, Riley positioned herself to avoid Sloan's wounded arm. She tightly hugged her father with unbridled warmth. Her arms remained locked around him when the door opened to a sea of bright lights and cameras.

Wayne Avrashow

Sloan walked through a passageway and onto the stage of the Mandalay Bay Hotel Ballroom with supporters loudly chanting, "Ty-ler, Ty-ler, Ty-ler."

Standing at the lectern, Sloan fixed his smile while nodding in affirmation. He raised his right fist in the air in triumph. The crowd's volume cranked loud.

The din of cheering partisans repeatedly chanted, "Ty-ler! Ty-ler! Ty-ler!"

Sloan waited for the right moment. "We're leading, barely, but we're leading. It's premature to declare victory." He grinned, his emotions unleashed. "And I'm certainly not declaring anything else."

Sloan waited for the roar to abate. He thanked vital supporters and members of his campaign staff. A collective cheer emitted from the room as CNN announced that Sloan's lead over Collins had increased to nearly two thousand votes.

"It's going to be a long night, maybe a long couple of days. But friends…we're going to change America."

Sloan walked off the stage. Out of public view, he tugged on his father's wrist to draw him closer to ensure their privacy. Zimmer stood a few feet away.

"Damn it, Dad," Sloan said passionately. "We can't have those bastards steal this election from me."

Mike leaned forward. Sloan was startled to feel the stubble from Mike's cheek scratch against his cheek at his father's kiss.

"I won't let that happen," Mike replied.

Sloan stuttered, then looked squarely at his father. Their lifetime relationship was a roller-coaster ride of twists and turns. At this moment, there were no tense yesterdays.

"I would have lost, but…you turned it around." Sloan's voice cracked.

"No. The candidate is always the most important weapon in a campaign." Mike beamed. "There will be a recount, but with your lead, we'll stay ahead."

"I've got to know about Rogers, Morgan, the video—"

"No," Mike sharply interrupted. "There's nothing you need to know or should know."

"You don't know, and you don't want to know," Zimmer chimed in as he moved closer.

"Damn it, Grant." Sloan's voice was sharp. "You're my lawyer, not my dad's. You both knew the video would leak. I know you guys did something. Spill it. What did you do?"

Mike shot a glance at Zimmer. It was the signal he would respond.

"How bad did you want to win?" Mike queried.

"How bad?" Sloan snapped back. "I gave up my career and put tens of millions in. Don't ask me that question."

Mike's hands dampened down as he accepted Sloan's verbal lashing. "Sorry, that didn't come out right." He exhaled. "Can you trust your father and your lawyer?"

"That's not the issue," Sloan said sharply.

"We gave you what you need—plausible deniability," Zimmer added.

"I want more," Sloan demanded. "Tell me everything."

Zimmer placed his palm out toward Mike. He would answer. He detailed how he had assembled sworn declarations from Rogers's staff, copies of Morgan's phone records disclosing calls between him and Rogers's campaign operatives, and copies of Morgan's bank accounts that confirmed the funds were wired from Rogers to Morgan. "It's an airtight case."

The fact that both men relished intrigue did not placate Sloan.

"I can't have this blow up on me." Sloan was firm. "Not now, not a year from now. Talk to me."

Zimmer methodically explained that before he met with Morgan, he attempted to "nicely" secure the video, but those measures left him empty handed. When they met, the singer confirmed he had sold a copy to Rogers for $200,000. Mike added that the same Rogers staffer who provided the Collins ad video took the ménage-à-trois video home since the campaign would not air it and thought it too risky to have at the campaign office.

"Rogers knew he couldn't win," Mike added. "He feared airing the video would destroy him with women voters, maybe all voters, if he ran again."

"We teed up Morgan for the presser," Zimmer chimed in.

Sloan motioned for more details.

"Morgan did what he was paid to do," Zimmer began.

"How much?" Sloan snapped.

"Three hundred large," Zimmer responded.

"From who?" Sloan demanded.

"A nontraceable source," Mike added with a prideful smile. "An old Cuban buddy of mine."

"Morgan disappeared, retired in Mexico—he'll never return," Zimmer continued.

"You have no guarantees; I have no assurances." Sloan stopped to absorb it all.

Zimmer allowed Sloan his moment before adding, "There's no notes, texts, or emails. No fingerprints. Write it, regret it, say it, forget it. It's forgotten. Morgan was a lone wolf."

"You were down eight points on Friday," Mike interjected. "I knew you'd nail it Saturday, but no speech can gain eight points four days before an election. I hoped the video would cut that lead in half, and then on Saturday—"

"I'd cut the other half," Sloan finished.

Mike began, "Remember, losers don't—"

"I heard it fifty times," Sloan interrupted with an edge, his patience gone. "Losers don't legislate."

Zimmer reminded Sloan of his own thoughts; one day the video would emerge. "We flipped the switch, from pain to gain. We capitalized on the opportunity."

Sloan raised his hand for silence. After a moment, he plaintively asked Zimmer, "Who made sure Morgan stayed on the script?"

"Prince Eddie," Mike said quickly.

"Jesus!" Sloan's voice thundered. "You kidding me? You can't trust him."

"He's an honorable thief. No one else knows." Zimmer's voice was a tad softer. "Take comfort—Prince has no clue you're aware of anything."

"Morgan could go off the rails; he's not right," Sloan worried. "What if this story leaks?"

"It won't leak," Zimmer replied.

"But if it does?" Sloan pressed.

"It won't, but let's play it out." Zimmer held firm. "It's a drug addict's word against mine and a former governor. We win that contest."

Sloan absorbed the details. It was too much. "Newcombe? What if he keeps digging?" Sloan asked tightly.

"He's chasing a ghost," Zimmer replied.

Sloan sighed wearily. He held an unyielding stare at his father. He placed his hand out to hold Zimmer back, signaling that he only wanted his father to answer. "Why did *you* do it?"

Mike sighed loudly and gazed upward as if drawing inspiration from above. "You once protected your mother and father, and this is how I protect my son."

Sloan stared at his father.

"I wanted you to win," Mike added with emphasis. "*You deserved to win.*"

Sloan repeated the phrase slowly, with a mix of confidence and uncertainty. "I deserved to win."

FORTY-ONE

September 5, Las Vegas

"This might shock a few people," Mike said to Sloan as the two walked up the stairs at Las Vegas's Bunkhouse Saloon Bar & Grill.

"Watch the faces when they recognize us," Sloan added. "Priceless."

Before they entered, Sloan reflected on all that had transpired in the two weeks since the election. He survived the recount. Martino's case was closed. Riley was living with him until Cindy was out of rehab. A lifetime of bad decisions with women had ended; he was secure with Bree. Zimmer was the new king of politics, and his father was wearing a perpetual smile. He gave grudging praise for Zimmer's and his father's billiard shots of playing angles; all issues were neatly resolved.

Raucous waves of applause rippled through the room at Sloan's entry. The location of the saloon affectionately termed the BH was both trapped and liberated between the Strip and downtown. The spirit selection had more tequila choices than wines. Hipsters sought refuge with its musical acts spinning like a roulette wheel, tonight landing on rockabilly.

Sloan walked amid the photographs of western heroes, real and televised. The singer for the onstage band enthusiastically waved for Sloan to join them. The drummer welcomed him with a drum roll, while the lead guitarist led an impromptu playing of Sloan's song "Believe."

Sloan walked onstage to loud cheers and a standing ovation. Standing at the microphone, he reminisced about playing similar clubs in his youth, recalling his first public gig at West Hollywood's Troubadour "open mic" night. He waited for the applause to simmer. "I'll be a little busy in Washington, so I won't be singing but thrilled to be back at the BH."

He playfully jested with a young woman in the audience's front row. The woman's blouse and cap were adorned with buttons screaming to save animals, genders, mammals, birds, and the environment.

"Hate to disappoint you," Sloan said lightly, "but it's not that bad. The world was simpler when Roy Rogers protected the West." Sloan gestured to the cowboy television star's photo on the wall. Yet few in the crowd understood the reference. He pointed at the wall photographs of Las Vegas at the turn of the twentieth century. "Maybe some of those desperados were the great-great-grandfathers of today's Democratic and Republican party leaders." He glanced at Mike, contently leaning back against the bar. "Those outlaws tried to steal my election." He paused. "I don't know if you *all* voted for me—"

"I voted for you twice!" one intoxicated voice yelled.

Sloan motioned to his father. "There's the man that made it all happen." The crowd turned as one to view Mike. "He was a great governor and an even greater dad."

The crowd responded with sustained and comforting applause. The ovation continued, stretching out as Sloan nodded in appreciation. He instructed the guitar player to switch his electric guitar for an acoustic one.

"I've had a lot of songs covered, but not like this one. I wrote songs before many of you were born, but this song was written before *I* was born. With the old one, I'll mix in a little of a new song I scribbled during the campaign, 'The Rising.' I'll give you a taste, mix in a little old and new."

Sloan cast a quick glance to ensure the band was ready. He nodded to the drummer, who began to brush the snare drum. He dropped his voice ever so carefully and started singing "Somewhere over the Rainbow."

He hit a few of the classic song's verses before shooting a glance at his father. Retaining the song's melody, a seamless transition to his new lyrics: "The years pulled us apart, time heals wounded hearts; we were the same, one last chance to win the game..."

He allowed himself a nanosecond of a smile.

ABOUT THE AUTHOR

Wayne Avrashow was campaign manager for two Los Angeles City councilmembers and served as chief of staff on two government commissions. He has an extensive background in California politics. His experiences in politics, government, business, and as a practicing attorney provide unique insight into the machinations and characters that populate political campaigns.

As a lawyer-lobbyist, he represented clients before numerous California municipalities and in Nevada and Idaho. He has lectured at Southwestern University of Law and taught at Woodbury University in Los Angeles.

He authored numerous op-ed articles that appeared in daily newspapers, as well as in legal, business, and real estate publications. He was chairman of Los Angeles County ballot proposition and co-authored ballot arguments. Wayne authored *Success at Mediation—10 Strategic Tools for Attorneys*, a book used by law students at the University of Southern California School of Law.

He is the proud father of two sons, Bret and Grant, and is a lifelong resident of Los Angeles.